Champion
OF
HER Heart

A BUENA HILLS ROMANCE

ALLISON GYGI

Published by Castlerod Press

Chicago, IL

Cover design by Raneé Clark of Sweetly Us Book Services

https://allisongygi.com

ISBN: 979-8-9860561-1-1

❀ Created with Vellum

For Mom
Thanks for reading every word I've written and saying they were all amazing even when they weren't. You're the best!

Chapter One

Last week of August

Mitch Skaggs shielded his eyes from the sun, tracking the volleyball sailing toward him over the net. As it cleared the tape, he took a running leap and spiked a hard shot back over. It landed with a satisfying thud in the sand at the back corner of the court. Cheers erupted from his teammates behind him before his feet even hit the ground.

Pumping his fist out in front of him, he let out a celebratory whoop. "That's how you finish a game, boys!"

It was only a friendly pickup game of four-on-four beach volleyball, but he couldn't help getting caught up in the moment whenever sports were involved. He'd met with the same group of guys every Sunday afternoon to play since he'd moved to Southern California for graduate school three years ago. Now a year after graduating, he still rarely missed a week.

His three teammates gathered around him, offering high fives and bro hugs before Mitch ducked under the net to shake hands with the other team.

His friend Jared slapped him on the back. "That was an awesome shot, man. Remind me to be on your team next week."

Mitch rubbed a hand over Jared's light brown hair. "Get here on time and maybe you will be."

Jared gave a hearty laugh, drawing a smile out of Mitch as well. His friend's quick sense of humor had led to a fast friendship when they'd met in athletic training school at Long Beach State. A year ahead of him, Jared had been the one to refer him for his current position at the SoCal Elite Sports Center outside of Buena Hills.

"See you tomorrow," Jared said as he turned toward his belongings.

"See ya." Mitch sauntered to the side of the court where his bag sat in the sand. He picked up his beach towel and wiped the sweat from his face before using it to brush off the sand stuck to his damp torso, waving to his friends as they headed toward their cars.

"Well, well, if it isn't the great Mitch Skaggs."

With his shirt in his hand, Mitch turned as three men approached. Recognition immediately dawned on him, and his mouth broke into a wide grin. "Tom Buchanan. Man, it's been a long time, hasn't it?" He accepted a handshake from the middle-aged man in the center.

"It certainly has." Tom lifted his sunglasses to rest on his tawny hair. "Eight years, right? What're you doing in California? Last I'd heard, you were still in Illinois."

Mitch shrugged, his smile still in place. "I got sick of the snow."

Tom chuckled and gestured to the guy on his right, who was several inches taller than Mitch's six foot four. A sling supported the man's heavily bandaged shoulder. "You remember Logan Carter?"

Mitch nodded toward him, receiving one in return.

Then Tom indicated the man on his other side. He was shorter than Logan, though still a couple inches taller than Mitch. "And this is Charlie Pratt."

Anyone who grew up in the beach volleyball community would recognize Logan Carter and Charlie Pratt. They made up one of the best teams in the country, frequently claiming the top spots in both the national and world rankings. During his years on the junior circuit, Mitch had looked up to both players, admired their work ethic, though his days as a pro had ended before he'd ever had the opportunity to play with or against either one at the senior level.

Mitch shook hands with them both. "I was sorry to hear about your injury," he said to Logan.

The man dipped his head in acknowledgment. "Those are the breaks." Disappointed resignation hung in his tone.

"That's why we're here," Tom said, drawing Mitch's attention back to him. "We've noticed that you come here to play a lot."

"Every week." Mitch bent to pick up his water bottle from the sand.

Tom inclined his head. "I like what I'm seeing from you. We're here to offer you an opportunity."

Mitch paused, his water bottle halfway to his mouth. "What kind of opportunity?"

Tom placed a hand on Mitch's shoulder, leaning closer. "How would *you* like a chance to get back on the professional level and try for a spot in the Global Elite Games?"

Mitch snorted. Were they out of their minds? The Global Elites were an international, multisport competition that took place in Switzerland every five years. The premier stage of professional athletics. "Are you serious?"

"Yes."

Mitch shook his head, trying to make sense of Tom's offer. "No, really. You've got to be punking me." He searched the man's face for any sort of a joke.

Tom didn't even crack a smile. "I'm completely serious."

"Why?" Mitch asked, narrowing his eyes.

"Charlie needs a new partner." Logan gestured toward his bandaged shoulder. "This injury came at the worst time. There's no chance I'll be healed enough before the Global Elites next year."

"Why me, though?"

"We've seen you play," Charlie said. "You had a lot of potential as a junior, and you're still good. We think with a little conditioning, you could work well with me."

They'd been watching him play? Mitch didn't know what to make of that. He shook his head again. Somehow his brain had stopped sending messages to his mouth to speak. He took a long swig from his water bottle, giving himself time to process what the heck was going on.

"Wow!" he said finally. "Thank you for the offer, but I don't think I can accept. I haven't played competitively for years. I mean, the Global Elites are less than a year away."

"There isn't a lot of time," Tom conceded. "However, we wouldn't be talking to you if we didn't think you were good enough. You were a junior world champion, after all."

Mitch removed his black baseball cap and ran a hand through his short, dark hair, upsetting some grains of sand that had lodged into his scalp. Sliding his hat backward on his head again, he said, "That was eight years ago. A lot has changed since high school."

A lot, indeed. Back then, volleyball had been his life. What could be better than traveling the world as a teenager, playing the greatest sport in the world and doing it all with his best friend? The summer he and Doug had won the junior world title had been a dream come true.

But only a few weeks later, that dream had turned into a nightmare.

He'd tried walking away from the sport completely after Doug …

Don't think about it. Dwelling on it only made Mitch sad, even after all this time. And he hated being sad. He pushed the memories aside where they belonged.

"Isn't there anyone else?"

Charlie shook his head. "With the Global Elites next summer, everyone is already teamed up. You're the only promising candidate left."

Tom clapped a hand on Mitch's shoulder. "You're a good athlete. If you'd continued playing after juniors, you'd be where these guys are right now. You're starting at a deficit, certainly. But you can be great. And these two have already racked up enough points to qualify for next summer. If you can be ready by the start of the World Tour in March, and place high enough in multiple tournaments to stay ahead of the other US teams, the spot is yours."

"You really think I'm good enough?" Mitch would be lying if he said he'd never pictured himself playing in the prestigious competition.

Tom nodded. "I do."

Mitch stared out at the ocean, his eyes squinting in the soft light of the descending sun. Finally, he said, "I appreciate your offer, Tom. I really do. But I don't think I'm your man." How could he explain his refusal? He couldn't ... it was too personal.

Tom seemed to read the words that Mitch hadn't said. He gave him a sympathetic smile. "Look, Mitch. I understand why you quit. But that was eight years ago."

Mitch grimaced. *Eight years tomorrow.*

"Don't let what happened keep you from moving on with your life. You have some real talent." Tom reached into his pocket. "Here's my card. Take a few days to think it over. Give me a call with your decision."

Mitch accepted it, studying Tom's contact information, if only to give him something to do while he sorted out his thoughts.

"Don't take too long, though," Tom continued. "We've got work to do."

Mitch pocketed the card and swung his bag onto his back. "I'll think about it."

"That's all I'm asking." Tom held out his hand for Mitch to shake. "I look forward to hearing from you."

With that, he turned and walked away. Charlie and Logan said goodbye and followed in his wake. Running a hand over his stubbled jaw, Mitch watched them go.

I should've called in sick, Mitch thought as he entered the front doors of the SoCal Elite Sports Center the next morning. A blast of cool air greeted him, replacing the late summer heat from outside. Normally, he loved his job. He'd started working at SoCal Elite a few months after completing his master's in athletic training the year before. The complex was so large—with multiple sports programs— that it had its own medical clinic staffed with physical therapists and athletic trainers. The wide variety of teams and classes available at the facilities assured that Mitch's days were never monotonous. Working with so many athletes of all ages made it the perfect job for an extrovert such as himself.

But he wasn't feeling it today. Holding back the grief was always harder on *the* day.

He made his way down the hall, taking deliberate breaths and running through the mental pep talk he always gave himself on the anniversary of Doug's death. *Don't think about it. Today is just like every other day.*

His phone vibrated in his shorts' pocket as he reached the clinic. He pulled it out; a FaceTime call from his mom flashed back at him. Strange ... she knew he had work. He swiped to answer. The picture came into focus on the screen, revealing his almost eight-year-old sister. His mouth immediately lifted.

"Hazelnut! How are you, kiddo? Shouldn't you be in school?"

"No, silly," she said, giving him a look like he should know that already. "I don't start until tomorrow."

Leaning his back against the wall, he checked his watch. He still had a few minutes before he had to clock in, so he returned his full attention to his sister. "Are you excited for second grade?"

Hazel made a face. "Not really. Aiden Jacobs is in my class again."

"Was he the boy who always chased you around the playground at recess last year?"

"Yes. He's so annoying."

Mitch smiled at her fierce look. She was a force, and he loved that about her. "Well, you tell that kid he better be nice to you, or your big brother will come protect you."

She giggled. "I heard Mamá telling Daddy that you'd be sad today. Are you sad?"

"I am a little sad today." No amount of mental pep talks ever succeeded in eliminating all the emotion of this day. Hazel wouldn't understand the reason behind his melancholy, but talking to her was exactly the pick-me-up he needed right now. Her surprise appearance in the Skaggs family had been the one bright spot during those awful first months after the tragedy. Though eighteen years younger, she'd given him a reason to keep going, even when he felt about to crumble. "Talking to you makes me feel better, though."

That brought a smile to her face, as he knew it would. "I'm going to draw you a picture today and send it in the mail."

"I'll hang it up next to the others." If he could find space. His refrigerator was already filled with her original artwork. He checked his watch again. "Hey kiddo, you'll never guess what happened to me."

Her eyes went wide with curiosity. "What?"

"You know how much I love volleyball, right?"

"Of course. I like watching it with you when you come home to visit."

He smiled. "I like that too. That's why I thought you'd get a kick out of this. A volleyball coach talked to me yesterday. He wants me to play on his team."

"Really?" Hazel asked. "Like the people on the TV?"

Mitch nodded. "Exactly like them."

Sunlight flashed across the grayish-brown carpet as the front door whooshed open a little way down the hall. He glanced up, his breath hitching in his throat as McKenzie Bowman and Aria Turner entered. They were two of the elite gymnasts who trained at SoCal Elite. His attention zeroed in on the former. The light at her back swathed her in a heavenly glow, making her even more lovely than normal.

Her gaze landed on him, and his mouth lifted into a slow smile. Blushing, she looked away. He bit back a frustrated sigh.

"Hello?" Hazel's annoyance returned his focus back to the screen.

"Sorry, kiddo," he said. "What was that?"

Hazel huffed, drawing a chuckle from Mitch. She'd give their parents a run for their money in a few years. "I said, what're you going to do?"

Well aware of McKenzie and Aria a few feet from him, he flicked his gaze back up to them. McKenzie seemed to be looking anywhere but at him. Aria, on the other hand, was hanging onto his every word.

He ignored them both for now. "What do you think I should do?" he asked Hazel.

"Well," she started, sounding more grown-up than her seven-and-three-quarters years, "I think you should do what makes you happy. Would playing volleyball in the TV make you happy?"

Eight years ago, he would've said yes without hesitation. Now, he wasn't so sure. Instead of answering, he winked at her. "How'd you get so wise for your age?"

In the background, his mother called out, her slight Ecuadorian accent detectable in her words.

Hazel turned her head to respond. "Just a minute!" To Mitch, she said, "Mamá says I have to hang up now. She'll call you later."

"I need to get to work anyway," he said. "I'm glad you called, though. You brightened my day."

"Me too. I hope you aren't sad anymore."

He smiled. "I could never be sad talking to you. I love you, kiddo."

"I love you too. Bye." Her face vanished from the screen.

"Who was that?" Aria asked, taking a step closer. She ran a hand down her mahogany ponytail. "And what was she saying about playing volleyball in the TV?"

He resisted the urge to move back. Her flirting had lessened in the past several months thankfully. When he'd first started working at SoCal Elite, it was no secret she held some interest in him. No official rule prohibited ATs from dating adult athletes, but he had his own personal standards. One of them being that he wouldn't date anyone who worked or trained at his place of employment. Only one person tempted him to go against his rule, and she was still trying to avoid his notice. Wonderful.

The idea of discussing Tom's offer with Aria didn't thrill him. She wasn't exactly known for her skill at keeping things under wraps, and he didn't want word to spread about his opportunity until he'd made a decision.

He sighed. It was his own fault for talking in a public area. "I was approached by a national volleyball coach. He wants me to get back on the pro circuit."

"Mitch, that's awesome!" Aria's tone rose several octaves. "You're going to do it, right?"

"Do what?" Jared asked, joining their little group.

What was this, social hour? Mitch had half a mind to look around to see if a water cooler sat nearby. He took pity on them and repeated the gist of his discussion with Tom.

Jared whistled low through his teeth. "Man, I wish I'd stuck around for that conversation."

Mitch made a noncommittal grunt and opened the door to the clinic, walking inside. Jared and Aria followed him. McKenzie hesitated outside for a long second before joining them.

Aria perched a hip against Mitch's desk, nudging the sealed box of medical supplies that had arrived over the weekend out of the way. "So, are you going to do it?" she asked again.

"I don't know," Mitch said. "There are complications I have to consider."

"What complications?" she pressed. Geez, did she have to be so nosy?

Mitch glanced at McKenzie, surprised to find her studying him, her brows pulled together. When she caught him looking, however, she quickly dropped her gaze to the floor. He frowned before redirecting his attention back to Aria. "Well, for one thing, I'd have to quit my job, or at least scale back to part-time. Which would be a shame because I wouldn't be here to see you lovely ladies every day." He flashed a friendly grin at McKenzie so she'd know the comment was meant for her.

She didn't even crack a smile. In fact, her discomfort was even more palpable than a second before.

Good one, buddy, he thought, wishing he could take it back. *Now you've freaked her out.*

To prove his point, McKenzie inched closer to her teammate. "We should get to practice." She spoke barely loud enough for Mitch to hear.

Aria shot an exasperated look at her training mate before saying, "Yeah, alright." Then she glanced at Mitch and rolled her eyes. He ground his teeth a bit.

The women turned to leave, and he beat them to the exit, holding the door open for them. Right before stepping out of the clinic, Aria turned to face him. "You have to do it. When are you ever going to get an opportunity like this again?"

"I'm thinking about it," Mitch responded.

Aria stepped into the hallway, and McKenzie moved to follow. As she brushed by him, he stopped her with a gentle hand on her arm. She flinched. Her whole body actually twitched, like she was repulsed by the simple friendly gesture. But why?

"How was your weekend?" he asked, attempting to keep his tone light, nonthreatening.

"Fine," she mumbled. Her mouth opened like she was about to say something, then closed again. "I h-have to go." She hurried away without another word.

He sighed as he watched her quick retreat.

"I don't know why you even try so hard to get her to talk to you," Jared said from behind him.

Mitch turned back to his desk and retrieved the box cutter from the top drawer. "I'm friends with her roommates. Good friends." He slid the blade across the box's seal and opened the flaps, taking out medical supplies and placing them on his desk. "I get that she's shy, but it's like I'm the grim reaper to her."

He placed the empty box on the floor by his chair, then filled his arms with gauze pads and medical tape intended for the cabinet along the back wall of the front office. The open room consisted of four desks for the ATs, who were responsible for keeping inventory of all supplies at the clinic. Off to the side were the private exam rooms and physical therapists' offices.

Jared twirled a pen around his fingers. "Why do you even like her anyway? Is it because she's playing hard to get?"

"I don't know. I mean, she's beautiful. There's no denying that. But there's something about her ... I can't describe it."

That wasn't exactly true. He remembered vividly the first time he'd seen her. It was his first day working at SoCal Elite. During his tour of the facilities, he'd entered the gym and was immediately drawn to her atop the balance beam, running through her routine. Her fiery hair made her impossible to miss. Every skill was executed with such artistry and grace, he hadn't been able to pull his attention away. After dismounting into the foam pit, she'd smiled at her coach's praise and Mitch felt the first stirrings of attraction for her. He'd wanted one of those gorgeous smiles directed at him.

When Gary had asked him to help spot McKenzie on a new sequence on uneven bars a few days later, Mitch truly got a glimpse of her fierce determination. She went through each skill over and over, never quitting or complaining, until she got them exactly right. He'd always admired that kind of inner strength. He liked to think he had the same in himself.

"Hey, who am I to judge?" Jared said, butting into Mitch's memories. "The heart wants what the heart wants."

"I just don't know why she dislikes me so much." It was the question he'd asked himself every day since he'd gone to visit his friend, Elise, and discovered McKenzie had moved in as the fifth roommate. At the time, he couldn't believe his good luck.

Despite his efforts to get to know her for almost a year, however, he'd been unable to coax more than a few words from her. Most of the time, she went to great lengths to avoid him.

It was a very good thing he wasn't one to give up easily.

Chapter Two

McKenzie flipped backward off the end of the balance beam, taking a step back to steady herself. Her coach approached her from a few feet away, where he'd been keeping a watchful eye on all his athletes.

"You've been more consistent in your tumbling sequence lately," Gary said. "I'm happy to see it. Let's try the standing Arabian again. It was a little wobbly on that last rep. Make sure to square your body directly over the beam."

McKenzie nodded. "Okay, Gary."

All around them, the creaks of uneven bars and thumps of tumbling gymnasts mixed with the pop music blaring from the gym's loudspeakers. Coaches milled about, calling out instructions to their athletes to point their toes or correct their form. On the beams adjacent to hers, Aria and Evie, the other women who trained under Gary, ran through their own skills.

McKenzie crossed to the end of the apparatus and rested her hands on top of it, pausing to take a centering breath. Pushing herself up, she straightened to a standing position, her back to the rest of the beam. After one more breath, she raised her arms above her head and leapt into a backflip, adding a half twist before landing in the opposite direction with knees slightly bent. Not even the slightest wobble.

"Yes!" Gary pumped his fist in the air. "That's my girl."

McKenzie smiled at his praise. His declaration was truer than most people realized. Having coached her since she was little, he was more father figure than her own dad. That wasn't saying much though. Sometimes she wondered if her actual dad even realized he had a daughter.

Gary walked over to her again and held up his hand. McKenzie leaned down and smacked a high five. "Let's move on to the next skill while you're up there. That was a little shaky too."

She performed a full turn on one leg right into a scissor jump, throwing her head back and losing sight of the beam. When she landed again, her feet stuck as if superglued to the leather-covered wood.

Gary nodded in approval. "Good. Now the full dismount." To Evie, he called, "I like what I see on that Wolf Spin. Let's try it one more time."

McKenzie walked heel to toe to the end of the beam. Her dismount required her to tumble the full length of the apparatus before performing two and a half twists off the end. She took a deep breath and started flipping.

A sharp pain shot through her ankle when her feet hit the mat. She gasped, doubling over and squeezing her eyes shut.

Her coach was next to her in an instant. He placed a hand on her back, leaning down to look into her face. "Are you okay?"

"I landed wrong on my ankle." Limping a few steps, she willed the throbbing in her foot to ease.

"I'm calling for medical," Gary said, pulling out his walkie-talkie.

McKenzie straightened and waved away his comment with both hands. "You don't need to do that. I'll just walk it off. It'll be fine." She was no stranger to pain; she'd push through it. Her career depended on it. And her mother expected it.

"Three weeks before nationals?" he scoffed. "No way. Let's get it taped up at least." He spoke into the walkie-talkie. The voice that responded was full of static, but she'd recognize it anywhere.

Anyone but him, she silently pleaded with some higher being. *Please send anyone but him.*

Two days had passed since she'd last seen Mitch in the clinic. She'd tried to talk to him. Really, she had. But her throat had dried up like the Sahara Desert. Typical.

Luck was not on her side. A few minutes later, he strode through the gym doors, his easy swagger exuding confidence. "I hear you hurt yourself." He crouched in front of where McKenzie sat with her legs outstretched, off to the side of the balance beams.

Trusting she was in capable hands, Gary left to work with Aria on a new skill she was practicing. But he remained close enough to step in if needed. McKenzie appreciated that about him. He'd always been a strong advocate for her, even more so since her almost-career-ending injury eight years ago.

She opened her mouth to tell Mitch that her foot was fine. No words came out, so she closed it again and nodded. Like a cheap bobblehead doll. *What is wrong with you?*

How was she able to perform complicated passes on a four-inch-wide balance beam, or risky releases on the uneven bars in front of thousands of people, but she couldn't muster the courage to talk to an attractive man?

And boy, *was* he attractive. The perfect blend of Latino and Caucasian genes—the epitome of tall, dark, and handsome.

"What happened?" he asked.

"I hurt my foot on my d-dismount," McKenzie mumbled.

Mitch lowered both knees to the mat. "Let's take a look." He gestured toward her foot. "May I?"

She nodded again. He took it in his hands, probing and manipulating it into different positions, testing its range of motion. A slow burn crept up her neck and onto her face. Her porcelain coloring had to be bright crimson by now. And blotchy. She wasn't cute when she blushed.

"Does this hurt?" he asked, flexing her foot. His chocolate eyes rose from it to her face. He had to notice her blush. Thankfully, he didn't mention it. He had his professional mask on. McKenzie knew him better than that, though. Underneath his respectful exterior was a guy who loved to tease.

"N-no." She forced herself to hold his eyes even though instinct told her to look away.

"How about that?" he asked, stretching it.

"No." That was a little steadier.

Mitch let go of her foot and sat back on his haunches. "It doesn't seem to be anything too serious. I'll tape it to give you more support. It might be a little sore for a day or two but that's all." He slid his bag closer to him and dug through it, pulling out a roll of athletic tape. He picked up her foot again. She fought another blush as his gentle hands wrapped the tape around her ankle.

He worked in silence, head bent to his task, giving McKenzie an opportunity to study him without being noticed. His olive complexion contrasted with the pasty coloring of her skin. A baseball cap worn backward covered his black hair. With his eyes focused on her foot, she had a perfect view of his long eyelashes—women would kill for lashes like his. The lightest dusting of freckles dotted his nose. Huh, she'd never noticed those before.

A moment later, he looked up and met her gaze. McKenzie's face flared at being caught staring. If her skin didn't start behaving, her feelings would be broadcasted across her entire face. And the one thing she didn't need was for Mitch Skaggs to know she liked him. Not with the Global Elite Games next summer and so much riding on making the team.

The corners of his lips twitched, and her stomach flip-flopped at that hint of a smile. He set her foot down and leaned back.

"How does that feel?" He didn't seem at all bothered at the prospect of her stare. On the other hand, McKenzie wished for a hole to magically appear and swallow her up forever. "Too tight? Too loose?"

She rolled her foot in the air, testing its range of motion. "I think i-it's good." She cringed.

Mitch surveyed his taping job again. Then he stood and held his hand out to her. She placed hers tentatively in his. A tingling sensation traveled up her arm as he pulled her to her feet.

"Will I see you at dinner?" he asked.

"D-dinner?"

"Elise invited me. She said you guys were inviting a few people over tonight."

Sometimes it was really inconvenient that Mitch and her room-mates were friends. Her home was supposed to be her safe place, but the amount of time he spent there seriously undermined that.

"Yeah, I'll be there," she said.

An irresistible twinkle appeared in his eyes. "Awesome. I'll see you then." He gave her shoulder a gentle squeeze, and miraculously, she managed to hold back a full-body shiver.

"Take care of that ankle." Slinging his bag over his shoulder, he walked away. McKenzie stared after him. A few paces from the gym's exit, he turned and flashed her one more smile before disappearing through the doorway.

McKenzie felt her lips involuntarily curve upward. Only slightly. Anything more than that could possibly expose her true feelings to anyone who looked in her direction.

That would ruin everything. And she couldn't afford to mess this up.

Chapter Three

McKenzie stepped onto the porch of the two-story bungalow she'd called home for the past year. The loud voices of her four roommates carried through the open front window as they sang off-key to the music. She smiled. How had she been so lucky to find such a perfect living arrangement?

At the beginning, her reservations about moving into a place where everyone knew each other had almost made her back out before signing the contract. She had firsthand experience with being the outsider. But these women had quickly accepted her into their group, making her feel welcome almost from the day she'd moved in. Boy, was she glad she hadn't listened to her fears. Which, for the record, didn't happen very often.

Laughter broke through the singing as she stepped inside the house. She dropped her bag by the door and kicked off her flip-flops before limping in the direction of the voices.

"What happened to your foot?" Hallie asked, pulling a loaf of freshly baked bread from the oven. The smell made McKenzie's mouth water. It was fitting that the aspiring baker would be making something yummy for tonight's dinner.

McKenzie looked down at her ankle. She'd swapped the athletic tape Mitch had wrapped it with for a simple Ace bandage. "I tweaked it on my beam dismount."

"Are you okay?" Elise turned away from the stove and paused the music. As Hallie's older sister, the two looked similar—long, blonde hair and blue eyes, though Elise's had more green in hers, causing them to change color depending on what she was wearing.

McKenzie crossed to the sink to wash her hands. "I'm fine. As long as I don't do anything too crazy, it should be okay by tomorrow."

"Did you see that reel of you on Instagram?" Kendall asked, looking up from the tomatoes she was chopping at the center island. "I follow the official Global Elite account. You're included in the list of gymnasts to watch on uneven bars."

"Wow, Zee. You haven't even made the team yet, and you're already landing on the highlight reels? It's like you're famous already." Beej nudged McKenzie's elbow with the arm that wasn't holding a baking sheet full of veggies on its way to the oven. Her real name was actually Bridget, but she'd been known as Beej since her younger sister was learning to talk and couldn't say her name.

Taking the stool next to Kendall, McKenzie scrunched her nose. Her roommates might think it was exciting, but she dreaded the attention. Maybe if all the stuff the media spouted about her was positive, she wouldn't hate dealing with it so much. She knew more than anyone how much doubt the gymnastics community held about her comeback. And reliving the darkest time of her life through constant questions at every single competition only added to her anxiety.

No, she'd rather stay far away from the limelight.

"I saw that too," Hallie said, mixing in the tomatoes Kendall dumped in the salad bowl. "You can do some crazy high-flying stuff. No wonder bars is your specialty."

McKenzie allowed a small smile at that. If it were up to her, she'd only do bars. And possibly beam. But Gary and her sports psychologist both seemed to think it was important to keep training vault, even after almost being paralyzed by the apparatus eight years before. The jury was still out on that decision.

"Do you think you'll be ready by next summer?" Elise blew on a spoonful of spaghetti sauce before taking a small sip.

McKenzie shrugged. "I hope so. I mean, I'll be twenty-three at the Global Elites. I'm older than so many gymnasts vying for spots. And yet, I feel like I have to work even harder than all of them."

Leaning against the refrigerator, Beej brushed a tight blonde curl from her face. "With age comes maturity though."

"You make me sound so geriatric."

Beej laughed. "I meant that you're older than them, so your instincts are better. Where a younger gymnast might make a mistake and fall off, you're experienced enough to correct it on the fly. Right? Isn't that how it works?"

"Maybe," McKenzie said. "But after all that time off because of my injury, I feel like I'm still behind everyone else."

"You'll do awesome." Elise flipped off the burner and moved the pot to the back of the stove. "You weren't a junior national champion for nothing."

Elise meant well, but her compliment still rubbed. It wasn't the first time someone had made that assumption when McKenzie had expressed her fears about her age compared to the rest of the competition field. Everyone was quick to mention that she *used* to be the best in the country without acknowledging that so many aspects of the sport had changed since she'd won the title at thirteen.

She was older now—very nearly past her peak. Routines were expected to be harder, packed with more complicated skills. Judges rewarded power and difficulty, focusing less on the gracefulness and fluidity at which McKenzie excelled.

Still, she should be grateful to be training again. That had once been a big fat question mark. It was a miracle she could even walk.

Constantly losing the top spots in competitions to teenagers stung every time though. It had been a long road back from injury. What if she couldn't make it to the top of the leaderboard again? What if she never got the chance to fulfill her lifelong dream of competing in the Global Elite Games? *Am I too late?*

She didn't voice her fears out loud. Instead, she turned to Elise and said, "How was work today? Only one week left, right? Are you ready for your trip?"

"I have a few things I need to pick up. And Kendall needs to start packing"—Elise scrunched her face at her bestie—"but we're basically ready."

Kendall rolled her eyes. "I enjoy the pressure. I'll be ready." Elise and Kendall had been planning their extended European backpacking trip for years as a reward for finishing college.

Elise raised an eyebrow at her before turning back to McKenzie. "I'll miss my job though. I love working at the museum. Except for all the summer camps. I swear every youth group in LA County decided today was the perfect day for a trip to the Buena Hills Art Museum. It's not even that big."

"Just one of the many reasons I'll never have kids," Kendall said, dumping more tomatoes into the salad bowl. "Too much noise. And they're sticky. But I'm looking forward to being the fun aunt for all your crazy kiddos."

Aunt was a loose term. Biologically, Kendall wasn't related to any of the women in the room. However, Elise and Kendall's friendship went so far back that they blurred all familial lines. As far as they were concerned, they were sisters, along with Hallie. And Beej was their cousin.

McKenzie rose from her stool. "I need a shower before dinner, and then I'll come back down and help. I don't think anyone wants Sweaty McKenzie at the table."

"I *love* Sweaty McKenzie!" Kendall called after her.

McKenzie laughed as she left the kitchen and headed upstairs to the bathroom. As the water ran over her body, she let the stress of her dreams—and the expectations heaped on her shoulders—wash down the drain. The warm spray felt nice on her stiff ankle, and she smiled at the mental image of Mitch's capable hands taping her foot. She only dared to indulge in her tiny crush on the man when she was alone.

She stepped out of the shower and toweled off before throwing on a pair of black shorts and a sleeveless shirt. Wrapping her ginger hair in a towel, she headed downstairs to see what still needed to be done to prepare for dinner.

Just outside the swinging door separating the hallway from the kitchen, McKenzie froze as a familiar male voice joined those of her roommates. Her shaky fingers pushed the door open harder than she'd intended, sending it clattering against the counter inside the kitchen.

Mitch looked up from the watermelon he was cutting at the center island, his mouth immediately turning up when he noticed her. "Hey, McKenzie." His eyes flicked above her head, then back to her face. "I like that look on you. How was the shower?"

What?

She lifted a hand to her hair, feeling the terry cloth turban holding it captive. "Oh!" Spinning wildly, she fled from the kitchen, ripping the towel from her head and frantically finger combing her locks while running for the stairs.

A strong hand gripped her elbow before she got there. "Wait, don't go."

Her cheeks on fire, she turned to face Mitch. He was quite a bit taller than her, and she couldn't bring herself to meet his eyes. Her vision settled at the level of his well-defined chest. That was even worse than looking in his face. The floor seemed the safest spot, so she focused on that.

"I'm sorry. I didn't mean to offend you," he said.

Was that really what he thought? McKenzie slowly forced her eyes up to his face. "You d-didn't."

Exasperation carved into his handsome features. "Then why won't you talk to me?"

"My h-hair ..." She started finger combing her wet locks again.

Mitch reached out and grabbed her wrist, lowering her hand. Her skin tingled at the contact. "Your hair looks fine."

"I'm so embarrassed." Mortified was more like it. She couldn't begin to imagine the state of her appearance.

Mitch shrugged. "Don't be. And you know what?" He dipped his head to look at her face.

As much as she wanted to, McKenzie couldn't look away. His brown eyes captivated her. "What?"

"Everyone gets embarrassed. It's a part of life."

McKenzie couldn't help a flicker of a smile. "You don't."

He leaned his shoulder against the staircase behind him. "I do embarrassing stuff all the time. I just don't let them rattle me."

It was hard to believe that the always self-confident Mitch Skaggs ever got embarrassed.

He raised an eyebrow at her doubtful expression. "You don't believe me, do you? How about I give you an example?"

She nodded mutely.

His mouth pursed to the side as he thought. Then his face lit up, as if a lightbulb had gone off in his brain. "I've got one. When I was thirteen, my grandparents came to visit from Ecuador—"

"Your grandparents live in Ecuador?" McKenzie flushed. She wasn't usually one to interrupt.

He didn't seem to mind. "Yeah. That's where my mom's from. She came to the States for college. After she met my dad, she never moved back."

How romantic. "I didn't know that," McKenzie mumbled. "Do you ever go visit?"

"About once or twice a year while I was growing up. My parents still go that often, but I haven't been back for a while."

McKenzie wrung her hands. The knot in her stomach that had formed when she first saw him in her kitchen was now doing some funny kind of Scottish jig. "S-sorry. You were thirteen ..."

Mitch hooked his thumbs in the belt loops of his shorts. "Right. When I was thirteen, my mom and abuela took my siblings and me to the community pool. We were about to leave, and I was standing by the edge, waiting for my family to finish packing up. I must've done something to make my abuela mad—I don't remember. She came over and gave me an earful before pushing me right in, towel and all."

McKenzie stifled a giggle. She struggled to picture anyone being angry enough with Mitch to do that. He always treated everyone like they were the most important person in the world.

"What did you do to make her so mad?"

He raised his arms, palms up toward the ceiling. "Probably mouthing off or something. I was thirteen."

"That doesn't sound like it would embarrass you that much. I mean, you *were* at a pool."

Mitch smiled, his eyes twinkling. "True. But it was also one of the hottest days of the summer in Illinois. I'm pretty sure most of Elmwood Falls—that's where I grew up—was there that day. As a brand-new teenager, it wasn't cool being pushed into the pool by my grandma in front of all my friends." He laughed, the sound warm and inviting, easing some of McKenzie's tension. "Your turn."

Her eyes widened, and she shook her head. Sharing embarrassing stories might not be a big deal to him, but there was no way she'd get into any of hers. "Uh-uh. I'd rather hear more of yours."

Mitch considered her. "Okay, here's another one. When I was in high school, I was at my buddy's house one night with a few other guys. There was a bet, and the consequence for losing was to streak across the front yard."

McKenzie gasped.

"Guess who the lucky loser was."

She bit down on her cheek to keep from smiling. "You didn't ..."

"I couldn't not do it. I would've been flamed for weeks," he said. "Unfortunately for me, my buddy lived across the street from our principal. She was probably the strictest person I've ever known. Anyway, she happened to come home at the exact moment to catch me. She didn't hesitate to call my parents."

McKenzie laughed at the tale even as she tried her hardest to imagine the principal's reaction and not the ... ahem ... reason for it. "Serves you right for streaking." She looked up at his smiling face— quite a feat due to his height.

Mitch's gaze on her squeezed her lungs, making it hard to

breathe. It was warm and full of ... what? She'd never been looked at in that way before. Especially by a man.

"I definitely learned my lesson." He chuckled. "I swear I couldn't look my principal in the eyes for the rest of the year. And I'd never seen my parents so mad. I'd gotten in trouble before, but that was the only time I've ever had my keys taken away. I was grounded for a month after that."

"Serves you right for streaking." McKenzie would've been punished for a lot longer than a month if she'd pulled a stunt like that. Not that she would. Even thinking about it was making her skin crawl.

Silence fell between them, filling the space with awkwardness. McKenzie studied her chipped fingernails. Keeping up her end of a conversation had always been a struggle.

She ran a hand over her hair, remembering her messy locks. "I-I should go do my hair." Ugh ... There was that stutter again. Talking to him was hard enough without that humiliating nervous tick.

"Okay." He touched her elbow, keeping her there. "But you'll come back down?"

Was he just being nice, or did he actually want her around? His hopeful expression stirred up small flutters in her chest.

"I'll come back," she squeaked out.

Those flutters turned into an entire butterfly colony zooming around her stomach at the relieved smile he gave her. Mitch was completely unaware of the power that smile had over her.

"See you in a bit," he said as she inched backward toward the stairs. Only when she'd reached them did he turn and reenter the kitchen.

McKenzie flew up the stairs, her smile so big it hurt. She thought over their conversation as she brushed her thick hair—braiding it in a loose plait over her shoulder.

Someone as cautious as she was didn't go through life without developing a keen sense of observation. It had served her well over the years. At times she'd even depended on it for survival in social situations. But she didn't know what to make of Mitch's friendliness. The looks he gave her, the way he touched her arm to get her attention ... What did it all mean? If she wasn't careful, her little crush was in very real danger of becoming a full-blown case of infatuation.

She couldn't have that.

But to have someone notice her, to want her around—especially someone like Mitch—she couldn't help but feel special. He was like that though—gorgeous, the type that women would flock to if he'd let them. However, it was his infectious energy and the way he treated everyone he met like they were VIPs that really drew her to him. It was nice to feel important.

Still, he could never find out about her true feelings. They shouldn't be difficult to keep from him. McKenzie was often overlooked. And besides, even on the small chance that he *did* feel something more than friendship with her, nothing could ever come of it. She couldn't lose focus on her purpose. Making the Global Elite team was the only thing that mattered. Nothing could come between her and this dream.

Everything depended on it.

Chapter Four

"Mitch Skaggs, former Junior World champion, future Global Elite star." Elise looked up from the food she was arranging on a card table set up on the back deck. "How cool is that?"

Mitch unfolded one of the chairs he'd found in the storage closet under the stairs. He set it down on the grass below her and gripped both his hands on the back of it. "It would be an awesome opportunity for sure."

In the three days since his conversation with Tom, it seemed that's all anyone wanted to talk about. News traveled fast apparently.

"So ... are you going to do it?"

That was the million-dollar question everyone, including himself, wanted to know. "I haven't decided yet."

The back door slid open, and Elise smiled when her boyfriend stepped outside. "Hey, there you are." She leaned into him as he kissed her cheek.

"Sorry, love. Traffic was murder on the way over, like." Rory's Irish brogue colored his words. "I think there was an accident."

Elise reached for the dish in Rory's hands. "No worries. Did you bring Seth with you?"

"Yeah, he's inside with Beej." He inclined his head in the direction of the kitchen.

"Shocker," Mitch teased as he climbed the four steps onto the deck. McKenzie's older brother was the fly to Beej's honey.

Elise laughed. "Yeah, I wouldn't go in there if I were you. You might catch them making out." She shuddered as if she'd experienced that very thing. To Rory, she said, "We're just waiting on McKenzie. She should be down in a minute."

"Grand," he said, extending his hand for Mitch to shake. "Howya, bud. What's the craic?"

Mitch had spent enough time with Rory to pick up on some of his Irish phrases. They'd had a bit of a rocky beginning when the Irishman had mistakenly thought Mitch was pursuing Elise, but even with their vast differences in personality, they'd since forged a close friendship. Rory's reserved manner balanced out Mitch's nonstop energy.

"Mitch talked to a volleyball coach last weekend." Elise wrapped an arm around Rory's waist where he'd tucked her into his side.

Rory's dark eyebrows went up. "Did ya now?"

Mitch nodded. "One of his players is hurt. Tom wants me to take his place."

"That's class!" Rory clapped him on the back. "Fair play to ya, mate."

Mitch couldn't help his smile. "They'd been coming every week to watch me play. Which blows my mind. They're just casual games. Hardly scout worthy. Not like the pro circuit."

"Have you decided to go for it, then?"

Mitch's eyes flew to McKenzie at the back door. How had she snuck up on him? His hands turned clammy at the mere sight of her. She was beautiful, her silky hair braided and hanging over one shoulder. He couldn't resist that hair. Like deep copper. If only he could plunge his fingers through it to see if it was as soft as it seemed.

The apples of her cheeks colored adorably when they made eye contact, but unlike most of their interactions, she didn't look away.

"Not officially, but I'm leaning toward no," he said.

She'd never initiated a conversation before. There had to be something to the fact that she'd talked to him first now, right?

McKenzie stepped out of the doorway, stopping a few paces away from him. She placed her fingertips in the front pockets of her shorts, her shoulders pulling forward as though she wasn't entirely comfortable being there. "Why not?"

Mitch lifted his shoulders. "For one thing, I love my job. Helping athletes achieve their dreams is my passion. I don't want to give that up. Plus, I haven't played competitively for years. I'd be going up against athletes far more experienced than I am."

"I know what that's like," McKenzie muttered to the ground.

Yes, she did. He didn't know the particulars of her past injury, but he was familiar enough to understand that she faced her own underdog situation.

"And there are ... other reasons," Mitch said, unable to keep the sadness from his tone.

She cocked her head to the side. "What do you mean?"

Shoot. Why hadn't he kept his mouth shut? He hadn't wanted her to think he was a chicken though. "It's personal." Did that sound as harsh to her as it did to him?

"Oh." McKenzie's face reddened. "Sorry." She took a step back, her eyes darting away.

Mitch could kick himself. He hadn't meant to hurt her feelings. "It's okay," he said, grabbing her hand before she could escape.

She flinched at his touch, glancing at their conjoined hands before lifting her gaze slowly, painfully, to meet his. Rarely was he at a loss for words, but as their eyes locked, all thoughts flew the coop. The air crackled between them, creating an energy that had nothing to do with the late summer heat. His heart pounded, attempting to break right through his chest. Out of the corner of his eye, he noticed Elise drag Rory away. Mitch would have to thank her later.

McKenzie didn't pull her hand away, but he could see the confusion and—if he interpreted it correctly—panic clearly on her face as she searched for ... something.

"I'm starving. Let's eat!" Kendall came through the back door. Beej stepped outside behind her, holding Seth's hand, laughing at something he'd said. None of them seemed to notice what was transpiring on the deck.

The moment broken, McKenzie pulled her hand away, mumbling about grabbing something from the kitchen, and escaped inside without a backward glance. Mitch watched her go, attempting to catch his breath, his skin still warm from her touch.

Mitch was no stranger to a woman's touch, but never had his body reacted the way it did while holding McKenzie's hand. Had she felt it too? It was hard to say since she avoided him during dinner. Every time he caught her eye, she quickly looked away, busying herself with cutting her food or reaching for her water glass on the grass next to her chair. No smile, no prolonged eye contact. It kind of made him wonder if he'd made up the whole interaction on the deck.

He had to find an opportunity to get close to her, to explore what happened a little more.

When he was about to leave, he spotted his chance. Standing alone on the deck, the glowing light inside the house framing her silhouette in the near darkness, she watched the rest of the group unsuccessfully hit croquet balls through hoops in the grass. It was just like her—never in the middle of the action, always off to the side and overlooked by the crowd.

Except by him.

He climbed the steps, stopping at the railing beside her. "Nice night, huh?"

"It is." She kept her gaze straight ahead.

They stood side by side, hands on the railing. The awkward game played out in front of them, punctured by laughs and groans from the players as they missed shot after shot. Mitch drummed his fingers on the railing in front of him, searching his brain for a safe topic.

"How's your ankle?"

McKenzie wiggled her foot back and forth in the air. "It's a little stiff, but it d-doesn't hurt m-much anymore. I guess I have you to thank for that."

What was it about him that made her so uncomfortable? She was quiet around everyone, but he hadn't noticed her stutter when she talked to anyone else. "Phew! Good thing it was just a strain. I was afraid I'd have to amputate."

Her mouth twitched. "I'm glad it didn't come to that."

He bit down on his bottom lip to keep his smile from breaking free. "You don't know how fortunate you are, McKenzie. I'm an expert at taping ankles, but my amputation skills are a little rusty."

The laugh that burst from her was so unexpected that Mitch stopped short. He could usually make anyone laugh. Except her.

Electricity charged through his veins, filling him with a new energy. Her laugh was a gold medal. He was already standing on top of the podium, hand over his heart, while the "Star-Spangled Banner" played through the loudspeakers.

"You're ridiculous," she said, amusement still crossing her face.

Mitch winked at her. "You laughed. What does that say about you?"

A rosy tint appeared on her cheeks, and the adrenaline running through him dimmed. Would she find an excuse to flee again?

Instead, she turned back to the yard, her hands on the wood railing. "Are you really not going t-to do the volleyball thing?" she asked after a few beats of silence.

Mitch hadn't expected that question to come from her. He blew out a breath as he formulated a response. None came.

"I m-mean, that coach wouldn't have approached you if he didn't t-think you were already good enough, right?" She craned her neck to look up at him. The light from the house gave her flawless skin a slightly ethereal glow.

"True." Where was she going with this?

She wrung her fingers on the railing in front of her. That mixed with her stutter pulled at his heartstrings. What could he do to help her feel more settled around him?

She pushed on though. "Well ... maybe you c-could work it out with your boss and the coach to keep your job part-time. You could t-train in the morning and work in the afternoon. Or vice versa. At least for now. It would be harder when you s-start traveling."

That was reasonable. "I could."

"Of course, if it's the other reason ... that's stopping you ..." She trailed off, staring at the deck, the wood black in the near twilight.

"I didn't mean to snap earlier," he said. "I just don't like to talk about it."

"I understand." Her hands pulled together in a tangle of fingers.

If Mitch wasn't careful, she'd retreat into herself again. That would be a shame after the progress he'd been making with her. "I'll think about it. I haven't made a final decision yet. But I need to soon."

"It's none of my business." She shrugged. "It's just ... volleyball seems important to you. Your career will always be there to fall back on. If you turn down this opportunity though, that's it. You might not get another shot."

She had a point.

He placed a hand on top of her ball of hands resting on the railing. Her fingers stilled their nervous movements. Mitch smiled at her when she turned toward him, that same look of confusion written on her face. "You're right. I'll give it some more thought."

She nodded, her eyes darting between him and various places around the yard, before turning back to the game winding down in front of them. Mitch stood beside her, afraid that if he moved even the tiniest bit, she'd realize he was still holding her hand. Nothing more was said, but there was a peacefulness in the moment that he hadn't felt in ages.

By the time he started the drive back to Long Beach, fatigue had begun to work its way through his body. Maybe he should consider moving closer to work. He spent most of his day up in Buena Hills anyway. The commute hadn't seemed like a big deal when he'd first started, but the drive—especially the traffic—drained more out of him the longer he had to do it. Especially after spending a few nights a week at McKenzie's, hoping to form some kind of friendship with her. It hadn't worked before now.

At least the long drive gave him ample time to think about their conversation. Back when Doug was still alive, they'd been the ones to beat. They were the New York Yankees of junior beach volleyball, minus the whole everybody-hating-them part. Playing in the Global Elites was his biggest dream. But he'd buried that dream along with his best friend.

Was it still there, waiting to be reignited after all these years?

Part of him worried that getting back into competition would stir up the all-encompassing sadness and anger that held him hostage for weeks after the crash. Grieving meant sadness, and he had too much life to live to be sad.

Still, putting a moratorium on competitive volleyball wouldn't bring Doug back, no matter how much he wished it would.

Mitch sniffed, his eyes stinging. He shook away the sadness. *Don't dwell on it. Let it go.*

His apartment complex was a series of four buildings scattered around a central parking area. He drove around to the back and pulled into his spot. After killing the engine, he shifted in his seat to dig the crinkled business card from his pocket.

He stared at the contact info printed beneath Tom's name. *Am I really doing this?* Inhaling a deep breath through his nose, he pulled out his phone. Then letting the air out slowly, he dialed the number before he lost his nerve.

It rang a few times, and Mitch began to wonder if he'd called too late. Then a click came over the line, and the coach picked up.

"Tom Buchanan."

Mitch took another breath. "Hi, Tom. It's Mitch. Is your offer still on the table?"

"It is. Are you interested?"

"I am. On one condition." He explained McKenzie's proposal.

"That sounds reasonable," Tom said after Mitch had finished. "Tell you what. Charlie is out of town until Sunday. Take the rest of the week to get your affairs in order. If your boss okays it, come in early on Monday morning and we'll get started. If you have any trouble, give me a call. I'll talk to him."

"I will. Thank you."

"My pleasure. I'm looking forward to it. I think you and Charlie will be good together."

After ending the call, Mitch leaned his head back against the headrest, peace settling over him. He'd made the right decision; he was sure of it. And he couldn't help the feeling that his whole life was about to change.

Chapter Five

"See you tomorrow, McKenzie," Aria said as they parted outside the gym Friday evening.

McKenzie waved and continued to her car with her keys in hand. The spacious parking lot was close to empty in the fading light, except for a few cars scattered here and there on the asphalt. Only the most serious athletes stayed this late.

After unlocking her car, she tossed her bag onto the back seat and slid behind the wheel, turning the key in the ignition. The engine rolled over but didn't catch. She tried again. No luck.

"No." She tried a third time. Still nothing. "No, no, no."

McKenzie squeezed her eyes shut and groaned. "This *can't* be happening." What a time to have car problems. She looked forward to going home every night to unwind after a full day of training.

Reaching for her bag in the back seat was an act of contortion. She dug through it, pushing aside grips, a bag of chalk for her hands, extra clothes, and other random stuff. When her hand finally closed around her phone at the very bottom, she pulled it out and climbed back to the driver's seat. A missed call from her mom lit the screen, which she ignored—now wasn't the time to face whatever issue the woman had to harp on today—and dialed her brother. It went straight to Seth's voicemail.

Where are you? Her fingers shook as she called Beej.

"Hello?" Beej's cheerful voice eased some of the panic McKenzie fought to keep under control.

"Hey, Beej. Can you come get me? My car won't start."

"Oh no! I wish I could but I'm working the night shift tonight."

McKenzie slumped back against the seat. "I forgot. Sorry. I hope you don't get in trouble for answering." Beej's boss on the pediatric floor of the Buena Hills Hospital had a strict no phone policy for nurses on duty.

"Don't be. It's fine. I'm on break right now."

"Do you know if anyone else is home?"

"Um ... I know Elise is out with Rory ..." No surprise there. "And I think Kendall had something tonight. But Hallie might be home."

"Thanks. I'll try her."

"Good luck," Beej said cheerfully.

"Thanks. See you at home."

McKenzie hung up and called Hallie, getting her voicemail.

Figures.

She leaned her head against the window and closed her eyes. Her stomach lurched at the thought of calling a tow truck. Talking to strangers over the phone was something she went to great lengths to avoid. But what else could she do? She couldn't sit in the parking lot all night.

Three quick taps on the window jolted her from her thoughts, and she shrieked, whirling to face whatever threat lurked outside.

Mitch's face stared back at her. At her alarm, his wide smile immediately turned apologetic.

McKenzie opened her door a crack. "You s-scared me," she said, raising a shaking hand to her chest. Someone needed to inform her heart that the danger was gone.

"Sorry, I didn't mean to." He held the door open as she climbed out of the car. "I was leaving the clinic just now and saw your car still here. I wanted to make sure you're okay."

McKenzie didn't know whether to be more touched about him coming to check on her or that he'd noticed when she'd left. "It won't s-start." Wrapping her arms around her middle, she tried to calm her racing heart. Was the rapid beating due to him standing next to her or that he'd scared the living daylights out of her?

Or both?

Mitch pursed his lips. "That stinks. Unfortunately, your present company knows nothing about mechanics. I could try to jump it, though I'd probably do more harm than good." His self-deprecating look lifted her spirits. "But I can call you a tow truck."

"You'd do that?"

"Of course."

The sight of his smile, warm and inviting, made her knees feel a little wobbly. She rested her hip against her car to keep from colliding with the ground. Or worse, toppling into him. She didn't need any more embarrassment after proving what a scaredy cat she was a moment ago.

Mitch pulled his phone from his pocket, looked up a number for a tow truck and made the call. Leaning his back against the driver's side door of McKenzie's car, he shoved his free hand into his pocket, completely relaxed. Of course he was. *He* had no problem talking on the phone.

As he spoke with the operator, he studied the ground, giving McKenzie the chance to study him. He was just as attractive from the side as from the front. The beige chinos and black polo he wore were at odds to his normally sporty style, though he wore them well. Especially the way his shirt pulled across his chest, showing off his lean muscles. Like a Greek god.

McKenzie lingered on those muscles for a drawn-out moment before her mind caught up to her sight. *Stop objectifying him!* She tore her eyes from Mitch's chest, flattening her back against the car harder than she intended. Ouch.

Sure, he was hot. She'd recognized that from the very moment he walked into the gym that first day. But he was also kind. Witty. And so playful. The whole package.

Oh my gosh, girl. Stop! If she kept thinking about his assets, her whole face would light up like Rudolph's nose on Christmas Eve. *Step aside, Rudy. There's a new reindeer in town.*

"I've got good news and bad news," Mitch said after finishing the call and returning his phone to his pocket. "Which do you want first?"

"Um ... good news?" she squeaked. Why did that sound like a question? She cleared her throat. "Always s-start with good news."

"I like your optimism. The good news is that the tow truck is coming."

"And the bad?"

Mitch angled his body toward her, his side still touching the car. "It won't be here for an hour."

"*An hour*?" She groaned. Some night this was turning out to be.

His smile turned sympathetic. "I'm afraid so. I can wait with you until it comes."

McKenzie's pulse went from almost back to normal to alarmingly elevated in less than a second. An entire hour alone with him? "Oh, you d-don't have to do that. I'll wait in my car, or go inside until it comes. I t-think Gary's still here."

Mitch shook his head. "I'd be happy to wait."

"I d-don't want to waste your time."

"Spending an hour with an awesome girl is never a waste."

Heat surged through her like flames in a fire, rushing from her stomach all the way to the top of her hairline. *This must be what it feels like to be burned at the stake.* Did Mitch notice that her face was as red as her hair? He had to. It wasn't that dark out yet.

Did he mean it, or was he only being nice? She'd heard him say stuff like that to her roommates a lot. It was hard to tell where his natural charisma ended and his true intentions began. She still hadn't been able to decipher the meaning of what happened out on the porch the other night. He'd held her hand. Twice.

Allowing him to get close to her wasn't smart. She should've pulled her hand away, but she couldn't deny the shock that connection had on her system.

Was it all just harmless flirting? McKenzie bit down on the disappointment of that sobering realization. She didn't even know how to flirt.

"Really, I'll be okay. I'm sure you have better things to do than wait for a t-tow truck."

Mitch grew serious, all flirtation gone in an instant. "McKenzie, I'm staying."

He held her eyes, and the tenderness she saw in his filled her with more heat. Out of arguments, she simply nodded.

"I'll bring my car around next to yours." He flashed her his pearly whites. "Don't go anywhere."

She rolled her eyes. "I don't think you have to worry about that."

His chuckle was a low rumble as he walked away. McKenzie reminded herself to breathe while she waited for him to come back. A whole hour with him. Piece of cake. She did harder things in practice every day.

Then why did she feel like hyperventilating?

A few minutes later, Mitch's black SUV pulled up beside her silver sedan. He hopped out and opened the hatch. "We can sit in the back while we wait," he said, motioning her over.

McKenzie climbed up and pressed her back against the side of the car, hugging her knees to her chest. Mitch sat on the other side, facing her, his long legs hanging out the back. She didn't dare look at him. Her parched mouth was full of that cottony feeling she always got on class presentation day in school. What she'd give for some water right about now.

The awkwardness grew thick as they sat in silence for a few minutes. She ventured a quick glance at him, staring out at the empty parking lot, apparently deep in thought.

Say something! Why couldn't she ever think of anything witty to break the ice? Scratch that, *any* line would work right now.

Mitch spoke first. "I thought about what you said."

"About what?"

"Volleyball. I've decided to go for it."

"Really?" She gave him what she hoped was an encouraging smile. "That's great, Mitch."

He returned her smile with one of his own. "Yeah. I think I made the right decision."

"Did you work it out so you can keep your job?" McKenzie straightened her legs out in front of her, bumping into his. The touch sent a shiver through her, and she pulled them back quickly.

"I'll train in the mornings and work in the afternoons and evenings," he said, shifting to give her more space. "It'll be busy, but I've got to support myself somehow. It's possible to earn a living from beach volleyball, but it'll take some time. Except for the teams at the top, there's not a lot of money in the sport. I'm sure you can relate."

McKenzie nodded. "Gymnastics is the same. Unless you do a lot of endorsements."

"You don't have endorsements?" Mitch asked.

She lifted her shoulders to her ears, pulling them forward and straightening her arms over her thighs. "I've modeled a bit for leotard companies, but mostly my parents pay for my t-training. I think my mother is more invested in my career than I am. Without their help, though, I wouldn't be able to keep doing it." She bit down on her tongue to keep from saying more. Where did all these words come from? And miraculously, she only'd stuttered one time in all of them.

"That's great they can help."

"Yeah." She swallowed the bitterness that came on whenever she thought of her parents. "When do you start?"

"Five a.m. Monday morning."

McKenzie made a face. "And I thought having to be at the gym by eight was early."

"I take it you're not a morning person." Mitch's lips twitched.

She snorted. "Definitely not. I sleep as late as I can on rest days. At least until nine."

"*Nine?*" Mitch whistled through his teeth. "I don't think I've slept that late ever. I was always the first one up in my house. Even my parents slept later than I did."

"Your poor parents," she said dryly.

"You have no idea. I definitely kept them on their toes."

McKenzie suspected he was referring to more than his sleeping habits. "I figured as much when you told me about your streaking experience."

His sudden crack of laughter made her jump. It was such a happy sound, and it eased a lot of her nerves. "I'm going to regret mentioning that to you, aren't I? Are you planning to hold it over me forever?"

"Until you die," she said, assuming her most somber expression. "I'll have it engraved on your tombstone."

He laughed, loosening more of the knot in her stomach.

The tow truck arrived quicker than McKenzie expected. Either that or the hour flew by. When it pulled up in front of them, Mitch retrieved her bag from the back seat of her car before the driver, a burly, tattooed man wearing a baseball cap and a blond, dagger-shaped beard, hooked it to the flatbed.

Once the car was loaded, the driver handed her a card. "That's the number for the auto shop where I'm taking your vehicle. Give them a call tomorrow and they'll have an estimate of when you can pick it up."

"Thank you," she said.

Mitch shook the man's hand. "Thanks so much."

"No problem. Good luck," the driver said in a gruff voice. He drove off in his truck, leaving McKenzie standing next to Mitch, watching her car leave the lot.

He nudged her elbow. "Come on. I'll drive you home."

Mitch navigated through the streets toward her house, chatting amiably about several topics. She chimed in occasionally, but for the most part, she was content to listen. How many times had she dreamed of meeting someone who accepted her shyness? She hadn't thought it would ever happen, but he didn't seem to mind that she was quiet.

When they pulled up in front of the house, he turned off the engine and faced her. "Here you go, home safe and sound."

"Thank you." McKenzie offered him a grateful smile. "I wasn't sure what to do before you showed up."

"I guess you could say I'm your knight in shining armor." He sat up straighter, puffing out his chest a bit. Smug pride took over his facial features.

She laughed. "I wouldn't go that far. But I'm thankful for your help."

He bobbed his head. "Do you need a ride tomorrow? I can swing by here on my way to work."

"That's okay. I can get an Uber. You've already done so much."

Mitch looked like he was going to protest, then thought better of it. "Suit yourself. I'll see you tomorrow."

McKenzie nodded and turned toward the passenger door. "Thanks again." She opened the door and swung her legs out.

His hand cupped her elbow, stopping her before she could hop out. "McKenzie, wait."

She turned back as something flickered in his eyes. Was he nervous? That couldn't be right. Mitch Skaggs never got nervous. He exuded confidence wherever he went. Not in a cocky way, but always self-assured.

He cleared his throat. "I was wondering ... Would you maybe ... go on a date with me this weekend?"

McKenzie's blood ran cold. A date? With *her*?

Bile rose in her throat. Finding things to talk about with him for an hour while waiting for a tow truck was one thing. But a whole evening was an entirely different matter. Not to mention her mother would never approve. And McKenzie really didn't need anything else to add to Mom's toxicity.

"I c-can't," she said.

"Oh."

McKenzie swiveled back to the door, grabbing onto the handle. She couldn't get out of there fast enough.

"Why not?" he asked.

When she faced him again, his eyes searched her. Confusion and something else—was it sadness?—appeared in the depths of his beautiful eyes. McKenzie didn't know what to make of it.

"I just ... don't think it's a good idea." She pulled her gaze from the heartbreaking look he gave her. "I should go."

She fumbled for the handle and threw the door open, catapulting herself from the vehicle. Without looking back, she flew across the lawn, onto the porch, and into the safety of the house.

Chapter Six

McKenzie pressed her back against the front door, leaning her head on the wood. Squeezing her eyes shut, she focused on the slow rhythm of her breathing—in, out, in, out—attempting to squelch the rising panic.

Mitch Skaggs asked her out. Mitch, who'd won her heart the day they'd met with his charisma and infectious positivity, wanted to go out with *her*. And she'd said no. Then she had to pour a whole bottle of hot sauce on his wound by bolting as fast as she could from the car.

She groaned. How was she supposed face him tomorrow?

The aroma of sugar and vanilla permeated the entryway, providing a tiny bit of comfort to her humiliation. Hallie must be baking. McKenzie pushed herself off the door and headed down the hall to the kitchen.

Hallie was indeed baking. She stood by the oven spooning balls of dough onto a cookie sheet. Elise and Rory sat close to each other on stools at the center island. Seth perched on another adjacent to Rory on the island's perpendicular side. They all looked up when McKenzie entered.

"What's wrong?" Hallie dropped another ball onto the cookie sheet. "You look upset."

"Nothing." McKenzie's attempt at a light tone fell short. "My car wouldn't start." She narrowed her eyes at her brother. "I called you. Why didn't you pick up?"

Seth pointed past her and McKenzie turned to see his phone charging in the outlet on the counter by the door. "Sorry, my phone was dead."

"What are you doing here anyway?" she asked. "I know for a fact Beej is working tonight."

"I know. I brought her dinner a while ago. Then I thought I'd come see if you were home yet. I'm staying for the cookies." He indicated the two on the plate in front of him.

McKenzie joined Hallie at the oven for a closer look. "Snickerdoodles?"

Hallie dropped one last dough ball onto the cookie sheet. "I tweaked my original recipe to make it better. You can have one if you want." She bent to open the oven.

She baked an assortment of goodies—cakes and cookies mostly —and sold them to customers and events all around town. Although her business was small while she made her way through college, she was working toward fulfilling her dream of having a brick-and-mortar bakery in the future.

"No thanks." The aroma was tempting, but McKenzie had to be extra careful about her diet. Mom's orders.

"Why didn't you call me?" Elise asked, her hand in Rory's on the countertop. "We would've picked you up."

"I didn't want to bother you. You only have a few more days together before you leave for four months. I thought you'd want to be alone."

Elise waved away her comment. "We would've come in a heartbeat. Right, Ror?"

Rory, his mouth full of cookie, agreed with a nod.

"It's okay," McKenzie said. "Mitch brought me home."

Elise shared a knowing look with Hallie, which McKenzie chose to ignore. Her crush was no secret among any of the girls in the house. Even if she'd tried to keep it one. She'd always been a terrible liar. Which was a problem when living with a bunch of roommates who were also related to each other. They were constantly up in everyone's business.

A knock sounded in the entryway, and five heads swiveled in the direction of the swinging kitchen door that led to it.

"I'd rather not answer that." McKenzie dropped onto the stool next to Seth.

Hallie cocked her head to the side, studying her for a few seconds, before dropping the oven mitt she held onto the counter and leaving the room. A moment later, the front door creaked open, and her muffled voice drifted to the kitchen. The low timbre of a male voice followed, though his words were indiscernible.

That would be Mitch.

McKenzie fought a blush, feeling three sets of eyes on her. She studied the veining on the marble countertop. Maybe she should've bypassed social hour with her roommates and gone straight to bed.

"That was Mitch," Hallie said when she'd reentered the kitchen. She turned to McKenzie. "You left your bag in his car. He was returning it."

Thank the heavens McKenzie hadn't been the one to answer. She'd have to see the guy soon enough as it was.

"He looked sad, so I asked him what was wrong." Hallie's blonde eyebrows pinched together. "He asked you on a date?"

Oh no.

"And you said no?" Hallie asked, not hiding the confusion in her voice.

"Zee, why?" Seth groaned, using the nickname he'd dubbed her when they were small. "You're not fooling anyone. The only person who doesn't know you like Mitch is ... Mitch."

McKenzie shot him her fiercest death glare. Her roommates constantly pushed her to go after Mitch, but Seth was supposed to be on her side. "He doesn't really want to go out with me. He's just a big flirt."

"Actually, he's not," Elise said. At McKenzie's doubtful expression, she added, "No really, he's not. Mitch is friendly and playful and otherworldly attractive—"

"Really, love?" Rory grumbled. "Otherworldly?"

Elise shot an amused look at him. He wasn't usually the jealous type. "You know I think you're cuter."

Rory cast his girlfriend a flirtatious glance. One that only Elise could pull from him. "I would if you showed me," he said, seductively. She giggled and leaned in to kiss him.

Seth tossed his balled-up napkin at them at the same time that Hallie held up a hand. "Please stop," she said.

"Okay, okay." Elise settled for a quick peck on Rory's mouth before turning back to McKenzie. "I've known Mitch a long time. He's always the life of the party. People are naturally drawn to him because he's so outgoing and happy all the time. But he's usually just being friendly. He only flirts with the girls he likes." She waggled her eyebrows.

McKenzie contemplated that for a minute. Could it be possible that Mitch Skaggs actually liked her? Not that he flirted with her much—there was no way she'd be able to reciprocate. Tonight, though, he seemed to be trying to.

Seth butted into her thoughts. "Stop overthinking things, Zee. If the date goes well, then you can worry about what to do next."

"What would we talk about?"

Her brother chuckled. "I don't know. Whatever comes to your mind."

McKenzie would definitely *not* tell Mitch about the thoughts swimming through her head. Those fantasies needed to stay firmly tucked away where they belonged. "Talking for an hour while waiting for a tow truck is one thing. How am I supposed to fill up an entire date?"

Elise's mouth twitched. "Mitch Skaggs has never lacked for conversation topics. By the end of the night, you'll probably wish he'd *stop* talking." They all laughed at that.

"It doesn't matter anyway," McKenzie said after the amusement had died down. "I already said no."

The timer went off, and Hallie rose to check on the snickerdoodles in the oven. "It's the twenty-first century. Why don't you ask *him* out?"

Panic traveled up McKenzie's insides, and she shook her head vigorously. "I could never do that."

"You might not have to," Elise chimed in. "I have a feeling you'll get another chance." She gave Rory a look as if she knew more than she was letting on.

Am I missing something? McKenzie rose from her stool. "I have practice in the morning. I'm going to bed."

"At least think about what we're saying," Elise said before McKenzie could make her escape.

McKenzie stopped at the swinging kitchen door and turned. "I will." The words emerged automatically, though she didn't need to think about it. Going on a date with Mitch wasn't an option, and no amount of thought or discussion would change that. "Good night."

She left the kitchen to a chorus of good nights from the others and headed upstairs to get ready for bed. As she pulled her pajamas from the bottom drawer of her dresser, a knock on her bedroom door interrupted the silence.

"It's open," she called.

The door opened a crack, and Seth poked his head into the room. "Got a second?"

She waved him in.

Seth shut the door behind him before crossing to her bed and sitting on the edge. "You okay?"

"I'm fine."

Both his ginger brows raised in doubt. "You sure? You seemed pretty shaken up earlier."

Her brother knew her way too well. But he was also the only person she felt safe to talk to about everything. She set her pajama bottoms and tank top on top of her dresser, then joined him on the bed. "Why would Mitch want to ask me out? I'm never anyone's first choice for dates."

"Hey, don't sell yourself short," Seth said. "Any guy would be lucky to go on a date with you. But he'd have to get past me first."

McKenzie swatted at his knee bent up on the bed before pulling her legs into a crisscrossed position, facing him.

"Do you …" He paused, and a question appeared in his gray-blue eyes. "Do you want to go out with him?"

She almost laughed. Seth had a right to be protective over her after all they'd been through together. But he'd never had to protect her from men. He didn't seem at all comfortable with the idea.

"I don't know," she admitted. "It doesn't matter because I can't. The Global Elites are *next year*. I can't have any distractions if I want to have a prayer of making the team."

"Bull. What's the real reason?"

McKenzie clenched and unclenched her teeth. Seth could be snarky and sarcastic with others, but he rarely allowed that side to come out with her. "That is the real reason. And you know Mom would never approve of me dating right now. Anything that isn't gymnastics is *forbidden*." She hissed the word with one hand at the corner of her mouth like a dirty secret.

Seth rolled his eyes, as he often did when they talked about their mother. "Last I checked, you were an adult."

She sighed. "An adult whose parents are still paying for her living expenses so she can focus on training. You know how controlling she is."

Her brother softened his tone. "Why do you think I chose not to go to college in Seattle and only talk to her or Dad when I absolutely have to?"

It was why McKenzie had moved to California as well. True, her mother never would've let her leave home at seventeen if Gary hadn't moved closer to his ailing mother. But a little distance was a good thing, even if her mom still managed to keep a tight hold on her youngest child.

McKenzie spent her entire life trying to live up to the woman's expectations—and always, *always* fell short.

"I really do need to focus on gymnastics," she said, steering the conversation away from Mom. "You know how important the Global Elites are to me."

Seth reached out and squeezed her shoulder. "Of course. But you also can't let that dominate your entire life. I was there after the accident when you faced the possibility of your career ending. You were completely lost. And it hurt so much to watch. I don't want to see my baby sister in that dark place again."

McKenzie hated thinking about those early days after the accident, and she knew he did too. He'd been her biggest ally back then. In a lot of ways, he still was. "I can't go out with Mitch."

"It's only one date, Zee. Mom doesn't even have to know."

McKenzie drummed her fingers on her knees. "It's not that."

"Then what?"

Warmth trickled up her neck and into her face. "He works at my gym. I don't want to be one of those athletes who dates the staff. Plus, he tapes my feet."

Seth tried unsuccessfully to cover up a snort. "I'm sorry, what? They're just feet." Then he really did laugh.

"Stop!" McKenzie shoved his shoulder, unable to hold in her own chuckle. "Have you seen mine? They're not pretty." She lifted her bare foot to demonstrate. Like the rest of her body, they'd taken too many beatings to be picture-perfect.

"I'm sure he's seen worse." Seth's amusement remained on his face. "Look, Zee, if you don't want to go out with him, fine. That's your choice. But you've been hiding behind gymnastics and Mom for too long. Whatever you do, it's time for you to take what you want from life. Be bold."

Be bold. That was the message that stuck with her after he'd left, and she lay in bed waiting for sleep to come. *It's time for you to take what you want from life.* Was she strong enough to do that?

Her entire life up to this point had been decided for her. Her whole world revolved around gymnastics. Around one dream that, whether she made the Global Elite team or not, would be over in less than a year. What then? Her mother's hold on her was strong. Did

McKenzie think it would end after she retired? If she didn't take control of her life now, would she ever?

But what did she want? She wanted to make the Global Elite team. That goal hadn't changed for years.

What else?

She wished to meet someone who could look past her shyness and accept her for who she was. She wanted companionship. Love.

She wanted a date with Mitch Skaggs.

Chapter Seven

Mitch slid into the booth across from Rory and Seth at The Burger Stop Saturday evening. "I'm surprised you wanted to hang out tonight. I thought you'd both be out with your women." He glanced at Rory. "Especially since you don't have much time left before Elise leaves for her trip."

Rory took a sip from his water glass. "It's girls' night, so I'm stuck with the likes of you two."

"They do that every week?"

Seth pulled his attention from the TV screen behind Mitch's head. "Every. Week." He rolled his eyes with a smile before turning back to the game.

The low roar of conversations rang through the restaurant. Several large TVs hung around the open room, broadcasting the Dodgers game. This burger joint was loosely considered a family establishment, but Saturday was game day, whether it be baseball in the summer, football in the fall, or any game in between. All around them, grown men—and a few women—stuffed their mouths with fries and burgers the size of their faces while cheering on the home team.

The server arrived, setting a water glass in front of Mitch before taking his order. Seth and Rory had apparently ordered before he arrived. Mitch handed back the menu and thanked her with a smile, making her blush as she scurried away to another table. He turned back to the guys, catching the amusement on Rory's face.

"Don't start," Mitch said through a laugh. He wasn't blind to the many women who found him attractive, and his buddies were more than willing to tease him about it. That was what guys did. And he couldn't help his looks. Besides, he only had one woman on his mind, and even after twenty-four hours, her rejection stung.

"Are you still licking your wounds after last night?" Seth asked at the commercial break, rubbing even more proverbial salt in said wound.

He thought it was funny, did he? That didn't improve Mitch's mood in the slightest. "I don't get it. She was finally talking to me. Why'd she say no?"

Seth's smirk changed to sympathy. "My sister is really shy. And inexperienced when it comes to dating. She's so driven to make it to the Global Elites that she's left little time for anything else."

"It seems like there's more to it though. She said she *couldn't* go out with me. That it wouldn't be a good idea. She seemed terrified about it actually."

Seth's mouth turned down in a frown, but he didn't respond.

"Sometimes McKenzie gets lost inside her own head," Rory chimed in. "She overthinks things." As Seth's roommate and Elise's boyfriend, he'd spent enough time with McKenzie to have developed somewhat of a close friendship with her. Lucky guy.

Mitch leaned forward, putting his elbows on the table and resting his chin on his fists. "I just wish I knew what she was thinking. The other day, I thought that maybe she could like me, but now I have no idea. It's like I'm stuck in a game of ping-pong." *I hate ping-pong.*

The server returned with their food. As a longtime athlete, Mitch preferred to eat healthy, so he'd passed on the jumbo burger. Even with the smaller size and sticking with water to drink, this dinner was heavier than he usually ate.

"Look," Seth said before biting into a fry. "If you really want to get to know my sister, you have to be patient. She doesn't open up quickly."

"I can be patient," Mitch grumbled. Even if frustration was the dominant emotion inside him right now. Seth's eyes narrowed, and

Mitch sensed the protective older brother coming out. So he turned to Rory. "How are you feeling about Elise's trip next week?"

Rory chewed and swallowed before answering. "Honestly, I'm not thrilled about it. But it's been her dream since long before she met me. I could never take it away from her."

"Why aren't you going with her?" Mitch bit into his burger.

"I've a deadline coming up. If I went, I'd not be able to get the score to the director in time. It's a girls' trip anyway." Under his breath, Rory muttered, "And Kendall scares me."

Mitch laughed and raised his water glass in a weird sort of cheers. Kendall's intensity scared a lot of people.

Seth wiped at the mustard dripping onto his hands with his napkin. "You know, if Elise were my girlfriend, I think I'd be worried she'd love it so much she might not come back."

Rory took a drink, contemplating. "She's a free spirit, that one. She needs space to be who she is. I'm not worried about her *or* us."

What would it be like to have that kind of confidence in a relationship? Mitch wanted that more than anything. "You two are great together."

Rory wasn't done. "Loving someone doesn't mean trying to change them into who you think they should be. We accept each other where we are and encourage each other to be the best version of ourselves we can be." He gave Mitch a pointed look.

"Why do I get the feeling you're talking about me more than you and Elise?"

Rory shifted his attention to Seth, who pursed his lips as if debating something. Finally, he spoke. "There's something you need to know."

That didn't sound good. "I'm listening," Mitch said.

Seth pushed his plate out of the way and crossed his arms on the table, leaning forward. "I'm going to be completely straight with you. I don't love the idea of you pursuing my sister. Her life has never been easy. Between her accident and our parents—particularly our mom—she's been through a lot."

"I get that." Mitch knew only the basics of McKenzie's past injury since it had happened before she started training at SoCal Elite, though he'd heard some things about it.

Seth shook his head. "I don't think you do. Not all of it anyway. There's a lot going on with her that she doesn't let anyone else see. She's under a lot of pressure. From our mom and from herself. The stress is a constant weight on her shoulders."

Mitch didn't miss the concern in Seth's eyes. Obviously, he carried that weight too.

"I'm worried," his buddy continued. "One more setback could very well crush her. I can't let that happen again."

Again? That sounded ominous. But Mitch didn't intend to break McKenzie's heart.

"Look, you're a good guy," Seth continued.

"Don't sound so shocked." Mitch couldn't keep the dryness from his tone.

Seth's mouth twitched. "Like I said before, I don't love the idea of you pursuing my sister. But at least I know you're not a jerk. All the same, please don't start something with her if you can't see it through. And if you truly care about her, find a way to take off some of her pressure. Don't add to it."

Mitch nodded. "I'll try."

"Good." Seth leaned back in his seat. "Then I have one other piece of advice for you."

"What's that?" Mitch asked.

A mischievous grin appeared on his buddy's face. "She doesn't train on Sundays. And she loves Indian food."

At home later that night, a heaviness settled in Mitch's mind as he sat at the scratched wooden table in his one-bedroom, shoebox apartment. He passed a stress ball from hand to hand, mulling over everything he'd learned from Seth. The last thing he wanted was to put more pressure on McKenzie. Especially if she was as fragile as her brother made her out to be. Was that the reason she'd rejected him? Had she felt pressured?

He thought back to their previous interactions. They'd all seemed to occur unexpectedly. He got her to talk to him and smile—and even laugh on occasion. McKenzie had seemed to enjoy being around him, then.

But how could he meet her where she was while still taking the glimmer of a relationship they had to the next step?

Mitch bolted upright as an idea came to him. The ball slipped from his hand, rolling off the table and bouncing across the floor, forgotten. A slow smile slid onto his face as he worked out his next move.

Chapter Eight

Sitting on her bed with her legs outstretched, McKenzie frowned at the headline staring back at her from her phone. *Former Junior National Champion Running Out of Time for Global Elite Comeback.* She didn't need to read the rest to get the gist of what the article was about. It was bound to be like all the others her mom insisted on sending her—stacking her against the rest of the field and reminding her that, at twenty-two, she'd made no world teams and had no national titles to her resume. She'd come close on uneven bars the year before, but her mom would never recognize that.

> Mom: You need to work extra hard in training to prove the doubters wrong. Don't let me down.

McKenzie rubbed her eyes with her palms. She couldn't possibly work any harder than she was already. Was her mom trying to cast more doubt on the likelihood of her daughter making the team? That wouldn't be surprising. McKenzie could never do anything right.

And why send this today? Sunday was supposed to be her rest day. The one day in the week she didn't eat and breathe the sport dominating her life. The only time she could push aside the road to perfection that sometimes threatened to break her.

She set her phone face down on her nightstand. If she really wanted to claim the rest she needed, she had to get off the phone. Her eyes landed on the dime-sized piece of aqua sea glass Seth had found years ago—a few months after the accident, in fact. Her brother had always loved hunting sea glass on the rocky shore near their childhood home in Seattle.

She picked it up, running her fingers over the smooth

surface, remembering the day he'd given it to her. McKenzie had been deep in the darkness of depression back then and facing the very real possibility that her career was over. She and Seth would often walk the few minutes to Lake Washington and talk for hours while combing the rocks for the little pieces of treasure. That day, their mom's verbal cruelty had reached a new height.

"The world can't be all bad," he'd said, holding it out to her, "if it can turn a piece of trash into something beautiful like this. Remember that. Better days are coming." With sorrow in his eyes, he'd turned back to the water.

Ever since that day, she'd carried it with her when she needed an extra dose of encouragement. She didn't think he even knew she still had it.

Sometimes it took hundreds of years for the ocean to polish a piece of broken bottle into glass. No matter how long it took, there had to be something good in store for her too. Right?

A soft knock floated up to her from the front door. She groaned. Her roommates were all off doing various activities that evening, and McKenzie had been looking forward to enjoying a quiet evening in an empty house. Maybe if she ignored whoever was at the door, they'd go away.

But then the creaking hinges signaled the opening of the door. "Hey, hey! Anyone home?" a familiar voice called.

Mitch?

After hesitating a few seconds, she placed the sea glass back on her nightstand and left the room, her body jumping with nerves. She paused halfway down the hallway, close enough to catch a glimpse of the entryway, but far enough away to go unnoticed on the upstairs landing.

Mitch, all six-foot-four-inches of perfection, packaged nicely in jeans and a green T-shirt, stood by the front door, a white take-out bag dangling from his fingers. He looked like he'd walked right off the cover of *Men's Health* magazine. She'd buy every copy of that edition and plaster them all over her wall. Like a shrine. Because that wasn't creepy at all.

Closing her eyes, she took a deep breath in through her nose and blew it out slowly through her mouth. *Be bold.* With that declaration, she continued to the stairs.

Mitch spotted her immediately, his face brightening. "There you are."

Fireworks erupted in her stomach, sending shock waves to every nerve ending in her body. "H-hi. What do you have?"

He held up the bag, turning it in his hands to survey it. "I was on my way home from playing volleyball with the guys, and I had a hankering for some tikka masala. But I think I got too much. Are you hungry? I couldn't possibly eat it all by myself."

His smile turned hopeful, giving him a boyish quality that somehow made him even more attractive. Mitch always radiated confidence. Did he even know the definition of doubt?

"You want to have dinner with me?" she asked.

"Why wouldn't I?"

Because I rejected you. McKenzie watched him for a beat before she made a decision. "I do like Indian food."

His smile grew. "Is that a yes?"

She nodded and turned away, motioning for him to follow. Unable to contain her glee, she grinned all the way down the hall. However, once in the kitchen, she faced him, her mask back in place.

Mitch plopped the bag on the center island. "I hope you're hungry."

"You came at the perfect time," McKenzie admitted. "I was just about to make dinner. If you'd come any later, you'd have to eat *my* food."

"Do you cook?" He reached around her and opened a cupboard, pulling out plates and cups with a familiarity of someone who'd spent a lot of time in that kitchen. A faint hint of his clean scent tickled her nose as his arm brushed her shoulder. She'd once imagined stealing one of his shirts so she could fall asleep to that smell. If anyone asked though, she'd fiercely deny it. That little fantasy was going with her to the grave.

He didn't smell like he'd spent the afternoon at the beach. *He must've showered before coming over,* she thought, then quickly steered her mind away from that mental image.

"I can hold my own," she said. They sat down on stools next to each other and dished out rice, tikka masala, and naan. McKenzie took the container of sesame green beans that Mitch handed her. "Are you a good cook?"

"I'm terrible." He shot her a self-deprecating smile. "My mom tried to teach me, but cooking is a lost art on me."

"What do you eat, then?"

He chuckled. "I have a handful of meals I know how to make. I won't starve."

"We wouldn't want that now, would we?" Wow, could she be any more awkward?

"Did you find out what was wrong with your car?" Mitch took a bite of masala.

With her mouth full of naan, McKenzie chewed, aware of how agonizingly slow each chomp of her jaw seemed.

"Sorry," he said. "Perfect timing, right?"

She waved him away, finally able to swallow. "It needs a new starter. Hopefully, I'll get it back sometime next week."

"I'm glad you could get it figured out."

"Me too. I'm not, however, looking forward to telling my parents." Her body gave an involuntary shudder.

Mitch's brows knit together. "They won't be happy?"

"No." McKenzie dropped her eyes to her plate. "My mother will think I broke the car on purpose. I swear, I can't do anything right." Shoot, why had she admitted that worry? Her shyness already made her weird enough. She didn't need to make things worse by airing her family drama.

He studied her with concern, turning up the heat inside McKenzie's body. She disguised her discomfort by scooping masala onto a piece of naan and taking a bite.

"I'd offer to give you a ride this week, but practice starts early tomorrow."

McKenzie swallowed, grateful for the change of subject. "Oh yeah. Are you excited?"

"Yeah." His tone gave away some reluctance. "I'm looking forward to it."

"You don't sound like it."

"No, I am," Mitch said hastily, bobbing his head for emphasis. "I've just been out of serious competition for almost a decade. It'll be … interesting." After a moment of heavy silence, he said, "So, what do you like to do for fun?"

Fun? She gave an exaggerated shrug. "I don't really have time for hobbies. Pretty pathetic, huh?" She clasped her hands in her lap, playing with her fingers. "I spend all my time in the gym."

Mitch pushed his empty plate away from him and leaned one elbow on the counter, swiveling his knees to face her. "I'll ask you this, then. If you had an entire week off from training, what would you do?"

McKenzie thought for a moment while she chewed. "Probably read a lot. Or binge-watch old movies. Maybe write a book." She didn't consider herself a gifted writer, but she'd always enjoyed her English classes in high school.

"You should write an autobiography," he said.

"About me?"

"That's what an autobiography is, right?"

"I know what it is." She fiddled with the napkin next to her plate. "But who'd want to read a book about me?"

"Gymnastics fans. Other athletes inspired by your journey." His pause drew McKenzie's attention back to him. "I'd read it. I've wanted to get to know you better."

His words weren't overtly flirtatious, but the way he said them, and the hint of a smile he gave her, caused her chest to swell, confusing her. This man was so out of her league, he practically had a different zip code. She was still trying to wrap her head around the fact that she was having dinner with him.

Alone.

Like a date.

What did this mean?

She shook her head to clear it, forcing a smile as her eyes rose to meet his warm, inquisitive ones. It was as if he could read her thoughts, gaining access to her innermost insecurities. Now was the time to change the subject. "Thank you for dinner."

"You're welcome." Mitch stood and reached for her plate. "If you still have room in your stomach, I know of a great smoothie place I'd like to take you to."

"Smoothies? Don't those places use a ton of sugar?" She snapped the lid over the leftover rice.

Mitch rinsed their dishes before depositing them in the sink. "I get it. You like to eat healthy. So do I. That's why I asked the first time I went, and the guy told me they're one of the only places in LA County that doesn't add sugar to sweeten their drinks." He lowered his voice to a stage whisper, that irresistible twinkle appearing in his eyes. "And if he lied to me, I promise I won't tell Gary."

It wasn't Gary that worried her. But Mitch's playfulness made her smile anyway. "I might be up for that. On one condition."

"What's that?"

"I'm buying." Mitch began to protest, but McKenzie cut him off. "You brought dinner. It's only fair that I pay for dessert."

"Alright," he conceded, waggling his eyebrows. "I'll let you be my sugar mama just this once."

Did she just giggle? She never giggled. It must be all the nervous jitters taking over her body.

After storing the leftovers in the fridge, McKenzie went upstairs to grab her flip-flops in her room. She slid her credit card into the pocket of her shorts, then stopped. She wouldn't hear the end of it if her mom found a charge for a possibly sugar-infested smoothie place on her credit card statement. The last time McKenzie had used her card to go out to eat with her roommates, she'd received an hour-long lecture about the evils of restaurant food and the importance of putting the right nutrients in her body to aid in her training.

Yes, checking McKenzie's credit card statement was one of Mom's favorite ways of making sure she stayed in line. It was right up at the top next to weekly calls with Gary.

McKenzie crossed to her nightstand and pulled some emergency cash from the drawer, then met Mitch by the front door. The last golden rays of daylight shone low in the sky as they stepped outside, casting a heavenly glow on everything it touched. They walked across the grass to his car parked at the curb.

"Thank you," she said when he held the passenger door open for her.

"You're very welcome." He waited for her to pull her legs in before shutting the door and jogging to the driver's side. She could add gentleman to his list of attractive qualities. Did the man have any flaws?

"Where is this place?" she asked when he slid behind the wheel.

He put the car into drive and pulled away from the curb. "It's here in Buena Hills. Elise and I discovered it a while back."

A few minutes later, they turned into a small parking lot lining a cluster of shops on Main Street. McKenzie got out and met Mitch on the sidewalk.

"It's up here a bit." Placing a hand on the small of her back, he pointed in the direction of the smoothie shop. She felt the simple gesture all the way to her toes.

The bell above the door announced their arrival in the brightly lit café. It took all of ten seconds for her to survey the space. The walls were painted in bright greens, pinks, and yellows, and framed paintings of tropical fruits adorned them. Three blenders lined the back wall behind the counter, waiting to be used to whip up delicious beverages for customers. Two high circle tables, each accommodating two plastic stools, were placed near the large window facing the street.

From behind the counter, a teenager watched their approach, his yellow-blond hair swooped over one eye. He wore a black shirt that said, *Got Smoothies?* McKenzie wouldn't be surprised if he'd come to his shift directly from surfing the waves. He gave them a lazy smile when they reached the counter. "Hey, bruh. What can I get you?"

They gave him their orders and paid before sitting at a table to wait. Surfer Dude dumped a bunch of ingredients into the blenders, and a loud grating noise filled the small café, making conversation impossible. When McKenzie's name was called a few minutes later, Mitch went to retrieve their drinks, handing one to her.

A burst of strawberry and banana filled her mouth when she took a sip. She almost groaned in delight. "Oh my gosh," she mumbled through a mouthful of fruity goodness.

"Good, huh?" Mitch took a large swig of his.

"This is the best smoothie I've ever had. How did I not know about this place?"

"It's easy to miss. Now that you know it's here, you'll want to keep coming back." He held the door for her, and they walked outside into the late summer twilight. "I don't recommend coming too often though. Your bank account might start a riot."

"It *is* pricey." Twenty dollars for two smoothies? *There better be fairy dust in these drinks.* McKenzie was grateful she'd had enough cash lying around. Mom definitely wouldn't have approved of that expense. "I'll make sure to save it for special occasions."

They wandered along Main Street, looking in shop windows as they passed. Where Los Angeles was large and impersonal, mom and pop restaurants and shops filled downtown Buena Hills, making it quaint and charming. As they walked, Mitch asked her questions about her interests, goals, and ambitions. Aside from the basics, he steered away from topics about her family. She was grateful for that —the last thing she wanted was to spoil the peaceful vibe with talk of her parents.

When they reached the end of Main Street, they crossed the street and entered a small park, wandering to the swings. McKenzie set her smoothie on the wood chips next to her and started pumping her legs forward and back, gaining momentum. The wind whipped through her hair and cooled her skin. Exhilaration coursed through her veins, the same way it did with every swing from the uneven bars. She loved this feeling of freedom.

Mitch chuckled from the next swing. "Hey look, we're married."

"What?" *Married?* She glanced over at him and noticed they were swinging in unison. "I forgot about that. It's been so long since I've been on a swing."

What would it be like to be married to Mitch? If it were similar to the way she felt right now, she'd say yes in a heartbeat if he asked.

Mitch's long legs easily pulled him higher, getting them out of sync. "And now we're divorced," McKenzie said. The happiness inside her dimmed a little. It was only a silly child's game, but the reminder that she could easily end up alone was a sobering one.

"No, McKenzie, don't leave me!" he cried in fake agony. "I can't live without you!"

That snapped her out of the blues. Her laughter rang out against the sound of creaking swings. Their teasing morphed into a competition to see who could swing the highest, trash-talking as they pumped their legs harder. She couldn't remember the last time she'd felt this light.

When she was too dizzy to keep going, McKenzie stopped pumping and coasted until her swing slowed.

Mitch did the same. Back on the ground, he picked up his smoothie beside his swing and took a long sip. "Thanks for hanging out with me tonight. I've wanted to get to know you better for a while," he said after swallowing.

McKenzie didn't know what to say. "You have?"

"Why is that so surprising?"

She didn't answer right away. The swing swiveled a bit as she bent to pick her smoothie up from the ground. She peeked up at him to find him still looking at her. "I know I'm shy. It's something I've tried changing about myself but ..."

Reaching over, he took her hand and gave it a squeeze. Warm tingles rippled up her arm. "Some things are hard to change," he said.

She kept her eyes on their entwined hands hanging between the swings. It wasn't the first time he'd touched her like this, but the excitement of it hadn't worn off. "Not that it matters."

"What do you mean?"

McKenzie hesitated. She wasn't often comfortable sharing the burdens she'd carried around her whole life. But something about his silent support urged her on.

"Gymnastics dictates every aspect of my life," she spoke slowly. "Anything that isn't moving me toward my goal of making the Global Elite team is an unnecessary distraction."

Mitch traced soft circles on the back of her hand with his thumb. "Says who?" His voice was quiet, serious. "You?"

McKenzie shook her head, still staring at her hand in his. The slow rotation of his thumb across her skin hypnotized her, breaking down the walls she'd worked so hard to build. Tears stung her eyes, mortification coming with them. She hadn't cried in years, and she wouldn't start now. Not in front of him.

Mitch bent down to put his smoothie back on the ground, never letting go of her hand. Pulling her swing closer to his, he lifted her face with his free hand. "Then who?"

She sighed, years of pent-up pressure expelling from her like the fizz of a shaken soda bottle. "My mother. And my coach to some degree."

"I know Gary. He doesn't seem so bad."

"Oh, Gary's great," McKenzie hurried to clarify. "To be honest, he's more of a father figure than my own dad. But in gymnastics, you're always striving for perfection. The pressure gets to me sometimes."

Mitch was silent for a moment, his expression unreadable. Finally, he said, "Do you still like gymnastics?"

"Of course. It's my life."

"But ..."

McKenzie blew out a tense breath. "My mother is so controlling." As if a dam broke, all her years of pent-up frustration came rushing out. "She thinks since she pays for my living expenses, she gets to make all my decisions. She's always been like this, but it's gotten even worse after my accident."

"Do you mind me asking what happened?" Mitch asked.

McKenzie rubbed her face with her free hand, fighting to keep her composure as all the memories of those dark days came rushing back. After a few shaky breaths, she spoke. "It happened at junior nationals when I was fourteen. Everyone expected me to repeat as all-around champion. Maybe the pressure got to me, I don't know. I got lost in the air on my vault and landed on my head, snapping my neck. The doctors said I was lucky I wasn't paralyzed."

Next to her, Mitch cursed under his breath.

"Because of some complications, it took two whole years to completely recover from it. But even after that, I struggled a lot mentally. I ended up quitting."

Though he was quiet, she knew he was listening. She hadn't had the courage to look at him during her tale, afraid she'd lose what little control she had over her raw emotions. When she finally snuck a peek at him, he was shaking his head in awe.

"Why'd you come back?"

"I was supposed to be at my peak for the last Global Elites. Instead, I sat on my couch watching, bawling my eyes out over a tub of Rocky Road, wishing I was there. Shortly after, I told my parents I was making a comeback. Gary had moved his family to LA to be with his sick mother, so I begged my parents to let me come down here to train with him again. Reluctantly, they agreed. I think having Seth going to school here helped. Now I'm twenty-two, competing with gymnasts five, even six, years younger than me. Next summer is my one shot before I retire."

"That's incredible," Mitch whispered.

"Tell that to my mother. She's always saying I'm too old."

"You're not the only gymnast competing in your twenties. There are plenty out there who are even older than you."

McKenzie sighed again. "I know that. But she expects perfection all the time. And I'm not that. It's hard to take her criticism all the time."

Mitch swiveled their swings so they faced each other, their knees touching. He took her other hand in his. "That's really hard."

"This was *my* dream. And now I don't even know if I want to keep going." She leaned forward, resting her face on their ball of hands in his lap.

Mitch removed one of his hands, using it to gently massage her neck. Could he feel the scar? It had faded a lot over the years, though not completely.

For a moment, she focused on the soothing pressure of his fingers working the knots from her shoulder. Then she wiped her eyes on her hand and peeked up at him. "Sorry. I really didn't want to cry. I don't talk about it much, so I guess the emotion was bound to come out eventually. And you're the lucky winner."

He chuckled at her dry tone. "Don't apologize. You can vent anytime. At least you're talking to me."

McKenzie sat up and gave him a small smile. "It takes me a while to open up to people."

"I know." He fingered a strand of hair that had come lose from her ponytail. "I mean it though. If you ever need to talk—about anything—I'll listen."

Comfort pooled within her. This man somehow knew exactly what to say to ease the pressure simmering right below the surface. "Thanks. Sorry I freaked out the other night when you asked me out." Pausing, she debated whether to go on. She'd already shared way more than she'd intended, so what was a little more? "I've never been on a date." Humiliation ignited her cheeks.

"Never?"

She looked away, thankful the darkness masked her face, which had to be as red as a tomato by now. "I wouldn't even know how to act."

Mitch bowed his head to look into her face, forcing her eyes on his. Even the shadow of his gaze was warm, compassionate. "This *is* a date. And you're doing fine."

The warmth of her cheeks turned to full burning, and she couldn't help the smile splitting her face. Did he realize the hold he had on her with his dreamy brown eyes and playful smile?

And the way he responded to her with tenderness and compassion, was it any wonder why he had her heart?

"We should get going." Mitch squeezed her hand. "We both have early mornings tomorrow." He stood, gently pulling her from the swing.

"Will you tell me how it goes?" she asked, disappointed when he dropped her hand as they started their walk toward the center of town.

"Of course."

All too soon, they arrived back at the car and drove to McKenzie's house. Mitch walked her to the door. "Thank you for dinner." She turned to face him. "And for introducing me to the best smoothie place in Southern California."

Mitch smirked. "They were pretty amazing, weren't they?"

"I can still taste it. Can I see you tomorrow?" *Look at me being bold.* "I want to hear about your first day."

He nodded. "I'll be in the office in the afternoon. You could stop by when you're on break."

He held his arms out, and she stepped in for a hug. His tall frame engulfed her. With her cheek pressed against his muscular chest, his heartbeat thudded against her ear. Its soothing rhythm picked up pace, matching her own rapid pulse. Losing herself in the comfort of his arms, the stress that seemed her constant companion evaporated, creating a feeling of security she hadn't felt in a long time. Probably never.

Mitch pulled away, shoving his hands in his pockets. "I should go." He held her eyes for a long moment and McKenzie's breath caught. Something had shifted between them tonight, charging the air with a new longing.

"Good night, McKenzie." He stepped back toward the porch steps.

"Good night," she answered on a breath, her sigh one of both disappointment and relief.

Leaning against the stone balustrade that overlooked the lawn below, she watched him saunter to his car. Long after his taillights disappeared, she stood there, replaying the most perfect date of her life. True, it was the only date of her life, though she couldn't picture another topping it.

And that hug! She'd never received one quite like it before. She shoved a hand in the pocket of her shorts, fingering the sea glass she'd placed there before they'd left for the smoothie shop. Hope surged in her heart. The very heart he held in his hands.

Chapter Nine

The next afternoon, McKenzie stopped outside the clinic on the way to her afternoon training session. Mitch should be done with his first practice by now, and she was dying to know how it went. Still, she hesitated, her hand shaking as it hovered over the doorknob.

In the past, when she'd faced something that terrified her, fear had almost always won. Too many times she'd used gymnastics as a cover for her insecurities. She didn't want to let that happen with Mitch. Not after last night.

But what if she was reading too much into their date?

For perhaps the millionth time in the last sixteen hours, their hug entered her mind, and the increasingly familiar buzz zipped through her body. Did a man usually hold a woman like that if he didn't like her? She didn't know, but she wanted to find out.

And that required walking into the clinic.

Be bold. Swallowing past the lump in her throat, she pushed the door open.

Mitch wasn't at his desk. In fact, there was no sign of him in the front room at all. Maybe he was with a patient. She'd have to come back later. She turned to go, relief washing over her.

"Do you need something?"

She whirled around. Jared sat at the corner desk, eyeing her curiously. Had he been there the whole time?

"Oh ... I ... um ..." She stopped talking and squared her shoulders. "I'm looking for Mitch."

Jared gestured with his thumb to another desk. "He's over there. On the floor."

"On the ... floor?"

Jared appeared to be holding back a laugh. "See for yourself."

McKenzie took hesitant steps in the direction he'd indicated. There was Mitch, laying spread eagle on the carpet behind the desk, his arms outstretched. His black baseball cap covered his face.

Approaching his horizontal form, she nudged his side gently with her toe. "Mitch?"

A grunt sounded from underneath his hat.

She bit back a giggle, crouching next to him. "Did they break you?"

A low, rumbling chuckle came from deep in his chest. "I'm not broken. Just very sore." He removed the hat from his face and sat up, dragging his long body a few inches to the desk. Leaning his back against it, he stretched his legs flat and patted the carpet at his side.

McKenzie dropped down next to him. "So ... how was it?"

A wide smile split his face. "It was *awesome,* Zee!"

Warmth filled her veins at hearing her nickname. Only her brother, and sometimes her roommates, ever called her that. She liked it best coming from Mitch. "Really? Even though you can hardly move?"

"Tom pushed me hard today. It felt good to be in training mode again. I didn't realize how much I've missed it."

"I'm glad. I was thinking about you all morning."

Mitch arched a dark eyebrow. "I *am* rather irresistible, aren't I?"

A blush crept up McKenzie's neck. To cover it up, she lightly smacked his arm. "I meant I wondered how your practice was going."

His lips curved into a devilish grin. "Oh, *that's* what you meant," he said before resting his head against the desk and closing his eyes.

McKenzie had the sudden urge to lean her head against his shoulder. She shook the temptation away. "Are you sure you're okay?"

He nodded, keeping his eyes closed. "Just tired. I was up early this morning. And a pretty girl kept me out late last night."

His teasing had a bad effect on her complexion. And yet, she was beginning to like his flirting.

They sat in silence for a moment until he rolled his head to the side and opened his eyes. "I had a great time last night."

The sincerity of his smile pierced straight to her heart. "Me too," she whispered, dropping her gaze to her hands clasped in her lap. "I haven't had that much fun in a long time."

He inclined his head closer and dropped his tone to match hers. "I'm glad. We should do it again soon."

McKenzie kept her eyes on her hands. She was having trouble breathing with him so close. "I'd like that."

He sat up a little straighter, and his voice regained its original volume. "Because let's be honest. Who wouldn't want to hang out with someone of my caliber?"

She threw her head back and laughed. It was impossible not to with his playful arrogance and infectious smile that sent a thousand warm fuzzies racing down her body when she looked at him.

He bumped her side playfully with his arm. McKenzie returned the gesture. Was it her imagination, or had he moved closer? She didn't think their legs had been touching when she'd sat down. They were now.

Mitch's phone went off in the pocket of the leg next to hers, tickling her thigh. He shifted away from her enough to pull it out. Despite her curiosity over who was texting him, she turned enough keep herself from snooping. Her gaze settled on Jared, who seemed about to fall out of his chair in shock. What was that about? His staring chased away all the warm fuzzies.

"Sorry," Mitch said, making her jump. He reached up behind his head to place his phone on the desk. "My brother wanted to know if I was still alive after this morning."

McKenzie forced a smile. "That's okay. I need to get to the gym anyway." She hurried to stand. "Gary won't be happy if I'm late."

Thankfully, Mitch didn't catch on to her discomfort. He reached out to her. "Help me up, will you?"

Clasping his hand, she ignored the spark traveling up her arm and pulled. He pushed off the carpet with a groan. "I'm *so* old. My body isn't seventeen like it was the last time I did this."

"Because twenty-five is so old," McKenzie said dryly. They walked to the door together.

"Hey, I'll be twenty-six on Saturday. Technically, I'm closer to thirty than I am to twenty."

"It's your birthday this week? I hadn't realized."

Mitch opened the door, letting her exit first, then leaned his side against the doorframe. "We didn't know each other this time last year. I started working here in September."

"I guess I'll wish you happy birthday now in case I don't see you before then."

"Thanks," he said. "But I hope you do."

McKenzie's heart fluttered all the way down the hall to the gym. Mitch wanted to see her again. Before the weekend. She never would've thought it possible even a few weeks ago.

Walking into the chalky air of the gym, she stripped off her T-shirt but left her tight shorts on over her sleeveless practice leotard, hurrying to where Gary and her teammates were prepping the uneven bars.

"You're late." The coach spared only the briefest glance from the bar he was spreading with chalk.

McKenzie clasped her hands behind her back. "Sorry, Gary. Bad traffic. My Uber was late."

He accepted her excuse with a nod. "Don't let it happen again."

"I won't."

Turning back to the bars, he motioned for Evie to go first. With his attention away from her, McKenzie breathed a sigh of relief.

"Bad traffic? My eye," Aria whispered in her ear, and McKenzie jumped. "You live less than five miles from here."

"Uh ..." McKenzie reached her arms above her head to stretch her biceps, avoiding looking at her teammate. "Buena Hills has traffic too. Have you tried driving past the high school when all the kids are coming back from lunch?"

Aria rolled her eyes. "I don't think that's it. I think a certain athletic trainer held you up." Her lips curled into a sneaky smile.

McKenzie elbowed her teammate sharply in the arm. "Aria!" she hissed. She jabbed a finger in Gary's direction. If her coach found out about Mitch, her mother wouldn't be far behind. She'd never underestimate Mom's ability to keep tabs on her.

Not deterred in the slightest, Aria gave her a knowing grin, though something lurked behind it that McKenzie couldn't identify. An uncomfortable feeling settled in her gut.

"So, were you with him?" Aria asked.

Before she could respond, Evie dismounted, and Gary called McKenzie over for her turn, thankfully ending the conversation. As she approached the bars, she tried to clear her head of all things Mitch. But an uneasiness remained. After months of keeping her crush on him under wraps at the gym—or so she'd thought—too many people were starting to notice.

It would be a frosty day in purgatory before she'd let a rumor about her and Mitch get back to her mother. Which meant there could be no more interactions with him at the gym.

Chapter Ten

When Mitch emerged from the clinic's conference room on Thursday afternoon, Jared was halfway out the door.

"Hey, man, are you busy right now?" he asked, stepping back into the room.

Mitch set his laptop on top of his desk. He'd just wrapped up a meeting with a teenaged diver and her parents, discussing the recovery plan he'd created to get her back to competition following a rotator cuff injury. "I have a conditioning session in"—he checked his watch— "thirty minutes, but I could spare a few before then. What's up?"

"I just got a call from the gym about a possible hamstring injury," Jared said. "I was heading there now, but I have an appointment with a patient in a few minutes. If you're not busy ..."

The gym? Mitch would welcome any chance to get a glimpse of McKenzie in her element. It wasn't the same as actually spending time with her, but a smile or wave—maybe even a quick conversation—would make up for the disappointing fact that she hadn't come to visit him at the clinic again in the past three days. "Sure, I can cover for you."

The corner of Jared's mouth twitched up. "It's not McKenzie."

Apparently, Mitch needed to work on his poker face. He ran a hand over his mouth, wiping away the smile. "I didn't think it was."

Jared laughed, the deep booming sound taking over the room. "Make sure to keep it professional."

Mitch scoffed as he lifted his AT bag onto his shoulder. "What're you talking about? I'm always professional." He ignored Jared's disbelieving smirk and left the clinic.

It was definitely professional the way he practically skipped all the way to the gym. Professional and manly. Oh boy, he really had it bad for this woman. *Is that even a surprise?*

Stepping into the gym, he immediately scanned the large area for McKenzie. He probably should've first located the athlete needing his assistance; she was his first priority after all. But searching for McKenzie had become automatic since he'd noticed her running through her beam routine on his first day at SoCal Elite almost a year ago. Like she was some sort of magnet, attracting him to her whenever they were in the same room.

He spotted her over by the uneven bars, chalking up her hands in preparation for her turn. As if sensing him watching, she looked up from the chalk bucket and met his stare. He lifted a hand in a wave.

Contrary to what he expected, she didn't seem happy to see him. Instead, her eyes widened and darted over to Gary, who was spotting Aria on the bars. Then she looked back at Mitch with an expression on her face that he couldn't even begin to interpret. She offered the tiniest wave known to man before turning back to the bucket of white dust in front of her. As if they hadn't just shared the best date of his life a few days before.

Odd. Attempting to act unbothered, he continued on to the gymnast who'd necessitated his trip to the gym in the first place, though his mind remained on McKenzie as he assessed the injury. Why had she acted like that? He'd thought after their date on Sunday, and her visit to the clinic the next day, that she'd warmed up to the idea of at least being his friend. And yet, she didn't seem even a little bit thrilled to see him just now. In fact, she acted as though those interactions had never even happened.

An unsettling feeling came over him. After all the progress he'd made with her, had something happened to cause her to shut him out again?

A guy shouldn't have to work on his birthday. Not that Mitch minded being at the clinic. He loved his job. Still, his current schedule didn't leave much time to celebrate the start of another trip around the sun. He could think of several things he'd rather be doing on a Saturday evening than working, and all of them involved McKenzie, even though her lackluster response to seeing him in the gym on Thursday confused him.

He sighed on his way back to the clinic after overseeing a conditioning session with the swim team—his final of the day. Had he done something to make her change her mind about him? Was it because he hadn't made much of an effort this week? It wasn't that he didn't want to. Early morning trainings followed by work had created a certain kind of exhaustion he'd never experienced before. An overabundance of energy was rarely something he lacked, but lately, he barely managed to make the drive back to Long Beach at the end of the day before collapsing for the night. It was a good kind of exhaustion for sure, but taxing all the same.

He opened the door as a burly athlete with the neck the size of Mitch's thigh was leaving. Backtracking out the door, he held it open. The athlete—probably a wrestler—thanked him, and Mitch nodded a greeting as he passed.

Jared exited an exam room as Mitch entered. "There's a box on your desk."

"A box?" Mitch tilted his head to the side. "What is it?"

"I don't know. It was left outside the clinic."

Intrigued, Mitch approached his desk. Sure enough, a small box, wrapped in shiny green paper, lay on top of the book of medical terminology he'd set down earlier. A folded index card with his name on it was tucked into the skinny, white ribbon. He plucked it out. Neat, loopy penmanship filled the entire inside.

I hope you can put this to good use.
   Happy Birthday!
   -McKenzie

A gift from McKenzie? Interesting. She couldn't possibly have changed her mind completely if she'd thought to get him a present for his birthday. Right?

Mitch set the notecard down and picked up the box, ripping off the wrapping paper and lifting the lid. A tube of Icy Hot was nestled in shimmery silver confetti. *What the heck?*

He pulled it out, placing it on the desk, then searched through the rest of the confetti for anything else that might be hiding underneath. Nothing.

Icy Hot? He picked up the note again. *Put it to good use?*

Then everything clicked, and he threw his head back and laughed. He'd complained about being old the last time he'd seen her.

The sound drew Jared's attention. "What's up?"

Mitch held up the tube. "It's from McKenzie."

"I didn't realize Icy Hot was so funny."

"Only if you understand the joke." Mitch couldn't wipe the smile off his face. McKenzie was thinking about him!

Jared leaned back in his chair, surveying Mitch like he'd lost his mind. "So ... you and McKenzie, huh?"

"I hope so." Mitch studied the feminine handwriting again. Almost a year ago, he'd lost his heart to her. Every discovery he made of her since only caused him to fall even harder. Here was another side of her—a wittier side, one he found insanely attractive. With each interaction, she was gradually gifting him each piece of her puzzle, and he wouldn't stop until he'd put together the whole beautiful picture.

Chapter Eleven

McKenzie closed her eyes and breathed in deeply. The pounding of her heart protested against her ribs as she clenched and then relaxed her sweaty, shaking hands. Not even the copious amounts of chalk dust she'd rubbed on them could prevent the clamminess.

I can do this. I will *do this.*

Opening her eyes, she stared down the runway, glaring at her nemesis. The vault stood unyielding at the other end. She took another deep breath, attempting to keep her panic at bay. She willed herself to take the first step, but her mind and body didn't seem to be on speaking terms.

Gary's voice called out above the other noises in the gym, though it all mixed together as a distant rumble in her ears. She was too focused on getting her feet to move to register what he was saying.

Finally, she rubbed her hands together, took one last steadying breath, and miraculously burst forward.

With every step, she picked up speed, the vault growing closer. She approached the end of the runway and dropped into a roundoff, jamming her feet onto the springboard and using it to power her handspring onto the vault. Pushing off the table, she exploded into the air, tucking her arms into herself as she flipped and twisted.

She landed in a heap of soft, squishy foam. All sounds of the gym, muted a moment earlier, flooded her ears. Relief pushed away the last remnants of negative energy inside her. She'd faced her fear, as she did almost every day. Some days, she lost.

Today was a win. Sort of.

"Come on out, McKenzie," Gary called.

Pushing her way through the large foam blocks reaching up to her shoulders, she made it to the side and took his hand. He pulled her from the pit.

"You had insane height on that vault," he said, patting her arm. "And your form was impeccable, as always. You could easily fit the extra twist and still land on your feet."

McKenzie's posture drooped. "I just can't get my body to do it." Even eight years and weekly sessions with her sports psychologist hadn't helped her work up the courage to attempt the vault that had almost ended her career and her life.

Gary's expression turned soft, and he laid both his hands on her shoulders. "I get it. It's a mental block. Thankfully, the World team selection committee will mostly be watching you on bars and beam. So you'll need to nail those routines at nationals. But I know you. You won't be able to truly get past this block until you've conquered that vault."

No matter how many times he'd said as much, McKenzie hated hearing it. He was right of course. Gary was always right, though that didn't make training on vault any easier. "I'll work harder."

"You'll get there." Gary patted her shoulders, then backed away. "Take a break. You can go again in a bit."

McKenzie walked to the side of the runway and grabbed her water bottle. She took a long swig of the cool liquid as she scanned the gym. Her breath caught in her throat when her eyes landed on Mitch, who was watching her with his hands on his hips.

What's he doing here? How was she supposed to keep her little crush on him a secret if he kept showing up, trying to talk to her? And yet, she couldn't help the little flutter of giddy excitement rising in her chest.

He gave her an enthusiastic two thumbs-up, a slip of paper crumpled in one of his fists. Then he crouched down in the area where she'd dumped her bag. When he stood again, his playful smile worked its way onto his face, stopping her breath. Oh, how she loved that smile.

She had to be careful. Risking a glance at Gary, she found him preoccupied working with Aria on her vault. Evie stood nearby, watching them. McKenzie turned back to Mitch, angling her body enough to block the small wave she gave him. She pointed to her bag. *What are you doing?* she mouthed.

His grin turned impish as his shoulders lifted. Then he waved again and left the gym.

She shook her head, fighting the amusement from showing on her face, as well as the urge to rush over to her bag and discover what was on the paper he'd placed in it. It would only take a moment.

She started toward it, then stopped. She couldn't have Mitch distracting her from her training. Whatever he had to tell her would still be there after practice was over. Changing directions, she joined Evie by the vault, instead. The note would have to wait.

By the time practice ended hours later, she'd forgotten all about the paper. Out of breath from her cooldown jog around the floor exercise, she walked off the mats to her bag and pulled out a pair of black joggers. The paper, caught in the folds of fabric, fluttered to the ground. She slipped on her pants, then bent to pick it up. The note was short and the writing so untidy she had to squint to decipher the words.

Thanks for the gift.

-Mitch

P.S. Passing notes is fun. You know what's more fun? Texting. Don't you think it's time you gave me your number?

The fact that he'd gotten a kick out of the joke pleased her more than she'd thought it would. His note was nothing special, but her insides still bubbled as if he'd written a steamy love letter.

"What's that?" Aria asked, peering over McKenzie's shoulder.

McKenzie jumped, clutching the note tight against her chest. Heat crept up her neck.

Aria snorted. "Like that's not obvious at all." Her peal of laughter drew several glances their way. "What does lover boy have to say?"

"*Aria!*" McKenzie hissed, hugging the paper to her chest. She shot a nervous glance at Gary. Her coach was chatting with one of the program administrators nearby and hadn't noticed the commotion. She breathed a sigh of relief. "He's not my lover boy. It's only a thank-you note."

"Is that why you're blushing like an overcooked lobster?" Aria's mouth curled upward in amusement.

McKenzie ignored her comment, though it was impossible to ignore the heat turning up on her skin. She shoved the note in her bag and zipped it up. "Really, it's nothing. I'll see you tomorrow." She walked out of the gym before Aria could say anything more.

Her training partner didn't know about the tense relationship McKenzie had with her mother. She was friends with Aria on a superficial level, not close enough to trust her with personal matters. Which was why McKenzie refused to discuss anything having to do with Mitch. She'd never admitted out loud that she liked him. Yet somehow Aria knew. And if Aria knew, soon everyone at SoCal Elite would find out.

It was getting harder every day for McKenzie to keep her growing attachment to Mitch private. Then again, maybe this was one secret she didn't want to keep anymore.

Chapter Twelve

It was raining by the time Mitch finally left the clinic on Monday evening. He lifted the hood of his rain jacket and made a mad dash to his SUV, instinctively scanning the lot for any sign of McKenzie's car. It wasn't among the few vehicles still scattered on the concrete.

Her simple birthday gift had helped ease some of his confusion after her lackluster reception to him when he came into the gym on Thursday. However, two days after it appeared at the clinic, she still hadn't responded to his note. Had he overstepped by asking for her number? *Maybe she was only being nice.*

He growled softly. These mixed signals could drive a guy mad. He'd never had to work this hard to get a girl to like him. He wasn't one to overthink things. Once he made a decision, he usually stuck with it. This constant second-guessing was making his head hurt. Maybe if he just aired his feelings out in the open, he'd figure out where she stood. *Ha, you'd probably scare her off completely.*

He backed out of his spot. He should go home; the morning would come soon enough, and he was bone tired. But Elise was leaving for Europe tomorrow, and he'd promised to stop by to say goodbye. The prospect of seeing McKenzie, even for only a few minutes, gave him extra incentive. Even if she didn't want to see him.

By the time he pulled up in front of the house, the rain had stopped. He walked across the wet grass, kicking up water droplets as he made his way to the porch. He gave a few quick raps on the door before opening it. "Yoohoo, anyone home?"

"In here," Elise called from the living room.

After stepping inside, he shut the door behind him, then headed toward her voice. She and Rory stood from the couch as he entered the room.

"Hey, Mitch," Elise said. "It's good to see you."

Mitch accepted her quick hug. "Sorry to interrupt. I came to say goodbye."

"Aw ... thanks. I'm glad you did."

"And I was also hoping"—he cleared his throat—"to see McKenzie."

Elise gave a giddy little clap. "Of course you did. She's upstairs. I'll get her." To Rory, she said, "I'll be right back, and then we can go."

Rory acknowledged her with a flick of his head, then extended his hand to Mitch. "Hey, mate. It's good to see you. How's your trainin'?"

"Can't complain." Mitch patted his friend's back. "Tom's been whipping me into shape. I've never been so exhausted though."

"Mitch? Exhausted?" Elise laughed from the stairs as she came back down, shoving her arms into a zippered hoodie. "You're like the Energizer Bunny. You just keep going. McKenzie will be down in a minute."

Mitch chuckled. "I've met my match, and his name is Tom Buchanan. Are you ready for your trip?"

Elise weaved an arm around Rory's back, and he tucked her into his side. "I'm excited. It's going to be great." But the smile she directed at her boyfriend held a hint of sad longing. "I'm worried about this guy though."

"I'll be fine." Rory's expression matched hers. No matter her excitement, it would be a tough four months apart for them both.

"Don't worry about Rory," Mitch said. "I'll look after him while you're gone."

Elise laughed. "Make sure he doesn't work too hard."

Rory rolled his eyes. The slight pull of his mouth betrayed his amusement, reminding Mitch, not for the first time, how perfect he was for her.

"You ready?" Rory asked, dropping his arm from her shoulders.

"Yeah." Elise stepped to Mitch and wrapped her arms around his neck. "I'm glad I got to see you before I left."

He gave her a tight hug, lifting her off the ground. "Things won't be the same around here without you." He set her back on her feet. "I'm proud of you for following your heart. I love seeing you so happy."

She smiled over at Rory, then looked back at Mitch. "Thanks, friend." She lowered her voice to a whisper, gesturing with a finger for him to get closer. "And I expect lots of updates on *you*. I might be leaving for four months, but I still have eyes in this place."

He knew exactly what she referred to. "I promise I'll keep you updated."

"Good. I expect you two to be engaged by the time I get back."

Mitch choked on his spit, rearing back to look in her face. A teasing glint appeared in her eye.

"Have the best time, Elise."

"Thanks. I plan to."

She held her hand out to Rory, who took it and led her from the room. Mitch followed them into the entryway as Rory pulled her close, planting a kiss on the top of her head. They left the house without a backward glance.

He didn't have to wait long before McKenzie appeared at the top of the stairs, her lips curving into a shy smile. His heart shocked into action as if she'd taken a defibrillator to it.

"What are you doing here?" She descended the stairs like a princess being presented at a ball. There was never any pomp or circumstance with her, but she might as well have been royalty—and Mitch her loyal subject. "I wasn't expecting you." She glanced down at her pajama bottoms and tank top.

He kept his focus on her as she approached, taking in her stunning eyes, her dainty nose, those kissable lips ...

He shook himself. Thoughts of kissing her had crept into his mind more than he'd care to admit lately.

"Sorry for stopping by unannounced." He wrapped her into a hug when she reached the bottom stair. The way her body melted into him eased some of his nagging doubts. "I would've texted you first but ..." He pulled out his phone and wiggled it in front of them.

McKenzie gave him a tight smile. "I'm sorry for not responding to your note. Training has kept me busy, and Aria is getting suspicious. I couldn't risk stopping by the clinic." She was rambling—a rare occurrence for McKenzie.

Inwardly, Mitch cringed. He'd never completely win her over if she worried too much about people at the gym finding out. He knew what a gossip Aria could be. He kept his mouth shut. Saying anything might cause McKenzie to retreat into her shell again.

They stood in the entryway for a drawn-out moment, staring at each other. *Get your head together, dude.* He'd never had so much trouble carrying on a conversation with anyone before. McKenzie was just so timid, everything he said had the risk of scaring her off.

Finally, she gestured toward the living room. "Do you want to come in for a minute?"

Yes, he did. More than anything. He couldn't think of a better way of spending his night, but another early practice loomed. He needed to hit the sack. And if he sat down on her couch, he feared he'd never leave.

"Actually, I can't stay. I only stopped by to thank you for your present."

McKenzie smiled. "Did you like it? I saw it at the grocery store the other day and thought of you. It'll help your *aging body.*" She put air quotes around the last part.

"My body appreciates your concern." He chuckled. "Now, about your number ... I really should've asked for it before now, but I didn't want to scare you off."

"I wouldn't have given it to you." Her lips were pursed, and the corners quirked upward as if she were holding back a smile.

He screwed his face into a smolder that more than a few women had found irresistible in the past. "How about now?"

She shrugged, that hint of a smile growing more pronounced. "I don't give it out to just anyone, you know."

Is she flirting with me? It was subtle, though he couldn't mistake the coy look on her face. He stooped closer, his mouth all but brushing her ear. "It's a very good thing I'm not just anyone," he murmured.

She shivered against him, and he smiled at that satisfying reaction before straightening to his full height and stepping back.

Narrowing her eyes a little, she scrutinized him for a moment before pushing out an overdramatic sigh. "Fine. Hand me your phone." She held out her hand, palm up.

Mitch stopped short of puffing out his chest in victory. A small victory, but one all the same. Pulling his phone back out of his jacket pocket, he unlocked the home screen before handing it to her. She glanced at the picture of a smiling Mitch, his arm slung around his mother, that made up the wallpaper. It was taken after his AT school graduation. Hazel clung to his back, his graduation cap hanging askew over her forehead.

"Is this your mom?" McKenzie asked.

"Yep. That's my mama." He pointed at Hazel. "And that's my baby sister."

"You keep a picture of your mom on your phone?"

He shrugged. "She's the most influential woman in my life. Why wouldn't I?"

"Aw." McKenzie puckered her lips in a small pout. "I didn't know you were so sentimental."

"I try." His frat brothers had given him a lot of heat in college for how often he'd talked to his family, but he didn't care. He rolled his shoulders in exaggerated movements. "Don't tell anyone though. It'll ruin my image."

Placing a hand on her heart, she lifted her nose in the air. "I promise your manhood is safe with me."

A laugh burst from him as her eyes grew as wide as golf balls.

"That came out wrong. I meant—"

He grabbed her hand, choking back another laugh. Sparks traveled up his arm. "I know what you meant."

Their eyes locked, and hers told him the giddy sensation wasn't one-sided. He wove their fingers together as the urge to kiss her reared its tempting head once again.

Her attention hastily returned to his phone before he could do anything about it. "Your sister looks so much like you," she said.

Mitch pushed away the mental image of his lips on hers and glanced at the picture. "I get that a lot. Out of the six of us, she and I look the most like our mom. When she came for my graduation, you wouldn't believe how many people thought she was my kid. I don't mind though. She's awesome."

"That's sweet." McKenzie entered her contact info into his phone and handed it back to him. "You can text me yours."

"Thanks." He pocketed his phone. "I should let you go to sleep."

She nodded slowly. "That's probably a good idea. Mornings are hard enough, even with plenty of rest. I'll walk you out."

Mitch opened the door, placing a hand on the small of her back to usher her through. They walked across the grass in silence, neither of them in any hurry to get to his car. The short time he'd spent with her tonight was nowhere close enough to satisfy his craving.

"Thanks for walking me out," he said when they'd reached his car.

McKenzie's smile was shy, and her eyes slowly traveled up to meet his. "I was hoping you'd come by tonight."

Her voice was quiet, but those words vibrated within him the same as if she'd spoken them through a megaphone. And yet, his uncertainty from the week made him say, "Really? You didn't seem too excited to see me at the gym a few days ago."

She dropped her gaze to her feet, scrunching her pert nose. "Oh ... that. My mother checks up on me constantly. I'm worried that if too many people see us together, she wouldn't be happy."

He should've known it had something to do with her mom. The woman could potentially prove a difficulty if he ever attempted to officially date her daughter. Which is exactly what he planned to do ... ASAP.

But he'd worry about that later.

"Phew! I was afraid I'd said something wrong the other day and you were ignoring me for being a pompous jerk."

Instead of the laughter he'd expected, she gave an emphatic shake of her head, her ponytail swishing. "That's not it at all. I just don't want my mom to get the wrong idea about us."

The wrong idea? At this rate, there wouldn't be any idea to get. He'd like to tell Mrs. Bowman exactly where to stick her unyielding control in her daughter's life.

He pushed down his silent grumbling. None of this was McKenzie's fault. He took a small step toward her, still leaning against the cool metal of the car. The desire to kiss her once again took hold of his senses. If she were any other woman, he'd have no problem going in for a little smooching. But she was different. Progress had been made with her but only recently. Moving at her pace was vital to his success, so he held back.

He settled for grabbing the hand that hung down at her side. Even the simplest act of holding hands was enough to set his heart racing. "I'll bet the next couple of weeks are going to be busy for you with nationals coming up."

She nodded. "I leave for Sacramento in two weeks."

"You ready?"

"As ready as I'm going to be, I guess." She lifted her shoulders. "I always get really nervous during competitions."

Mitch squeezed her hand. "I've seen you in practice. You'll do great."

"Thanks." She offered him a small smile, though he didn't miss the hesitation in it.

With his free arm, he pulled her close. She rested her cheek against his chest, and he marveled at how perfectly she fit in his embrace. They stood that way in silence, the steady chirping of crickets in the night air providing the only sound. Her warm vanilla scent wrapped him up like a blanket.

"I should go." Mitch lifted her hand to his mouth, kissing her fingers softly before letting go.

"Yeah," McKenzie said. She seemed as reluctant as he did for their few minutes together to end. She remained on the sidewalk as he made his way to the driver's side.

After folding himself behind the wheel and shutting the door, Mitch glanced down at the hand that, moments before, held hers. It already felt strange to be empty.

Looking to the sidewalk where McKenzie had been, he watched her walk back across the grass, the porch light briefly illuminating her before she disappeared inside. Grinning from ear to ear, he started the ignition. No matter how long it took, he was even more determined than ever to win her over.

Chapter Thirteen

Over the next two weeks leading up to nationals, not a day went by that McKenzie didn't receive at least one text from Mitch. He was just as playful in his texts as in person. She loved that about him. No matter how busy or challenging his life became, he always found a way to enjoy it. It was infectious, and he'd dragged her into it as well, making her laugh even when the stress threatened to boil over.

On the morning of the finals, the vibration of McKenzie's phone woke her early. With the window shades down, the morning sunlight had not yet permeated the hotel room. The clock on the bedside table flashed 6:07 in neon red numbers.

She groaned. Who could possibly be calling now? Anyone who knew her well knew she didn't answer the phone until she'd pumped her body with caffeine. And besides, she still had an hour of good sleep left.

Grumbling, she fumbled for her phone on the nightstand. Mitch's name flashed across the locked screen, immediately improving her mood. Careful not to wake Aria in the next bed, she felt her way to the bathroom, stumbling a little on a shoe on the floor.

After shutting the bathroom door with a soft click, she accepted the video chat. "Hey." She slid down to the floor and sat with her legs outstretched, back against the door.

"Good morning, sleepyhead." Mitch's teasing smile filled the screen, sending her heart into backflips. "Did I wake you?"

"No, of course not. I've been up for hours." A yawn snuck out, and she covered her mouth with her free hand.

"I can see that." He chuckled. "I wanted to tell you to knock 'em dead today. I'll be thinking about you."

"Thanks." She clamped down on another yawn. "That means a lot."

Someone shouted in the background behind him, drawing a booming laugh from Mitch. He waved them away with an arm behind his head.

"Where are you?" McKenzie asked.

He tossed a volleyball at someone out of camera range. "I'm in Hermosa. Tom and Charlie think I'm ready to start scrimmaging with other teams. The first one's this morning."

"Wow, that's great!" McKenzie said. "You've only been training for a month. It looks like I should be wishing you luck too."

"Maybe you should pray for me instead." He gave her a self-deprecating look. "How're you feeling about tonight?"

McKenzie shrugged. "Nervous. But as ready as I've felt for nationals in a long time. I just want to get out there."

"You'll do great." Mitch's smile sent a ripple through her that had nothing to do with nerves. "No matter what happens, let's celebrate when you get home."

"I'd like that," McKenzie said.

Another shout and a few cheers sounded in the background. Mitch turned away from the phone and called out before directing his focus to McKenzie again. "I'll let you get back to sleep. We're about to get started."

Did he have to go already? They'd been talking for less than five minutes. Would they always have to settle for small bits of time together? "Thanks for calling. I'm glad I got to talk to you for a few minutes."

"Me too. Good luck tonight. I know you'll do great." He paused for a few lingering seconds, studying her, before ending the call, leaving McKenzie staring at the screen until it went dark. She pushed herself off the floor and made her way back to bed.

Crawling under the covers, she replayed the last five minutes. He'd chosen to call despite his lack of time. That had to count for something, right? She had very little experience with men. She had no idea how they reacted around women they viewed as more than friends. But it was getting harder by the day to equate the way he acted around her to his naturally friendly personality.

And she liked the way she felt around him. Mitch brought out a different side of her—one she was often too timid to show. He'd made her laugh harder than she ever had before. He'd listened to her vent, without running away when she cried.

And how could she not be affected by the way he looked at her with his dazzling brown eyes, like she was the only person in the room? It was only natural to fantasize about kissing those smiling lips as she fell asleep at night.

McKenzie pulled the blanket tighter around herself. She'd never admit those thoughts out loud. As much as she wished things were different, Mitch hadn't actually pushed for anything between them. They were just friends. Even if his arms around her made her feel safe and secure. Like the world could be crashing down around her, and she'd be okay as long as he was holding her.

Don't get distracted. She'd had to remind herself of that hundreds of times over the past few weeks. *We're just friends.* But what she felt for him was starting to seem much stronger than friendship. She suspected it felt a lot like falling in love.

Chapter Fourteen

Every muscle in Mitch's body tensed, his eyes alert and watching, as the opposing team prepared to serve. The sand was cool on his bare feet, the midmorning sun not yet heating it to blistering levels. He bent his knees, bracing his hands on his thighs. A few paces to his right, Charlie did the same.

Mitch glanced to the side of the court, making eye contact with Tom. His coach nodded in silent encouragement. A still-recovering Logan, who'd embraced his new role as team cheerleader, stood next to Tom, filming the action. A small gathering of avid fans surrounded the court, cheering on the teams—women in tiny bikini tops and cutoffs, men carrying energy drinks, even a few families with young children playing in the sand while their parents watched. They'd all been enthusiastic supporters for both sides the whole game, firing Mitch up when he needed it most.

He turned his attention back to the court. On the other side of the net, the server spun the ball once, twice, three times between his fingers before holding it up to his face in his pre-serve ritual. Then he tossed the ball into the air in front of him. Mitch straightened, preparing for action. When the ball rocketed over the net, he dove to his left. His forearms connected with the ball, sending it back toward the middle of the court seconds before his chest hit the sand. Not the prettiest shot, but it did its job.

"Yes! That's what I'm talking about!" Tom's excited voice was barely audible above the adrenaline roaring in Mitch's ears. "Way to get in there!"

As Charlie chased after the pass, Mitch popped to his feet, ready for the near-perfect set at the net. Taking three running steps toward the ball, he leapt, swinging his arm behind his head then slamming the heel of his hand into the leather. The blocker was ready for it and the ball ricocheted off his wrist, bouncing onto Mitch's shoulder on its way to the ground.

Game over.

The spectators let out an *ahhh,* and a smattering of applause broke out. After congratulating the other team on their win with handshakes and bro hugs, he turned and brushed the sand off his damp chest and arms.

"Not bad for your first time," Charlie said, clapping Mitch's sweaty shoulder.

Mitch straightened and slapped his teammate's hand twice. He shook his head with a small laugh. "Geez, that was hard. You didn't tell me the first scrimmage would be against the big guys." The team they'd played had taken over the top US spot now that Logan was out.

Charlie nudged Mitch in the stomach with the back of his hand. "Hey, the first one's behind you now. You'll only get better."

They made their way over to the sidelines where Tom and Logan had their heads bent over the camera, already studying the game. Logan held up his uninjured arm for a high five as Mitch and Charlie approached. "I got it all on film for us to analyze next week. You had some awesome shots. Reminiscent of a certain Mr. Dig Man, I'd say."

Mitch chuckled as he accepted a towel from Tom. "I haven't heard that nickname in years." He tossed his sunglasses on top of his bag and wiped his face with the microfiber.

Tom looked up from his clipboard. "I sensed some nerves in the first set, but you seemed to shake them off. By the end, you really started to hit your stride."

"Thanks, Coach." Mitch wasn't about to tell any of them the real reason he'd had so much trouble in the first set. What would everyone think if word spread that the former junior star had been fighting back tears behind his Oakleys? He couldn't even blame the nerves. Memories of the good times from the junior circuit with Doug had hit him out of nowhere, the grief making him sluggish to react. He'd had a lot of practice pushing the sadness to the back of his mind over the years, but it always resurfaced at the most random times.

As much as he loved training again, playing without Doug felt wrong. It was irrational—volleyball players swapped partners all the time—but the guilt refused to go away, confirming in Mitch's mind that returning to competition was somehow abandoning his friend.

And yet, Doug had been dead for eight years, and Mitch was still very much alive. There had to be some way to get off this hamster wheel of grief. Because that's what it was: a never-ending loop. One minute, he was fine. And the next, he was transported back to senior year, going through the cycle all over again.

Blinking back the moisture in his eyes, he pulled his CamelBak from his bag and took a long swig. As he lowered the bottle from his mouth, his gaze fell on a young boy who appeared to be around the same age as Hazel. He watched Mitch curiously from a few feet away.

Mitch pasted on a smile and approached, scanning the sand for anyone who might be the boys' parents. A woman stood watching, far enough away to give her son some freedom, but close enough to intervene if needed.

"Hey, buddy," Mitch said. "What's your name?"

"Jonah."

"It's nice to meet you, Jonah. I'm Mitch." He held out a fist.

The boy bumped his small hand against his knuckles. "I know who you are. I watched you win Junior Worlds."

That didn't sound right. Jonah likely wasn't alive when Mitch and Doug had dominated the junior circuit. He glanced up at the boy's mother, who'd approached. "Jonah lives and breathes volley-ball. He loves watching old games on YouTube."

Returning his attention to the boy, Mitch crouched in front of him. "Do you like to play too?"

"Yes," Jonah said. His posture dipped. "I'm not that good though."

Mitch gave the boy's shoulder a squeeze. "That's okay. You're still learning. If you keep practicing, I know you'll get better. And you know what?"

"What?" Jonah lifted his eyes, hope entering them.

"The most important part is having fun. As long as you're enjoying it, nothing else matters."

Some of the melancholy lifted from the boy's demeanor. "Are you really going to the Global Elite Games?"

"I'm going to try."

"That's *awesome.*" Jonah's expression turned to pure hero worship. "Can I have your autograph?"

Mitch eyed the scrap of paper and Sharpie the boy produced from his pocket. He could remember the euphoria of meeting his volleyball idols as a kid. He'd begged his parents to take him to Oak Street Beach to watch the tournaments whenever the American pros came to Chicago. Maybe he could make a difference in Jonah's life. "I'll do you one better. Hang on, I'll be right back."

Jogging over to his duffel bag, he rifled through it, pulling out the extra ball he kept inside. When he returned to Jonah, he crouched in the sand again and took the Sharpie, scribbling a message before signing his name and handing both items back to the boy.

Jonah bounced on his toes with barely concealed excitement as he took them. "Wow! Thanks!" He turned to his mother behind him. "Mom! Look!" She smiled at her son, then looked at Mitch. *Thank you!* she mouthed.

He nodded to her before turning back to Jonah. "No problem, buddy." A quick glance at Tom and Logan showed them gathering up equipment. Charlie was down by the water with a dark-haired woman Mitch had never seen before. Judging by their body language, whatever they were discussing wasn't good.

Mitch turned back to Jonah and smiled. "Hey, listen. I need to run, but it was nice meeting you."

Jonah tucked the ball securely under his arm. "Thanks for the autograph. Bye."

Mitch waved as the boy slipped a hand into his mom's and they walked away. The day had grown hot, the midmorning sun beating down on him. Lifting weights in the air-conditioned gym would be a relief. He started toward Logan and Tom.

"Hi, Mitch," a breezy voice from behind stopped him, and Mitch turned. A woman in a neon pink bikini top and cutoffs stood facing him.

"Hey," he said.

"You were great out there. You almost had them at the end." An alluring smile appeared on her tan face. Running a hand through her beachy blonde waves, she looked up at him through her long lashes —a difficult feat as she was only a few inches shorter than his six feet, four inches.

"Thanks for coming out to watch." He gave her what he hoped could only be interpreted as respectful friendliness. The last thing he needed was to give an enthusiastic fan the wrong idea. This woman was gorgeous, and she knew it, if he interpreted the way she looked at him correctly. But he'd never been interested in the flashy, runway model type. His preference lay with McKenzie's classic beauty.

Just thinking of Zee brought a pang to his heart. He missed her. She'd been in Sacramento for six days, and the few minutes they were able to talk that morning had gone by way too fast.

The woman took a step toward him. "I like watching the pros practice here sometimes. It's so refreshing seeing that intensity again. I played indoor at Long Beach State … outside hitter."

"Did you really?" Mitch asked, his tension easing. He placed his hands loosely on his hips. "I went to grad school at Long Beach."

Her face lit up, and she brushed a hand on his arm. "No way! I graduated last spring." Her touch sent shivers up his spine, and not the good kind.

"We were there at the same time, then. I completed my master's the year before. I probably saw you play. I went to several women's games."

Charlie came up beside him, clapping a hand on his shoulder.

"Ready to hit the weights?" An unmistakable weariness lurked behind his smile.

"Let's do it." Mitch held his hand out to the woman. "It was nice meeting you ..."

"Chelsea," she said, accepting his handshake.

He nodded. "It was nice meeting you, Chelsea."

"Can I get a picture with you before you go?" She batted her eyelashes. "I want to be able to say I met you before you became famous."

That was laying it on a bit thick. He briefly glanced at Charlie, who appeared to be trying not to laugh, then back to Chelsea. "Sure."

If he'd thought she was flirting with him before, he was even more sure by the way she cozied up to him for the picture. With an arm stretched behind his back, she pressed her bikini-clad chest into his side and placed a freshly manicured hand on his stomach. Her skin was silky smooth on his bare abs. The sensation sent little pinpricks radiating uncomfortably from the point of contact.

It's just a picture, he reminded himself. Posing with fans was one part of being a professional athlete he'd have to get used to. He had no reason to feel guilty. Still, his gut churned as the image of a crest-fallen McKenzie etched itself firmly in his mind.

That picture stayed with him an hour later through his last reps in the weight room. Sweat slid down his bare back as he pushed the lever of the chest press, the faint scent of body odor that normally accompanied the gym accosting his nose. Metal clanking against metal from the nearby weight machines echoed through the room.

He blew out a breath and pushed again, his muscles burning as he worked out his chest and shoulders. He'd always had an athletic build, but the last several weeks of regular training had put him in even better shape than before.

Charlie approached the machine next to him and adjusted the weights. Mitch spared him a quick glance before continuing his rhythm: deep breath in, push the bar forward, release breath, bring the bar back.

"Was that your girlfriend you were FaceTiming with this morning?" Charlie asked casually after a few reps on his machine. "She sounded cute."

Is she my girlfriend? They'd never put a label on whatever was happening between them.

Mitch blew out another breath and pushed the lever forward. "She's just a friend." He said it with conviction, but that didn't stop his smile. "Maybe someday."

Charlie put his hands on his shorts and faced him, his brows arching upward. "Yeah? You're sweet on her?"

A laugh bubbled from deep in Mitch's chest. "Only since the day I met her." He let go of the lever and relaxed in the seat. "Was that your girl I saw you with earlier?"

Charlie bobbed his head. "Addison."

"Everything okay? You two seemed tense."

Charlie's face fell as he stood from his machine and walked a few paces to the stack of towels on a cart by the wall. Grabbing two, he tossed one to Mitch. "Honestly, I don't know. Sometimes I wonder if we're going to last much longer."

Mitch stopped wiping down his machine to look at him. "What makes you say that?"

Charlie sighed. "She doesn't like how much I have to travel to tournaments. It's been a huge source of conflict our entire relationship."

Mitch couldn't ignore the unease that pricked his subconscious. "How'd you meet?" He tossed his dirty towel into the laundry room and followed Charlie into the locker room.

"We dated in high school," Charlie said. "After graduation, we lost contact. I came down here to play for UCLA, and she went to school back east. We reconnected at our ten-year reunion three years ago." He sat on the bench, untying one of his shoes. "For some reason I thought it would be different this time."

"What do you mean?" Mitch sat down on the bench opposite

him and took off his own shoes. He pulled off his socks, balling them up and stuffing them into his shoes.

"Addie never understood my dream of being a pro volleyball player." Charlie retrieved his flip-flops from his bag and slipped them onto his feet. "She thought I was only attracted to the idea of parties and girls and all the perks of being a professional athlete. But I don't believe in that party lifestyle the media, and even the fans, attribute to beach volleyball. It takes hard work to be successful in this sport. The guys who spend every night drinking and chasing skirts aren't going to make it very far."

Mitch couldn't agree more. He'd never even touched a drop of alcohol. How could he with the way Doug died? "Hey, you don't have to worry about me. I'm just here to play."

Charlie nodded his approval. "That's why we make a good team. I've seen your drive. You're dedicated to getting better." He stood. "And I'm not saying all this to discourage you from dating anyone. Many guys do and it's fine. Every couple has its issues. It just seems Addie's and mine are getting too big to work through. I love her, but man it's tough. I don't want to keep hurting her."

What began as a small prick of discomfort when they'd started talking about Addison had swelled to something much larger. And it found its home right in Mitch's gut. If all went well this year, continuing to play after the Global Elites could be a very real possibility. Despite his lingering guilt over playing without Doug, he still loved the game. What affect would his career have on a possible relationship with McKenzie?

Charlie clapped him on the back. "I need a shower. See you tomorrow?" he asked before heading in the direction of the showers.

"See ya."

What Charlie said about his relationship resonated deeply with Mitch. Once he was alone in the locker room, he slumped forward on the bench, resting his chin on his closed fists, his heart heavy. He cared for McKenzie. If anyone would understand the demands of a professional athlete, it would be her. But she was retiring once the

Global Elites were over. After the ups and downs of the last several years, she deserved to have some normalcy in her life. Dating him would be the exact opposite of that.

He'd promised Seth he wouldn't start something if he couldn't follow through. And he'd assured him he wouldn't add to her stress. Between her mom, overcoming her fear of the vault, and the pressure of gymnastics in general, she had enough troubles heaped on her shoulders. Would having a boyfriend jet-setting around the world every weekend to play volleyball be too much of a burden on her?

Even the possibility of that unsettled him.

Chapter Fifteen

McKenzie was having the National Championships of her life. After three rotations on the final night, she still held the top score on uneven bars. She'd followed it with an almost flawless balance beam routine, besides the small hop on the landing. And her performance on floor exercise was the best of her career, up to this point. Only the vault stood in the way of a near perfect night.

On the outside, she was a vision of absolute calm, the slight clenching of her fists at her sides the only indication of her nerves. But inside, a storm brewed. Memories of her accident ran through her brain like a highlight reel. The hours of surgery, the lengthy recovery, the all-consuming depression when she'd thought her career was over. The only recollections she had of the actual vault came from replays she'd forced herself to watch alone in the darkness of her own bedroom.

She swallowed the bile rising in her throat as she stared down her nemesis. She'd never puked at a competition before, but there was a first time for everything. Curling her toes under her right foot, she pushed down gently against the mat to stretch them out. Then she did the same with her left foot. Nervous energy coursed through her, and her body refused to hold still.

The waiting was always the worst part of competitions. She wouldn't receive the go-ahead from the judges to start until they announced the previous gymnast's score. Sometimes the pause was excruciatingly long, like it was now. What could be causing such a lengthy delay?

I can do this. Shaking out her arms, she closed her eyes, taking a breath and holding it. She visualized her routine from takeoff to the moment her feet hit the mat at the other end. Then she released the breath slowly and opened her eyes to stare down her Goliath again.

Cheers rang around the arena as, somewhere on the competition floor, an athlete finished her routine on another apparatus. And still, McKenzie waited.

Finally, the previous gymnast's score was announced to a smattering of applause, and the green flag went up, signaling McKenzie's turn. Light puffs of chalk dust flew from her hands as she blew on her fists for good luck. She acknowledged the judges with straight arms raised over her head. After one more deep breath, she willed herself forward.

Her body went into autopilot as she accelerated faster and faster with each step. She hardly registered catapulting herself off the vault and through the air. The next thing she knew, her feet connected with the mat, the momentum of her twisting propelling her body forward. Her stomach swooped as she took a giant leap, almost landing face first on the mat. Somehow, she managed to stay on her feet.

McKenzie raised her arms above her head, her chest heaving at her attempt to breathe. Any other gymnast would be disappointed with that giant hop. There was a time when it would've bothered her too. But tonight, she only felt relief.

"We'll need to work on controlling your landing," Gary said when she stepped off the raised competition floor and accepted a hug. "Your form in the air was good, though your feet were crossed a smidge. We'll work on that. Overall, I'm proud of you tonight. I'd say this was your best competition yet."

"Thanks, Gary," McKenzie said. She was proud of herself too.

As she awaited her score, she walked to her bag to retrieve her warmups. Aria was on the floor, legs outstretched, reaching to touch her toes.

"Good job," she said, pushing herself up to give McKenzie a half-hearted hug. Though Aria's mouth lifted in a smile, the gesture fell flat. Then she dropped back onto the floor and resumed her stretching without another word.

McKenzie felt for her. While she was enjoying a boost of confidence after a job well done, Aria landed on the opposite side of the spectrum. Her fall on bars in the first rotation had been a huge blow to her confidence, and she'd struggled the rest of the night. To McKenzie, that congratulatory hug had felt more out of obligation and less from happiness that her teammate had performed so well.

McKenzie tried not to let it bother her. She'd had her share of flops in the years since her return to the sport. It was unfortunate that Aria's had happened tonight when the World team would be selected, but she'd bounce back stronger than ever. McKenzie was sure of it.

The large step on her vault reflected negatively in McKenzie's final score, dropping her down on the leaderboard to sixth place, but she couldn't be disappointed with her overall performance. And she still had a chance to be selected for one of the specialist spots on the World team. Hopefully, she'd impressed the committee with her bars and beam scores alone.

When the last routine had concluded and the final scores announced, McKenzie waited in a room with the rest of the competitors as officials deliberated behind closed doors. Her knee bounced uncontrollably while she scrolled through her phone. There were a few messages from former teammates from Seattle, who'd gone on to compete for various college teams and therefore were not there tonight, offering their congratulations. Rory had texted, as did Kendall and Elise all the way from Greece. But nothing from the one person her heart truly hoped to hear from. Why hadn't Mitch reached out?

She immediately shook the thought away. He had a lot on his plate trying to balance volleyball and work. And he'd already called that morning to wish her good luck. Expecting more from him was just plain needy.

Once the World team was announced—her name included—

McKenzie, duffel bag slung over her shoulder, left the athlete's area with her head held high. After eight long years and countless hours of hard work after that horrible day, it was finally her time to shine. There were always areas to improve upon, but with the Global Elite Games less than a year away, she seemed to be peaking at the perfect time.

Spotting the small group of family and friends in the waiting area, she headed toward them. Hallie and Beej noticed her first. They'd made the six-hour drive from Buena Hills that morning to see her compete. McKenzie was touched, though she couldn't help but wish Mitch had joined them. The highs and lows of competition night always left her emotionally drained. She could use one of his magic hugs right about now.

"You did awesome!" Hallie said as she and Beej crushed McKenzie in a three-way embrace.

"And you made the World team!" Beej squealed. "I'm so proud of you."

McKenzie beamed. "Thanks. I'm glad you both could come."

"We wouldn't miss it." Hallie pulled back and waved a hand in the air. "I wanted to come to prelims too, but I had a class I couldn't miss. We talked to Elise and Kendall on the car ride up here. They said to tell you they were cheering for you too."

"They texted me a bit ago," McKenzie said, adjusting the strap of her bag so it sat more comfortably on her shoulder. "They stayed up late to follow the live feed."

Beej nodded as if she already knew this. "We can talk more later. I think your family wants to congratulate you." She smiled at Seth, who'd come up beside her and placed a hand on her back. Mom stood a few feet away. Dad was nowhere in sight. No surprise there.

McKenzie refused to let his absence dampen her mood. She approached her mother. "Thanks for coming, Mom." She accepted the stiff hug her mother offered. "It means a lot that you're here."

"You have more work to do on that vault," Mom said, without

even so much as a hint of a smile. "I'll talk to Gary about giving it more time during your workouts."

And that was all the words McKenzie's mother had for her. No gushing praise for clinching the national title on uneven bars. No acknowledgement of her career high on floor exercise or beautiful beam routine. No heartfelt congratulations for making her first World team. Only criticism of her flaws. But this was nothing new. "I'm proud of you" never came from Debbie Bowman's mouth when referring to her kids.

McKenzie's gaze dropped to the floor. With those few words, the wave she'd been riding high on a moment before came crashing down on her, drenching her in negativity and self-doubt. What did she have to do to earn the affirmation she craved from her parents? She held back a heavy sigh as she forced herself to look at Mom. "I'll work harder."

The woman gave a curt nod and turned away.

It didn't take long for Seth to swoop in to the rescue. He wrapped his arms around McKenzie and held on tight, both to offer encouragement and to give her a moment to compose herself before the tears took over.

"Don't listen to her," he growled loud enough so only she heard. "You did an amazing job tonight. Don't you dare let that woman rob you of that."

McKenzie nodded and looked at her brother, noticing the angry glint in his eyes. She bit down on her wobbling jaw.

What would she do without Seth? She may not have the love and approval of her parents, but even in the moments when she'd wished for any other family than the one she had, she'd never take for granted her relationship with her brother.

He never seemed as bothered by Dad's neglect and Mom's criticism. He was so unapologetically Seth no matter who was watching.

If only McKenzie could be more like him. She was twenty-two. Old enough to decide what was best for her life. She shouldn't be so concerned with what her parents thought.

She couldn't help it though. Was it too much to ask that her parents love her enough to be proud of her?

Chapter Sixteen

The more Mitch contemplated the wisdom of pursuing a relationship with McKenzie, the heavier the weight lodged in his gut became. All weekend, it spread like wildfire, eventually engulfing his entire body.

By Monday afternoon, his doubts had grown so loud he couldn't focus on anything else. The swim team expected him in the weight room in ten minutes to supervise their conditioning session, and he'd hoped to finish the report he was working on before then. But he'd stared at the same blinking cursor for the last quarter of an hour without making any progress.

Squeezing his eyes shut, he pressed his fingertips to his eyelids then puffed out a breath and opened them to stare at the computer screen again.

She'd been back from Sacramento for twenty-four hours, and it had taken an exorbitant amount of willpower not to storm her doorstep last night and confess his feelings before kissing her senseless. But he'd held back. After all she'd been through, she deserved a partner emotionally available to her when she needed him. If he continued playing volleyball, he wouldn't be able to give her that. As much as he wanted more, the possibility of hurting her, even unintentionally, didn't sit well with him.

As much as he hated the idea, he had to take a step back. Remain friendly but distant. And absolutely no touching. Groaning, he rolled his eyes. He was probably the only guy on the planet to put *himself* in the friend zone.

That would be an easier feat if he could only stop thinking about kissing her. But the more he attempted to push the image of her lips mingling with his away, the tighter his mind held onto it.

He tapped his pen against the desk repeatedly, the metal casing hitting the wood hard enough to leave little silver streaks on the surface. *Focus, idiot.*

The door to the clinic opened a crack, taking matters from bad to worse. McKenzie, of all people, poked her head through, hesitantly at first. The pen flipped out of his hand, ricocheting off his ear before landing on the carpet a few feet away. *Ouch.*

When she realized he was alone, her face relaxed, and she entered the room. A strangled groan died in Mitch's throat at the sight of her in one of those high-chested sports bras many of the gymnasts trained in. Way too much of her perfectly sculpted stomach was exposed for him not to be tempted to take her in his arms and relish in her smooth skin against his hands.

Stay in the friend zone. He already hated the friend zone.

Why couldn't she be wearing a hoodie and sweats? Or better yet, a muumuu. Then again, he'd still be attracted to her if she wore a paper bag.

She hurried over to him, her duffel slung over her shoulder, plopping down on the chair on the other side of his desk. It was a good thing something solid stood between them to keep him from reaching for her. He slid his hands underneath his legs just in case.

"Mitch, guess what?"

His mouth twitched at the way she practically bounced in her seat. He bit down on his cheek to keep his smile in check. The metallic taste of blood landed on his tongue. Several weeks ago, he couldn't get her to talk to him. Now there wasn't even a trace of the timidity that once held her hostage. She had truly come out of her shell. Which made the situation he was in that much more agonizing. "What's up?"

"I made it!" Her eyes lit up. "I'm going to Worlds!"

"That's great, McKenzie." He couldn't disguise the tightness in his voice. Should he confess he already knew she'd made the team, that he'd watched both nights of the competition? "This is what you've been working toward. I'm ... happy for you."

"Thanks." Her hand moved to stroke the end of her fiery ponytail, some hesitation entering her baby blues. "So ... when do you want to celebrate?"

Mitch blinked. "Celebrate?"

"Yes?" Confusion flickered across her lovely face. "You said you wanted to celebrate when I got home."

He did say that. He'd been so preoccupied with his dilemma, he'd forgotten all about the phone conversation on the morning of the finals. Had it only been two days ago? It felt like more.

Spending time alone with her probably wasn't the best idea if he wanted to keep things between them on a strict friends-only level. He was literally sitting on his hands because he couldn't trust that he'd keep them to himself. And they were in a public place. Sure, no one was in the clinic at the moment, but someone could enter at any time. Obviously, his self-control was lacking. What would keep him from giving in when they were in private?

He forced a smile. "I can't this week. I've got a lot on my plate."

"Oh." She stopped fiddling with her hair and dropped her hands to her lap. "Okay. No problem. Do you ... do you at least want to stop by for dinner on Wednesday? Seth and Rory are coming too."

That might work. He'd have to eat anyway. And dinner was a neutral setting where he could spend time with her while still keeping things on friendly terms. A safe environment surrounded by people. Exactly what he needed to prevent him from doing anything to push them out of the friend zone.

"Uh ... yeah ... sure." He rubbed the back of his neck. "I think I can squeeze that in."

Her brows knit together as she tilted her head to the side. "Are you okay?"

"Yep." He coughed. "Dandy." *Dandy?* That word had never come out of his mouth ever in his life. To disguise his awkwardness, he leaned over to pick his pen up from the carpet. On his way back to a sitting position, his funny bone connected with the corner of the desk.

Rubbing his elbow, he groaned. What was wrong with him?

"Are you sure you're okay?" McKenzie asked, her confusion turning to alarm.

He dropped his arm to his lap, the movement aggravating the throbbing in his elbow. "Yeah. Uh … I should get back to work."

She stared at him for a few more seconds before leaning forward to grab the strap of her bag. "Okay. I guess I'll see you on Wednesday, then." She stood.

"Mm-hmm. See you." He watched her go.

She paused at the doorway, turning back to give him one more odd look, before stepping out of sight into the hallway.

Mitch stared at the doorway for a few seconds before dropping his forehead to the desk, bouncing it in a slow rhythm on the wood, groaning. Could he have made himself look any more like a fool?

The friend zone was going to be the death of him.

Chapter Seventeen

Even forty-eight hours after her interaction with Mitch at the clinic, McKenzie's head still spun. She'd never seen him act so uncomfortable. So different than his usual confident demeanor. For two whole days she couldn't shake the worry that he'd seemed reluctant to spend time with her. Why? Had something happened to make him change his mind about her?

True, they weren't actually dating. She'd reminded herself for weeks that they were just friends. Which was exactly how it should remain. But the dread in her stomach every time she thought about him was enough to convince her that her reminders weren't working. She liked him, and the disappointment that had followed her since Monday wouldn't go away.

You're worrying about nothing, she reminded herself again. He probably had a lot to do. Balancing training with work couldn't be easy. Besides, a few months before, she'd never have thought it possible a guy like Mitch would give her more than a passing glance. Now, after only a few weeks of attention, was she really so selfish that she expected him to drop everything to hang out with her when he had so many responsibilities to juggle? *Stop overanalyzing this to death.* Then again, she wouldn't be McKenzie Bowman if she didn't.

After her shower following practice Wednesday evening, she descended the stairs to help put the finishing touches on dinner. Rory and Seth were already in the kitchen, and Mitch should arrive any minute. Something wiggled in her stomach, hinting that maybe her mental pep talk hadn't made it all the way to her heart. *You have no reason to be nervous.*

As her foot hit the floor in the entryway, the little wiggle turned into full-fledged backflips at the knock on the door. Seconds later, it opened, revealing Mitch about to call out his usual greeting. When he spotted her, his familiar smile slid onto his face. "Hey, Zee."

His smile chased her nerves away. This was the Mitch she knew and admired. Maybe she had read too much into their interaction the other day. "Hi. I'm glad you made it."

He opened his arms for a hug and she stepped toward him, anticipating the same connection she felt the last few times he'd hugged her. But at the last minute, something in his smile changed from delighted to, dare she say it, regret. He dropped one arm to his side and held the other out for a high five.

What?

Even when McKenzie had tried her hardest to keep him at a distance, he'd never initiated *that* kind of physical connection. She could count a few times when he'd brushed her arm to get her attention, even tapped her knee if he somehow ended up sitting next to her. But a high five? How ... not romantic. Slowly, unable to mask her confusion, she hesitantly tapped his hand with hers.

He cleared his throat. "Are the others here?" he asked, flicking his eyes above her head. Why was he in such a hurry to get away from her?

"In the kitchen," she said absently, still attempting to wrap her mind around the high five. "We're about ready to eat."

Mitch nudged her arm and smiled, though it didn't quite meet his eyes. "Great."

Without another word, he headed down the hall, leaving McKenzie in the entryway staring after his retreating back. *What was that?* she wondered, trudging toward the kitchen.

She pushed through the swinging door as the others were putting the food and plates on the center island.

"Have you talked to Elise yet today?" Beej asked Rory as she scooted her stool a little closer to Seth's.

McKenzie sat, intentionally leaving a space in between her and

Seth. Despite Mitch's unusual greeting in the entryway, she still hoped he planned to sit next to her.

Rory spooned some rice onto his plate. "She rang earlier. We talked for about an hour before she and Kendall had to leave."

"That's great that you get to talk to her so often," Mitch said, taking the seat next to Hallie.

McKenzie's heart sunk, and she took out her disappointment by stabbing a piece of chicken in the baking dish with her fork and dropping it onto her plate. Some of the juice splattered onto Seth's arm as he reached for the rice.

"Dude," he said, glancing at her, his hand holding the bowl stationary in the air.

"Sorry," she mumbled to her plate.

"Did she show you the view from their hostel?" Hallie asked, continuing the previous conversation. Though the question was posed to Rory, she cast a confused glance at Mitch. Then her focus pinged to McKenzie and back to Mitch, who took particular interest in the mixed veggies he was dishing onto his plate. Hallie turned back to Rory. "It looks gorgeous there."

"It is, that," Rory responded. "Elise said they're having a grand time."

McKenzie tuned out the rest of the conversation. Elise and Rory's connection was evident by the way he spoke of her. They had a deep bond that not even half a world between them could sever. She was happy for them, but she'd give anything to have that level of companionship with someone. Up until two days ago, she'd thought she was heading in that direction with Mitch.

Obviously not.

She kept her eyes on her chicken and rice, attempting to give off the impression that her mind wasn't tumbling down a rabbit hole of doubt. Was Mitch just being friendly these past few weeks? Had her crush on the man caused her to misinterpret his intentions as being stronger than they actually were?

McKenzie ate quickly while attempting to make it appear that she wasn't eating quickly. Once she finished, she announced her fatigue to the rest of the group and, after placing her dishes in the sink, left the kitchen without making eye contact with anyone in the room. Especially not Mitch.

She didn't make it far before someone grabbed her arm, and she tensed. *Please don't be Mitch.* She couldn't talk to him right now. But she turned around anyway and let out a breath.

Seth's concerned face studied her. "Are you okay? You seem quiet tonight, even for you."

"I'm fine," McKenzie said trying to convince herself too. Her doubts were totally winning the battle. "Just really tired. Practice was hard today."

Her words didn't ease her brother's concern. "Are you sure? Did you talk to Mom today? You seem bothered by something."

McKenzie shook her head forcefully. "She called, but I didn't answer. Really, I'm okay." Though she trusted Seth, she didn't want to get into what was bothering her. Especially since it may have simply been the case of her getting it wrong. "I just need a good night's rest."

Seth pursed his lips, looking her up and down before giving her a resigned nod. "Okay. But you know you can talk to me, right?"

"I know." She forced a smile. "Good night."

After getting ready for bed, she crawled under her covers and turned out the light. She sighed, frustrated with her inability to let go of the disappointment. It made no sense to fall head over heels for the first guy to truly see her. She and Mitch were simply not meant to be. And it wasn't as if she had time to devote to an actual relationship right now. After the Global Elites were over, she'd worry about dating. Maybe she'd have better luck finding her soulmate then. Mitch was just another guy—one of millions in Southern California.

But would she find someone as cheerful or playful as him? Or with a smile that made her heart bubble over with happiness ...

Oh. My. Gosh. Get a grip, girl! McKenzie shook her head, firmly. She couldn't spend any more headspace worrying about Mitch's intentions. With World Championships next month and the Global Elite Games in less than a year, she couldn't allow herself to lose focus. Now was the time to forget about him and train harder than ever.

At least there was one silver lining in all of this: Mom couldn't flip out about a relationship that didn't exist.

Chapter Eighteen

Mitch took the steps two at a time up to his apartment on the middle story of the three-level building. Balancing his cell phone between his ear and shoulder, he dug his keys out from the pocket of his gym shorts. "So when are you finally coming out here to visit?" he asked his brother, letting himself inside. Dumping his bag on the floor, he flipped on the light before crossing the open front room to his bedroom.

"As soon as you buy me a plane ticket," Sebastián responded. "You're the one with the career. I'm just a starving grad student surviving on cheap cereal and Mom's Sunday dinner leftovers."

Mitch put the phone on speaker and set it on his bed. "Mmmmm ... I could really go for a home-cooked meal right about now." Having lived in the States since she was eighteen, his mom's cooking repertoire went far beyond the cuisine of her homeland. It didn't matter what she made; he loved it all. "Sunday dinners are one of the things I miss most about living so close to home."

He tossed his baseball cap next to the phone, then pulled off his sweaty T-shirt. He'd stayed at SoCal Elite after finishing up at the clinic to get in an extra workout, hoping it would ease some of the tension that had been building since his conversation with Charlie. He understood the wisdom of putting the brakes on his pursuit of McKenzie, even if he didn't like it.

"How's training going?" Sebastián asked as Mitch chucked his shirt in the laundry basket by the closet and picked up the phone again. "Are you going to be ready by the time next season starts?"

"I think so. Charlie and I are finding a good rhythm." Mitch left his room, heading toward the kitchen, which only consisted of a single counter along the front wall of the apartment sandwiched between the refrigerator and dishwasher. Retrieving the protein shake he'd made earlier from the fridge, he gave it a good shake before opening the bottle and taking a swig. "We're not as smooth as Doug and I were, but we're getting there." His heart pinched as it always did at the mention of his friend.

"True. You two were practically unbeatable back in the day. But you don't know if you'd still be partners ..." Sebastián cleared his throat, obviously aware they were steering into difficult waters. "If he were still alive."

"Yeah." Mitch set his shake on the table and sat. "I know."

Sebastián was silent for a moment, and Mitch braced himself for whatever was coming next. His brother knew him better than anyone. They'd always been close, despite the two years that separated them, but Doug's death had cemented their bond even more. Sebastián was the one person Mitch allowed himself to open up to about what happened, though he only did when he absolutely had to.

"Mitch, buddy, it's not your fault you weren't there that night," Sebastián said gently. "And even if you had been, you couldn't have prevented the accident."

Mitch drummed his fingers on the table. "I was supposed to be driving. I could've—"

"You could've been killed too," Sebastián forced out. "Or landed in the hospital, fighting for your life ... like Jules."

Mitch placed his elbow on the table and dropped his forehead onto his hand. Intellectually, he knew all this. The likelihood of preventing Doug's death was minuscule, but grief had a funny way of making him hold onto irrational guilt.

Why hadn't he been there that night? Why did Doug have to die when the driver of the other car walked away with hardly a scrape?

"Have you heard from her lately?" Mitch asked. Growing up, Jules had been as much a part of their friend group as the rest of them. She was one of the guys until high school when Doug finally admitted his feelings and asked her out.

"No." Sebastián's tone held a hint of regret. "I tried checking up on her a few years back, but she'd changed her number. I still worry about her."

"So do I."

A knock on the door broke through the heavy silence that followed. Mitch lifted his eyes to the ceiling and mouthed a silent thank-you. His heart had been heavy enough all week as it was. Hashing out the what-ifs about Doug wasn't helping.

The clock on the stove flashed a few minutes after nine. Weird. He wasn't expecting company. "I gotta go. Someone's at the door."

"I should get to bed anyway. It's late here. But first ..." Sebastián went quiet.

"What?" Mitch asked.

"Selfishly, I'm glad you weren't there that night. I wasn't ready to lose my big brother."

Mitch swallowed, emotion clogging his throat. "Thanks for being here all these years, Bas." His voice cracked.

"Always," Sebastián said right before hanging up.

Mitch sat at the table for a long moment to compose himself. Another knock forced him to make his way to the door. He opened it to find Rory standing on his outside porch.

"What's up?" Mitch asked, opening the door wider so his friend could enter.

"I should ask you the same question." Rory looked him up and down before rolling his eyes. "Geez, mate, would you put on a shirt? Or at least suck on a stick of butter. You make the rest of us mere mortals feel bad about ourselves."

Mitch snorted out a laugh. Seth and Rory took great pleasure in roasting him for being an athlete. It was all good-natured teasing; Mitch let it roll off his back. "Hey, you showed up unannounced, so it's not my fault you caught me like this. I was about to hop in the shower. What're you doing here anyway?"

Rory sat down on the couch, crossing his ankles on the coffee table. "I couldn't help but notice things were a little strange between you and McKenzie last night. And I wasn't the only one."

Sinking onto the other side of the couch, Mitch rubbed a hand over his mouth. Strange was the understatement of the year. Downright awkward described the entire evening more accurately. And he still felt horrible about it. Hence the extra workout. "I think I blew it, Ror."

Rory studied him for a minute. "You've been chasing after McKenzie for over a year. What gives?"

Mitch sat up, bracing his hands on his shorts. "I'm in love with her." The past few days of trying to keep a friendly distance had made his feelings even more clear.

Rory's brows shot up. "Is this primary school, then? You like a girl, so you completely ignore her? Come on, mate."

A humorless laugh came from Mitch before he could stop it. "I just don't know if it's fair to keep pursuing her."

"Why not?"

Mitch thought about all the same reasons he'd used to convince himself why a relationship with McKenzie wouldn't work. "If I continue playing volleyball after the Global Elites, I'll be traveling a lot. It's a long season, and sometimes tournaments are back-to-back. We're talking weeks at a time on the road. McKenzie deserves more than that."

Rory looked at the ceiling, muttering something under his breath.

"What?" Mitch asked.

"I said it's no wonder you and Elise are close. You think the same."

"I don't get it."

Rory looked as if he were speaking with someone a few players short of a football team. "Elise did the same thing to me before we got back together. She was so worried I'd get tired of her constant need for adventure that she didn't give me the option of deciding what was best for me."

"I remember."

Rory fixed Mitch with an intense stare. "Don't do that to McKenzie. She's stronger than a lot of people give her credit for."

Mitch leaned forward, resting his forearms against his thighs. "She's probably one of the fiercest people I know." He'd witnessed that countless times watching her in training, and he was even more convinced of it after hearing her talk about everything she was constantly forced to overcome. "That's why I don't want to put any more burdens on her. I mean, you were at The Burger Stop when Seth made me promise not to add to her stress."

Rory was shaking his head as soon as Seth's name came out of Mitch's mouth. "I don't think even he realizes how strong she is. He's been in the protective big brother role for so long he doesn't know how to see her any other way. There's this automatic reaction inside him to swoop in every time there's even a hint of a threat to his little sister."

That was something Mitch could relate to. It was hard to get out of the protective brother role no matter how old his sisters became.

"Let McKenzie decide how much she can take," Rory continued. "She's had people telling her what's best for her all her life. She doesn't need it from you."

Mitch gnawed on the inside of his cheek as he mulled it over. Rory's words held a lot of sway. He'd been friends with McKenzie longer than Mitch had known either of them.

"Talk to her," Rory insisted. "And really listen to what she has to say. She doesn't trust easily, but it seems she trusts you."

Trust. The tiny morsel of hope sparking inside of Mitch crumbled with that one word. "Maybe she trusted me before. But I doubt she does now." Not after he'd made things so weird between them.

Rory removed his feet from the coffee table and sat up straighter, turning toward Mitch. "Since when are you so quick to give up on something?"

"Like you said, she doesn't trust easily." The magnitude of that statement made the guilt even harder to swallow. She'd given him a piece of herself she normally kept tightly guarded. She had to be questioning that decision now. He'd let the shiny allure of the Global Elites and a career in beach volleyball cloud his judgment, making him forget McKenzie had been in his sights long before all that. He put his face in his hands and groaned.

"So you'll have to work a bit harder to earn it back." Rory stood from the couch and took a step toward the door before turning back. "She hasn't fled the country, so you've got that going for you." His lips quirked up in amusement.

Mitch had to smile at that. It was good to see his buddy laugh about the early days of his relationship with Elise.

"I'd start by telling her how much you've bungled things," Rory said. "Groveling might also be a good tactic."

Mitch raked a hand through his hair, his chuckle more sad than humorous. He rose from the couch and followed Rory to the door. "It's going to take a lot of persuasion to get her to open up to me again."

Rory pointed to the phone still on the table. "How about you start by picking up your trusty mobile and giving her a ring, yeah? See ya."

Mitch shut the door behind him and retrieved the device on his way back to the couch. Collapsing onto the worn leather, he stretched out, kicking his feet onto the coffee table and thought about how to regain McKenzie's trust. It was going to take effort on his part, but he was willing to do whatever it took to make it up to her.

He dialed her number. Her voicemail clicked on after the fourth ring. Mitch hung up without leaving a message. Maybe a nonthreatening text would be an easier way to open up the lines of communication.

Mitch: I'm sorry for making things weird last night. Can we talk?

He set the phone on the coffee table and headed for the shower. Another early training loomed, and he needed to hit the sack.

By the next morning, she still hadn't responded.

Chapter Nineteen

McKenzie's phone buzzed from the center console as she pulled into the parking lot of SoCal Elite on Saturday for her afternoon practice. Letting her car idle, she picked up the device and froze when Mitch's latest text flashed across the screen.

> Mitch: Hope your day is going well. I miss you.

She stared at the message. Above it were two others just like it, both unanswered. Her bottom lip caught between her teeth. She knew she was being immature—and probably a bad friend—for ignoring him.

But that was the thing. She didn't want to be his friend. He had a way of making her feel seen like no one else did, not even her room-mates or brother had that ability. Her lonely heart had taken that attention and run with it, imagining more to their relationship than was actually there. And she'd assumed he'd felt the same way. How could she settle for being only friends when her heart wanted so much more?

No, it was better to cut all ties than let him back in and be forced to face her unrequited feelings. She'd felt her focus slipping over the past few weeks anyway. She couldn't afford to get distracted again.

Reluctantly, she read his text again. *I miss you.* Leaning the back of her head against the headrest, she closed her eyes. She missed him too. His devastating smile, and how he was always ready to laugh. The way he seemed to know when she needed a hug, and how he really listened.

She missed the way he brought her out of her shell.

She lifted a hand to pinch the bridge of her nose. Yes, distance from him was the best solution.

Three weeks. She only had to push through for three more weeks. Once she left for the World team training camp, she wouldn't return until after the competition ended in Portugal. That would give her some solid time away from California to clear her head of all things Mitch. Maybe then she'd have an easier time letting him go.

Sighing, she shut off the engine and got out of the car, retrieving her bag from the back seat. Her phone buzzed again on her way to the entrance. She looked at the screen and groaned. Nothing brought her out of the zone faster than a call from her mother.

Seconds before tossing her phone in her bag, she stopped. Mom would call back. She always called back. Maybe it was better to get it over with now than be chewed out for not answering later.

McKenzie pushed talk right before it went to voicemail. "Hi, Mom," she said with forced cheerfulness.

"McKenzie? Why are you answering your phone? Shouldn't you be in the gym already?"

McKenzie rolled her eyes. *Then why are you calling?* She didn't dare say it out loud. That would only lead to a lecture on respecting her elders.

"I just got here," she said instead. "We were on break for lunch. I'm not late." She made sure to add the last part. Mom always hounded her about being punctual. McKenzie wasn't sure where she got the idea that her daughter was incapable of making it anywhere on time.

Mom clicked her tongue. "I hope you ate something healthy and low calorie."

Here we go. McKenzie pulled open the doors to the facility and walked toward the gym, forcing her eyes forward as she passed the clinic.

"McKenzie, you need to be very careful about what you put in your body. You're several years older than the other gymnasts, so you need to work harder to keep your body in the best shape for competition."

McKenzie rolled her eyes again. "I know, Mom. You don't have to—"

"The competition is younger, faster, and more athletic than you are."

McKenzie bobbed her head side to side, mouthing silently along with her mom's lecture.

"You need to spend even more time training than they do. You can't afford a single distraction."

Pausing outside the gym, McKenzie leaned her hip against the wall, massaging her temple with her free hand as she pretended to listen. There was no interrupting her mom when she got on her high horse.

A knot formed in her stomach, and she lowered her hand to rest flat against her abdomen. "I'm not distracted." At least not anymore. "And I'm already spending more hours than most. If I train any harder, I'll crack."

"You can't crack," her mom scoffed.

McKenzie leaned her back against the wall and squeezed her eyes shut. After a few calming breaths, she said, "Mom, I'm trying." She couldn't mask the desperation in her voice. "You don't understand how much pressure I'm under right now. Sometimes I wish I could just be normal."

Her mom sighed, the sound laced with disappointment. "You were never meant to be normal. You were meant to be a champion. I expect nothing less from you, McKenzie. Don't let me down."

McKenzie blinked at the stinging in her eyes. She didn't used to be a crier. But it seemed the dam had snapped, and she had no control over her emotions anymore. "I won't."

"Good. Now, don't keep Gary waiting." The line went dead.

McKenzie turned her phone completely off and dropped it to the bottom of her bag. A text from Mitch and that unsettling phone call was all she could take from the annoying device today.

Why did she even try? She'd never please anyone. Never make it onto the Global Elite team. Not when every other gymnast had a better resume than she did. Making her first World team at twenty-two was nothing to brag about. She wouldn't bring in enough international competition experience to be considered for an event as important as the Global Elite Games. The selection committee was bound to pass her by.

Maybe it was time to give up.

Things went from bad to worse when she walked into the gym and headed over to Aria, who was pulling off her sweatpants and stuffing them into her bag. She gasped as McKenzie approached. "Oh my gosh, did you see that picture of Mitch on Instagram?"

McKenzie slowed her steps, surprised by the greeting. "You know I stay off social media as much as possible." There was already too much speculation about her comeback around the gymnastics community. She didn't need the constant bombardment from social media as well.

Sitting down next to her teammate, she pulled off her T-shirt, revealing her racerback tank top underneath. She straightened her legs, reaching forward to grab her toes.

The sound of Aria digging through her bag drew McKenzie's attention in her direction. "I was scrolling through earlier today when I saw it," Aria said. "I was shocked. I thought you two had something going." She pulled out her phone.

"What are you talking about?" McKenzie asked. She hadn't told Aria about the awkward turn her relationship with Mitch had taken, and she wasn't planning to. Her teammate's reputation as a gossip made McKenzie uncomfortable with the idea of confiding in her. That uneasiness had only grown since nationals.

Without warning, Aria shoved the phone in McKenzie's face, giving her a good view of Mitch at the beach in all his shirtless glory, with his arm slung around a leggy, blonde bombshell in a bikini and cutoffs. McKenzie's heart dive-bombed to the floor. The woman's perfect hand, with its long fingernails the exact shade of neon pink as her tiny top, rested nauseatingly on his washboard abs.

McKenzie glanced down at her own unpainted fingernails. Her palms were dry and calloused from countless rotations on the uneven bars. She picked at a patch of broken skin next to the two new blisters she'd noticed that morning.

Mitch obviously wasn't too disappointed in the situation either. In fact, he seemed to be enjoying it, judging by the broad smile on his face. The same one that never failed to make McKenzie want to melt into a puddle on the floor. The only sensation she felt now was the bile burning its way up her throat.

Women would line up to get a chance to date him. Why would he choose quiet, red-headed little Zee when he could have a tall, gorgeous woman like the one snuggled up next to him in the picture?

But what about his texts? Why had he ended them saying he missed her when he clearly wasn't suffering too badly?

"What a snake," Aria said, her tone full of indignation. But when McKenzie looked at her, the smallest of satisfied smirks played at Aria's mouth. "I'm sorry, McKenzie." She dropped her phone in her bag and went back to stretching.

"It's fine. Mitch can hang out with whoever he wants. We're just friends." McKenzie spread her legs apart and stretched to her side facing away so Aria wouldn't see her disappointment. "That's all it's ever been between us."

The realization stung.

The first lesson an athlete learned in gymnastics was how to fall without getting injured. Sprawled on her back across the mat, staring at the unforgiving underbelly of the balance beam, McKenzie had obviously failed that lesson. Even laying still, every muscle in her abdomen screamed in pain as she attempted to catch her breath.

This wasn't the first time she'd had the wind knocked out of her from a fall, but it never got easier. Why did she willingly put her body through so much torture? Was making the Global Elite Games worth all this?

It has to be.

"Are you all right?" Gary crouched beside her, his expression a mixture of concern and frustration. He hadn't been pleased with her efforts this afternoon.

"I think so," McKenzie panted. Another figure knelt on her other side and the stomach spasm that occurred had nothing to do with her pain. Of course Mitch had to witness that humiliating fall. There'd been nothing pretty about it. She squeezed her eyes shut, blocking out his worried look. She took a slow breath in, and another stab of pain shot through her abs. "I'm okay."

Mitch went into full trainer mode, checking her over to make sure nothing was broken. McKenzie swatted his hand away, rising onto her elbows with a groan.

"Really, I'm fine. I got the wind knocked out of me. I'll be okay once I've caught my breath." To prove it, she slowly got to her feet. Her stomach throbbed but the fall had spared her ribs, so at least there was one positive.

Mitch's lips pursed into a straight line, and he placed a light hand on her arm. "Are you sure, Zee?" She bristled at his touch "It would be a good idea if I checked you over—just in case."

McKenzie forced herself to meet his eye, clamping down on her jaw to keep it from trembling. She had to be strong, couldn't show any weakness. She'd trained through pain before, she'd do it again. But when she looked at him, though his expression was serious, the image of his devastating smile and the bikini babe tangled around him was all she saw.

"I'm fine," she repeated firmly.

"Zee—"

"Seriously, Mitch, stop fussing over me," she snapped. "I know you're only doing your job, but believe me, I've had worse falls than this one."

His brows shot up in surprise, and he lowered his arm, taking a step back.

She turned to Gary. "I need a minute to catch my breath, and then I'll be ready to go again."

Her coach shook his head. "After a fall like that, no way. You've been distracted all afternoon. You need a break."

Indignation took over. *I don't need a break, I need to train harder, do more reps.* "Gary, I'm fine. It's only a bad practice. I have to keep going. With Worlds coming—"

"McKenzie, no." Gary's tone, stern and full of authority, cut her off. She shrunk back a little, lowering her eyes to the mat, hands fisted at her sides. She didn't need to look at Mitch to feel his serious gaze—not at all like the fun-loving man he was. He was all business.

Gary sighed, and his composure changed from authoritative coach to concerned father. "McKenzie, if your head isn't one hundred percent in the gym during practice, it's not safe for you to be here. You, more than anyone, should know what could happen. I care about you too much to go down that road again."

McKenzie kept her focus on the blue mat she stood on. "Yes, sir."

"Good." His tone softened even more. "Take the rest of the afternoon off. Clear your head and rest your body. I expect you back Monday morning ready to train."

Tears stung in McKenzie's eyes. It was bad enough to be rebuked by her coach, but to have Mitch present to witness it all, she didn't think she'd ever recover from the humiliation.

Keeping her head down to avoid glancing at the men in front of her, she turned and gingerly fled the gym. As soon as the large metal doors closed behind her, she stopped fighting the tears and let them cascade down her cheeks as she made her way to the exit.

Right before stepping outside into the early October afternoon, she stopped. *My bag.* It was still in the gym where she'd left it. Which meant her keys were also in the gym. Shoot. Hadn't she faced enough humiliation for one day?

She couldn't face everyone after the last few minutes. Couldn't bear to see the smug look on Aria's face with this latest failure. Not yet. McKenzie ducked into the narrow hallway leading to the maintenance closet. Sliding to the floor, she buried her face in her knees and let the sobs take over her battered body.

Chapter Twenty

Mitch watched McKenzie's escape from the gym, his heart fleeing with her. He didn't believe she was okay for a second, no matter how much she insisted otherwise. His front-row view of her terrifying fall had sucked the breath from him, almost as if he'd felt the effects himself. The nauseating dread ripping through him as her body crashed onto the beam was like nothing he'd ever experienced before. It was a miracle she hadn't ended up with a broken rib or two.

He exchanged a few quick words with Gary before the coach sighed and walked away to continue working with Evie and Aria.

Alone by the beam, Mitch removed his baseball cap and ran a hand through his hair in frustration before sliding it backward onto his head again. He tossed his bag over his shoulder and headed toward the exit.

This was more than a bad practice. He was sure of it. Every time he'd caught a glimpse of her this week, she'd seemed so burdened. She could brush it off all she wanted, but he saw right through it. And his gut twisted at the idea that he'd played a part in her inability to focus.

She hadn't responded to his texts. He'd opened the door of communication on his end, but hers was still shut and locked with at least a dozen deadbolts. Understandable after the way he'd ignored her at dinner. Still, he wasn't about to give up.

On his way to the exit, Mitch stumbled over something on the floor, and he looked down at McKenzie's bag at his feet. She'd have a hard time driving home without her keys, which he knew she kept inside. He muttered an inaudible thank-you at the perfect opportunity to approach her.

Mitch checked his watch. He had twenty minutes until his next appointment. Enough time to check on her before he had to be back at the clinic. Slinging her bag over his other shoulder, he left the gym.

He searched for her all the way down the hall toward the front exit. Right before stepping outside, muffled sobbing met his ears, and he stopped. Following the sound, he found McKenzie tucked into a narrow hallway, hugging her legs to her chest, face in her knees. Her shoulders shook as she cried.

Mitch's protective instincts took over. He dropped both bags onto the floor and stepped into the hallway. Squeezing his tall frame into a sitting position next to her was almost comical. Somehow, he managed it, although uncomfortably. She didn't acknowledge him next to her, but her body stiffened, so he knew his presence hadn't gone unnoticed.

"You left your bag in the gym," he said after a few minutes. He kept his focus on the wall in front of him. "I brought it out for you."

When McKenzie didn't respond, he glanced at her. She hastily wiped at the tears on her blotchy face and turned her body away from him, resting her cheek against her knees. Her ponytail brushed over her bare legs like a fiery wall, blocking the rest of her from view. The quiet stretched on, the air growing more uncomfortable as the seconds ticked past. His fingers itched to reach for her, to initiate some connection. But he held back. She, no doubt, wouldn't appreciate it.

"What's wrong, Zee?"

McKenzie still refused to look at him, though she turned her head enough to give him a view of her profile. "I'm having a bad day." She swiped at her wet face. "And my body hurts."

"You could take a bath in Icy Hot," he said, remembering the tube of medicated ointment she'd given him for his birthday. "Might make it feel better."

She pierced him with a fierce glare.

He sobered. "Sorry, bad attempt at a joke."

More silence danced around them, and he wiggled a little, searching for a more comfortable sitting position. He was too tall to cram himself in a tight spot like this, but he wasn't about to leave her.

"Zee, please talk to me."

She shook her head. "You don't want to hear about my problems."

"Sure I do. I'm worried about you."

"Why?" she mumbled before burying her face again.

"Because I care about you."

Her head shot up, then jerked in his direction, anger flashing across her face. "Tell me something, Mitch. The whole time you've been hanging out with me and texting me ..." She kept her posture stiff, maintaining eye contact. "Did you have a girlfriend the whole time?"

"What?"

"Were you just entertaining your options?" She looked away. "Or maybe I'm so stupid that I misinterpreted everything."

He opened his mouth to speak. No response came so he shut it again. When had he given her the impression he had a girlfriend? "Zee, what are you talking about?" he finally asked.

Her frustration only grew. "It's okay. You don't have to spare my feelings. Aria already showed me the picture." A faint flush appeared on her cheeks.

Picture?

And then everything clicked into place. His first scrimmage, talking with Chelsea, that stupid photo. She'd tagged him on Instagram a few days ago.

He sighed, dropping his head back against the wall. "I think I know what you're talking about."

His knee brushed hers as he struggled to adjust his sitting position enough to dig his phone out of his pocket. She scooted over to avoid his touch. After a lot of difficulty, he finally had the device in hand and found the incriminating photo, holding it out to her. "Is this the picture you mean?"

Her gaze flicked to the screen before darting away again with a barely visible nod of confirmation. "She's pretty. And tall. You're cute together."

"She's not my girlfriend. I hardly know her. She comes out to watch the pros scrimmage sometimes. She was there last week and asked for a picture. I had no idea she'd get so ... cozy." He cleared his throat. "It made me uncomfortable."

"Why?"

Mitch set the phone on the floor between his legs and interlocked his fingers between his knees. "Because I didn't want you to get the wrong idea." He dropped his voice to a whisper. "There's only one girl I'm interested in dating, and she's not very happy with me right now."

His words didn't have quite the affect he was hoping for. Her gorgeous blue eyes, still red-rimmed from crying, flickered back and forth between his, full of questions. "Why have you been so weird around me, then?" He could hear the hurt in her quiet tone.

He pushed out a breath, then lifted his shoulders to his ears. Now was his chance to put Rory's advice into action. "I like you, Zee. And I want you as more than a friend. But I also know this isn't all about me. The last thing I want is to put more stress on you."

"I don't understand." She leaned forward to rest her chin on her knees.

He studied her profile for a moment before continuing. "I know how much you crave normalcy. If I continue playing volleyball, a relationship with me wouldn't give you that. Once the season starts, I'll have tournaments almost every weekend. Sometimes back-to-back. I'll be gone a lot."

She didn't respond right away, but she turned toward him again, her eyes searching his face for ... something. He didn't know what. Her life had already been riddled with so much heartbreak—her almost career-ending injury, the constant paralyzing pressure from her mother, her emotionally absent father. Mitch wanted nothing more than to take away all of it. To somehow help her realize how incredible she was.

"Thanks for bringing me my bag," she said. "I didn't want to go back in there."

Mitch swallowed his disappointment at the sudden change of subject. "I figured."

McKenzie sat up, placing her elbows on top of her knees. She rubbed circles over her temples with her fingers. "It's probably for the best that Gary kicked me out of the gym. I didn't want to practice today anyway." A lone tear trailed down her cheek, and she brushed it away.

"I guess you could say I saved the day." He quirked an eyebrow at her, nudging her arm with his elbow. "Maybe I should get a cape and start wearing my underwear on the outside of my pants."

She snorted, the sound half laugh, half sob. She glanced at him, her pursed lips failing to hide a smile. "You're ridiculous."

A morsel of relief lightened his heart. "But I made you laugh. At least I think that's what that was."

She laughed for real this time.

"Hey, I did it again. I'm on a roll." He flashed her a smile, and pink stained her cheeks.

She drummed her fingers against her cheek, as if considering something. "My mom called before practice. That's why I was so distracted."

Mitch waited for her to continue.

"I don't know why I even try sometimes. She's so negative." She adopted a high-pitched voice and screwed her face into a scowl as she imitated her mother. "McKenzie, you're too old. McKenzie, you're too weak. You're supposed to be a champion. Don't let me down." She shook her head and rolled her eyes at the ceiling.

Her bitterness surprised him. In the time he'd known her, he'd never seen her like this. Discouraged, frustrated, yes. But never bitter.

"Why doesn't she come right out and say it? I'm a failure as a daughter and she wishes I was never born." She buried her face in her hands. A minute later, she lifted her head again. "Sorry, I'm just so over this."

Mitch reached over and took her hand in his. "I'm sorry, Zee. That's really hard."

She looked at their entwined hands, and for a brief moment, he thought she appreciated his show of support. Then she pulled hers away.

That gesture spoke volumes. She still didn't trust him even after he'd been honest with her. Earning back her trust would obviously be a marathon, not a sprint. Good thing he was in it for the long haul. And she was talking to him again so ... baby steps.

"It doesn't matter how much I achieve, "McKenzie grumbled. "I'll never be good enough for her."

Listening to her vent made Mitch want to call his own parents to thank them for everything they'd done for him throughout his life. And apologize for all the times he'd taken them for granted. As far as parents went, he'd hit the jackpot.

As he thought about what to say to her, he moved his torso from side to side, attempting to work out the kink forming in his back. Painful prickles shot up his foot, which had fallen asleep sometime during their conversation. "Zee, you *are* enough. You're a talented gymnast, and you work harder than most people I know. Just because your mom can't see it, doesn't mean it's not true."

McKenzie stared at him, and the vulnerability he saw in her face pricked at his heart. "Thank you for saying that. It's hard to remember sometimes when she calls me every day and reminds me of what a disappointment I am."

"I have some choice words for your mother right about now," Mitch grumbled, smiling at her when she laughed quietly. "You've been under a lot of pressure lately. You were bound to crack eventually."

Her chin quivered, and she kept her focus on the wall in front of her.

"Life isn't meant to be all about work," he continued. "You need to have a little fun once in a while to give yourself a break."

"I don't spend all my time in the gym. Sundays are my day to take my mind off gymnastics."

"I'm not talking about days off, Zee." Mitch gave her a pointed look. "When was the last time you did something simply because you wanted to and not because it was expected of you?"

McKenzie shrugged and said nothing, swiping at the wetness lingering on her porcelain cheeks.

An idea emerged in Mitch's mind. "You don't train tomorrow, right?" She shook her head. "Clear your schedule. I want to take you somewhere."

"I don't think that's a good idea," she said hastily. She looked away, reminding Mitch of the first time he'd attempted to ask her out. At least this time he blocked her exit. She'd have to literally crawl over him to get out of this cramped hallway.

"McKenzie, I'm worried about you." He reached out and lightly touched her chin with his fingers, turning her face toward him. He spoke barely louder than a whisper. "It breaks my heart to see you cry."

McKenzie remained fixated on his face, and the sound of her breath catching caused his heart to pound in his chest.

"Please say yes. I'm not asking you to trust me right now. Just let me do this for you. We don't have to talk about gymnastics or annoying parents, or anything else you don't want to talk about."

She pursed her lips, clearly mulling over his proposal.

Static coming from Mitch's walkie-talkie broke their connection. Jared's voice cut through the crackle informing him that his four o'clock appointment was waiting.

Mitch unclipped the device from his belt loop and brought it to his face. "Tell him I'll be right there." He clipped it back onto his pants before turning to McKenzie. "I have to go. But please say you'll go out with me. I'm not above begging." To prove it, he clasped his hands together and gave her his best puppy dog look.

"We wouldn't want that, would we?" She blew out a dramatic sigh. "Fine, I guess I'll go out with you."

It wasn't a glowing acceptance, but he'd take it. "Great, I'll pick you up at one." He gave her knee a gentle pat before pushing himself off the floor. His body protested the movement after so much time crammed in that tight space. "Wear your swimsuit." Then he picked up his bag and stepped out of the hallway.

Chapter Twenty-One

When McKenzie's official World Championships apparel arrived in Gary's office the day before, she'd stuck the box in her car, eager to open it at home. After her disastrous fall on beam, however, she'd no longer had the heart. The box sat locked in her trunk overnight.

Now, somewhat removed from the emotional toll of the day before, she felt more equal to the task. She sat cross-legged on her bed, four long-sleeved competition leotards and five sleeveless practice leos laid out around her. Reverently, she touched the tiny American flag at the wrist of her favorite one—all-white, metallic, with paper-thin threads of shiny red and blue running throughout, that gave it a slightly iridescent look. Goosebumps rippled across her arms as she ran her finger along the tiny silver rhinestones that made up the USA emblem at the hem of the right hip. Renewed determination flooded over her. Despite her horrible practice yesterday, and the constant pressure from her mom, she *would* make her country proud.

The knock on her open door drew McKenzie's attention away from the leotard. Beej entered, surveying the items on the bed. "Those are gorgeous!"

"Aren't they? This one's my favorite." She held the all-white one against her torso for Beej to see. "It's so surreal to finally get to wear one of these."

Beej picked up a leotard—navy with red accents and tiny gemstones arranged to look like an exploding firework on the front —and plopped down on the bed across from McKenzie. "You deserve it after how hard you've worked."

"It's been a long road." McKenzie spoke mostly to herself. "And it's not over yet."

Beej patted McKenzie's knee. "You'll get there. I know you will."

McKenzie was touched by her friend's immediate show of support. Surprised by the sudden lump in her throat, she swallowed. "I don't think I've ever thanked you for picking me to be your roommate. You all are the best friends I've ever had."

Beej smiled and reached forward to give her an awkward hug, both of their laps still full of spandex. "I'm glad it worked out too. You're part of our family now. And as your best friend, I should tell you that Mitch is downstairs waiting for you."

McKenzie gasped, pulling back quickly, and tossed the leotard onto her bedspread. "It's one already?" She snatched her phone from under her pillow where it had landed when she'd flung it on the bed earlier. A text from Mitch saying he was on his way appeared underneath the clock that showed ten after one.

She placed a hand on her stomach, attempting to steady the nausea bubbling there. A dull pain still throbbed in her abs from her fall, though it had faded a lot since the day before. "Tell him I'll be right there. I have to change."

Beej rose from the bed, pausing before making her way to the door. "Remember to trust your instincts, Zee." Then she left.

Trust her instincts. Easier said than done when McKenzie didn't know what they were telling her. As far as Mitch was concerned, her thoughts and emotions were all over the place. She was still embarrassed at being caught in the middle of an ugly cry by the one guy she'd been trying to avoid. On the other hand, he'd sought her out. His obvious concern for her welfare had touched her more than she'd willingly admitted the day before. And his confession about wanting to date her? She still hadn't unpacked her thoughts about that.

The squeamish feeling in her stomach only grew as she hurried out of her tank top and leggings and into her swimsuit—a green-striped, one-shouldered bikini that complimented her small but athletic figure. The high-waisted bottoms covered most of the ugly purple bruise on her lower abdomen, though a tiny bit still showed over the top. She threw on a flowy halter-top cover-up that fell a few inches above her knees and tied around the neck, then gathered her hair into a ponytail. Tucking a few wisps of hair behind her ear, McKenzie assessed herself in the mirror hanging on the back of the door. *Not bad,* she thought before hurrying from the room.

She took a few calming breaths at the top of the stairs, fortifying her emotional defenses. Mitch had said all the right words in that cramped hallway, and she wanted to believe him, but there were so few people in her life she could truly trust. Only time would tell whether he was one of them.

When she finally entered the living room, Mitch was lounging on the couch with one arm slung along the back of it. He glanced up from his phone as she approached, his mouth immediately lifting into a knee-buckling smile.

McKenzie broke into an answering one against her will. It seemed that even though her head warned her to be cautious, her heart had other plans. No wonder she was so confused.

He stood and approached her. "Hey. I was beginning to think you'd stood me up." After a slight hesitation, he wrapped an arm around McKenzie's shoulders in a side hug.

She returned the gesture, pushing down the desire to move in for a more substantial hug. "Sorry, I lost track of time."

"No worries. We're not in a hurry." He pocketed his phone, drawing McKenzie's gaze for the first time to his swimsuit. The navy shorts were dotted with white shapes scattered all over. Except they weren't shapes at all.

"Are those llamas on your swimsuit?"

Mitch glanced down at his shorts. "They're alpacas, actually."

A giggle escaped before McKenzie could stop it. "I have so many questions."

He chuckled at her response. "I found them at the back of my dresser this morning. I didn't realize I still had them. I was hoping they'd cheer you up. It's not possible to be sad around alpacas."

His comment shouldn't have surprised her. Mitch would do anything for a laugh, especially when someone he cared about was hurting. The fact that he'd spend a whole day in those ridiculous trunks to get her to smile touched her. "Be honest. You know they're your favorite."

His wink knocked down more of McKenzie's defenses. "You caught me," he said. "Are you ready?"

She nodded, and they made their way to the front door. "Where does one find an alpaca swimsuit anyway?"

Mitch held the door open for her. "I have no idea. They were a gift from my sisters a few Christmases ago."

"There has to be a story there."

He stepped outside behind her and shut the door. "Let's just say there's an alpaca wandering around the Ecuadorian countryside missing his cuddle buddy."

McKenzie pursed her lips to hold back a smile. "And that cuddle buddy would be ... you?"

"Ding ding ding." He touched the end of his pointer finger to his nose. "You're a smart one. I was the unwilling participant, of course. He kept following me on a hike the last time I was down there. I named him Alberto."

"Alberto the alpaca." She laughed. "I like it."

She glanced at him, and the wide smile he gave her stopped her in her tracks. How was she supposed to keep her walls strong when he had the power to weaken them so quickly?

They walked across the grass to his car parked at the curb. A jet ski sat atop a metal trailer hitched to the back.

"We're going jet skiing?" she asked.

"Have you been?"

"No." Jet skis meant open water, which always made her nervous. "Do you even know how to work that thing?"

Mitch eyed her sidelong. "It can't be too difficult. I should be able to figure it out."

McKenzie stopped short, her eyes widening.

He laughed and placed a hand on her back, urging her forward. "I'm kidding! I grew up near Lake Michigan. My buddy's family had a few of these babies. When I wasn't playing volleyball, I spent my summers taking them out on the water."

After fighting the Southern California stop-and-go traffic, they finally made it to the beach. The afternoon sun shone down from a cloudless sky. An ocean breeze cut through an otherwise warm day, sending goosebumps down her arms. A few boats already dotted the ocean, though with the summer season long over, the crowds were manageable.

Mitch had opened the back hatch and was pulling out life jackets and wet suits when McKenzie joined him by the trailer hitch. He handed her a black suit. "I had to guess your size at the rental place." He shrugged apologetically. "I hope it fits."

"Thank you."

Mitch smiled in response, eliciting more flutters in her stomach. She pulled the wet suit as high as it would go before removing her cover up and slipping her arms into the sleeves. For some reason, having Mitch see her in a bikini seemed a little too intimate for her liking. She could already feel her defenses slipping in the short time they'd spent together that day. It scared her, and she wasn't ready to throw caution to the wind just yet. But it was the only suit she had.

Mitch, on the other hand, had no qualms about stripping down to only his hilarious alpaca trunks. In one fluid motion, he reached behind his neck with both hands and pulled off his shirt, tossing it into the back of the SUV. McKenzie's eyes stretched wide, and she hastily turned away, though that one look was all she needed to burn the shirtless image of him into her mind forever.

The man was ripped. If McKenzie were to look up washboard abs in the dictionary, she wouldn't be surprised to find a picture of Mitch Skaggs' stomach as the definition. No wonder that fan couldn't resist snuggling up to all that. McKenzie wouldn't mind doing the same.

Her face burned. Yes, Mitch was hot. She'd recognized that the first day he'd walked into her gym. That immediate awareness of him had made her work hard to avoid him in the beginning. But there was so much more to him than sculpted muscles and a gorgeous face. As cliché as it sounded, his genuine heart was his most attractive feature.

But he was still nice to look at.

"Do you want me to zip you up?"

McKenzie startled, whirling around to face him. "W-what?"

Mitch raised an eyebrow, his lips pursed as if holding back a laugh. The sleeves of his wetsuit were peeled down at the waist, and she made sure to keep her eyes on his face instead of his glorious stomach. Had he noticed her ogling him? Gosh, she hoped not.

He twirled his finger in a circle, motioning for her to turn around again. "I'll zip you up," he repeated.

"Oh, right." Her cheeks burned as she complied. As he raised the zipper, his fingers brushed her back, sending little prickles radiating outward across her skin. Her body gave an involuntary shiver in response to his touch.

"How does it fit?" His eyes traveled up and down her body as he assessed her.

McKenzie straightened the neck with a finger. "I t-think it's okay." She cleared her throat. She hadn't stuttered around him for weeks. "Apparently you have a knack at guessing women's sizes." She squeezed her eyes shut. *What kind of comment is that?*

Mitch laughed. "It helps that you're about the same size as my sister, Andrea. I asked her what size she wears." He lifted his suit over his torso—finally covering his distracting abs—and shoved his arms into the sleeves. McKenzie's breath returned to normal. "Will you zip me up?" he asked.

He turned around, and McKenzie caught sight of the tattoo on his back. Interesting. Mitch didn't seem like the type. Not that there was anything wrong with it. She'd always thought a well-placed tattoo upped a man on the scale of hotness. Although Mitch was already off the charts.

With a tilt of her head, she gave it a closer look, stalling with one hand on his zipper. A volleyball covered his left shoulder blade with the letters DTJ written through it and a date right below.

What could be so important to him that he'd have it permanently inked on his body? The volleyball made sense. It had always been a huge part of Mitch's life, even during the years he hadn't played competitively. She didn't know what the letters signified, though she had a strong hunch they had something to do with why he'd stopped playing on the pro circuit.

Very slowly, she reached out a hand toward his shoulder blade, itching to trace her fingers across the symbol.

Inches from his skin, she froze and jerked her hand back. *What am I doing?* She hastily raised the zipper.

Once they were out on the water, McKenzie's nerves faded. Mitch was right—doing something simply for the fun of it was exactly what she needed to clear her head. And she had no complaints about sitting with her arms around him and her hands resting on those tantalizing abs.

But even the wind in her hair and the ocean spray hitting her face couldn't stop her mind from staying transfixed on his tattoo. That symbol, so simple in appearance, hinted at a deeper layer to the fun-loving man she knew. Whether out of mere curiosity, or her growing feelings for him, she couldn't ignore the desire to dig deeper, to uncover the mystery, if she could only find the courage.

And while her head screamed at her to fortify her wall and shut him out, her heart stood at its base holding a stick of dynamite poised to blow that wall to the ground.

Chapter Twenty-Two

Mitch wasn't sure when he'd get another opportunity to spend a day with McKenzie, so he was determined to draw it out for as long as possible. After returning to the boat launch and securing the jet ski back on the trailer, he suggested a walk on the beach, thrilled when she agreed without hesitation.

Soft sand caressed his bare feet as they headed toward the waves crashing against the shore. The sound was a soothing touch to a day made perfect by the beautiful woman beside him. McKenzie's flip-flops dangled from the tips of her fingers poking out of the sleeve of his navy University of Illinois hoodie. The jacket dwarfed her tiny frame, the ocean breeze rustling the hem of her cover-up hanging barely longer than the hoodie.

Mitch nodded toward the volleyball tucked in her other hand. "Why'd you bring that?"

She glanced at the blue and white ball. "I was hoping you'd show me some of your moves."

"How about I teach you something?" he asked.

She tilted her head to the side, her mouth pursed in thought. "Will you show me how to jump serve?"

"Sure." A heavy breeze sent goosebumps up and down his arms, despite his long-sleeved shirt.

The late afternoon sun had begun to dip in the sky and a few people still wandered about, though the crowds had mostly dispersed for the day. They wandered past a few kids chasing after kites and groups of teens and twenty-somethings tossing around frisbees until they found an empty patch of beach a few yards from the tide line.

Mitch dropped his flip-flops onto the sand and gestured for the ball. She handed it over. "Watch me first, then you can try."

With McKenzie watching his movements from his side, he turned his back to the water. There was no net to work with, so he zeroed in on a spot up the beach, passing the ball between his hands. Then he held it in front of his face and puffed out a deep breath. He flicked his wrist as he tossed it high in the air in front of him, putting a good spin on it. After three running steps, he jumped and swung his arms back. Bringing his right above his head, he snapped the ball forward. It landed exactly on the sweet spot.

McKenzie slow-clapped behind him. "That was impressive."

He threw a cheeky grin over his shoulder. "That? Nah, it's easy. Anyone can do it."

"Oh yeah," she said with amused sarcasm. "Piece of cake."

Mitch jogged over to retrieve the ball, before returning to her side. "Here. You try."

She unzipped his hoodie and tugged it off, letting it fall to the ground. "Okay, coach, what do I do?"

"Take the ball in your left hand." He handed it to her. "Then toss it up and swing with your right. Make sure you throw it up high enough so you have time to get a good jump."

"Wait, but you used the same arm to toss it as you did to serve. Are you going easy on me because I'm a girl?" Somehow, even being over a foot shorter than he, she still managed to look down her nose at him.

"Me?" He scoffed, putting a hand on his chest in overblown dramatics. "Of course not. It took me years to perfect my serve. I'm teaching you the easier way."

"I don't want to learn the easier way," she said. "Teach me the better way."

Her determination was hot. "If you say so. Drop the ball, and I'll teach you the motions. Then you can try it for real." He moved behind her, using his hand to extend her right arm out in front of her. The sweet scent of her hair filled his nose, and his pulse drummed through his body. It would be so easy to lean down and kiss the soft spot below her ear.

He took a stuttering breath, squeezing his eyes shut to regain his control. She was way too tempting. Still, as much as he wanted to kiss her, he had to wait for the right time. Only twenty-four hours before, she'd had him at arm's length. He wouldn't risk losing the ground he'd made with her just to get what he wanted.

After several minutes of practicing the rhythm, Mitch said, "You're a fast learner. I think you're ready to try it with the ball." He picked it up from the sand and tossed it to her.

McKenzie threw the ball into the air and jumped, her feet barely leaving the ground. She swung and ... missed it completely. Glancing at him, she shrugged with amusement.

"Pretty good for a first try." Mitch bobbed his head in a slow nod, his voice shaking with suppressed laughter. "This time try hitting the ball."

That pulled a hard laugh from her—a rare occurrence, especially lately. He took a few seconds to enjoy the sound of it.

"Maybe I will try it the other way," she said.

"Good idea."

McKenzie tried again. This time, she executed an awkward serve that only went a few feet—but it *was* a serve.

Mitch clapped his hands together. "There you go. That's how you get it done."

After a few more practice serves, they started volleying back and forth. Mitch went easy on her, feeding passes he knew she could hit. To her credit, she picked up the sport quickly. She missed plenty of balls, sure, but Mitch was still impressed. The urge to scoop her up in his arms and kiss her overwhelmed him once again. He was getting to be an expert at resisting temptation. But the longer he spent with her, the harder it was to summon the willpower.

Wrapped up in his distraction, he didn't notice the pass coming his way until it ricocheted off his arm. The ball flew behind him toward the water.

"So, the superstar isn't invincible after all!" McKenzie shouted as he chased after it.

He reached the ball as it rolled into the incoming wave. "I was distracted by your beauty," he called back, picking it up and trotting back to her. He wasn't lying.

Instead of giving her a soft pass he knew she could return, he served it hard in her direction. She screamed and ducked out of the way.

"Mitchell Skaggs!" She popped both fists on her hips. "You could've hit me!"

Mitch choked back a laugh at her glare. This feisty side of McKenzie was new, but no less attractive than every other aspect of her.

"Come on, Zee," he said, sauntering over to her. "You know I'd never hurt you. My aim is too good for that."

"You're so full of it." She continued staring him down as she picked up the ball, her eyes narrowing even more at his cheeky grin.

Was she actually mad? *Real smooth, man.* If he'd ruined his chances of winning her back, Mitch would never forgive himself. He didn't need to give her any more reasons to hate him.

"I'm sorry, Zee. I was just messing around."

Her lips lifted a tiny bit. "Got you," she said, chucking the ball hard at his head. The catlike reflexes that had made Mitch the best American defender on the junior circuit kicked in, and his hands flew up to catch it.

"That's it!" He dropped the ball and charged. She shrieked as he easily slung her over his shoulder, then took off at a run down the beach.

"Foul!" McKenzie squealed, barely getting the word out through her laughter.

Mitch sprinted several yards up the beach while enjoying the sound. After a minute, he turned around and ran back to their starting point. He set her gently onto her feet, breathing hard from his run. There was nothing like a jog on the beach to get the blood pumping.

"Show me in the rule book where it says you're allowed to fling your opponent over your shoulder like that." McKenzie picked up the hoodie, brushing it off before slipping it back on. She sunk down onto the sand facing the water. "I don't know much about volleyball, but I can't believe that would be allowed."

Mitch joined her, leaning back on his hands, chuckling. "Man, if you'd used my middle name back there and added an accent, you'd have sounded like my mother."

She elbowed his arm. "What *is* your middle name? You know, in case I need to call you out again."

"You'll absolutely need to call me out. Skaggs men are known to cause trouble." He flashed her his most devilish smile and was rewarded with a laugh. "It's Javier."

"Is that a family name?" she asked, copying Mitch's position by leaning back on her hands, their pinkies mere inches apart.

He nodded. "I'm named after both my grandfathers. Mitchell from my dad's side and Javier from my mom's."

"I like hearing you say it. It sounds so ... Spanish."

"Surprising, isn't it? So different from my Chicago twang? If you're nice to me, I might even speak sweet nothings to you in Spanish and really blow your mind." He smiled at the adorable shade of pink that appeared on her cheeks. "What's yours?"

"Eliza." A hint of her blush still touched her skin. "Don't ask me why my parents insisted on using double Zs in my name. It's such an ugly letter."

"Nah, I like it," he said. "A beautiful name for a beautiful woman."

She looked away but not before Mitch caught the pleasure on her face. They fell into silence, watching the waves roll onto the shore, the sound lulling him into contentment. He'd always found solace near the water. McKenzie sitting next to him only added to the peaceful comfort of the ocean.

He snuck a peek at her. In the soft glow of the golden hour, her face—turned up toward the sun—was a picture of complete calm. The light shone on her hair, turning her long, beachy waves into a fiery halo. As he watched her, he couldn't help but feel he was intruding on a deeply personal moment. Apparently, he wasn't the only one who found reverence from the ocean. Try as he might, he couldn't pull his gaze from the goddess next to him.

Just kiss her already. If he didn't do something about this building desire soon, he was bound to combust. He dropped his eyes to their hands, still separated by only inches of sand. Crawling his fingers to hers, he hesitated a second before interlocking their pinkies. He gauged her reaction. If she showed any sign of discomfort, he'd break the connection.

Instead, her soft smile, still turned toward the sunlight, sent his pulse racing. Such a gorgeous smile.

Encouraged, Mitch inched sideways until his upper arm brushed hers. "Zee—"

"What does DTJ stand for?" she asked at the same time, turning toward him and opening her eyes.

Mitch froze. She'd noticed his tattoo. Of course she had. He hadn't exactly tried to hide it. And she wasn't the first person to ask about its meaning. He'd promised Doug's mom shortly after the accident that he'd never forget her son. Getting the tattoo had seemed a fitting way to commit to that. But never forgetting didn't mean he was willing to talk about that night to anyone.

Except vulnerability was a two-way street. And McKenzie had trusted him with her deeply personal struggles, even when it was difficult. Hadn't she earned the right to be a confidant to him?

Staring out at the sun dipping closer to the horizon, he gathered his strength. "Douglas Todd Jepson." His voice cracked, and he swallowed the emotion clogging his throat. "He's my ... was ... my best friend. And volleyball partner before ..." He hung his head and took a shuddering breath, forcing himself to blurt out the rest. "He died. But it should've been me."

Chapter Twenty-Three

"What?" McKenzie asked.

Mitch couldn't look at her. "I was supposed to drive that night. It should've been me who died."

"Mitch, you're not making sense." McKenzie's voice held a note of desperation.

He kept his focus on the waves rolling onto the sand in front of them. His composure was already tumbling out of his control, and he knew if he looked at her, he'd lose the battle completely.

"Mitch." McKenzie slid her pinkie out from under his and turned his hand palm up, weaving her fingers through his. The soft pressure drew his attention to her. Concern shone in her eyes. "Please tell me."

The calluses on her palm rubbed against his skin, anchoring him in the present and preventing him from getting lost in the all-encompassing grief that filled those early days after Doug's death. He breathed in the ocean air, releasing it slowly. "It was a few weeks after Junior Worlds. We'd just started our senior year of high school. You remember how seniors are."

She shook her head. "I'd already moved to LA by then. I was living with Gary's family and doing my senior year online."

"I forgot about that."

She shrugged. "Go on."

He gave her hand a squeeze before continuing. "Anyway, we were on top of the world. Invincible. Like nothing could touch us." He swallowed. "Then everything changed."

His breathing came in stutters, and he blinked hard to clear the moisture from his eyes. McKenzie remained quiet, didn't press him for more. She seemed to be waiting for him to continue at his pace.

"The night of the first home football game, Doug, his girlfriend, and I were all planning to go together. I was the only one with my own car, so I was supposed to drive. But at the last minute, I decided not to go."

"How come?"

Mitch shrugged. "My girlfriend and I broke up earlier that week. And Doug and Jules were nauseatingly cute. The perfect couple. Don't get me wrong, they were my best friends, but I was a hormonal teenager who'd just been dumped. I really didn't want to be the third wheel to the shoo-ins for Prom royalty."

The shame of his petty jealousy threatened to take over like it always did whenever the memories boiled to the surface. This was exactly why the past belonged firmly buried where he couldn't dwell on it. How did it always work its way to the surface?

He'd sacrifice anything to go back in time and redo that entire week of his life. Maybe the outcome would be different. "Doug was irritated that I refused to go, but he didn't push it. He borrowed his mom's car instead. On the way home, a drunk driver barreled through a red light and T-boned the driver's side. Doug died on impact."

A single tear escaped, and he swiped it away quickly with the back of the same hand that held McKenzie's. Flashbacks of that tragic night ran through his mind. Suddenly, he was seventeen again, back in the Jepson's living room, sitting next to Mama B as the police officer informed her of how her only child had died. Mitch had held her hand while she sobbed, desperately attempting to hold back his own grief, to be strong for her.

He cleared his throat and forced himself to finish. "Jules survived, thankfully, though barely. She was in the hospital for weeks. My brother and I visited her as much as we could, but she struggled." He sniffed. "Her family moved to St. Louis shortly after she was released. I haven't heard from her since." She'd told him her dad's work transferred him, though Mitch had always suspected he'd requested it so Jules wouldn't have to live with the memories.

"Oh, Mitch." McKenzie's tight whisper brought him back to the present. "You couldn't have known that was going to happen. It wasn't your fault. You had a perfectly valid reason for not going."

He glanced at her, immediately wishing he hadn't. The tears in her eyes nearly broke him. He turned away. "Believe me, Zee, I've been telling myself that for years. It's hard not to feel responsible though. If I'd been there, maybe the timing would've been different."

"Maybe. That doesn't mean you're to blame for any of this. You weren't the one driving drunk."

Mitch didn't respond. No matter how many times he'd hashed out that exact argument in his brain, the guilt never went away. He could mask it, even ignore it, but it always lingered over him. His own personal nightmare.

McKenzie let go of his hand and shifted closer, leaning her head on his shoulder. "That's why you gave up playing competitively, isn't it?"

He rested his cheek against the top of her head. "At first, the grief was too strong to keep playing. Those months immediately after it happened were really dark. And Doug was my partner. As more time passed, I couldn't stomach the idea of returning and having everyone on the circuit asking about it when I was trying to forget. It seemed easier to stay away."

"I'm sorry, Mitch." McKenzie lifted her head, resting her chin on his shoulder to look at him. "I shouldn't have pushed you into going back."

He pulled his legs up to his chest, wrapping one arm around his knee and the other around her shoulders. "You didn't push me. You helped me reconsider."

"What was he like?" She returned her cheek to his shoulder. Hastily, she said, "Sorry, I shouldn't have asked."

Mitch swiped at his eyes again. "It's okay. He was the golden boy, everyone's favorite. It didn't matter if he'd known someone for ten minutes or ten years, he always made everyone feel special." He cleared the emotion from his throat. "Man, people like him shouldn't be allowed to die."

McKenzie didn't speak for a moment before she said quietly, "You have the same effect on people though."

Mitch gave her shoulder a squeeze. "I haven't always been like this. Especially right after he died. I was really closed off."

"What changed? I mean, you're such a positive person now."

He thought for a moment. "My family's my saving grace, especially my baby sister. Hazel was born a few months after the accident. When she was a baby, she had this scream-cackle that was the cutest sound ever." He chuckled remembering his sister back then. "I could always make her laugh. She made me realize that when I brightened someone's day, even just by making them smile, it made me happy too, even if only for a little bit."

A heavy breeze whipped through the beach and McKenzie snuggled closer to him. "I can see that in you."

Mitch stared out at the darkening water, clinging to the last remnants of his composure. "Sorry. I promised no hard conversations on this date."

"No, you promised no gymnastics or annoying parents. There was no ban on all heavy subjects." She gave his leg a little shove but turned a compassionate smile on him. "Thank you for telling me."

As they watched the sun make its last descent before disappearing below the horizon, their conversation gradually switched to lighter topics. The sadness gripping Mitch's heart faded little by little with each minute that ticked past, though some of it lingered even after they'd left the beach. But somehow, McKenzie's quiet demeanor provided a peaceful presence.

Much too soon, they arrived back at her house. Mitch held her hand as he walked her to the door. "I hope I didn't put a damper on the day earlier." They stopped underneath the glow of the porch light.

McKenzie shook her head. "I haven't had this much fun in a long time. You were right. I needed a day away."

His heart jump-started into overdrive when he took her into his arms, and she rested her cheek against his chest. "Let me know when you need another break. I'll gladly escape with you."

"I'd like that." She pulled back, resting her hands lightly on his biceps. "As long as we can go jet skiing again. And next time, I want my own." She nudged his chest with the back of her hand.

Mitch chuckled. "Hey, I'd love to see you drive one again. That was hot."

Her face flushed, and she looked away. A few seconds later, her shy gaze returned to his face. "You know how yesterday you told me you were only interested in one person?"

"Yeah." His pulse sped up a notch, his intuition charged.

Her bottom lip caught between her teeth, drawing his eyes to her bow-shaped mouth. The desire to kiss her reared its not-so-ugly head once again. "I was too overwhelmed to say this yesterday but ... I feel the same about you."

That was all the invitation he needed. Keeping one hand at her waist, he brought the other to cradle her jaw. Her eyelids fluttered closed as he stooped toward her, and she raised onto her tiptoes to close the gap.

A shrill whistle rang through the quiet night, startling them both. McKenzie jumped back, her face a deeper red than he'd ever seen on her.

"Seth!" Beej protested as she and Seth ascended the front steps onto the porch. She gave him a shove before offering Mitch a sympathetic look.

Of course Seth would show up at the exact moment Mitch was putting the moves on his little sister. He should've realized McKenzie's front porch was *not* the ideal spot for a first kiss.

"Sorry. I tried to get him to go in through the garage, but he wouldn't have it." Beej narrowed her eyes at her boyfriend.

McKenzie covered her face with her hands. "How embarrassing," she muttered.

"I had to check up on this guy." Seth firmly gripped Mitch's shoulders with both hands and gave him a few shakes. "You remember what we talked about a few weeks ago?"

Mitch read the warning in Seth's eyes. His protective side was coming out, despite the amused smile on his face.

"Yes, sir," Mitch said.

Seth nodded in approval, removing his hands. "Good. Make sure you don't forget."

"Oh, leave him alone, babe." Beej rolled her eyes, though she passed a flirty look in his direction. She nudged him toward the door. "Let's go inside. I need food."

Before the door shut, Seth poked his head back out, alternating pointing to himself and then to Mitch and back to himself with two fingers. "I'm watching you, man." He disappeared again, and the door snapped shut.

"What did you talk about a few weeks ago?" McKenzie asked, bringing Mitch's attention back to her.

He reached out for her again, and she stepped into him willingly. "He was only reminding me to treat you right."

She groaned and dropped her face into his chest. "I wish I were an only child."

He chuckled. "He's only looking out for you."

"Sometimes he's a little *too* protective."

"As a guy with three sisters, I can tell you it's a brother's job to be annoyingly overprotective of his sisters. *Especially* if they're younger."

McKenzie laughed into his shirt. He held her for a moment before somehow managing to release her. "I suppose the mood is killed now, huh?"

"And buried six feet under," she said, regret in her voice. "I'm sorry about my brother."

He waved off her apology. "Don't worry about him. At least I know how you feel now." He cupped a hand around her chin, bending to press a lingering kiss to her forehead. It wasn't the kiss he'd hoped for, but it was better than nothing. For now. "Good night, Zee."

Her mouth puckered down slightly. "See you tomorrow?"

Keeping his eyes on her, he whispered, "Can't wait." He backed a few steps away before turning to go down the front stairs.

"Mitch!" she called when he was halfway across the grass.

He turned around. McKenzie was sprinting across the lawn to him. Before he knew what was happening, she grabbed his shirt in her fists, pulling him down to her. Their lips connected. Shock seized control of his body, making it impossible to react. *Do something, idiot!*

Was this the same woman who was so shy that a few months ago she couldn't string more than a couple words together when speaking to him? And now *she* was kissing *him!*

Get it together, man! Finally, his instincts kicked in and his arms came around her, pulling her up to him until every inch of distance between them disappeared. He lost himself in the feel of her lips, as soft as he'd imagined they'd be, inviting him to soak in every drop of their deepening connection.

People could say what they wanted about her quiet personality, but right now, her hands were not shy. They roved up his chest, along the planes of his shoulders and down to his biceps, like a seductive temptress marking her conquest. And Mitch was here for it. All of it. A trail of heat scorched every inch her hands touched.

Mitch straightened to his full height, lifting her off the ground. McKenzie wrapped her legs around his waist. He was vaguely aware of his hat sliding off his head, replaced with her hands running through his hair. Not even the most vivid fantasies of this moment even cracked the surface of how perfect reality was.

He loved her. Oh man, did he love her. And the way she kissed him, he couldn't imagine she didn't feel the same.

Gradually, the kiss slowed from long and passionate to soft, sweet pecks. He lowered her to the ground, keeping her in the circle of his arms as he trailed kisses along her jaw. His chest heaved while he attempted to catch his breath.

McKenzie peeked up at him through her lashes, a bashful smile gracing her swollen lips. She made no move to go inside, which was fine with him. He'd do anything to prolong this night as long as he could.

Mitch's pulse jackhammered in his neck. Reaching out, he fingered a strand of her silky hair before tucking it behind her ear. "That was ..." He trailed off, his mind still jumbled in one of those slide puzzles he always came close to solving but could never quite figure out. Never in his life had he experienced a spark like that. He leaned in to kiss the tip of her nose.

That kiss turned into one on her lips, then another, and another before she reluctantly pulled back. "Good night, Mitch," she said before backing up toward the house. She didn't break eye contact until she reached the bottom of the steps.

"'Night," he whispered, watching her go. At the door, she turned, sending him one more smile, made visible by the porch light. He waved.

Once she was safely out of sight, Mitch could no longer hold in his enthusiasm. Raising his arms above his head, he lifted his face to the black sky. "And the crowd goes wild!" he whisper-shouted. He cupped his hands around his mouth, quietly imitating the sound of a roaring crowd.

He'd remember this kiss for the rest of his life.

Chapter Twenty-Four

That kiss, and the ones that followed, carried McKenzie through the next three weeks of intense World preparation. The day before she left for team training camp, Mitch met her in the parking lot after her last practice. They walked together to her car, the darkness making the hour seem a lot later than the early evening it was.

McKenzie adjusted her duffel bag to her back and zipped up her jacket. The afternoon had been even warmer than normal for early November, but a chill had fallen now that the sun was down.

"Do you want to come over tonight?" she asked as they stopped in front of her car. She unlocked it with the key fob, then tossed her bag onto the back seat. As she turned to face him again, she clasped her hands together to keep from reaching for him. They'd held hands so many times in the last few weeks that the gesture had become almost automatic. While at the gym, however, the strict no-PDA policy she'd placed on them was necessary.

Mitch leaned his hip against the side of the trunk, shoving his hands deep into the pockets of his pants. "I have a few things to wrap up here before I can leave. It shouldn't take more than an hour, and then I'll be over. Do you want me to bring dinner?"

She shook her head. "I have stuff at home. I'll get started and you can help when you come."

His expression turned playful, and he bumped her shoulder with his arm. "Are you saying you finally trust me in your kitchen?"

The snort that escaped her mouth wasn't attractive at all. "Absolutely not. I've seen you in action. I'll be watching you the whole time."

"Ooh, I like that idea," he purred, low and seductive. One side of his mouth quirked up in a devilish smile that made McKenzie's breath catch. She loved it when he looked at her that way, as if she were the only person in the whole world that mattered. Still, she stiffened when he stepped closer, bending to her level, his lips hovering near her ear. His breath tickled her skin.

"*Mitch*," she hissed, backing up hard to create some distance. The sedan's side mirror jabbed into her side, sending shock waves of pain vibrating across her back. She grimaced. "Not here."

Her eyes darted around the parking lot, checking for any nearby witnesses. Even if the darkness gave them a slight disguise, the streetlight positioned next to her car shone down on them like a spotlight. They'd be easy to see by anyone walking nearby.

When she was sure the coast was clear, her body relaxed, and she faced Mitch in time to catch the tiny flash of frustration that crossed his face. Less than a second later, it was gone.

"Ow," she said, rubbing at her throbbing side. "Did you have to pin me against the mirror?"

"Sorry." Then he sighed. "You know we won't be able to keep us" —he waved his hand between them—"a secret forever."

McKenzie shoved her hands into the pockets of her windbreaker, her shoulders pulling forward. She understood his frustration, but he didn't have the same reservations about making their relationship public that she did. "I know. I just don't want my mom to find out."

"You're going to have to tell her, eventually." He leaned his hip against the car again.

McKenzie had confided in him a little more about her relationship with her mom since their beach date, so he knew more than most people why she had a hard time standing up to her. And yet, she detected more than concern in his voice.

"Besides," he said, "I know Gary. He doesn't seem like the type to meddle in things that aren't distracting you during training. And I wouldn't dream of ever doing that. I know how important the Global Elites are to you."

How could she make him understand? Her mother was relentless. A master interrogator. She had a subtle way of luring unsuspecting victims into surrendering their deepest secrets. If Gary found out about them, it was only a matter of time before Mom did too. And McKenzie planned to do everything in her power to keep the woman in the dark about her love life.

Love life. The term shot giddy shivers down McKenzie's spine.

"Gary's not the problem," she said finally. "I'm worried about how Mom will react. She can be really manipulative when she thinks something is getting in the way of my training."

"What does she consider 'getting in the way'?"

McKenzie attempted to act unbothered. By the way he searched her face, she could tell he didn't buy it. "There's a reason I haven't gone to college and don't have a job. I'm not this spoiled rich kid willingly mooching off my parents."

"I never once thought that."

"Some people have." She kicked at a black pebble on the cement near her flip-flop. "I'm *so* close to my goal. As soon as the Global Elites are over, I promise I'll tell her." That was, if they were still together by then. *Don't think like that.* "Just ... not yet, okay?"

Mitch's brows knit, and his concerned scrutiny made McKenzie squirm. Then his posture relaxed. "Okay. I'll respect that." Even as he spoke, his hand came out and caught hold of her side, giving it a gentle pinch.

She swatted his hand away, a giggle slipping out before she could stop it. "Mitch," she said as a warning.

"Sorry." He didn't look sorry. "I'll behave."

"You better." McKenzie shot him an exasperated smile. Involuntarily, she reached out and grabbed a chunk of his rock-hard abs. Mitch yelped and doubled over before retaliating, resulting in an impromptu tickle fight. They obviously needed to work on the whole no-PDA thing.

As McKenzie darted away from his latest advance, her gaze slid past him, instantly cutting off her laugh. A short distance away, Aria

crossed the parking lot, her focus trained on them with thirsty interest. Too much interest. She scowled when she noticed McKenzie
watching.

McKenzie straightened quickly, dropping her hands to her sides.
"Oh no," she muttered.

How much had Aria seen? The tension brewing between them
since nationals still hadn't improved, and the constant cold shoulder
and passive aggressive comments whenever McKenzie made a
mistake in training were getting old. She didn't need more kindling
for the fire.

Why couldn't I keep my hands to myself? McKenzie had called Mitch
out for the same thing only a few minutes before.

"What is it?" He turned to see what had captured her attention.
Immediately, Aria's scowl turned into a playful smile just for him.

McKenzie only managed to hold back an eye roll. Of course Aria
would act innocent in front of him. She hid her true colors well.

Mitch lifted a hand in greeting, and she wiggled her fingers in a
wave before climbing in her car and driving off.

"What was that about?" he asked, turning back to McKenzie.

This wasn't a conversation she wanted to have right now. Physical exhaustion from her grueling training session had begun to set
in, and emotional fatigue from having to deal with this unwanted
feud with Aria was on its way.

"It's probably nothing." McKenzie placed a hand on the driver's
side door. "I'll see you at home?"

He nodded and held the door open for her as she slid behind the
wheel. With the door blocking them from view, he stooped down to
give her a quick peck on the lips before shutting it and backing away.

Uncertainty percolated in her mind all the way home. Aria had
already suspected her growing attachment with Mitch, and there'd
be no doubt in her mind now. McKenzie couldn't shake the feeling
they were heading toward dangerous waters.

When Mitch came over a little while later, he saw right through her measured cheerfulness almost as soon as he walked in the door. McKenzie tried to play it off as exhaustion and nerves about Worlds, but her worries finally spilled out halfway through consuming their lemon chicken.

"I thought you and Aria were friends," he said after they'd finished eating, looking up from the pot he scrubbed at the sink.

Though his cooking skills left much to be desired, he proved his worth in the cleanup. With his sleeves pushed up to his elbows, the muscles in his forearm bulged through the soap suds as he attacked the chicken pieces caked onto the skillet with a dish wand.

McKenzie snapped the lid onto a Tupperware full of zucchini noodles and walked it to the fridge. "I wouldn't call us friends, but we've always gotten along. She's been acting weird ever since I made the World team and she didn't." She set the noodles in the fridge and shut the door. "It bothers me."

"Why?"

"I don't know. For some reason she's always showed a lot of interest in us. I thought she was only being nosy at first, but now I think she's up to something. I mean, she was the one who showed me that picture of you and that fan. You know the one."

He nodded.

"She had this gleeful look on her face while she did it too. Like she knew it would hurt me and was happy about that."

Mitch turned off the faucet, slipping the dish towel from the rack on the oven door, and wiping the skillet dry. "Do you want me to slash her tires? I can make it look like an accident."

She laughed in spite of her worry. "You're sweet, but no."

"Look, Zee, she's probably frustrated with how she did at nationals and projecting those feelings onto you." He took their dirty dinner plates McKenzie handed him and placed them in the dishwasher. "I watched both nights. You completely killed it. I'm sure Aria sees you as a threat."

McKenzie had already come to that conclusion, though the realization hadn't made training with Aria any less awkward. "I don't get it. She's been picked to be on several international squads over the last five years we've trained together. Teams I would've given anything to be on. Even though I was disappointed for myself, I've always been happy for her. And now that it's finally my turn, she gets jealous. It's like she's only willing to be supportive when she knows she can beat me." She sprayed the stove with cleaner and began scrubbing so hard soapy suds squeezed from the sponge.

"Rivalries are an age-old thing in sports," Mitch said, not looking up from the last dishes he loaded into the dishwasher. "Take it as a compliment."

McKenzie didn't hold back the heavy sigh as she abandoned her cleaning and walked to the center island, dropping onto a stool. "I don't want a rival." She propped her elbows on the countertop, dropping her chin into her upturned hands. "My life is already stressful enough without one."

Mitch closed the dishwasher and dried his arms before approaching her. "Come here." He took her hand and pulled her into a hug.

Some of McKenzie's frustration melted away as she snuggled into him, slipping her hands around his back. "Sorry, I really didn't want to talk about this on our last night together. I'm just tired. Things are already hard enough with my mom the way she is. I don't need any more reason to not want to train every day."

"Hey." Mitch placed two fingers under her chin and tipped her head up to meet his gaze. The intensity she saw in his eyes surprised her. "You have nothing to apologize for. Tomorrow, you leave for training camp and then Portugal next week. So that's two whole weeks you don't have to worry about Aria. I'm sure it'll blow over by the time you get back. And even if it doesn't, that's on her, not you. You've worked your butt off for years. You deserve to be on that team." He chuckled. "If you ever need a reminder, you could always read those articles about you Gary has tacked up all over his office."

"Ugh, I hate those articles. Why does he have to draw more attention to me? I always sound like a complete moron whenever I have to talk to the media. It's like I've forgotten how to speak. And I'm so tired of talking about my accident. How am I supposed to move past it when they keep bringing it up?"

"You have the classic comeback story." Mitch ran his hand in soothing circles around her back with one hand while ticking off the reasons with the other. "Top junior gymnast, destined for success, tragic accident, odds stacked against you ... The media was bound to sensationalize it. That's what they do." His tone drooped. "I get that it's annoying though. That's why it took me so long to come back to the pros."

McKenzie sensed the weight settling on his shoulders, so she changed the subject. Without lifting her head from the safety of his chest, she asked, "Will you watch me at Worlds?"

"Of course. I've watched all of your competitions since we met, and I definitely won't miss this one."

She pulled back to look at him. "You have?"

He brushed a hand over her cheek and brought his face closer to hers. "I don't think you realize how long I've been fanboying over you, Zee," he said, his voice a low rumble.

His words gave her that same thrill she got every time she conquered a difficult release move on bars. Like she was flying. Or diving off a cliff, falling deeper for this amazing man. She raised herself a little and kissed his stubbled jaw.

"I think you're going to surprise a lot of people leading up to next summer," Mitch said when she was back to resting her cheek against his heart. "I can't wait to watch. I'll miss you while you're gone though."

"Me too."

"And this time," he said through a chuckle, "I mean it when I say we need to celebrate when you get home."

McKenzie propped her chin on his chest to stare up at him. "Promise?"

Her stomach performed a full twisting backflip as the fondness in his expression turned to unmistakable desire. "I promise. And to prove it, I'll seal it with a kiss."

McKenzie slipped her hands around his neck and let him do exactly that.

Chapter Twenty-Five

McKenzie had competed in front of a lot of crowds over the years, but none as big as the one gathered for the women's team final at the World Championships in Lisbon. Standing in front of the uneven bars, she adjusted the wrist straps of her hand grips, more out of nerves than actual necessity. The two Americans that had gone before her in the lineup had done their jobs, earning good scores that would help the team keep the top spot on the leaderboard. Now it was her turn.

Be bold. McKenzie pressed a hand to her stomach, attempting to settle the nerves dancing inside. If there was ever a time to nail a routine, this was it. Her team was counting on her. Mom was expecting greatness. And her future as a Global Elite athlete could very well depend on what happened in the next minute.

When the green flag went up, she blew the excess chalk off her fists for luck, then raised one arm to the ceiling. With one more cleansing breath, she mounted the apparatus.

Her routine started with a couple of skills on the low bar before transitioning to the high bar. She swung once, then changed her body's direction to swing backward up to a handstand. Letting go with one hand, she pirouetted on her wrist, and grabbed the bar again to go into her first release. With her back parallel to the ceiling, she let go, flipping forward, her body somersaulting between her split legs.

Reaching out to latch onto the bar again, her fingertips brushed the flexible wood and fiberglass. But something was off, and she couldn't get a good grip. The weight of her momentum peeled her hands off, sending her crashing to the mat with a sickening smack. Her skin stung at the contact as a gasp came from the crowd.

Fighting back tears of frustration, McKenzie pushed herself up and made the walk of shame to the basin of chalk dust at the edge of the mat. *What happened?* she wondered as she plunged her hands inside. She'd performed that release perfectly so many times in practice. What was different about this time?

She only had thirty seconds to remount and continue her routine, so she quickly chalked her hands and approached the low bar. After a few deep breaths, she climbed up and hopped to grab the high bar. She took an extra swing to gain speed and repeated the same release she'd fallen on a moment before. Despite being rattled, this time she managed to get a better grip when she caught the wood-covered fiberglass and went right into her next skill.

The rest of the routine went without another hiccup until the dismount. After swinging three times to gain speed, she flipped off the high bar, under rotating and landing low on the mat. She took a giant step to the side.

McKenzie clamped down on her trembling jaw as she saluted the judges and walked to the side of the competition floor. Gary met her as she descended the stairs down from the podium.

"Shake it off," he said, giving her shoulders a squeeze. "We need you back in the game for balance beam."

McKenzie nodded mutely and stepped away, accepting hugs from her four teammates. Although she refused to look at any of the cameras nearby, it was impossible not to feel them focused on her. She didn't need the reminder that it wasn't only the packed arena that saw her huge mistake. No, thousands, maybe even millions, of fans from all around the world were tuning in at this very second to witness her fall from grace. How devastatingly humiliating.

Turning her back to the competition floor, she bent to retrieve her warm-ups from her bag, thus hiding the tear trickling down her cheek from view.

She blew it. Her skill on uneven bars had landed her a spot on this team. And at the moment it counted most, she'd let her team down. Why would the selection committee trust her to deliver at the even more prestigious Global Elite Games?

She'd have another chance to prove herself. Her uneven bars score during qualifications had already earned her a spot in the event finals a few days from now. Her only hope was to go out there and deliver then. But would it be enough?

Somehow, she kept it together through the rest of the competition. She had a few nervous bobbles on balance beam, but thankfully, she stayed on, and the US still miraculously found themselves at the top of the winner's podium. No thanks to her. First place was little consolation.

McKenzie stood next to her teammates during the national anthem, her hand covering her heart, watching the Stars and Stripes rise in front of her. The hardware around her neck felt extra heavy, more like a ball and chain used to weigh prisoners down than the badge of honor it was meant to be. She'd dreamed of this moment for so long. But the feeling accompanying this experience was so far from what she'd always imagined. Glancing down, the gold medal gleamed accusingly at her. She hadn't earned it. She hadn't done the job she came to Portugal to do. Did she even deserve to be considered for the Global Elites?

Chapter Twenty-Six

Mitch sat at his desk in the clinic, updating the rehab notes on the patient he'd just seen. His right leg bounced uncontrollably as he stared at the laptop screen, reading over the last few lines he'd written. No matter how much he loved his job, the afternoon was passing slower than usual. Each hour felt like twenty. All because any minute now, McKenzie's plane was due to land in LAX, and he was stuck at work. Wonderful.

Propping his elbows on the desk, he clasped his hands together, resting his mouth against his knuckles. His eyes traveled to the clock on the wall, then over to his phone near his left elbow. He unlocked it to see if maybe he'd missed a notification in the last few minutes. He'd checked that thing at least every five minutes for the last hour, hoping for something, anything, from her.

Stupid plane delays.

The article he'd read earlier still filled the screen. *Former Junior National Champion Bounces Back to Silver in Uneven Finals of World Championships,* proclaimed the headline.

Bounced back was right. McKenzie had faced adversity during the team finals, but she hadn't let that failure hold her back. It was that strength of character that had caught his eye from the very beginning. Was it at all surprising why he was so in awe of her?

Right as Mitch finally succeeded in bringing his focus back to his work, the most beautiful sound caressed his ears—the unmistakable vibration of an incoming call. His hand flew to the phone, and he smiled when McKenzie's name lit up the screen. All the other trainers were carrying out their responsibilities around the building, leaving the front room empty, so he accepted the call.

"Hey, chica." He leaned back in his chair, resting his free hand on his thigh. "How was the flight?"

"Bumpy," she said. "I don't think I've ever been so grateful to see a plane land. But I made it. Hang on."

Mitch waited as a muffled announcement came over the PA system. After being forced to settle for five-minute conversations whenever they could squeeze them in for the last three weeks, it felt good knowing they were finally on the same continent. He understood why she hadn't been able to call often. Her days were packed with training, competitions, and media engagements. Add in the eight-hour time difference between Portugal and California, their free time simply didn't match up. When she called right before lights out, he was in the middle of his workday. Still, those few minutes were sacred.

"Sorry," she said, coming back on the line. "It's hard to hear in here. I should go anyway; my bags will be here soon. I only called to tell you I made it."

He picked up his hat from the desk and twirled it with the fingers of his free hand. "I won't keep you since I'll be seeing you later." His smile grew as he imagined their reunion. Hopefully there'd be some kissing involved. He'd missed her.

Another announcement came over the PA system before McKenzie said, "What time do you think you'll be over?"

"I'm not sure yet. I have a few appointments and some loose ends to wrap up." He wished he could drop everything and get over there right now. If it weren't for his patients, that's exactly what he'd do. "It'll be a couple hours still. Sorry."

"No worries. I'll have time for a shower *and* a nap before you come over. I'm falling asleep on my feet." More airport commotion. "I need to go. Gary's coming back from the bathroom and they're starting to bring in the bags from my flight. I'll see you tonight." She hung up before he had a chance to say goodbye.

The rest of the day dragged on until he finally packed his things and left the clinic. His phone vibrated in his pocket as he slid into the driver's seat of his car. He considered ignoring it. Whoever it was, he'd call back later. Nothing would keep him from holding McKenzie in his arms again. He was *so close.*

He fished the device out of his pocket anyway. His mother's number flashed on the screen. With his other hand, he started the ignition. It took roughly ten minutes to get to McKenzie's house across town. *That should be enough time to see what Mom wants.*

"Hey, Mom," he said, after accepting the call. He put the phone on speaker and slid it into the holder on the dash before backing out of his spot.

"Hola, Mitchito. How are you, my boy? You've been so busy we haven't heard from you."

He smiled at the term of endearment from his childhood. *Little Mitch.* He towered over his petite mom now, and yet the nickname still stuck. She could get away with it though. If anyone else called him that, there'd be trouble. "I know. I'm sorry I've been out of touch. My days are so packed, I barely have time to breathe. How is everyone?"

"We're all fine," Mom said, her soft accent coming through her words. "Hazel and I visited Brenda earlier this week to drop off cookies for Doug's birthday. She's been struggling. You know how lonely she gets living all by herself. I think she appreciated the visit and the card Hazel made. I'm assuming you called her? You always do."

Mitch brought a palm to his forehead. No, he didn't call. Mama B hadn't even crossed his mind. He could count on one hand how many times he'd missed calling her for Doug's birthday or the anniversary of his death. It was the least he could do for the woman who'd had a hand in raising him.

Lately though, Mitch had been burning the candle at both ends. Between early morning training sessions, work, and squeezing in what little time he had left with McKenzie—while trying to keep their relationship secret—he didn't have the mental headspace to spare. And Mama B was the casualty. He knew how much his calls meant to her.

Guilt wiggled into his stomach, and he hung his head. "I forgot." Sadness pierced those two incriminating words. The grief loomed like a thunderstorm, ready to rain its oppressive drops on him. He fought so hard to keep it at bay, but it always reared its ugly head during moments of weakness. "I blew it."

"Oh, mijo," Mom said, her voice full of compassion. "You have so much on your plate these days. She'd understand that. I'm sure she'd love to hear from you though."

Mitch pulled up in front of McKenzie house and put the car in park, letting it idle. He leaned his head back against the headrest. "Yeah, I'll call her."

"That would be wise." Mom paused. "But don't beat yourself up about this, son. You're doing the best you can."

No matter how many stupid things he'd done over the years—and there'd been a lot—his mom had always been his fiercest ally. His biggest fan. "I love you, Mom," he managed to get out.

"I love you too. Chao, Mitchito."

"Chao." He tossed his phone onto the passenger seat and buzzed his lips, hanging his head in his hands. It was always hardest to fight the sadness on days like this one. Days when Doug should be alive and well, celebrating another year of life.

But he wasn't here. And Mitch didn't even have the decency to check in on the woman who still deeply mourned his death. With both Doug and her husband gone, Mama B had no real family left.

He looked toward the house and sighed. McKenzie was waiting for him inside, but he had to make this right first.

A tear trickled down his cheek, and he didn't bother wiping it away as he took a moment to compose himself. Mama B needed him to be strong. Pushing down the grief, he picked up his phone again and made the call.

Chapter Twenty-Seven

"*What?*" Hallie shrieked, her question directed at Kendall over video chat. "You got mugged?"

McKenzie caught the laptop before it slid off her roommate's lap and over the edge of the bed where they sat side by side. She pulled it onto her legs to keep it safe.

"It sounds worse than it was," Kendall assured them. "We left most of our things locked in the hostel. The guy only got away with a few euros."

The video feed jerked a little and Elise's face appeared on the screen. "Still, no one tells Rory. He doesn't need to know about this."

Hallie leaned in closer to McKenzie to be seen in the camera. "You're keeping secrets from Rory? Don't tell me there's trouble in paradise."

Elise rolled her eyes. "We're fine. He just has enough on his plate right now with his job and finishing his album without also worrying about my safety. I don't want him to drop everything and rush over here."

"He totally would too." McKenzie placed the laptop onto the bed in front of her and pulled her legs into her chest. "Do you regret coming to Lisbon then?"

"Of course not," Kendall said. "We were planning on going to Portugal later anyway. When you told us you made the team, it wasn't a big deal to switch around our travel plans."

"And it was so fun catching up and hearing your exciting news." Elise raised her eyebrows, suggestively. "Speaking of ... where's Mitch tonight? By the way you talked about him, I thought he'd be over as soon as you touched down in LAX."

Where *was* Mitch? It was already after nine. He'd texted more than an hour ago to let her know he'd wrapped up at the clinic and would be over soon. A trickle of worry bubbled in her stomach, and she couldn't help but think back to the last time she'd returned from a competition. Was he having more doubts?

No.

Their relationship was in a better place now. Something must be holding him up. She forced the worry down where it belonged and shoved her hands into the pockets of Mitch's hoodie. He hadn't asked for it back after their beach date, and she didn't plan to return it. She liked having a little piece of him to snuggle in when they were apart. It made her feel as if he weren't so far away. Her fingers brushed the sea glass she'd slipped in there earlier. "I'm sure he'll be here soon."

"You're video chatting without me?" Beej asked, entering the room, her usually tight curls made straight from her shower. The other two women scootched over to make space for her on the bed. She dropped down, leaning across Hallie to speak to McKenzie. "Did you know Mitch is outside?"

"He is?" McKenzie's heart did a giddy flip.

Beej nodded. "I noticed his car parked out front when I went into my room just now."

Kendall whistled, then called, "Get it, girl!" That sent off a chain reaction of cheers and whistles from the other three women.

A blush traveled up McKenzie's neck. She shook her head quickly before burying her face in her knees, her smile so wide it hurt.

She couldn't help but be pleased, and not only because Mitch had come after all. Until now, she'd never had a group of friends to share in the excitement of her relationship. She lifted her head again, biting her bottom lip nervously.

Elise laughed. "What're you waiting for? Go be with your man."

My man. It still sounded so strange to think of him that way. The smile returned to her face as she said goodbye and climbed off the bed. She forced herself to calmly make her way down the hall, despite the temptation to fly down the stairs. In the entryway she stopped, peeking out the tall, thin window on the side of the front door. Mitch's car was parked at the curb, though she couldn't see him. She opened the door.

Her excitement died at the sight that greeted her. Mitch sat on the top step, his face in his hands, the porch light illuminating his back. The bill of his backward hat was the only part of his head visible.

"Mitch?" she asked, barely above a whisper.

He didn't respond. Not even the smallest twitch to indicate he'd noticed her there.

McKenzie stepped onto the porch, closing the door quietly, and approached him with hesitant steps. She placed a light hand on his back. He flinched.

"Are you okay?" *What kind of question is that?* Obviously, he wasn't.

Mitch slowly lifted his head, and the bleak look he gave her sucked the air from her lungs.

"I promised I'd never forget him," he said, his voice hoarse.

This must be about Doug. They hadn't talked about him since that night on the beach, though she'd thought about him a few times since. She'd never forget the haunting sorrow piercing Mitch's eyes when he'd talked about his friend's death—the same look she saw in them now. The guilt exuding from him was so uncharacteristic of his usual optimistic outlook on life. While the world saw someone who would do anything to make others happy, he'd been hiding his own secret heartbreak.

The weight of responsibility settled in McKenzie's gut. He'd chosen to share a piece of himself he normally kept hidden. She could only hope to provide even a tiny bit of comfort to him in his time of need. It was the least she could do after all the times he'd been there for her.

She dropped down beside him and wove her fingers through his. They sat in silence for a few minutes, both staring out at the darkness beyond where the porch light carried.

Finally, Mitch blew out a heavy breath. "It's been eight years. I thought I'd be past this crushing sadness by now."

"There's no expiration on grief, Mitch."

"Most days it feels like he's been dead for decades, and I can go on with my life like I'm fine. But other times the grief hits me with so much force it's like it happened yesterday." His voice cracked.

Letting go of his hand, McKenzie slid her arm over his muscular back, hooking her other around the front of his shoulder closest to her. He hung his head toward her, pinching the bridge of his nose with his fingers.

She searched her mind for something, anything, to say to somehow relieve his burden. "That's the way grief is. Most of the time you can hold it at bay, but sometimes it still pushes its way out."

"You sound like you're speaking from experience."

"Sort of." When he glanced at her, the question was clear in his misty eyes, so she continued. "All my life, I've had this idea of what I wished my family was like." As soon as the words left her mouth, she realized how callous she sounded. Mitch grieved a death, she only mourned her silly ideals of a perfect family not coming true. "I know it's not the same."

Mitch reached over and gently squeezed right above her knee, leaving his hand there. "It's still valid."

McKenzie leaned against his shoulder, and his head came down to rest against her hair. More silence. The quiet was comfortable, however, even with the heavy sadness hanging in the air. Much like the evening they'd spent on the beach watching the sun go down.

"What brought this on tonight?" She asked.

"I forgot his birthday," he said, guilt thick in his words. "Ever since he died, I've called his mom every so often to check on her, but especially on his birthday and the anniversary of his death." He removed his hand from her knee and placed it on his own. "It's unfair for one person to go through so much tragedy. First, she loses her husband to an early heart attack, and then her son is taken much too soon."

McKenzie could practically feel the emotional weight crushing him. "That's so sad."

"I promised I'd never forget him ... or her," Mitch continued. "I told her she could count on me—that I'd always be there for her. And I let her down."

McKenzie ran slow circles along his back, desperately seeking for some way to comfort him. "I think you're being a little too hard on yourself—"

"I've been so busy with work and volleyball and ... you that I don't have enough headspace for anything else."

Her hand stilled its movement. Was he regretting their relationship?

Mitch turned an apologetic look to her. "Zee, I didn't mean it like that." How was he so good at reading her? "I just mean that maybe I did the wrong thing going pro. It's taking away from the things that really matter."

McKenzie's hand resumed its slow circuit along his back. "Tonight isn't the time to make a hasty decision. At least put some thought into it. If you still feel this way in a few days, then you can make that call."

After a few beats of silence, Mitch spoke. "I should probably listen to you."

"See? You're thinking already." She allowed a tiny teasing smile to slip through. Mitch's lips twitched in response. "Have you called her yet?"

"Right before you came out here," he said. "She's really struggling right now."

McKenzie's heart went out to him. Not only was he trying to work through his own grief, but he also had other people expecting him to carry theirs. Although she'd never think less of a mother grieving a son, McKenzie's defensive side crept up all the same. Her loyalty was with Mitch, and it broke her heart seeing him in so much pain.

"What about you?" she asked.

He looked blankly at her. "What about me?"

"Who do you turn to when you're struggling?"

Mitch adjusted his position, stretching his long legs out in front of him. His expression turned desperate. "She needs me. I have to be strong for her."

McKenzie placed a hand on his forearm. "You are strong, but even you shouldn't have to carry your grief alone."

He didn't respond, though he didn't turn her away either.

"Put it on me, Mitch. Let me help you shoulder it."

He shook his head. "I can't place this burden on you all the time. You have enough problems without taking mine on too."

Removing her hand, she placed it in her lap and turned away from him. She knew he was sincere, and she appreciated that he wanted to be a source of strength for her.

Still, his response irked her. All her life, people constantly underestimated her. She was the baby sister needing protection, the gymnast taking guidance from her coach. And, worst of all, the daughter who couldn't be trusted to make her own decisions. She didn't want that kind of relationship with Mitch.

"I've upset you," he stated.

McKenzie kept her eyes on the pavement ahead of her.

"Zee." He grabbed her hand. "Please, what did I say?"

His pleading tone pulled the thoughts she'd been mulling over from her mind. "I don't want you to treat me like this weak person who needs protecting. I get enough of that from Seth. I want to be your equal. And that includes being trusted with the hard things, not just the good things."

"I do trust you."

She finally turned to him. "Then let me in. You've already told me about Doug so even if you refuse to talk about him, I'm still going to worry." She gestured between them with the hand not holding his.

"This is a two-way street. I don't want you to pretend to be happy if you're not. You don't have to be my champion all the time. I just want you to be real."

Mitch considered her before understanding dawned on his face, and he nodded. "Okay."

His response was only that one little word, but the way he said it convinced her that he wasn't trying to simply get her off his back. Rather, it was said out of acceptance to her request and, dare she say it, relief.

He didn't express that relief with words, but she sensed it in the way his body relaxed into her when she wrapped her arms around him. They sat that way in silence for a few minutes until she felt his shoulders shake, his breaths becoming stuttering sobs. McKenzie pulled his head down into her lap, shielding him as he succumbed to eight years of suppressed grief.

With a tear trailing down her cheek, she slipped his hat from his head, setting it on the step beside her. Gently, she stroked her fingers through his thick hair, her heart breaking again for him. Yet somehow, she felt completely at peace in the moment. He'd been her rock so many times in the past months. Now was her opportunity to be his. She couldn't take away his grief, but she could hold him like this when the burden became too much.

She wasn't sure how long they sat there before his emotion stilled, and finally, he wiped his eyes and sat up. He turned to her, and she noted some embarrassment by the way he cleared his throat.

"Sorry, tonight was supposed to be a celebration of your awesomeness." One side of his mouth lifted in a crooked smile. "A silver medal at your first World Championships. Am I even worthy to be in your presence?"

"Stop," McKenzie said, the tiniest bit of laughter in her tone. She could see the optimistic side of him fighting to get out. Slipping a hand into his, she curled her other one around his bicep, tugging him closer. "We can celebrate another time. I'm just glad you're here. And

I have something for you." She pulled the piece of sea glass from her pocket and held it out to him.

"What is it?" he asked, taking it in his palm and running his thumb over the smooth surface.

"It's sea glass. Seth gave it to me years ago when I was going through a really hard time. I want you to have it. A reminder that better days will come."

He pressed a tender kiss to her temple before looking down at the stone again. "Thank you." He kept it in his hand as they settled back in their cozy position with her head on his shoulder. After some minutes of peaceful silence, Mitch spoke again. "Zee?"

"Mmm?"

"My family is renting a beach house in San Diego for Thanksgiving." He hesitated a few seconds. "I'm driving down to stay with them for a few days. Will you come?"

Her pulse thrummed faster. "You want me to come ... with you?" Their relationship was still so new. Thanksgiving was still two weeks away, but wasn't it a little soon to meet the family?

Mitch shrugged, bouncing her cheek a bit. "Of course I want you to come."

A storm of emotions brewed in her. They had so little time together. This could be the answer to that problem. A thrill went down her spine at the idea of spending a few uninterrupted days with him.

But what if spending that much time together pulled them apart? What if they ran out of things to talk about. What if Mitch realized he didn't want to date the shy girl?

And what if his family hated her? Racing after that thought was the realization that her mother would take this as another reason to accuse McKenzie of being distracted. As if she hadn't already had plans to go home for Thanksgiving. She wouldn't be training then either. But Mom was bound to overlook that little detail.

Mitch apparently took her internal deliberation as a rejection. "Sorry, it's probably not a good—"

"I'd love to," McKenzie blurted out before he could finish.

He glanced over at her. "Really?"

She smiled at the boyish anticipation on his face. "Really." Then another worry surfaced, and she grabbed his arm with both hands. "Are you sure your parents won't mind if I came?"

"They have six kids. Six loud, obnoxious kids. I think they'll see you as a relief." His mouth lifted in a teasing smile. "And besides, my mom already threatened to drive here herself and kidnap you if you said no."

McKenzie laughed at that. "In that case, it's settled." Almost settled, at least. Now she somehow needed to figure out how to tell her mom.

Chapter Twenty-Eight

On Thanksgiving Day, McKenzie paced the living room floor, her phone in her hand. She breathed deeply, attempting to appease her rising anxiety. Any minute now, Mitch would arrive to pick her up for their weekend in San Diego. Three and a half days away from the gym and the pressures of training for the Games. Eighty-four uninterrupted hours with the man of her dreams, give or take a few.

The idea of meeting the very large Skaggs family terrified her, but Mitch had assured her more than once in the weeks leading up to this day that they'd love her. She was trying to trust that.

Her pacing brought her to the wall, and she pivoted back the other direction. It wasn't Mitch's family that currently had her insides in knots though. No, the issue now lay with the fact that she still hadn't told her mother she wasn't coming home. A big problem, as the flight McKenzie was supposed to be on was due to land in—she checked the clock on her phone—one hour and thirty-two minutes.

She hadn't meant to leave it to the last minute. But it wasn't like Mom was the easiest person to talk to. And McKenzie didn't need another reason for the woman to jump down her throat.

McKenzie's pacing brought her back to the front window. Still no sign of Mitch. She lifted her phone again, swallowing the bile burning up her esophagus. It was time to pull up her big girl panties. Even if she'd rather let Mom discover that one less guest was coming for Thanksgiving dinner when the plane landed at Sea-Tac without her daughter on it.

McKenzie gave herself a pep talk as she resumed her path around the living room. *You can do this. It's just a quick call. Say, "Mom, I'm staying in California for the weekend." End of story. It'll be fine.*

Even thinking about it, she knew her mom wouldn't let it be that simple.

Once again, McKenzie wished she could be more like her brother. Seth had no problem telling their parents he wasn't going home. The only reason he kept any relationship with them at all was to protect her.

Maybe I should call him and see how he's doing. If she thought meeting the Skaggs seemed an overwhelming prospect, it didn't hold a candle to Seth's weekend. Somehow, Beej had talked him into attending the famous Abernathy Thanksgiving get-together. Not only would he be meeting Beej's immediate family, but her enormous extended family as well. McKenzie was surprised he even took that step. He'd never let a relationship progress that far.

Focus! Now wasn't the time to contemplate Seth's relationship phobias. Her hand shook as she lifted the phone again and toggled through her contacts until she got to her mother's. Her pointer finger hovered over the call button at the same time something caught her attention outside the window. She glanced up as Mitch's black SUV turned into her driveway.

She couldn't make the call now. As much as she trusted him, a phone conversation with her mother wasn't something she wanted him to witness. Opening up a new message, McKenzie sent a quick text instead.

> McKenzie: Not coming home today. Decided to spend Thanksgiving with a friend. Sorry.

"You're nothing but a big fat chicken, McKenzie Bowman," she reprimanded herself. "When are you ever going to change?"

Mitch's knock interrupted her grumbling. Seconds later, the door opened. "Honey, I'm home!" he called. A crack of laughter followed.

McKenzie scrunched her nose, disgusted with herself, before pasting on a smile and turning toward the entryway. She was in for a very unpleasant phone call when Mom finally checked her texts.

Oh goody.

As they pulled up to the white, spacious beach house, Mitch gave a long whistle. "Dang, Mom and Dad went all out for this weekend." He parked behind his parents' rental van and killed the engine before glancing over at McKenzie in the passenger seat.

She'd grown quiet the last few miles of the drive to San Diego's La Jolla neighborhood. One knee bounced rapidly, and her fingers knotted together so tightly on top of it that all color had fled from her already pale knuckles. Her gaze didn't stray from the short fan palms lining the driveway on the passenger side.

Mitch could appreciate her nerves, even if he didn't completely understand them. The prospect of meeting a family as large as his would be daunting for any introvert, even more so for someone as shy as McKenzie. He took one of her hands in his, finally drawing her attention away from the window. "You okay?"

"Uh-huh. Fine." Her tight smile did little to convince him.

"It'll be great." He squeezed her hand before getting out to retrieve their bags from the back. The house, and the abundant foliage in the front yard, hid the ocean from view, but the sound of crashing waves in the distance promised it was nearby.

He set their wheeled suitcases on the clay-tiled driveway and shut the hatch. McKenzie still hadn't left the car, nor did she look at him when he opened her door. Her hands were back to their white-knuckled embrace.

Bracing one of his palms on the back of her seat and the other on the dashboard in front of her, he leaned in, catching the look of terror in her eyes. "Are you planning to get out?"

"Uh-uh," she squeaked. "I think I'll stay here, thank you."

He bit back a smile and reached across her to unclick the seatbelt. "Come on. My family is loud, but they won't eat you."

"Are you sure?" she whispered. "They might be hungry."

He chuckled and kissed her temple before taking her hand and helping her from the car. "It's Thanksgiving. They wouldn't feast on you when the menu is so much more satisfying."

"That's a relief," she said dryly.

Mitch fought to keep a straight face as he bumped her side and muttered, "They'll save *you* for tomorrow." He laughed when she shoved him.

They made their way up the walkway to the porch, wheeling their bags behind them. His stomach rumbled at the mouthwatering smells coming from the house.

"It smells so good," McKenzie said, stopping at the front door. "It'll be nice to actually enjoy a holiday meal without my mother watching my calorie intake."

He pushed down the handle of his suitcase and faced her. "She really does that?"

McKenzie didn't say anything, but the knowing look she gave him answered his question.

"Well, there's no place for counting calories in this family. You're in for a real treat. My mom's an amazing cook."

The chirping of McKenzie's phone cut off her response. "Sorry." Digging it out of her jacket pocket, her mouth tugged down in a frown. Mitch knew the caller without needing to ask.

"Do you need to take that before we go in?" *Please say no.* Mrs. Bowman needed to learn her daughter wasn't always at her beck and call.

He could see McKenzie's frustration flash to determination and then defiance in the way her posture straightened, her chin lifting.

"No." She silenced the ringing and slid her phone back into her pocket. "I'll call her back later."

"Did you tell your mom why you're not going home this weekend?"

"I took care of it," she said, avoiding his eyes.

Far from reassured, he let the subject drop, despite the temptation to push for clarification. She was already nervous enough. He lifted their clasped hands to his lips and pressed a kiss to the inside of her wrist. "Let's go, then. Get ready to meet the circus."

He pushed the door open, and they stepped into the entryway. Setting his suitcase onto the floor next to McKenzie's, he looked around. Straight ahead of them, a wide hallway led into what appeared to be an open living area, complete with an ornate chandelier. Off to the right, a circular dining table and chairs sat in a room with floor-to-ceiling windows. Voices carried to them from another room.

Mitch cupped a hand around his mouth. "Hola, mi gente linda!"

A child's shrieks immediately followed and seconds later, his baby sister came racing through the dining room. He caught her as she launched into his arms.

"Hazelnut! I've missed you so much, kiddo."

"Me too. I've been waiting since yesterday for you to get here." She looked past his shoulder, assessing McKenzie. Hazel dropped her voice to a whisper. "Is that your girlfriend?"

"Yes." Mitch matched her tone. He angled his body to include McKenzie in the conversation. "This is McKenzie."

Hazel leaned close to Mitch again. "She's pretty."

He glanced at McKenzie, an adorable shade of pink rising on her cheeks, and winked. His eyes didn't stray from her as he resumed speaking to his sister. "She's very pretty." Then he finally turned back to Hazel. "Actually, I have an important job for you."

"What is it?" she asked, wiggling a bit in his arms.

He set her down, crouching in front of her. "I need you to help me make McKenzie feel welcome in our enormous family. Can you do that?"

He had no doubt his family would be as welcoming to McKenzie as they were with everyone. But he also knew his sister often struggled with youngest child syndrome—a fear of constantly being left behind—especially as a child in a family of mostly adults. Those feelings would only intensify when Gabe, the next youngest sibling, left for college the following August. Mitch liked making Hazel feel important.

"I can do that," she said, nodding once for emphasis.

"That's my girl." Mitch tugged gently on one of her dark braids and rose to his feet.

Hazel stayed by his side as an eruption of happy chaos broke out with the arrival of the rest of the Skaggs from all over the house. Mitch lost sight of McKenzie in the frenzy of bodies, though he took comfort in knowing that his family didn't wait for introductions to be made before welcoming her with warm greetings.

For the next few minutes, he basked in the enjoyment of finally hugging his family again. First his dad, followed by Andrea, the oldest, with her two-year-old son, Luis, in her arms. His younger sister, Lorena, came next, then Gabe.

When he got to Sebastián, he threw his arms around him, slapping him on the back. "It's about time you showed your face on the West Coast, Bas."

"I would've come sooner but I'm still waiting for that plane ticket you promised me." He smirked, slugging Mitch's shoulder.

Mitch retaliated by slinging his arm around his brother's neck in a headlock. "I never promised you anything."

"Boys," his mother called, halting the impromptu jostling that followed. She hurried through the dining room, removing her apron and tossing it neatly over the back of one of the chairs. "You'll have three whole days to wrestle. It's Mom's turn for a hug."

Mitch dropped his arm from around Sebastián's neck and stooped to wrap his mom's tiny frame in a bear hug. "Hola, Mamá."

"It's good to see you, Mitchito." She kissed both his cheeks before stepping back, keeping hold on both his arms. "Let me look at you." Her eyes moved up and down, assessing him fondly. "You're too skinny. We need to fatten you up."

He rolled his eyes with a smile. "You know I'm training again. It takes effort to keep up this impeccable physique."

She swatted his chest with the back of a hand. "Don't give me that. It's because you're a terrible cook. I tried to teach you." She cast her eyes to the ceiling and muttered under her breath in Spanish before giving him a look that was more loving than scolding.

"Really?" Mitch said, pretending to be offended. "You're mocking me in front of my girlfriend?"

McKenzie's voice came from somewhere behind him. "She's not saying anything I don't already know." Her statement was met with chuckles from the rest of his family.

"Ooh, I like her already," Lorena said.

Mitch sighed dramatically. McKenzie was supposed to be on his side. For someone who was almost paralyzed with nerves only a few minutes before, she certainly didn't show it now. He had an inkling that the combination of her and the headstrong women in his family would be lethal for his ego. Was it strange to admit he was looking forward to that? Probably.

His mom quickly moved him aside as if finally remembering the real reason she'd wanted the family to spend Thanksgiving in California. She made a beeline for McKenzie with outstretched arms. "Oh, McKenzie. Bienvenidos. Welcome, welcome to our home away from home." She pulled her into a tight hug.

At first, McKenzie seemed surprised by the embrace, and even more so at the double cheek kisses—the customary greeting among loved ones in Ecuador—that followed. Mitch weaved over to them in case she needed a rescue. Underneath the calm façade she wore on the outside, she had to be overwhelmed. He'd watched enough of her competitions to appreciate her skill at hiding what truly went on beneath the surface.

But then her body visibly relaxed, and she returned the air kisses. "Thank you for having me."

"Of course! It's been so long since Mitch has brought a girlfriend home to meet the family."

Oh, here we go.

His mom continued with a twinkle in her eye. "I was beginning to wonder if he still knew how to woo a woman."

"Mom!" *This is exactly why I don't,* he thought, glancing at McKenzie. She was biting her lip, trying unsuccessfully not to laugh. "You're embarrassing me."

"Oh, mijo," Mom said, patting his cheek twice. "Don't be silly. You don't get embarrassed."

Mitch shook his head, unable to keep his smile from breaking free. Mom had a way of keeping her children humble, while still making it perfectly clear they meant the world to her.

"Well, what are we waiting for?" she said after another minute of mingling. "We'll worry about taking the bags up to your rooms later. I need everyone's help getting the food on the table. Dinner is ready." She linked an arm through McKenzie's and led her toward the dining room. Hazel claimed the position on McKenzie's other side, holding her hand.

Mitch followed behind them with the rest of the family. The weekend had started out even better than he'd planned, and for the next two days, he had no obligations except McKenzie. He fully intended to make the most of them.

Chapter Twenty-Nine

In the days leading up to Thanksgiving, McKenzie had to physically remind herself to breathe anytime she thought about meeting Mitch's family. She'd been fully prepared to superglue him to her side so she wouldn't have to face even a minute alone with them. The prospect of spending an afternoon in the kitchen with the Skaggs women by herself was completely out of the question. And yet, a little over twenty-four hours after arriving, she stood at the kitchen counter placing little doughy trees on a cookie sheet with Mitch's mom and sisters while he played basketball outside with his dad and brothers. That she didn't feel the urge to dry heave was even more surprising.

"Keep it in the bowl, Luis," Andrea instructed her son, barely taking her focus off the shortbread dough she was rolling out for the alfajores cookies. "Don't get the flour on the floor."

McKenzie had never tried the Latin American treat before. Cookies in general were high on her mother's list of evils. They looked tasty.

Luis looked up at his mother from his spot at her feet, scooping flour from one bowl to another with a measuring cup. An ample amount of the white powder had missed the bowl completely, covering the hardwood floor around him. His angelic face broke into a toothy grin before he dumped the full cup over his head, turning his dark hair a patchy white. Andrea groaned.

"Ah, let him have his fun. I'll sweep it up later." Mitch's mom, who'd quickly insisted McKenzie call her Cristina, bent down and pinched her grandson's cheek with the hand that wasn't holding the pan of sugar cookies heading into the oven. He giggled.

"Did Mitch really come into our room before sunrise this morning?" Lorena asked, reaching for the snowman cookie cutter amid all the ingredients taking up space on the center island. "Or was I imagining that in my sleep?"

"It wasn't your imagination. He said he wanted to watch the sunrise." McKenzie giggled. "Geography is obviously not his best subject. The sun doesn't rise over the Pacific."

She placed another tree-shaped cookie onto the baking sheet in front of her, then lifted her eyes to the game happening outside the open kitchen window. Sebastián's shot swished through the basket, and he slapped hands with his dad while Mitch and Gabe groaned. Hazel sat watching on the grass near the court. She'd abandoned the kitchen early in the cookie-making process, preferring to be near her favorite big brother.

"I don't think Mitch ever sleeps." Andrea's sandy-brown ponytail swished over her shoulder as she shook her head in bemusement. Out of all the children, she looked the most like their Caucasian father, though she was the only one who hadn't inherited his height. "Even Luis sleeps later than he does." She crouched in front of her son. "You're a good little sleeper, aren't you, buddy?" Taking his chubby cheeks in her hands, she kissed the top of his head. Luis squealed in delight.

"Are you a morning person, McKenzie?" Cristina came up beside her, thumping a bag of powdered sugar onto the counter.

"Not normally."

The other women laughed. Luis looked up from his bowl, a cherubic smile lighting his flour-dusted face, though he certainly didn't understand the humor in McKenzie's comment.

Truth be told, she hadn't minded being pulled from slumber while the world was dark, and the rest of the family was still asleep. She'd never felt so secure as she had snuggled against Mitch's side on the back patio couch while the waves played a soothing rhythm in her ears. It was like a big cocoon of happiness she wanted to stay in forever. That's how it always was with him; warm and safe—her happy place.

Her attention strayed once again to the game outside. Hazel rode on Mitch's shoulders, holding onto his backward baseball cap as he dribbled toward the basket. He handed the ball up to her and she made the short shot, throwing her hands up in the air when it swished through the net. Her dad and brothers all cheered.

Mitch was clearly a doting older brother. Hazel adored him. Even little Luis seemed completely enamored. A fierce battle had raged between McKenzie and her ovaries last night as she'd watched the toddler use his oldest uncle as a human jungle gym, jumping and crawling all over him. While she tried to keep a level head, those darn female organs screamed, *Marry this man! Don't let him get away!* She felt another battle brewing now.

"Those two are like peas in a pod," Cristina said, startling McKenzie from her thoughts. "Every time he comes home, Hazel latches onto him like a shadow. And he doesn't mind one bit that she never leaves his side."

"They're cute together," McKenzie said, not missing the knowing look she received from Mitch's mom. Had her thoughts been that transparent on her face?

Cristina walked to the fridge and pulled out a gallon of milk, then returned to McKenzie's side. "I'll tell you what, having a baby after forty wasn't easy, especially while also raising teenagers. Alex and I thought we were done after Gabriel." Her mouth twitched up, though her attention remained on the liquid she poured into the bowl of powdered sugar. "Unlike Vegas, what happens in Mexico doesn't stay in Mexico."

"*Mom.*" Andrea gasped at the same time a surprised laugh burst from McKenzie.

Cristina waved away her daughter's objection with both hands. "Oh mija, you've had a baby. You know how it goes."

Andrea blushed. "I just don't think McKenzie wants a rehashing of your anniversary trip with Dad," she said quietly, keeping her eyes on the thick layer of dulce de leche she was spreading on the small alfajores.

Mitch had told McKenzie enough about Andrea's situation to know that Luis's father had never been in the picture.

"I'm initiating her into the family." Cristina picked up a rubber spatula and began mixing the icing. To McKenzie, she said, "After all, I expect you'll be one of us for real before long."

Her comment did nothing to help the inferno raging on McKenzie's face. They were really talking about marriage? Already?

Cristina turned back to the icing. "Anyway, Mitch helped me a lot when Hazel was small. I was tired all the time and struggled waking up in the middle of the night. She wasn't even a week old when I got up to feed her and found Mitch already snuggling her in the rocking chair. He said, 'I've got this, Mom.' So I made him a bottle and went back to bed. This happened for months until Hazel started sleeping through the night. He never complained once."

No wonder Mitch and Hazel were so close. McKenzie's ovaries gained the upper hand once again. She set one last Santa on the baking sheet and turned to Cristina. Fondness shone in the woman's eyes as she watched her husband and four children out the window.

"I felt guilty about letting him do it," she continued when she'd gone back to her mixing. "Teenagers already have so much keeping them from getting the rest they need. I don't think he was sleeping much anyway though. This was after ..."

"After Doug died," McKenzie mumbled to herself. Her gaze traveled out the window again as Mitch performed an odd sort of celebration moonwalk around his dad, completely unaware of the serious conversation taking place inside. He'd told her once that Hazel had been his saving grace. She could vividly imagine the eighteen-year-old kid grasping for anything to help him alleviate his grief. The twenty-six-year-old man outside hadn't changed in that regard.

A tug on her capris and Luis's sweet voice saying, "Up," brought her attention to the boy. McKenzie lifted him into her arms, and he immediately lunged toward the batch of completed alfajores next to the unbaked sugar cookies.

"Can he have one?" McKenzie asked before realizing for the first time that all three women's eyes were on her. "What?"

Andrea shook herself from her apparent shock. "Yeah, sure. He can have one."

McKenzie handed Luis a cookie as Lorena asked, "Mitch told you about Doug?" Her hand clutched the handle of the half open oven door. "He doesn't talk about him to any of us."

McKenzie hadn't realized she'd spoken Doug's name out loud. "He's told me a few things when I've asked. But he never brings it up himself."

"I've been worried about him," Cristina said. "He was such a naturally happy child, always making us laugh. After the accident, he fought a lot of darkness for a while. I've seen him coming back to us more the last few years, but he still won't allow himself to fully grieve."

McKenzie knew that was true.

Cristina reached out, and McKenzie accepted the hug with Luis still in her arms. The way Mitch's mom embraced her—so reverently, lovingly—surprised her, as did the words that came next.

"You've been a good influence on him. I can tell," Cristina said. "He's different around you. More content than I've seen him in a long time. Like he's not trying so hard to be happy. Thank you for loving my son."

Tears stung McKenzie's eyes as she melted into the embrace. For years she'd craved this parental affection, never once receiving it from her own mother. Mitch's family had been so kind and welcoming since the moment she'd arrived. How could she be so easily accepted into a group of people who hardly knew her when her own parents forced her to earn their love?

"There, there now." Cristina backed away and squeezed McKenzie's upper arms. "Dry your tears. There's a man outside who won't be happy if he knew you were crying."

McKenzie laughed and swiped her free hand across her cheek.

Seeing her tears, Luis leaned his head on her shoulder, offering comfort in the only way a small child knew how. It was enough.

As they finished their baking, the conversation steered toward other things, but her mind stayed fixated on one thing.

Thank you, Cristina had said, *for loving my son.*

In that moment, McKenzie realized the truth of that statement. She was no longer *falling* in love with Mitch. She *was* in love.

And she wanted to be part of this family.

Chapter Thirty

"You've been neglecting your basketball skills, old man," Sebastián gloated after scoring another basket for his team. "What? You only have energy to be good at one sport these days?"

"*Old man*?" Mitch scoffed. "Nah, that was a lucky shot."

"What about the dozens before that?" Dad held up both hands and Sebastián gave him a double high five as he came near him.

Gabe trotted to the edge of the grass and accepted the ball from Hazel, who was sitting cross-legged nearby. "You're only winning because Dad's on your team." He tossed it to Mitch.

It was true. Alex Skaggs might have been past his prime on the court, but the former college basketball star hadn't lost his competitive edge. And he was definitely to blame for passing that trait on to all six of his children.

"Last play," Dad said, wiping the sweat from his face with the hem of his shirt. "I need to go in and see if your mother needs help."

Mitch faced the basket and bounced the ball to Sebastián, who caught it and bounced it back. Then Mitch glanced at Gabe. Dad had him well covered, all but putting him in a headlock to keep him away from the ball. The youngest Skaggs brother would be no help in this play.

Dribbling, Mitch took a few steps forward, then retreated out of reach when Sebastián attempted to intercept him.

Sebastián's eyes flicked past Mitch's shoulder. "McKenzie's behind you."

Mitch continued dribbling, though he couldn't help the smile sliding onto his face. "Nice try." He darted forward, then back again. "But your distraction tactic won't work on me." With that, he spun past his brother into a layup on the right side of the hoop. The ball bounced off the backboard and went in, eliciting cheers from Hazel and Gabe.

"That's how you do it, baby boy," Mitch said, moonwalking around Sebastián. "I hope you're taking notes."

A familiar laugh stopped his celebration, and he whirled around to face McKenzie, standing at the edge of the patio. She bent to pick up the ball that had rolled to her feet.

Andrea stepped outside behind her, Luis in her arms. Crumbs covered his flour-dusted face, most likely from the cookies he clutched in both hands. "Hazel, we saved the large Santa cookie for you to decorate."

"Yeah!" Hazel hopped up from the grass and ran toward the house, her long braids flying behind her. Andrea followed her inside, leaving McKenzie on the patio alone.

"I liked your moves back there." She bounced the ball against the pavement between her bare feet. Her awkward dribbling was adorable. "How long did it take you to come up with that victory dance?"

"Probably as long as you've spent learning to dribble," Mitch said. "You're a natural."

Her nose crinkled in amusement. "And you're a terrible liar." She threw a Hail Mary toward the hoop. He watched the ball hit the backboard and bounce onto the rim before sinking through the net.

"No way!" His full laugh broke free as his dad and brothers hollered with glee. Mitch wrapped his arms around her waist, bending to kiss her cheek. "Where'd you learn to shoot like that?"

She accepted his outstretched hand, and they walked over to the other men. "Seth and I used to play H-O-R-S-E a lot when our parents ..." She cleared her throat. "We played a lot of hoops," she finished quietly.

Mitch could see the melancholy begin to set in as it often did when she talked of her parents. He searched his mind for a joke to lighten the mood. "You know, after you retire from gymnastics, you should switch to basketball."

Her mouth twitched in a tiny smile. That was a start. "Those women are at least twice my size. They'd trample me."

"Nah, you could be their secret weapon," Sebastián chimed in.

Gabe jumped in next. "Yeah, you're so tiny you could dribble right through the other team's legs. They'd be too shocked to stop you from getting off a straight shot to the basket."

Sebastián pointed to him, his brows raised in silent agreement while Dad chuckled.

McKenzie laughed, her sadness evaporating instantly. Mitch had never been more grateful for his brothers' lighthearted humor. She fit in so well with his family that he might as well hand over the remaining pieces of his heart that didn't already belong to her. It wasn't difficult to imagine her being a part of them for real. And not only for the weekend.

The game broke up after that, and the others headed back inside, leaving Mitch and McKenzie alone for the first time since that morning. He kicked off his shoes, balling his socks inside, and left them on the edge of the patio, then took her hand. They walked in the direction of the beach.

The sand was soft between his toes, and a steady breeze blew off the ocean, creating a slight chill. He slung an arm around her shoulder, letting it hang down as he tucked her in close. "You've been a good sport with my family. Especially with Hazel hanging around all the time."

McKenzie snuggled into him, latching onto his fingers with one hand and circling her other arm around his back. "I don't mind. She's adorable. Besides, we had a little time alone this morning, even if you did wake me up earlier than I wanted." She pinched his side gently.

Mitch squirmed a little at her tickling. "It's not like you were awake for long. You were back asleep within minutes of coming outside."

She smiled at his teasing, as he'd hoped she would. "Can you blame me? I was already wrapped in a puffy blanket, and your voice droned on and on. Add in your warm body, and that's all it took put me to sleep."

"It's humbling to know how boring you think I am." He glanced down at her upturned face and winked. "I was right in the middle of a gripping story, and I looked over to find you passed out with your mouth open and drool—"

"I've never been a drooler." She laughed and shoved him away.

Mitch chuckled. "Okay, okay, no drool." He pulled her back to his side, resuming their cozy position. He hadn't minded one bit holding her while she slept during their cuddling session on the patio couch. Normally, his restless energy made him anxious after being motionless for too long. But with McKenzie in his arms, he'd found a rare contentment in the stillness.

They reached the edge of the waves, and the cool water lapped at their feet. The sun hung low in the sky, inching closer to the horizon as the afternoon faded into evening. Nothing could disrupt the perfection of this moment.

Nothing except the faint vibration of McKenzie's phone.

She hastily reached into the pocket of her hoodie and silenced it before pulling her hand out and latching onto his fingers again. "Sorry, I meant to leave that at the house. I was texting with Beej earlier. Seth dumped her."

Mitch reeled back slightly to look McKenzie in the face. "He did?"

"Apparently, he thought they were getting too serious, so he ended it. Right before they were supposed to leave for her parents' house too." Under her breath, she said, "I'm not surprised."

"Poor Beej."

McKenzie's phone buzzed again. This time, she pulled it out and groaned. "Why can't she leave me alone for one weekend?"

Uneasiness came over Mitch as he glanced at the screen in McKenzie's hand in time to catch "Mom" on the call banner before she turned the device completely off and slipped it back into her pocket.

She sighed. "This is the seventh time she's called since we've been here. You'd think after a few times, she'd realize I'm not going to answer."

Mitch didn't respond, instead turning to stare out at the weak beams of sunlight skipping across the waves. McKenzie had assured him she'd talk to her mom before Thanksgiving. And when they'd arrived at the beach house, she'd also said she'd taken care of it. Why did he feel like she wasn't being honest with him?

"Hey." McKenzie patted his waist to get his attention. "What's wrong?"

Dropping his arm from her shoulders, he slid it into his shorts' pocket, keeping his gaze focused on the sand in front of him. He didn't want to ruin their precious alone time talking about her mom. But neither could he let this issue go ignored anymore. "Zee, what did you tell your mom about this weekend?"

Her shoulders pulled forward when he glanced at her, and he could sense her preparing her proverbial bricks for wall construction. He'd have to tiptoe lightly around this conversation.

"I told her I was spending Thanksgiving with a friend and wasn't coming home." She turned to face him, and her gaze settled somewhere between his chest and his navel.

Mitch chose his words carefully. "I know we agreed to keep us a secret, but what could your mom honestly do if she found out? Don't you think it would be easier if you just told her?"

"No," she said automatically. When he sighed, her posture slumped. "Mitch, you will never understand what it's like growing up in a family like mine. Your family is full of amazing, beautiful people, and mine is ..." She trailed off and took a shuddering breath.

"Zee—"

"All my life, I've had to reconcile with a father who barely acknowledged my existence." She looked up at him, her eyes brimming with tears. "While at the same time tiptoeing around a mother who disapproved of everything I did and always found some reason why I'm not the daughter she wants."

Mitch didn't know what to say. She turned to face the ocean, wrapping her arms around her middle.

"You have the kind of family I've always dreamed of having," McKenzie continued quietly after a moment. "But being here has been a humbling reminder that I'll never have that." With that, she stalked off toward the house.

Her words had the effect of a sucker punch to the gut. Mitch's thoughts churned about like the foamy tide at his feet, and he didn't immediately go after her. He watched her trudge back to the house, a tightness forming in his chest that could only be caused by guilt.

She was right. He didn't understand what she'd had to live through. And he'd mistakenly thought he knew what was best for her.

He jogged after her, catching up as she reached the back patio. "Zee, I'm sorry. I was being insensitive."

Her chin wobbled as she sank onto the sofa—the same one they'd snuggled on that morning, though the vibe wasn't the peaceful contentment that had existed then.

McKenzie hugged one of the gray pillows to herself. "Why can't I ever be good enough?" she asked in a strangled whisper.

Mitch sat down beside her. "You *are*. Just because your parents don't recognize your worth, you can't discount the opinions of everyone who knows better."

She looked unconvinced.

"Think about it. You charmed my family within five minutes of being here. Gary talks about you like you're his favorite child. Your roommates think the world of you. So do Seth and Rory and ..." He leaned forward, ducking his head to look into her downcast eyes. "... me."

Her breath caught in the tiniest of sobs, but she held his eyes. Mitch took that as his cue to continue. Leaning his back against the couch cushion, he said, "Do you remember that time I helped spot you on bars?"

She shifted to face him, curling her legs onto the couch. Her knees nudged his thigh, and she kept them there. "That was right after you began working at the clinic."

Mitch placed a hand on her knee. "You were just starting to train your current routine. You know the tricky part with the release into the spinny thingy down to the low bar, and then the other spinny thingy back to the high bar, followed by another release?"

McKenzie snorted a laugh that had him convinced wasn't intended. "They should have you naming the skills. You'd be good at it."

He chuckled. "I think I'll stick with the job I have. Anyway, you went over that sequence over and over, falling more times than not. Some of those falls were pretty hard too. But you always got up and did it again without complaint until you nailed it." That was the day he'd fully lost his heart to her. "Watching you back then ... I realized immediately that you were something special."

"Really?"

"You have this quiet strength about you. Like no matter how hard life knocks you down, you're going to get back up and keep fighting. I *see* that in you."

A glimmer of relief appeared on McKenzie's face. "Thank you."

"Have you ..." He hesitated. "Have you talked to your psychologist about your mom?"

She shook her head. "We mostly talk about how to overcome my mental block on vault."

"I think you should," he said, taking her hand and resting it with his on his thigh. "I can give you all the pep talks you want, and I'll absolutely walk beside you as you go through the process, but I don't have the training to actually help you heal from a lifetime of abuse."

Her eyes flew up to his. "My mom is controlling and vindictive, but I wouldn't call it abuse."

"Zee, she uses emotional manipulation to control you."

McKenzie leaned forward, dropping her head in her hands. Mitch placed a reassuring hand on her back, his fingers sliding underneath her hair to massage the skin on her neck. The slight outline of the scar from her surgery met his touch, a reminder of the hard road she'd walked.

Finally, she turned her head to the side to look up at him. "Deep down, I think I knew that all along, I just couldn't stomach the thought of admitting it."

"Naming it is the first step to stopping it." Mitch gently wiped at the tear hovering on her lashes with the pad of his finger. "You should really discuss this with your therapist. I know she'll help you sort through everything you're feeling."

McKenzie swiped at the trail of tears making its way down her cheek. "I'm tired of feeling so broken."

"You're not broken." He took one of her hands in both of his. "And you deserve so much better than what you've received. I'll do everything I can to change that."

She exhaled and nodded. "I'll talk to my therapist."

"Good." Lifting her hand to his mouth, he kissed her palm. "For now, what can I do to help you feel better?"

She studied him for a few seconds. "I really need you to support my decision to keep us from my mom until I feel it's the right time to tell her, even though you don't agree."

He lifted his shoulders in resignation. "Okay. I won't press anymore."

She leaned against him, resting her chin on his shoulder. "And I could use one of your magic hugs."

"Magic hugs, huh?" That was a nice little boost to the ego. He slipped his arm around her as she curled into him, her cheek resting against his chest. "Are you sure you're not just using me for my warm body and soothing voice?"

The rolling waves in the distance were no match for the sweetness of her laughter. Once again, Mitch sat in awe of her. Even when life threatened to kick her in the teeth, she still sought reasons to laugh. He loved that about her. He loved *everything* about her.

His heart pounded in his chest so hard he had no doubt McKenzie could feel it. He'd tossed that three-word phrase around in his brain for weeks, waiting for the right moment to tell her how he felt. This was it. He could feel it. He pressed his lips into her soft hair. "Zee, I lo—"

"Come inside, you two," Lorena called from the back door, startling them both. "Dinner's ready."

Mitch hissed a curse that made McKenzie giggle. "Rena! Can't you see we're having a moment?"

"You can make out later," Lorena said, and Mitch could practically hear the eye roll in her voice. "Andrea wants to have the Christmas house contest before Luis goes to bed so he can help. Which means we have to eat now."

Mitch hung his head for a moment before glancing at McKenzie. Her face rivaled the color of the poinsettias decorating the dining room, and she pursed her lips, attempting not to laugh.

"There are some drawbacks to having a large family," he said.

She stood, holding out her hand to him. "They're not that bad. Come on, I'm hungry, anyway." She laced their fingers together, pulling him up while he pushed off the couch. "What were you about to tell me?" she asked on the way to the back door.

He'd have to find another time to tell her. *Thanks a lot, Lorena.* "Would you be my partner for the contest?"

Apology shone in her eyes. "I'm so sorry, Hazel already asked me."

"What? When?"

"In the kitchen earlier. You were playing basketball."

"I can't believe it." He sighed. "Bested by my own baby sister. Well then, Bowman, you'd better get ready to lose."

"Not a chance, Skaggs," she said, her blue eyes narrowing into a glare. Too bad it looked more adorable than fierce. "I might be small, but I'm just as competitive as you are."

Mitch tucked her securely to his side and stooped close to whisper in her ear. "In that case, let the best house win."

Chapter Thirty-One

The Skaggs family sure took their crafts seriously. They were only making little houses out of graham crackers and icing, but an outsider wouldn't be able to know that with the amount of hilarious trash-talking being dished out among the siblings. At one point, McKenzie had been sure a candy fight was about to break out when Andrea had attempted to sabotage Gabe and Lorena's house by stealing all their peppermints. They'd retaliated by eating her cinnamon bears.

Loud and chaotic was the only way to describe this annual Skaggs holiday tradition. And McKenzie, who was neither loud or chaotic, couldn't help joining in the antics.

"Wait, where'd my icing go?" Mitch asked next to her, moving bowls of various candies around the table.

She pursed her lips to disguise her smile.

"I swear it was right here a second ago." Her snort brought an end to his search, and his head jerked in her direction. "Where'd you put it, Zee?"

"I don't know what you're talking about." She gave him her best innocent expression. "Did you check behind the gumdrops?"

His eyes narrowed, though he was clearly more amused than skeptical. "You're sitting on it, aren't you?" He slid his chair closer to her, sliding an arm around her shoulders. "I will find it," he purred in her ear before brushing a light kiss on her cheek.

Warmth radiated through her, and she couldn't look away, held hostage by his captivating gaze. Who knew a little game of hide the icing could be so ... sensual? And in front of his family?

"Come on guys, cut it out." Gabe tossed a peppermint at them, nailing Mitch in the ear. "You're making me want to gag."

"Yeah, keep it family friendly," Andrea said. "There are children present."

McKenzie's cheeks flamed, and she hastily slid her chair a few inches from Mitch, unable to make eye contact with the other members of his family. She pulled his piping bag of icing from behind her back and handed it to him.

Fake indignation took over his gorgeous features. "I knew you had it. You better watch yourself."

Luis wandered over, pulling on Sebastián's arm. His uncle lifted him onto his lap. Attracted to the tasty sweets covering their house, Luis lunged for a gummy bear attached to the roof. His little hand made contact with the house to brace himself, but he only managed to flatten it to pieces.

Rather than be upset, boisterous guffaws came from his uncles. "Well, I guess we lost this contest," Mitch choked out through his laughter. "Though I think we should get bonus points for our King Kong demonstration." That brought on more chuckles from the rest of the family.

McKenzie and Hazel were soon declared the winners, and Andrea left to put Luis to bed while everyone else cleaned up.

"Do you want to watch a movie or something?" Mitch asked once the rest of the family had dispersed and only he, McKenzie, and Hazel were left at the table.

"Yeah!" Hazel shouted. "Can I pick?"

"You sure can." Turning to McKenzie, he asked, "Is that cool with you?"

She nodded. "I just want to change into my pj's first."

Mitch leaned over and kissed her cheek. "Go ahead. We'll wait."

"I'll hurry." She smiled at him before leaving the dining room and heading up the stairs.

Entering her empty room, she shut the door, crossing to the dresser to retrieve her pajamas. Her phone buzzed on the nightstand as she changed out of her clothes. Even without looking, she knew who was calling. Her mom had been relentless ever since McKenzie arrived in San Diego. For a fraction of a second, she debated letting it go to voicemail again. After avoiding the woman for the last two days, what was one more night?

On the other hand, she knew the woman wouldn't let up. And the longer McKenzie let it go, the worse the conversation would be.

You have this quiet strength about you, Mitch's voice from earlier spoke to her. And Seth's advice from months ago followed right after. *Be bold.* She'd repeated that mantra to herself over the last several weeks any time she had to do something hard. She needed that reminder now.

Taking a deep breath, she braced herself for the onslaught she knew was coming. "Hi, Mom," she said, congratulating herself for keeping her voice steady. Sure, she'd only said two words, but it was something.

"So, you've finally decided to answer your phone." Mom's words held no warmth.

McKenzie dropped onto her bed, hugging her pillow to her chest for comfort. "Um ... I ..."

A knock on the door interrupted her stuttering. McKenzie looked up as Lorena poked her head in the room.

"Sorry." Lorena cringed an apology. "I didn't know you were on the phone. Can I grab my pj's? I'll change in the bathroom."

Nodding, McKenzie mouthed, *Go ahead,* then rested her chin onto the pillow. Lorena crossed the room and retrieved her pajamas from her side of the dresser.

"McKenzie?" her mother's grating voice came through the phone. "Why didn't you come home? Where are you this weekend?"

McKenzie waited until she was alone again, contemplating repeating what she'd said in her text. But she'd thought a lot about her conversation with Mitch earlier. She could tell he was frustrated with having to keep their relationship a secret. If she were being honest with herself, she was tired of tiptoeing around too. He deserved more from her. Maybe it *was* better to come clean.

She swallowed. "I'm in San Diego, Mom."

"San Diego." A long, tense pause followed. "And whom are you with?"

Be bold. "My ... boyfriend."

"Your *boyfriend?*" Mom spat. "Young lady, you know you don't have time to date right now. And you certainly shouldn't be taking trips to San Diego with random men."

"Mitch isn't a random man, Mom." McKenzie attempted to keep her emotions in check. Lashing out would only make things worse for her.

"He's a distraction." Mom's voice grew more grating by the word. "You don't need anything else taking you off your path."

"He's not *taking me off my path*," McKenzie insisted, directly quoting her mother. "Mitch is an athlete too. He knows firsthand about the pressure I'm under to make the Global Elite team, and he's been helping me work through it."

Mom scoffed. "You don't need a boyfriend to help you deal with the pressure. That's what Gary and your psychologist are for. You're still seeing her, aren't you?"

"Yes." Every week since McKenzie had moved to California at seventeen. She'd be even more messed up if she didn't.

"Good. Keep it up. You can worry about dating after the Global Elites are over."

McKenzie would probably have her pick from a Debbie-Bowman-approved list of Ivy League grads and heirs of old money. An athletic-trainer-turned-pro-volleyball-player certainly wouldn't make her mom's cut.

Could she expect anything else though? It was just the way of things in the Bowman family. Her mom had married her dad because he was her parents' choice. And where had that gotten her? Unhappily married with a son who rarely talked to her and a daughter who wished she could do the same.

"I wish you'd just trust me, Mom," McKenzie said. "Mitch would never distract me from my goals."

"That's not how it appears to me. Running off with him to San

Diego, wishing to be normal when you're anything but. Your father and I have been very generous in paying for your living expenses all these years. Is this how you want to repay us?"

Generous isn't the word I'd use. Perhaps when McKenzie was a naïve teen moving away from home. Back then, she'd been more than happy to accept her parents' money. And why not? She hadn't even graduated from high school.

Now she saw it for what it was: a way for her mother to control every aspect of her life. After McKenzie had completed her senior year online, she'd tried to take back some control. She'd made some money from endorsements while modeling for a few leotard lines, which her mother allowed since it related to gymnastics. Gary had even convinced Tamryn, the director for the whole gymnastics program at SoCal Elite, to offer McKenzie a part-time job teaching a few beginner's classes. But her mom had insisted it would spread her too thin.

If only McKenzie had been more forceful back then. Maybe she'd feel a little less stuck now.

She didn't bring up any of that. Instead, she said, "You *have* been generous. I couldn't have come this far without—"

"However," her mother cut in, "if you insist on repaying our generosity with your ingratitude, I see no point in continuing to support this ... dream of yours."

McKenzie's blood ran cold. *No!*

Mom kept talking, completely unaware of the panic rising up her daughter's spine. "I don't want to take away your funding, but if you don't get your priorities in the right place, I'll have no choice. Do you understand?"

Yes, McKenzie understood completely. If she didn't toe the line without wavering, she'd be cut off, left with nothing. As much as she hated relying on her parents' money, she shuddered at the prospect of not having it. How would she pay her rent? Or feed herself? And what about her training?

She could talk to Gary. Perhaps the offer to teach some classes was still on the table. But beginning coaches barely made minimum wage, even with her experience as an athlete.

Heck, McKenzie would even be willing to clean the bathrooms at SoCal Elite if it meant being free from her mother's clutches. She could pick up odd jobs here and there to scrape enough money to pay for her living expenses. She'd have to shave a few hours off her training, and it wouldn't leave much time with Mitch, but surely he'd understand.

What about her car payments though? And insurance? Utilities? And on and on. This was Southern California. Teaching gymnastics to young children and scrubbing toilets part-time wouldn't pay the bills. And besides gymnastics, she had no useful skills, no training that would allow her to find a job that paid enough to cover everything.

The panic thickened as her mind continued to spiral. She'd have to quit gymnastics. And probably move back home. How would she ever get out from underneath her mom's thumb?

"McKenzie?" Mom cut into her anxiety-ridden thoughts. "I said, do you understand?"

McKenzie sighed. "Yes, Mother. I understand."

"Good. I hope you think long and hard about this. I expect more from you. Don't disappoint me again." The line went dead.

McKenzie placed her phone on the bedside table before curling her legs to her chest and dropping her face into the pillow. What was she supposed to do? She wanted Mitch. Oh boy, did she want him. But continuing to date him would mean an end to a dream she'd been training for her entire life. How could she quit when she was so close to her goal?

But how could she give up the possibility of sharing love, maybe even a future family, with Mitch?

Another knock on the door interrupted her sobs. Hastily, she wiped the tears from her cheeks as the door flew open. Mitch entered, carrying Hazel on his back. "The movie is all cued up, Hazel's choice"—he bounced his sister a little, making her giggle—

"the popcorn is ready, we're just waiting for a certain hottie to join us." He flashed a flirty grin in McKenzie's direction. It died as soon as he caught sight of her trembling jaw.

McKenzie stood and tossed the pillow onto the bed. When she crossed to them, Mitch's hand brushed her arm. "Are you okay?" he whispered so only she could hear.

No, she wasn't even a little bit okay. Mom was like the obnoxious neighbor crashing the party she wasn't invited to. McKenzie knew she needed to talk to Mitch about their conversation, but not in front of Hazel. She forced a smile as she met his eye. *Later,* she mouthed.

His brows knit together as he studied her for a drawn-out moment. He seemed like he wanted to say something else, then masked his concern as he turned his head to look at Hazel on his back. "You ready to get this party started, little sis?"

In response, she squeezed his back with her knees, bouncing up and down once. "Giddyup, horsey!"

Mitch shot McKenzie a last worried glance before literally galloping from the room with a "yeehaw!"

McKenzie stifled a sob watching them trot down the hall. This man, this family, was the life she wanted. Why did it have to be so out of reach?

Chapter Thirty-Two

Whoever came up with the idea that emotional releases made a person feel better must've been drunk. After crying herself into an exhausted sleep—silently so she wouldn't wake Lorena—McKenzie woke the next morning to some unpleasant nausea thanks to the ache practically splitting her forehead in two.

Groaning, she rolled over and jammed her pillow over her head to block out the light seeping through the blinds. She opened her eyes and peeked at Lorena's bed from the slit created between her pillow and mattress, then tossed the pillow aside upon seeing it empty. Her head throbbed in protest when she sat up.

After a few deep breaths to ease the pounding, she stood and retrieved her suitcase from the closet. Moisture pooled in her eyes as she tossed items into it. How did she have any tears left after last night?

A few raps on the door permeated the quiet of her bedroom. She turned toward it as it opened. Mitch poked his head in. "Hey, you *are* awake. Breakfast is ..." His gaze shifted from her to the open suitcase on her bed. "You're leaving?"

She responded by tossing her toiletries into her suitcase.

"Why? How?"

"I'm taking the train," she said, barely sparing him a glance as she continued her packing.

He entered the room, shutting the door behind him, and crossed to her bed. "Were you going to tell me, or were you planning to sneak out the back?"

McKenzie grabbed the sweater off the back of her chair and folded it loosely before tossing it on the top of her things in the suitcase. As bad as it looked, she absolutely had planned to talk to him. She knew once she ended things with him, it would be too heart-breaking to then have to come upstairs to pack. No, it was best for them both if she made a clean exit.

"Can we please talk about this?" His pleading tone forced her gaze to his face. The painful expression she saw there as he sat on the edge of her bed sucked an audible breath from her lungs.

"I can't do this," she finally squeaked out.

"What?" he asked, equally as breathless.

"This." She gestured between them, then dropped her eyes to the bedspread. She didn't dare look at him after dropping that bomb-shell. "I can't date you anymore."

The silence between them stretched on for what seemed like forever. Finally, Mitch whispered to his hands, "I don't understand. I thought this weekend—"

"The last two days have been the best in my life. The whole last month with you has been a dream, really." She shouldn't have said that, but she couldn't let him think he didn't mean the world to her. Against her better judgment, she dropped onto the bed and laced their fingers together. "But it's time for us to wake up. We both need to focus on our careers. And you'll be going on tour once the new season starts anyway."

Mitch scrubbed his free hand over his face. "Is that what this is about? Because I'm leaving? I know I'll be traveling a lot, but I'm sure we can make it work."

McKenzie shook her head forcefully. "That's not what this is about."

"Then what is it?"

"I can't afford to get distracted."

His eyes narrowed. "That sounds like your mom talking." Though subtle, she could sense the bitterness and it stung. "I take it you spoke to her finally?"

"Last night," McKenzie mumbled.

He bobbed his head slowly, though it was far from an acceptance. "That's why you seemed so bothered during the movie."

Apparently, she hadn't done a very good job of hiding it. "She's right though. The Global Elites are in seven months. I can't let anything get in the way of making that team. It's all I've ever wanted."

"In other words, *I'm* the distraction." He pulled his hand away, bracing both of his on his knees. "McKenzie, I understand the position you're in. You *know* I do. I wouldn't do anything to keep you from reaching your dream."

She stood, needing to create a little more distance between them.

"So our talk yesterday meant nothing?" Forced calm gripped his words.

She whirled to face him, throwing her hands up in desperation. "What choice do I have, Mitch? I tried standing up to her. I told her about us, about what I wanted. You know what I got?"

He waited, not looking at her.

"She's going to cut me off if I keep seeing you." She pressed her knuckles to her mouth to stifle a sob.

Mitch swore under his breath. McKenzie crossed to her suitcase and flipped the top closed. Her eyes snagged on his troubled expression.

"Okay, let's consider our options." It was so like him to search for the positives in an impossible situation.

"We have no options. Don't you get it?" She sank onto the bed again. "There's too much at stake for me. If I get cut off, there's no way I'd be able to keep paying for training. I'd have to quit. I've been doing gymnastics my whole life. I don't have any marketable skills. No job I got would pay the kind of salary to cover all my living expenses, even if I cut out all unnecessary costs." Years of her mother's manipulation had already taught her to be a minimalist. "I'd have to leave California."

Mitch blew out a long sigh, then took her hand. "I refuse to let that happen. You can stay with me if it comes to that."

"I won't be a charity case."

"Charity case?" He pushed a hand forcefully through his hair. "Zee, part of being in a relationship is taking care of each other."

McKenzie pulled her hand out of his and wrapped her arms around herself. "You know we can't do that. Now that you've cut your hours at work, you can barely cover your own bills. I can't expect you to help me with mine too."

"But I love you."

Those three words hurt more than a hundred hard falls off the balance beam. *I love you too,* she wanted desperately to say. She'd hoped for weeks to hear him say it to her. Somehow, she'd imagined the moment being way more romantic than this. Once again, her mother had ruined what should've been a beautiful experience.

"I'm sorry." That was all McKenzie could manage before bending over and dropping her head into her lap.

They sat in heavy silence, not looking at each other, until she couldn't resist the temptation any longer. She snuck a glance at his profile. His Adam's apple bobbed slowly up and down as he swallowed once and then again. The sight of his clenched jaw and misty eyes shattered the small piece of her heart still intact.

This is so wrong. She'd finally found her person. Her other half. How was she supposed to give him up?

"I should go," she said in a strangled whisper.

"Can I at least drive you to the station?" He spoke to the carpet.

"I have an Uber coming."

He finally met her gaze. The bleak resignation in his eyes was too much. Standing, she grabbed the handle of her suitcase and started for the door.

Mitch followed her out of the room. At the stairs, McKenzie went to pick up the bag, but he beat her to it, his hand brushing hers. She longed to grab hold, to hang onto it for dear life. He picked up the suitcase and carried it down the stairs.

They passed the dining room on their way to the front door. The rest of the Skaggs were gathered around the table for breakfast. She'd hoped to leave without making a big fuss. It was hard enough saying goodbye to Mitch. She didn't think she could face the whole family.

Cristina entered the room from the kitchen, a bowl of scrambled eggs in her hand. She glanced up as she set it in the middle of the table. "Are you leaving?" she asked, striding to the entryway.

McKenzie nodded. "I need to get back home. Thank you for everything."

"At least come in and have some pancakes before you go."

McKenzie didn't think she could eat even if she tried. "I can't. My ride will be here soon."

Cristina wrapped her in a hug, and it took all of McKenzie's will power not to crumble in the motherly embrace.

"It's been a pleasure having you here, McKenzie," Cristina said. "I hope we'll see you again soon."

McKenzie forced a smile, biting down on her cheek to keep her chin from wobbling. "Thank you."

Mitch grabbed onto the suitcase again. "I'm going to walk her out. I'll be right back," he said, sharing a heavy look with his mother.

McKenzie didn't trust herself to speak as they made their way down the driveway, past the palm fronds and around the bend. Mitch kept his free hand in his pocket, and she hugged her arms around her middle, attempting to comfort herself. There was no affection, no playful banter.

He turned to face her as they reached the sidewalk. "I don't want to say goodbye to you." His voice broke, bringing more tears to her eyes.

Before she could stop herself, she wrapped her arms around him. He enfolded her in one of his hugs, though this time, it didn't have the effect it normally did. It only hurt more. Still, they clung to each other, neither willing to let go. Finally, McKenzie stepped back.

"Is there anything I can do to change your mind?" he asked when McKenzie finally stepped back. Her Uber pulled up to the curb, and the driver got out to grab her suitcase, placing it in the trunk.

With all her heart she wished Mitch could whisk her away. The place didn't matter as long as it shielded her from an unfair world where her life wasn't her own. Where they could be together.

"I'm sorry," she whispered.

"Me too," he said just as softly. "Take care of yourself, McKenzie."

After settling into the back seat of the car, she braved one last look at the sidewalk. Mitch had already disappeared.

Chapter Thirty-Three

Flying home for Christmas was a mistake. Mitch should've expected that with how quickly McKenzie had charmed his family in San Diego. The only thing worse than having to say goodbye to the love of his life was having his family present to witness the aftermath. His mother's reaction had killed him the most. She'd been supportive of his heartbreak, of course, but he could tell she'd already had the flowers picked out for their wedding.

The four weeks since had been brutal. Memories of his time with McKenzie ran through his mind constantly, mocking him almost every waking moment. He'd assumed going home would be the lesser of two evils.

He was dead wrong on that score.

Mitch wasn't usually the type to dwell on failed relationships. Sure, all breakups were hard. But none of his past girlfriends had reached the serious, start-to-think-about-the-future stage. Until McKenzie. She *was* his future. At least he'd begun to think so.

Those two days in San Diego—up until she'd left—had only cemented in his mind what his heart already knew. He loved her. With every piece of his heart, he loved her.

And now he'd lost her.

The fact that he worked in the very place she trained didn't help. This was exactly why he'd made the rule not to date people from work. At any given moment he could run into her, which put him on guard every second of the workday.

At least he had volleyball. While the rest of the pros spent December recouping from the long season, there was no rest for the weary in Mitch and Charlie's case. March would come soon enough, bringing Mitch's first official season back on the pro circuit with it. In all honesty, he was grateful for something else to pour his heart into other than missing McKenzie. Pounding the snot out of a ball made good therapy.

Now, the day after Christmas, Sebastián couldn't resist bringing her up again. "I'm still shocked, man," he said in the car on their way to Mama B's to deliver a plate of their mom's Christmas pastries. "You looked like a solid couple."

Mitch bit back an irritated sigh as he shifted into the left turn lane. But he couldn't keep his frustration off the brake pedal. The car lurched to a stop.

His brother hissed a curse, grabbing hold of the plate in his lap before the pastries collided with the floor. "Dude."

This time, Mitch really did sigh, though not from irritation. "Sorry. I've been a little on edge lately."

"I can see that. What happened anyway? You never really explained why McKenzie didn't want to go out with you anymore."

Mitch buzzed his lips. "It's not her. It's her mom." He left it at that. As much as being without Zee still hurt, he refused to share the real reason why they couldn't be together. He understood the impossible situation she was in. He didn't like it, but he wouldn't betray her trust.

Sebastián lifted the plastic wrap from the plate and snitched a pastry. "Her mom doesn't like you?" he asked through a mouthful of food. He held out the treat to Mitch, who waved it off.

"Her mom's a—" He caught himself before vocalizing his true assessment of the insufferable Debbie Bowman. "Never mind. It doesn't matter. There's no use talking about it."

"I've never seen mom so crushed about any of *my* failed relationships," Sebastián said, brushing the crumbs off his fingers. "She was already thinking of names for your kids."

Her immediate love for McKenzie didn't go unnoticed by Mitch either. "Well, she'll have to wait to meet little Sara and Victor."

Sebastián chuckled. "She'll get over it. And so will you. You'll bounce back."

Mitch pulled up in front of Mama B's house and cut the engine. Forcing a smile, he said, "I always do." He could only hope that was true this time. "Come on. These goodies won't deliver themselves."

The smile on Mama B's face when she opened the door was bright. "My boys, I'm so glad you're here." She didn't bother inviting them inside before embracing Mitch.

He bent down to make it easier for her to wrap her arms around his neck. "Hey, Mama B. You look good."

"I feel good. A special guest came to visit today. Come in out of the cold, both of you. There's someone here I think you'll be eager to see." She took the dessert plate from Sebastián as he stepped inside and gave him a warm hug with her free arm. "This is so sweet. Please thank your mother for me."

Mama B took their coats and ushered the men down the hall. When Mitch reached the family room, he stopped in his tracks at the sight that greeted him. "Jules?" he asked as Sebastián crashed into his back.

What was Doug's old girlfriend doing in Mama B's house? She hadn't stepped foot in Elmwood Falls since her family had moved away after the accident.

Jules looked up from the photo album on her lap, and her hand found the thin silver chain around her neck, the same one Mitch had helped Doug pick out for her seventeenth birthday. She looked older, but Mitch would recognize those hazel eyes and honey-colored hair anywhere.

"Mitch." A tentative smile slid onto her face as she stood. "Sebastián. It's so good to see you guys."

Mitch grinned and threw his arms around her in a bear hug that lifted her from the ground. "What are you doing here?"

"My parents are taking a cruise for New Year's. They left for Florida this morning, so I thought I'd come up and visit Brenda on my way home." She accepted a hug from the younger Skaggs. "I live in Chicago now."

"Wow!" Mitch was still in shock. "I can't believe it."

"Sit down, all of you." Mama B pulled the men further into the room. "I'm sure you have a lot to catch up on. We were just talking about Doug."

Mitch froze. As happy as he was to see Jules after all this time, his heart, still hurting for McKenzie, couldn't muster up the strength to be the emotional stronghold for not just one but two of Doug's women.

"Actually, we don't have a lot of time," he mumbled, trying to think of any excuse to make his escape. "We only stopped by to drop off that plate from my mom."

Mama B rose from the armchair by the fireplace. "Nonsense, I'm sure Cristina won't mind if you stay and chat for a while."

"Yeah, come sit, Mitch." Jules scooted closer to Sebastián on the couch, patting the empty cushion.

"No, really." The force in Mitch's words surprised even him. "Come on, Bas. We should go." As he turned toward the hallway leading to the front door, he caught the worried glance Jules gave his brother.

"He still won't talk about it." Sebastián's whisper hadn't prevented Mitch from overhearing.

Jules nodded, sadness entering her eyes as she stood. She approached Mitch and slid her arms around his middle. "It took me a long time to be able to talk about him too."

Emotion gripped Mitch like a chokehold, and he clenched his jaw to keep it in check.

"When I finally opened up to people who care about me," Jules continued, "the accident and Doug's death became a little easier to face."

Mitch attempted to swallow, but it was no use. "I don't know if I can."

Jules gave him a small smile. "No one can force you to. I'm only giving you something to think about. I'm sorry for pulling away for so long. Maybe if I'd stayed in Elmwood Falls instead of convincing my parents to move, we could've helped each other through it."

"It's not your fault." Mitch could barely get the words out. "I should've been driving. If I'd gone, maybe he'd still be alive. What if it's because of me that he's not."

"I pulled away because the memories were too strong," Jules said. "It's taken me until now to work up the courage to come back here. I never thought you were to blame."

A gentle touch on Mitch's back caused him to turn. Mama B took him in her arms, tears welling in her eyes. "You've been such a strength to me since Doug's passing. Sometimes, your support has been the only thing to get me through these dark years. The whole time, I had no idea how much you were struggling. It was unfair of me to place such a burden on you. Especially when you were so young."

Mitch blinked hard to clear the emotion from his eyes. "I wanted to be there for you. I still do." He glanced at Jules. "For both of you."

Mama B touched his cheek. "And you have. But you don't have to be the strong one all the time. It's okay to admit you need help too."

McKenzie had said something similar a few weeks ago. Hearing it again made him miss her even more. She was the only person who made him feel safe to not be okay every minute of the day. Like he didn't need to be the strong one all the time. He was always the protector, the one to lift everyone else's burdens. He hadn't realized until now that he needed someone to lean on too. And McKenzie had been that for him.

As Mitch glanced at Jules again, his attention landed on a picture frame on top of the fireplace mantle. He wandered over to it and studied the seventeen-year-olds immortalized in the photo. It had been taken shortly after the Junior Worlds victory ceremony. He and Doug had their arms slung across each other's shoulders, their other hands holding the top corners of the American flag draped around their backs. Gold medals hung from their necks and colossal grins took up half their faces.

A small smile tugged at his mouth as he picked up the picture. "Man, I haven't seen this in ages."

"That was such an exciting day." Mama B placed a hand on his shoulder blade. "You both worked so hard to get there. I remember the two of you talking all the time about winning Junior Worlds and then dominating the senior circuit. There was no doubt in your minds you'd get there one day."

Mitch chuckled at the memory of those carefree days. So much had changed since then. "We used to pretend every tournament was the Global Elite Games."

Mama B laughed. "It wasn't just tournaments. I can still picture the two of you in the backyard passing the ball back and forth imagining you were in the gold medal match of the Global Elites. And you always won. You two were dreamers. I'll give you that."

Mitch joined in for a second before the amusement died again. "I wonder what he'd think about my comeback."

"I know he'd be proud of you." Mama B took the photo from him and reverently placed it back on the mantle. "Just like I know you'd be proud of him if the situation were reversed. Would you want him to give up on the dream?"

He shook his head. If Doug were alive, Mitch would absolutely want him to keep playing, even if he couldn't. The realization eased some of his guilt.

"Do it for him." Mama B placed both her hands on his arms, giving them a gentle squeeze to gain his attention. "I can't think of a better way to honor Doug's memory than to dedicate your journey back to competition to him."

Mitch could no longer hold back the tears. He only managed a nod in response.

"And we'll all be here for you." Jules sat back down next to Sebastián. "Like your own personal fan section."

Mitch smiled for the first time since he'd realized Jules was in the house. "Does that mean you plan on keeping in touch?" He wiped at his eyes.

"Yeah." She glanced at Sebastián, then back at Mitch. "I've

missed you guys. And anytime you need to talk—about anything—please call me."

Mitch thought about their exchange for a long time after he'd returned to his parents' house. For years, he'd bottled up his grief, never letting it fully come out. As if surrendering to it would force him to accept that his best friend was truly gone.

Seeing Jules tonight had been therapeutic in a way. He was glad she'd found some peace. Though the way she talked about Doug clearly showed she hadn't forgotten him. Even Mama B, who still deeply mourned her son's death, had come to accept it, even on hard days.

Maybe accepting didn't have to mean forgetting.

And maybe it was time Mitch started searching for his own peace.

Chapter Thirty-Four

All winter, McKenzie worked hard to prove to the world, and herself, that she wasn't slowly dying inside. Day after day, she played the part of the perfect athlete, throwing every ounce of her mind and body into her training. To everyone else, she was the poster child of focus and determination.

She deserved an Oscar for her stellar acting abilities because truthfully, her passion for gymnastics had dwindled long before she'd ended things with Mitch. That fateful day had only cemented in her mind that her life had no purpose except bowing to her mother's will. And she had no idea how to claw her way out of that vice grip.

On the first Saturday of March—a little over three months post-breakup—McKenzie sat amongst the other elite gymnasts after practice, staring up at the three coaches standing in front of them. With her chin propped in her hands, she counted down the minutes until the end of the team meeting. These monthly info dumps often became long-winded, and she stifled a yawn as Gary droned on about the invitational in Las Vegas the following week.

"We'll have two days of normal training before we leave for Vegas on Wednesday," he said, consulting his clipboard. "The bus leaves from here at six a.m. sharp. It's up to you to make sure you're here on time. Don't make us wait for you."

McKenzie groaned along with her teammates.

Sonya, the coach standing nearest Gary, gestured for quiet. "Trust me, we don't want to get up that early either," she said. Laughter rang through the group.

"You'll have plenty of time to sleep on the bus," Gary said, once he'd regained control of the group. "In fact, we have a training session that evening, so I suggest you do." He looked to Sonya and Mark, the third coach. "Do you have anything else to add?"

They shook their heads.

"Okay, that's it. Have a good day off tomorrow," Gary said in dismissal. "We'll see you back here on Monday."

Chatter broke out as the gymnasts separated off into smaller groups, leaving McKenzie and Aria alone on the mat.

"Six a.m.?" Aria complained, digging through her bag. "Why so early? I'll have to wake up at three to get ready." She pulled out her flip-flops and shoved them onto her feet.

McKenzie stopped searching for her keys and scrunched her face in confusion. "It's an eight-hour bus ride. How dressed up do you need to be?" Once she'd found what she was looking for, she stood, lifting her bag onto her shoulder.

"I suppose you plan on showing up in your pajamas." Aria scoffed in disgust, her perfectly sculpted brows furrowing.

Her response wasn't all that surprising, both what she said or the way she'd said it. While the rest of the gymnasts hardly wore any makeup at practice, Aria's face was always competition ready. And it was only one of the backhanded comments she'd given McKenzie that day alone.

"McKenzie," Gary called, saving her from responding.

Turning to her coach as he approached, she breathed a silent sigh of relief for the rescue. She wasn't in the mood to act as Aria's passive aggressive punching bag anymore today.

"I'd like a word with you in my office before you leave," he said. "It won't take long."

"Sure, Gary."

He nodded and left to chat with the other coaches.

Aria sneered in her ear. "Oooh, someone's in trouble. What did you do?" The smugness in her eyes was impossible to miss.

McKenzie shrugged it off. She had no idea, and she wouldn't share it with her teammate if she did. "See you on Monday." She walked away without waiting for a response.

Gary's office door was still locked when she got there a few minutes later. She leaned against the wall to wait for him, wiping her clammy hands on her leggings. A summons to her coach's office shouldn't make her this nervous. He'd known her since she was a toddler for crying out loud. They were practically family.

"Sorry it took me a minute to get here," Gary said, coming up beside her and digging his keys out of his pocket. He unlocked the door and motioned for her to enter first. "I got stopped by Tamryn on my way. Have a seat."

Mutely, McKenzie sat. She kept her eyes on the navy and gray carpet in front of her feet so they wouldn't accidentally stray to the framed articles from the Buena Hills Gazette on the wall facing her. Those articles never provided the motivation her coach thought they should.

Gary perched a hip against his desk. The window looking into the gym framed his figure. "I'm impressed with your hard work on vault the last few weeks. Your confidence has really improved it seems. I think you're ready to add the extra twist."

McKenzie sucked in a breath, panic settling in her gut. That meant attempting the vault that had caused her accident. "Gary, I don't—"

Her coach lifted his hands out in front of himself, cutting off her argument. "McKenzie, I know you don't want to, but it's time. You've performed that skill perfectly on the trampoline. There's no reason you wouldn't be able to do it off the vault."

Flipping on the trampoline was different though. Without the added element of catapulting herself off the vault, the skill seemed like any other she was attempting to learn. But trying it off the vault? She wasn't ready for that.

"I'd love to see you compete it at the Global Elite trials. Which means it needs to be ready to go long before then. I wanted to meet with you now, so you'd have the weekend to mentally prepare to try it on Monday."

McKenzie picked at the ripped cuticle of her right pinky finger to give her an excuse not to look at him. "Do I have to? I'm a bars specialist. Why do I even have to train vault at all? Can't I skip it altogether and focus on the other events?"

Gary's silence forced her gaze up to him. The look of compassion on his face eased some of her anxiety, though it didn't mask the determination also lurking in his eyes. "That's an option, certainly," he said finally. "However, I don't want you to retire and spend the rest of your life wondering if you could do it. This isn't about improving your all-around scores. This is about proving to yourself that you can move on from what happened."

She blew out a deep breath. She hated when he was right. The memory of her accident would continue to hang over her head unless she found a way to face it head on. Even if it took her out of her safety zone.

He approached her, placing a hand on her shoulder. "You can do this, McKenzie. You have the skill and the consistency. Now it's time to train your brain to believe it too."

"I'll try," she said, trying to convince herself as much as him.

"Good." Gary gave her shoulder another pat and smiled as he shooed her from the office. "Go on. Get out of here. I'll see you on Monday."

She left his office, trying to shake the unsettling jitters rippling through her body. Worrying about that vault was a problem for future McKenzie. There was nothing she could do about it now.

A few lights remained on, casting shadows on the trophy cases along the walls of the wide hallway. As McKenzie passed the weight room, something drew her focus inside. A trio of large punching bags hanging in the corner were the only part of the room illuminated. And a familiar figure stood facing the one nearest her.

She gasped, her hand flying to her mouth to stifle the sound. With his back to the exit, Mitch's focus didn't stray from his sparring. The tiny white buds in his ears further made sure her surprise went unnoticed.

She stood in the doorway, transfixed on the strained muscles of his bare back as he delivered blow after blow on the vinyl bag. Sweat glistened off his skin in the low light, drawing her eyes to the tattoo on his left shoulder blade, a visible reminder of his loss.

She hadn't seen much of him since Thanksgiving. Surprising, since they spent six afternoons a week in the same place. He, no doubt, was avoiding her too.

She glanced down the hallway, then back into the room. Every second she stayed, she risked being discovered. But the firm lecture her head gave her heart faded into the void because her feet refused to budge. Those stupid appendages cemented to the floor as if they were stuck in concrete. And her eyes superglued themselves to his deltoids.

For several minutes she watched him, her whole body crying out louder for him with each punch of the bag. He had a grace to his movements that seemed out of place for someone as tall as he was. McKenzie knew he often used boxing as a stress reliever when dealing with heavy things. Was grief for Doug driving him back to it? Or was it her?

His movements slowed, a major cue she had to scram. Any minute now, he'd turn around and catch her staring. Still her feet wouldn't move.

Mitch reached for his towel on the bench nearby, turning enough for the side of his face to come into view.

That little glimpse of his handsome profile spurred McKenzie into action. She turned toward the exit and miraculously, her feet followed. If she moved quickly, maybe she'd get out of there before he spotted her.

"McKenzie?"

She froze at the sound of her name on his tongue. She'd been caught. Very slowly, she turned back around.

Chapter Thirty-Five

"You're here late," Mitch said, unable to hide his surprise. The towel he was using to wipe the sweat from his skin hovered motionless in front of his stomach.

McKenzie stared at him, and her eyes traveled down the length of his torso before widening and snapping back to his face. If not for the shock over discovering her there, he would've found her obvious ogling amusing.

"T-team meeting," she stuttered, blushing.

"Ah." So she was back to being nervous around him? That was disappointing.

He slid the towel down his stomach before moving to his arms, unable to resist the temptation to flex his muscles a bit. Zee's gaze flicked to his bicep before darting away again and settling on something past his right shoulder.

"Your training seems to be going well," he said. "You were tearing it up on bars when I was in the gym the other day."

"It's going okay." Her eyes pinged around the deserted weight room before settling on him again. "How's ... how's volleyball?"

He crossed to the dirty laundry bin, keeping his body facing her so she didn't take his distance as a dismissal. Seeing her in the doorway, so close and yet so emotionally and physically out of reach, was more than a little uncomfortable. Even after more than three months, his arms still itched to hold her. He knew he was only making things harder for himself by wanting her there. But he'd couldn't let her leave. After blowing out a breath, he tossed the towel into the bin.

"It's good," he said, taking pity on her and picking up his T-shirt from the nearby bench. He removed his hat and threw the shirt on before replacing the cap backward on his head. "I'm leaving in the morning for my first set of tournaments." Not a day too soon. He couldn't wait to get out of California for a while.

McKenzie interlocked her fingers in front of her, turning them about. Mitch grabbed his water bottle and took a long swig, clenching it hard to resist the urge to take her hand. A few months ago, that simple act had been enough to calm at least some of her anxiety.

He didn't have that right anymore.

"Where are you going?" she asked.

Mitch swallowed. "The first one's in Rio. Then we're heading to Cancun and finishing up in Salinas, Ecuador—"

"Ecuador? That'll be nice for you."

The way her face lit up like she was genuinely excited for him made him smile, despite the uncomfortable feeling growing in his stomach.

"I'm pretty stoked," he said, nodding. "I have family coming from Quito to watch. It'll be nice to see them again. It's been a while." He set the bottle down on the bench.

"Nice." McKenzie looked away. A heavy silence fell between them. After several long seconds, she raised her eyes to him again. "Rory and Elise got engaged over Christmas break."

An odd conversation shift, perhaps, but it was innocuous and safe, two things he knew she needed. "I know. They told me." They'd stopped by his apartment to share the news shortly after returning from spending Christmas with Rory's family in Ireland. Mitch had been thrilled for his friends, of course, even if everyone had seen it coming. But a little part of him had also been sad for himself, knowing that he wanted the same happily ever after with McKenzie.

"Oh, right," McKenzie said, looking down at her feet. "They're your friends too."

Yes, they were. Even if their friendship had changed since Mitch's relationship ended. Rory and Elise remained loyal to both Mitch and McKenzie, though Elise's role as the roommate made it difficult to remain as close to Mitch as they once were. Aside from losing McKenzie—the most tragic part of the whole situation, of course—distancing himself from the rest of the group had been an unfortunate casualty.

"I hate that one of my favorite people is forced to avoid coming to the house," Elise had bemoaned one evening when Mitch stopped by Rory and Seth's apartment. "I still don't understand it. You were perfect together."

"Tell that to McKenzie," Mitch countered. "If it were up to me, we'd still be together."

Elise's look of pity hadn't made him feel any better. "I did. She won't talk about it. She's back to being shy and withdrawn like when she first moved in. We're all worried about her."

Mitch had been worried too. He still was. He just didn't know what to do about it.

McKenzie cleared her throat, snapping his attention back to her. She brought a hand up to finger a wisp of hair that had escaped her messy bun. "I should g-go." She glanced at the door and back at him. "I didn't mean to bother you."

"You didn't," he pushed out hastily. Was it crazy that he didn't want her to go, even if it meant suffering through this painful conversation? *Yes, it is.* Apparently, torture was the preferred activity tonight. Sweet torture in the name of McKenzie Bowman. "It's nice to see you."

Her head bobbed once in acceptance of his comment as she tucked the wisp back behind her ear. The sight of it stirred a memory from months ago when those same slender fingers gently worked through his own hair as he gave into his grief. He missed the comforting safety of her affection. If only they could go back to that.

Neither of them moved. Mitch couldn't pull his eyes away from her, and she seemed reluctant to as well. They stood there, staring at each other as the AC system purred through the room. The silence between them rang louder than a stadium full of wild fans.

There was so much more he wanted to say to her. He wanted to tell her he was finally confronting his grief. Some days were brutal, reminding him why he'd buried it for so long. Still, he was working through it with the help of his family and Jules.

He wanted to tell her he missed her. That he still loved her.

She found her voice first. "T-take care, Mitch."

He lifted a hand. "Bye."

Backing up a few steps, she bumped into the doorframe, stumbling a bit. She glanced at it and then back at him before turning and dashing out the door.

Mitch pushed out a tense breath and sank onto the bench nearest him. Oh yes, sweet torture was definitely the name of the game tonight.

He dug through the small pocket of his bag, searching for his keys. His hand brushed the sea glass McKenzie had given to him months before. He'd forgotten he'd stashed it in his bag. Pulling it out, he ran his thumb over the smooth surface. *I want you to have it to remind you that better days will come,* she'd said.

He could only hope that was true.

Chapter Thirty-Six

McKenzie shouldn't be trusted to make rational decisions when this tired. Bone-crushing fatigue was the only logical way to explain how she found herself standing on Mitch's doorstep in the middle of the night. She hardly remembered making the drive down to Long Beach. And yet, here she was. Just hours after their uncomfortable encounter in the gym too.

The dim glow of the porch light illuminated his blue door, one of two on the middle floor of the three-level complex.

When you can't sleep, you should take a melatonin, she lectured herself, the voice in her head sounding a lot like her mother's. *Not drive to your ex's apartment on a whim.*

She wrapped Mitch's hoodie more tightly around herself for comfort. What was she doing here anyway? Looking for closure? A clandestine meeting with her forbidden love? She didn't even know.

But something shifted for her after their conversation in the weight room earlier. And though she hadn't had any luck banishing the gorgeous image from her mind, that shift had nothing to do with the fact that he'd been shirtless.

She missed him. And she hated that in her first real encounter with him since the breakup, she'd gone back to her skittish tendencies.

She had to see him again. Before he left for Brazil.

The flutters rumbling in her stomach were reaching vomit-inducing levels. Worrying about the possibility of throwing up only made her anxiety over the situation worse. It wasn't too late to get back in her car and pretend this little excursion never happened. In fact, that's exactly what she should do.

But was it what she *wanted* to do?

She took a deep breath in through her nose and blew it out slowly. The flutters settled enough to ease her temptation to puke. She knocked, quietly at first, then louder. Several minutes slogged by in agonizing slowness.

A throat clearing signaled the first signs of life on the other side of the door. Seconds later, it opened and there was Mitch, hair sticking out in places and sleep lines on one side of his face. Day-old stubble aside, he looked adorably boyish standing there squinting at her. He rubbed his hands over his face, then stared at her again like she'd lost her mind.

Which, for the record, she had.

"I'm s-sorry. I shouldn't have woken you up," she said, turning to go.

Mitch grabbed her hand before she'd taken a step. "Zee, wait." His voice was still raspy from sleep. "What're you doing here?"

He hadn't posed the question in an unkind way. And McKenzie had asked herself the same thing dozens of times on the way over. Still, her composure weakened. She clamped down hard on her jaw to keep her chin from wobbling. *Don't cry. Do. Not. Cry.*

She stared down at the cement porch, knowing she'd lose it if she looked at him. No good. All the negative emotions she'd been holding inside, all the pressure of the last few weeks—scratch that, her entire life—came crashing down on her all at once. She was helpless to stop the deluge of tears that began to flow.

Mitch's strong arms came around her, bringing her in close. She leaned her head against his chest and focused on his heartbeat thudding against her ear. Strong and steady, like the man himself.

Without letting go of her, he pulled her inside the apartment and shut the door. His hands ran soothing circles along her back, and she matched her breathing to the slow rhythm.

Once she'd composed herself, she pulled away and wiped her cheeks on her sleeve. "I don't want to do this anymore." More tears stung the backs of her eyes, but she willed herself to stay strong.

Mitch was fully awake now. "Do what?"

"Be without you."

His brows twitched in surprise.

She blew out a slow breath, taking strength from it. "I hate that I've hurt the only man I've ever loved. You're worth more to me than some silly dream."

"It's not silly," he said, holding his hand out to her. She accepted the gesture and followed him to the couch. Once they were seated, bodies angled facing each other so only their knees touched, he asked, "What about your mom?"

"I don't care about my mom. I don't care about gymnastics. None of it matters anymore if I can't have you."

He chewed on his bottom lip, pondering. "There has to be some way for us to be together without you being cut off," he said after a minute.

McKenzie shook her head. "I don't see how. My mother will absolutely make good on her threat. As soon as she finds out about us, that's it. I'm done."

"She won't find out." He reached for her hand again.

"You can't underestimate her."

"Believe me, I'm not." But uncertainty crossed his face. "Did you mean it a minute ago when you said you loved me?"

"With all my heart," she choked out.

The joy that lit his face warmed her to her core. Holding her gaze, he lifted her hand to his lips and pressed a kiss to her fingers. "That's all I need for now. You're retiring in a few months, right? Your mom won't have anything to hold over your head after that. I'm okay keeping things casual until then."

If only it were that easy. "I'm sure she'll find something else. I doubt she'll give up control just because I'm no longer competing."

"True, but we can cross that bridge when we come to it."

He leaned forward and pressed a kiss to her forehead. A new kind of flutter emerged in her stomach. She'd missed his forehead kisses. They made her feel cherished, treasured in a way she'd never experienced before.

"What did you tell me the night you returned from Worlds?" He slid an arm around her, pulling her close. "Better days will come?"

McKenzie snuggled deeper into him. "Sometimes you have to fight hard for them."

"I'll fight with you," he said. "I mean it. I won't give up on us if you won't."

She looked up at him, soaking in all the love in his gaze. "It's us against the world, then?"

His lips grazed hers, his breath hot against her skin. "Exactly." He gave her mouth another peck. And then another.

"Are you sure you're okay with this though?" she asked, snuggling into him again. "My family is messed up. It's not fair for me to drag you into all of that."

"Us against the world, Zee." He placed his hand over hers where it rested on his chest. "Whatever comes, I'll fight with you, no matter how ugly it gets."

"I feel bad asking you to keep us a secret again."

He gave an exaggerated sigh. "It'll be difficult. That's for sure. How will I ever manage?" He winked down at her.

McKenzie barely kept a straight face as she said, "Especially with all those gorgeous volleyball babes swarming you on tour and not knowing you have a girlfriend. You might find your soulmate."

His mouth twitched. "Nah, I've found my soulmate."

If she hadn't been sitting, she would've melted into a puddle of happiness. She reached a hand up to smooth the strands of hair sticking out of the side of his head as his gaze dropped to her mouth. When his eyes raised to hers again, they lingered on her so intensely it forced a small gasp from her.

He leaned in, and his lips brushed hers once before capturing them in a real kiss. McKenzie willingly surrendered to him, pressing her body firmly against his chest and sliding her hands around his neck. Their lips moved as one, a reunion of sorts, the kiss so passionate it made her toes curl.

Her mother's voice returned to her mind. *This isn't smart. It will only lead to more pain later.*

Maybe, but she clamped down on the fear anyway. In this moment, kissing him felt right. Like coming home. Except not hers. One radiating a happiness she only felt when she was with him. For once in her life, she was going after what *she* wanted.

Mitch broke the seal of their mouths, moving on to explore more of her with his delicious lips. He trailed kisses down her cheek before continuing to her neck and the soft spot behind her ear. She kept her eyes closed, attempting to stop the room from spinning.

"Is this casual?" she asked after several minutes, her voice pitchy.

He brushed another tantalizing kiss on her jawline. "I thought we could be casual with perks," he purred, soft and low. "You know, like friends with benefits?"

McKenzie giggled but shook her head.

Mitch stopped nuzzling her ear and sighed, dropping his forehead onto her shoulder. "You're right. Sorry." He turned his face to plant one last kiss to her neck before moving back, keeping an arm around her.

She leaned her cheek against his chest. "Thank you for being willing to do this for me. I know it isn't the best situation."

"Hey, I can be casual." He ran his hand along her ponytail. "The volleyball world might know me as Mr. Dig Man, but *you* can call me Mr. Casual."

She laughed harder than probably was necessary. The late hour and lack of sleep must be catching up to her. "Mr. Dig Man? Is that really your nickname?"

"Isn't it great? I earned it after setting the junior record for most successful digs in a single season. That was the year before I left the circuit." He settled her more comfortably against his chest. "I still hold it by the way."

McKenzie smiled at his smug tone. "Are you going to expect me to use it when I'm talking to you? Maybe I should call you Mr. Cocky instead."

"Me? Cocky? Never." His low, rumbling chuckle vibrated against her ear. "In all seriousness though, you're right. This situation isn't ideal. For either of us. But you're my future, Zee. I know that. And I'm willing to do everything in my power to fight for it. Besides, my season is starting this week. And your training schedule and competitions will keep you busy. We won't be seeing much of each other for the next few months at least."

That realization dimmed the happy feeling swirling around her. "I wish you didn't have to leave so soon." She just got him back, and she already had to say goodbye? It hardly seemed fair.

It's only a month. A month seemed like an awfully long time.

"I promise to call. Every day." He kissed the top of her head. "I'll miss you, though."

"I'll miss you too."

With his protective arm around her, everything felt right for the first time in months. Eventually, she'd need to get in the car and drive home, but what was the hurry? He was leaving in the morning, and she planned to soak up every minute left with him she could. Burying her face into his chest, the warm firmness of his skin underneath his T-shirt lulled her into a dreamlike bliss.

But mention of the junior circuit, as brief as it was, brought one of McKenzie's worries of the last few months to the forefront of her mind. "How are you handling things?" she asked, her fatigue quickly catching up to her. "With Doug, I mean. I've been worried about you."

He didn't answer right away. She sat up, surprised to see contemplation on his face in the place of the sadness she'd expected. She reached a hand up to stroke the nape of his neck with her fingernails.

Mitch leaned his head toward her, closing his eyes, obviously enjoying her touch. A small smile teased his lips. After a minute, he looked at her. "Some days are easier than others. I ran into Jules over Christmas, and she's been helping me work through it. I've found that talking about happy memories is actually kind of therapeutic. We had a lot of good times. I think Doug would've liked you."

"I wish I could've met him." McKenzie yawned. "Will you tell me more about him?"

"Anytime you want." He slid his arm out from under her. "Except right now. You look like you're about to crash." Standing, he held out a hand to her. "Come on. Take the bed. I'll sleep out here."

McKenzie was too tired to argue. It probably wasn't smart for her to drive home right now anyway. She took his hand and followed him to his room. Once she'd settled underneath the covers, Mitch knelt next to the bed and pressed a kiss to her temple.

"Good night, Zee," he whispered before quietly leaving the room, the door clicking shut behind him.

Relaxing deeper into the pillow, she closed her eyes, listening to the sounds of Mitch settling onto the couch coming from the front room. His familiar scent lingered on the pillowcase, and she breathed it in, longing for a day when she'd be able to wake in his arms.

Their problems were far from over, and she couldn't predict the future. Tomorrow, her world could very well blow up in her face again. But for the moment, she finally felt safe.

Chapter Thirty-Seven

Mitch knocked lightly on the bedroom door, covering a yawn with his other hand. Morning had come quickly, and the couch hadn't been the best sleeping spot for his tall frame. He didn't regret the lack of rest one bit though. How could he when it was McKenzie who'd kept him up? He wouldn't trade the time he spent with her for all the hours of sleep in the world. He'd nap on the plane.

When no answer came from the room, he poked his head inside. She slept soundly, the light streaming in from the living room falling on her porcelain skin. He slipped into the room and crouched next to the bed, nudging her shoulder. "Zee."

She didn't budge, which was no surprise. If he'd learned anything from San Diego it was that she slept like a rock.

He shook her a little harder. "McKenzie, wake up."

This time, she stirred with a sigh before finally opening one eye a crack. "What time is it?" she slurred.

"Just after six. I have to leave for the airport soon. I came in to get some clothes so I can shower before I go."

She rubbed a hand over her face and yawned. "Do you want me to drive you?"

Mitch smoothed a strand of hair off her forehead. "I have an Uber coming. You go back to sleep. I just didn't want to leave without saying goodbye."

McKenzie's arms snaked out from underneath the blanket to wrap around him.

Sliding an arm over her, he touched his forehead to her temple. "Will you watch my games?"

She nodded into his neck.

"I'll text you my schedule when I have it." He pressed a kiss to her hair and started to move back.

McKenzie tightened her grip around his neck. "Not yet," she mumbled, still not fully awake.

How could he argue with that? He lingered a moment longer in her arms. Twenty-four hours ago, he couldn't wait to get on tour. Now, he was reluctant to go. Once he was on his way, the excitement of his first tournament would most likely catch up with him. But man, leaving her was tough.

Somehow, he managed to break away. "My extra key is on the counter by the door. Lock up when you leave?"

She gave him a thumbs-up before slipping her hand back underneath the blankets. He forced himself to stand and made his way to his dresser. After pulling out a T-shirt and pair of black joggers, he headed toward the door.

"Hey," she said before he left the room. At the doorway, he turned around. She'd lifted her head off the pillow, propping it against her hand. "Win or lose, I'm proud of you for doing this."

He smiled, fighting against the internal struggle to return to her side for one more hug, one last kiss. He'd like nothing more than to hold her in his arms and soak in the quiet calm of the morning. Unfortunately, he had a plane to catch. "See you in a month."

Following a last lingering glance, he left the room, already counting down the minutes until he'd see her again.

McKenzie was still giddy when she arrived at practice on Monday morning. After kicking off her flip-flops and shoving them into her bag, she approached the group of gymnasts already stretching and dropped down onto the mat beside Aria.

"Why are you smiling?" her teammate asked.

"Am I?" McKenzie touched a hand to her cheek. She was totally smiling.

In fact, she hadn't stopped since leaving Mitch's apartment yesterday morning. He'd been gone for only a day, and they'd already talked on the phone twice—during his layover in Houston and then after his training session that morning.

She barely managed to squelch the giggle that almost bubbled over thinking of his butchering rendition of "Good Morning" from *Singing in the Rain*. The man was perfect in many ways, but he was no Gene Kelly. McKenzie was surprised he even knew the words. He didn't seem like a classic movie kind of guy. She planned to remedy that the next time they had a few hours together.

"Something amazing must've happened for you to be so happy. You've been such a grump lately." Aria paused in her stretching to scrutinize McKenzie with narrowed eyes.

McKenzie stretched her legs out into the splits and reached forward. "Do I have to have a reason to smile? I'm just looking forward to another training day."

The words weren't completely untrue, even if they didn't convince her teammate. After talking things over with Mitch Saturday night, and their subsequent phone conversations, a huge weight had lifted, even if most of McKenzie's circumstances remained the same. She was still in danger of being cut off, and today was still the day she'd attempt the dreaded vault since almost dying.

But those challenges didn't seem so daunting now. Not when she and Mitch were on the same page. Waiting until after the Global Elites to make anything official sucked, but his commitment to her boosted her resolve to keep going.

That resolve stayed with her for most of the morning training session. Through every swing on uneven bars and every tumbling sequence on balance beam. Right up until the moment Gary announced it was time to move to vault. As soon as he mentioned the word, those positive vibes fled faster than a cheetah chasing its prey.

Taking her place at the end of the vault runway, McKenzie waited for Gary to finish moving the blue landing mat over the foam blocks on the other side of the apparatus. He rarely had his athletes land vault outside of the pit during practice to eliminate some of the pounding on their bodies. But even that was little reassurance to the anxiety chomping away at her confidence.

I almost died, she thought, fighting hard to keep the memory at bay. *I'm lucky I can walk, let alone compete.* She firmly shook the thought from her head.

Gary gave her the signal, and she took off running. With each step, the internal tug-of-war of anxious thoughts grew louder, stifling their rational counter arguments. Quick bursts of mental pictures flashed in her mind like those crime shows Kendall liked to watch. Twisting in the air. Crumpled on the mat surrounded by medical staff. Unconscious in a hospital bed with tubes stuck in her nose. Her brother's worried look. Mitch's gorgeous eyes marred by grief.

She gasped. That image was not from her past.

Instead of dropping into her roundoff at the end of the runway, McKenzie stepped to the side and sprinted past the vault. She lurched to a stop, doubling over to catch her breath.

You're safe. She repeated the words to herself several times, her hands covering her face as she willed the panic to subside.

A hand on her back stopped her internal self-soothing. Gary crouched in front of her. "How're you doing?"

She finally looked at him. "I can't do this, Gary," she pushed out, still trying to catch her breath. She straightened and crossed her arms over her middle to further calm herself. "It's too hard. I'd rather stick with the easier vault."

"This isn't a matter of what you can't do," Gary said, cutting off her spiraling. "You're more than capable of conquering this obstacle."

Shame prevented McKenzie from meeting his worried look. "I can't get the image of what happened out of my head. It's been almost nine years. I've been working with the psychologist every week." Tears stung her eyes. "I've been doing what everyone tells me to do. Why can't I forget it?"

Her coach placed both hands on her shoulders, then straightened his fingers and inched her chin up so she was forced to look at him. "The goal is not to forget about the injury. That's impossible. Overcoming a fear, especially one as big as yours, comes in stages. And each one is harder than the one before. This is just another stage to work through. Today, you made it down the runway. The goal is to get closer with every repetition. Yeah?"

She nodded silently.

"You need to trust yourself," he continued, removing his hands from her shoulders. "I wouldn't push you to do this if I didn't know for sure you could."

How was she supposed to trust herself when she'd been given so little opportunity to in her life? She thought about that as she walked off the mat and watched Evie take her place at the end of the runway.

As Gary walked away to work with Evie, Aria came up beside McKenzie. "Looks like the coach's favorite isn't Little Miss Perfect on everything," she said, a haughty tilt to her head.

McKenzie balled her fists at her sides, biting back the retort she was tempted to make. Why did Aria take such pleasure in belittling her? If she focused on her own training, she had the potential of being one of the best in the world. She didn't need to be threatened by anyone else.

And what had McKenzie done other than make the World team when Aria didn't?

With measured breaths, McKenzie turned to her teammate. "I've never claimed to be perfect."

She stalked off without another word, turning her back to the gym as she stretched her arms over her head and tried to reclaim calm. This sport already made her vulnerable enough, exposing every one of her weaknesses even while she strove for perfection. On top of that, she had to deal with having those flaws mocked by someone who was supposed to be in her support system. Aria's true colors came out with every practice, and each backhanded comment made it harder for McKenzie to be the bigger person.

Only a few hours earlier, she was on a high after talking to Mitch. Now that dreaded vault and her insufferable teammate had knocked her back to her place in the slumps. What did she need to do to catch a break?

Chapter Thirty-Eight

Even non-contact sports had their job hazards. Getting clocked in the face by a ball going seventy miles-per-hour was definitely high on that list. The lightning-fast reflexes that had made Mitch so good as a junior defender were useless in helping him get out of the way of the Dutch player's rocket serve. The force of the blow knocked Mitch off his feet. Pain radiated from his cheek so intensely that little pinpricks of light danced around his peripheral vision.

He remained on his side in the sand for a few seconds, taking stock of his surroundings. The hush of the crowd, the faint crashing of water onto sand from the other side of the makeshift grandstand, the suffocating heat of the Brazilian afternoon. Finally, he rolled to his knees and sat back on his haunches, waving off the medical personnel making their way onto the sand.

"Are you okay, man?" Charlie asked, crouching in front of him.

"Yeah. I just need a minute." Mitch pushed himself off the sand. Claps and cheers rippled through the crowd as he stood, boosting his spirits. The fans had been electrifying in their support the entire tournament, and this quarterfinal match was no exception.

Charlie gave him a fist bump, their post-play ritual whether they'd won or lost the point. Mitch brought a hand to his cheek, stretching his jaw in different angles to test the pain. Good thing he'd turned his face to the side before getting nailed. He'd probably have a nice shiner, but on the flip side, his nose wasn't broken.

He located his sunglasses in the sand where they'd landed after flying off his face during the collision. A large crack ran through the right lens, and he frowned. At least they hadn't shattered. He could've injured his retina.

Raising his shades toward the head referee, Mitch pointed to the lens, a silent request to replace them. The woman, whistle still in her mouth, acknowledged him with a nod. He trudged over to the side-line. It was hot—like being locked in a sauna with no way out—and he'd jump at any chance for a mini timeout.

Not to mention the break in action would hopefully stop the scoring spree the other team was currently enjoying. The number one seeded Dutch team had won the first set easily. And that ace-serve, courtesy of Mitch's face, had brought up match point in the second. A demoralizing end to such a strong tournament for his first as a senior.

He tossed his useless Oakleys onto his chair and retrieved his backup shades from his bag, wiping them clean with a towel. Heading back to the court, he slapped Charlie's outstretched hand before taking his place on the left side of the court.

"Let's go, baby!" Charlie shouted, slow clapping a few times to pump them up for the next point. His energy amped up the crowd, and Mitch as well. They made a good team, feeding off each other's enthusiasm, especially when one of them struggled, as he was now. He'd been the serving target for most of the game, the Dutch team no doubt trying to wear him down, get into his head, and capitalize on his inexperience.

The shrill squeal of the ref's whistle cut through the rumble of the crowd, and the background music faded, signaling the start of the next rally. This time, Mitch was ready for the serve. His forearms connected with the ball near the baseline, and he bumped it toward his teammate. As he jogged toward the net, his eyes tracked Charlie's pass.

"Angle!" Charlie screamed as Mitch leapt.

Mitch hammered a crosscourt spike past the blocker, proving to everyone in attendance that he wasn't afraid of a showdown at the net. The ball hit the sand, kissing the edge of the out-of-bounds tape on the other side. Charlie wanted angle? That was about as much angle as he could get.

"Nice one, buddy!" Charlie yelled. He trotted over to Mitch and held his hands up for a double high five.

"Thanks for that call, man." Mitch patted his teammate on the back. "I was planning to go line."

"That was all you," Charlie said as they turned and walked together to the baseline. There wasn't a lot of time to discuss the game between points, so they had to make each second count. "Not many people can make that shot. Let's get the next one too."

"You got it." Mitch slapped his hand again and Charlie went back to serve.

The ball sailed over the net, and Mitch relaxed his posture, still razor focused on the opposing team passing the ball back and forth. As the Dutch spiker went to deliver an offensive blow over the net, Charlie was there to meet him. The ball ricocheted off his fingertips.

Mitch sprinted toward the opposite side of the court and dove, but it wasn't enough. The ball landed in the sand, barely out of reach, officially ending his first World Tour tournament.

"I'm bummed we lost," Charlie said after their recovery session with the athletic trainer. "All things considered though, we really had no business making it as far as we did. I mean, the quarterfinals in our first tournament together? Not to mention your first as a senior? Crazy."

"I have good teachers for sure." Mitch followed Charlie out of the training facility, the heat immediately engulfing him. The early evening still hadn't brought a relief to the temperatures, and he was grateful for the reprieve of the air-conditioned building after a grueling game. He rubbed some beads of sweat off his forehead with the crook of his arm. His cheek was still tender from getting hit with the ball, though the worst of the pain had faded. "Those guys better watch themselves because we're coming for them next time."

Charlie whooped. "You know it, baby!" He turned to give Mitch a high five.

A trio of teens—two boys and a girl—approached them. One of the boys held up a phone. "Please? Picture?" he asked, excitedly, in heavily accented English.

"Sure, no problem." Mitch took the phone in his hand. It hadn't taken long for him to get used to being approached by people after his games. Standing beside the boy, he gestured for the others to crowd in. He snapped a few selfies, before handing the device back to the owner. "Did you watch the match?"

The other boy nodded, his eyes lit with excitement. "We cheer for you."

The girl looked at Mitch with a shy expression that reminded him a lot of McKenzie when he'd first met her. Had they only known each other for eighteen months? So much had happened between them that those days when she hardly talked to him seemed like a lifetime ago.

"Thanks for coming out to cheer us on," Charlie said. "We appreciate the support."

After a few autographs, the elated teens left, and Mitch and Charlie continued their walk to the bus that would take them back to their hotel. They'd only made it a few steps when they were stopped again, this time by a woman who looked vaguely familiar.

"It's good to see you playing on the world stage again," she said, sticking out her hand. "I don't know if you remember me. I'm Tara Nielson from *Stars of the Sand*. I did an interview with you and Doug shortly after Junior Worlds."

Mitch shook her hand. "Oh yeah, it's nice to see you again." If he remembered correctly, Tara was one of the founders of *Stars of the Sand*, the official fan magazine and podcast of beach volleyball.

"Listen," Tara said. "If you're up for it, I'd love to sit down and talk with you about your return to competition. You caused quite the stir when you left the circuit." Her expression sobered. "My condolences on Doug's passing."

"Thank you." Mitch's voice cracked. Mention of Doug's name pricked at his heart, though not as much as it would've a few months ago. He glanced at Charlie a few feet away, chatting with the Brazilian duo who'd just arrived for the first semifinal match. Talking to the media had never been an issue for Mitch, even if it still felt strange how much of a stir he'd caused on tour already. He turned back to Tara. "That sounds great. I'd love to talk with you."

"Perfect." She pulled out her phone and tapped away at the screen. "Why don't you give me your contact info and I'll be in touch with the date?"

He gave her his email address and exchanged a few more pleasantries before saying goodbye. Then he joined Charlie for the short bus ride back to the hotel.

Two hours later, Mitch stepped onto the balcony of his room for privacy and called McKenzie. *Please answer,* he pleaded. Their free time hadn't matched up much since she'd left for Vegas, and the few texts they'd shared in the last few days hadn't been enough.

After a few rings, she accepted the video chat. He smiled as soon as her face filled his phone screen.

"What happened to your face?" she asked.

He gingerly touched his cheek with two fingers. His quick assessment of the injury before his shower hadn't shown anything too noticeable. "I got hit by the ball. I didn't think it looked that bad."

"Your right cheek is swollen. I can tell by the way it puckers when you smile."

She'd noticed something so minuscule? "You must spend a lot of time checking me out."

She shrugged. "You're nice to look at."

Her lack of hesitation made him chuckle. "Are you back from Vegas yet?"

"Not yet. We go home tomorrow. My meet was earlier today."

"How'd it go?" Turning the deck chair to face the ocean, he lowered himself onto it.

Seagulls bickered with one another in the fading light as they circled the hotel's private beach ten floors below him. Despite the earlier loss, he couldn't be anything but grateful. He was in Brazil, playing the game he loved.

"I placed fourth. Can you believe it? I haven't finished that high in a competition since I was a junior." She flashed him a brilliant smile. "And I won bars and beam."

"Zee, that's amazing!" He stretched his legs out in front of him. "I'm so proud of you."

"If I'd scored just a few tenths higher on vault, I would've won the whole thing." McKenzie pursed her lips to the side and then sighed. "If only I could do the harder one …"

Mitch's heart went out to her. He couldn't imagine how hard it would be to have to face her fear every single day. "Hey. You've got to celebrate the small steps. Today was a win. Be proud of that."

Her mouth lifted in a tiny smile.

"And think of it this way, you finished higher in your competition than I did in mine."

She cocked her head to the side before understanding dawned in her eyes. "You lost today? I'm sorry, Mitch. You were doing so well."

He lifted one shoulder. "I'm disappointed, but there are some takeaways to improve on. I mean, we were the obvious underdogs."

"You weren't expected to win yesterday either," she said, shifting onto her side on her hotel bed.

"You watched?"

She nodded. "I caught the replay on my phone when I was supposed to be sleeping last night. You're so fun to watch. And the commentators were singing your praises."

They weren't the only ones. Mitch shook his head in disbelief. "I can't believe all the hype already. When I showed up at our qualification match on Wednesday, it was like Charlie and I were already playing in the finals instead of trying to earn a spot in the Main Draw. I mean, I knew word had gotten out that I was making a comeback, but I didn't expect it to be this big of a deal. Today I was asked to do an interview with *Stars of the Sand*."

"What's that?"

"It's a magazine. They interview players to give fans an inside look at their favorite athletes. They also cover news stories around the beach volleyball community. It's crazy. I've only played in one tournament."

"I believe it." McKenzie sat up. "It's not even about how good you are. You're so likable that everyone wants to root for you. I love that about you."

Leaning forward in his seat, he brought the phone closer to his face and flashed her a teasing smile. "Gosh, Zee. You're making me blush. What else do you love about me? My witty sense of humor? How about my rugged good looks?"

"Certainly not your ego." Her laugh was light, happy, and Mitch loved hearing it. Talking to her was exactly what he needed after a tough loss. "Don't let this interview go to your head."

"I won't," he said, chuckling. Then he stopped as a sudden wave of homesickness washed over him. Not for home, necessarily, but for her. He studied her lovely features on the screen, wishing she were there with him in person. She could watch his games during the day, and they'd sit out here in the evening as the sun went down. It wouldn't matter what they talked about, or if they talked at all. He just wanted her here.

"What's wrong?" she asked.

He shook his head. "Nothing. I miss you is all."

Her smile turned soft. "I miss you too. But I should go. Aria wanted to see The Strip, so she dragged Evie along with her. They'll be back soon."

Did she have to go already? The temptation to convince her to throw caution to the wind, to forget the secrecy, threatened to overwhelm his reason. He couldn't do that to her though. The repercussions would be a lot more severe for her than for him if word got out. There was wisdom in taking the slow route. Not to mention he'd promised to keep it casual until after the Global Elites. And a promise to McKenzie held more weight than any other to him.

"Call me when you get home tomorrow?" he asked. "I'll just be watching the matches. We don't leave for Cancun until Monday."

McKenzie nodded. "I will."

Silence came over them, though neither moved to hang up. Would he always miss her this much when he was gone? That would make a volleyball career difficult to pursue. But he also never wanted to become complacent about being away from her.

A sound in the background jerked McKenzie's attention from the screen. She turned back to the phone, her eyes wide. "That's Aria. I have to go. I'll call you later." Then she was gone, leaving Mitch with only the sound of the waves and squawking gulls to keep him company.

Chapter Thirty-Nine

The Thursday following the Vegas invitational, McKenzie spent her birthday in the gym. She stood next to Evie near the uneven bars, watching Aria train a release skill that had been giving her trouble all week. Her fingertips grazed the bar as she attempted to catch it again, but the force of her momentum ripped them off before she could get a good grip, and she crashed to the mat.

The sound of skin splatting against the leather-covered foam sent sympathy tingles across McKenzie's arms, and she grimaced. She'd been there too many times to count—it never felt good.

"Try it again," Gary's authoritative voice called from a few paces away. His stone-faced expression made his displeasure obvious.

Aria grumbled and pushed herself up from the mat, brushing chalk dust off her legs. She mounted the bars and tried the release again with the same result. Her scream of frustration rang through the gym.

Gary sighed, running a hand down his face. "That's enough for today. You're up, McKenzie. Aria, pay attention to her technique on that release."

McKenzie squeezed her eyes shut, letting out an almost audible groan before opening them again. Could he have said anything worse? On her way to chalk her hands, she stopped next to her teammate.

"You're letting go too soon. It's bringing your body too far from the bar," she said. Even though she hated being the object of Aria's grudge, learning new skills never came easy for McKenzie, and she understood the frustration that came with not being able to get it right. "I can help you work on the timing if you want."

Her teammate's glare caused her to shrink back a little against her will.

"I know how to do it," Aria hissed under her breath. Her eyes flicked to Gary, but he was busy rubbing chalk dust on the high bar.

Way to make things worse, McKenzie chided herself. She shrugged, attempting to appear unbothered by the coldness. "I was only trying to help."

"I don't need your help," Aria snapped. "You're not my coach." She bumped McKenzie's shoulder as she passed.

McKenzie sighed and stepped up to the bars. Ever since this stupid feud started back at nationals, she'd tried her best to let it roll off her back. Mitch still seemed to think Aria's resentment would fade eventually. He obviously underestimated her ability to hold a grudge.

McKenzie left the gym a few hours later, eager to get home. Dinner with her roommates at Curry & Spice, her favorite restaurant in Buena Hills, was a far more preferable way to spend her birthday than being with Little Miss Negative Nelly.

As she walked to her car, motion to her right caught her attention. A man leaned against a gray sedan a short distance away. His focus zeroed in on her, and he pushed off the car, heading toward her. A camera hung around his neck, not quite hiding the lanyard holding some form of white tag underneath.

Goosebumps prickled against her neck. Occasionally, the program directors at SoCal Elite would invite the press to do a story leading up to a big event, but McKenzie hadn't heard of anything like that happening today.

A few years before, a swimmer training at SoCal Elite had broken a longstanding world record, and every sports journalist in Southern California had swarmed the facility, searching for an exclusive interview with the athlete. There were so many people buzzing around the entrance, no one could get inside the building. It had disrupted everyone's training. Ever since, reporters weren't even allowed in the parking lot without an invitation.

All this was fine with McKenzie. She got more than enough exposure to the media at competitions without having to worry about dodging them every day at training.

What was she supposed to do about *this* man here right now? Walk faster until she got to her car and lock herself inside? Dart back into the building until he left? She could be waiting for quite a while.

Her heart thumped faster as he approached, and she clutched her keys tighter in her hand. What did he want with her anyway? Compared to other athletes training at SoCal Elite, she was small fries.

He stopped in front of her. "Are you McKenzie Bowman?"

"Y-yes?" *Confidence,* she reprimanded. *Journalists can smell fear.*

The man stuck out his hand. "Lance Harrison. I'm a writer from—"

"You're not supposed to be here." She stood a bit taller, though it didn't eliminate much of the height difference.

Lance ignored her. "I have a few questions for you about Mitch Skaggs. He works here, right?"

Alarm bells went off in her mind. "N-no comment." She kept walking in the direction of her car. Unfortunately, Lance followed.

"Rumor has it you two are an item."

That stopped her. Word couldn't possibly have gotten out so quickly. She hadn't even seen him since the night before he left on tour. Unless ...

No. Mitch had promised he wouldn't say anything. She turned to Lance. "Who did you say you were?"

"Lance Harrison from *Stars of the Sand.* I wanted to get your thoughts on Mitch's quick rise to stardom on the World Tour. How does that make you feel to see him become such an instant fan favorite?"

McKenzie's blood chilled. *Stars of the Sand?* Wasn't that the same magazine Mitch had mentioned on the phone the other day? She fought against the urge to run. *Don't break down. Not here.* Holding her head high, she turned to Lance, attempting to exude more courage than she felt. "I have nothing to say. Excuse me." She continued to her car, not looking back to see if he'd followed. Thankfully, he didn't.

She couldn't get out of the parking lot fast enough. Her mind swirled the entire drive home. *Had* Mitch mentioned her in the interview? She knew he'd never intentionally do anything to hurt her, but maybe something had slipped out by accident.

With a firm shake of her head, she stopped the accusations before they went any further. After all, she hadn't asked Lance where he'd heard the rumor. And stress often had a tendency of sending her on a running leap down the slippery slope of conclusions.

Her hatred of the media aside, if she were any other person, their relationship leaking out to the press wouldn't be a big deal. Then again, if she were any other person, they wouldn't need to keep it a secret at all. But the worry of being cut off before she'd figured out her plan B still lived rent-free in her brain. What was she going to do?

Don't overreact. Mom didn't even follow volleyball. Even if an article did come from this, the chances of her mom reading it were slim. Everything would be fine as soon as McKenzie cleared things up with Mitch.

When she arrived at her house, the driveway was already occupied by her roommates' cars, so she parked at the curb. Unable to take the stress any longer, she pulled her phone from her bag and opened her latest text thread with Mitch.

> McKenzie: Have you already had your interview with Stars of the Sand?

Thankfully, three dots immediately popped up, and she held her breath, waiting anxiously for a response.

> Mitch: No, we're still nailing down the date. Why?

Should she tell him about the reporter? It wasn't the sort of thing she wanted to get into over text messages, and he couldn't do anything about it from so far away, so what was the point in bringing it up?

McKenzie: Just curious.

She clicked off the screen, feeling slightly better about the situation. Lance was probably just grasping for a story that wasn't there. Well, technically it was, but the status of her relationship with Mitch was no one's business but their own.

After retrieving her bag from the back seat and locking her car, she cut across the grass to the house. A large cardboard box sat on the edge of the porch. McKenzie climbed the stairs for a closer look. It was addressed to her.

Interesting. She wasn't expecting anything. It had been a long time since her parents had sent her a birthday present. In their eyes, paying for her living expenses was enough of a gift.

Carrying both the box and her bag through the front door was a struggle, but somehow, she managed to get them both upstairs. Once in her room, she dropped her duffel down near the door and sat on her bed with the box on the floor in front of her. She slid her house key through the tape to break the seal. A card with two words printed on it rested on the top layer of sparkly silver and blue tissue paper.

Hug me.

"What the heck?" She set the card down next to her and tugged on the tissue paper. She kept pulling, and pulling, and ... Sheesh, there was a lot of it. When she finally cleared the box, she reached inside.

Soft fur caressed her hands as she pulled out a large brown teddy bear with a blue bow around its neck. She laughed. What was she supposed to do with a stuffed animal this size? "Hug me?" Still chuckling, she awkwardly wrapped her arms around it and squeezed.

"Happy birthday, Zee." Mitch's deep voice sounded odd coming from such a fluffy bear, sending McKenzie into a fit of giggles. "I'm sorry I can't be there to celebrate turning twenty-three with you in person, but whenever you're missing me, just give Cuddles the Bear some love and it's like I'm right there with you. I love you."

This cheesy gift was so *him*—doing whatever he could to get her to laugh. Even thousands of miles away, he'd gone the extra mile to make her feel special. No one had ever done that before. She loved him even more for it.

Setting Cuddles aside, she walked over to her bag and retrieved her phone. She didn't expect Mitch to answer, but she dialed his number anyway. After the fourth ring, it went to his voicemail.

"It's me," she said after the beep. "Thank you for the birthday gift. No one has ever given me a giant talking teddy bear before." She reached over and wrapped an arm around Cuddles. "But I love it. And I ... I love you."

The words still felt strange in her mouth. Not because they weren't true. They were absolutely cemented in stone. But aside from that night at his apartment, she'd never said them out loud to anyone besides her brother.

"Anyway, good luck in your game tonight. I'll be cheering for you over here. Talk to you soon." She hesitated, keeping the phone to her ear, not wanting to break the connection with him, even if he wasn't on the other side listening. Then she lowered it, ending the call. She glanced at the bear staring back at her. "Well, Cuddles, I guess it's just you and me now."

She moved the stuffed animal to the corner of her bed, her hand lingering on the soft fur for a moment. Then she left her room to get ready for dinner, all worries of the media replaced with thoughts of Mitch.

Chapter Forty

McKenzie hated being late. It always drew attention to herself, something she tried hard to avoid. Yet, a week after her weird encounter with that reporter, she found herself rushing home after practice to shower before meeting up with the rest of the girls at Behind the Veil. If she skipped washing her hair, she might make it before Elise found *the dress*.

Stepping out of the shower, she hastily toweled off and scrambled into her clothes. On her way to her room, she sent off a quick text to Elise.

> McKenzie: Sorry, practice ran long. I'm leaving in five.

She didn't wait for a reply before swiping the mascara wand over her eyelashes. Elise wouldn't mind her tardiness, McKenzie was sure of it, but it wasn't every day she got to help a good friend pick out her wedding dress.

After gathering her hair into a simple ponytail, she grabbed her keys and wallet and hurried from the room. She flew down the stairs and threw the door open, freezing at the sight that greeted her.

"Mom," McKenzie sputtered. "W-what are you doing here?"

Her mother stood on the porch—her pert nose angled in the air as critical as ever—dressed to the nines in a cream-colored pantsuit. Expensive jewelry adorned her wrists and around her neck. Not a strand of her auburn hair was out of place, perfectly styled in an elegant chignon. She lowered her arm, which had apparently been about to knock when McKenzie opened the door.

"Is that the way to greet your mother?" Mom looked to the

ceiling with a disappointed sigh. "I taught you better manners than that. Aren't you going to invite me in?"

"I was actually on my way out ..." One glimpse at her mother's stern look forced McKenzie to open the door wider. She wouldn't be leaving anytime soon. *Maybe I should text Elise and tell her I can't make it.*

Her mother strode past her, not stopping until she reached the living room. McKenzie followed mutely, because she knew Mom expected it, and not out of any desire to be in the same room as the woman.

McKenzie had counted on the distance from Seattle to Southern California keeping her mother's visits to a minimum. For the most part, it had worked like a charm. In the five years since she'd moved to the Golden State, she could count on one hand the amount of times the woman had shown her face. Which was perfectly fine, thanks very much. Mom had her own methods of making sure her daughter toed the line.

Which made her sudden appearance now so surprising. And it could only mean one thing.

She knew.

"I thought I've made myself clear you were not to let anything get in the way of your training," Mom said. "You told me yourself you'd ended things with that boy. And I trusted you were telling the truth. Not only were you dishonest with me, you've also brought the media into it."

The media? "Mom, what are you talking about?"

Her mother slipped her phone out of the dainty purse dangling from her shoulder and tapped at the screen. "Our new neighbors, Carl and Melanie Swanson—you remember them, don't you? You met them when you were home for Christmas."

McKenzie vaguely remembered meeting them in passing. They seemed like her mother's type: filthy rich and proud. That was all the information McKenzie needed to know about them.

"Anyway," Mom continued, without waiting for a response,

"they have a daughter in high school. She's quite the volleyball player, according to Melanie."

McKenzie's premonition went on full alert. Mitch had told her about how tight-knit the volleyball community was. She brought a shaking hand up to stroke her ponytail.

Mom continued. "I was having lunch with Melanie the other day. Imagine my surprise when she showed me an article in some magazine that was all about my daughter."

"W-what?"

Mom thrust her phone into McKenzie's hands. "You lied to me."

McKenzie looked down at the screen, her eyes immediately drawn to Mitch's body sprawled out inches above the sand as he dove for the ball. She scrolled down to the headline below the photo.

Beach Volleyball's Newest Superstar Off the Market

No! Nope, nope, nope. *This can't be happening.* Where had that reporter gotten his information for the story? It certainly hadn't come from her. Not to mention *Stars of the Sand* must be hurting for news if they decided to print something as insignificant as the relationship of a couple of athletes. She scrolled even further and started to read.

American Mitch Skaggs delighted the beach volleyball community with his return to professional competition earlier this month. The former Junior World champion had stepped away from the circuit shortly after his long-time teammate and best friend, Doug Jepson, passed away in an automobile accident. Though Skaggs only has two tournaments under his belt this season, he is exciting spectators and commentators alike with his scrappy defensive skills and lightning arm. And his charisma and infectious enthusiasm off the court have already cemented him near the top of the list of fan favorites, particularly with the female audience. But don't get any ideas, ladies, because this well-appointed heartthrob is taken. Here's what we know about the lucky woman who has captured his heart.

McKenzie kept scrolling, mortification fueling the flame engulfing her body the more she skimmed. This article wasn't about Mitch's return to competition. It was all about *her*. Including detailed information about her accident, her comeback, and the relationship she and Mitch had attempted to keep under wraps.

The first few pictures scattered through the article weren't so bad: her official national team headshot, receiving her silver medal after the uneven bars final at Worlds, an action shot of her on beam at the most recent National Championships.

Then she reached the final picture. As she stared at the image of her and Mitch embracing on her doorstep—the night before McKenzie left for Worlds, if she wasn't mistaken—all air escaped her lungs. It literally felt like her trachea had been reduced to the size of one of those tiny straws used in coffee shops. They might be suffi-cient to prevent burning the mouth but were worthless when trying to restore her oxygen levels.

Someone had been to her house. Months ago, judging by that last picture. Mitch hadn't even come over since November. Whoever had taken this photo had been watching them—taking photos of them—without her even knowing. What others were out there that she didn't know about? And why was all of this coming out now?

Nausea bubbled in her stomach as anger and panic flared red hot in the edges of her vision. This article wasn't even the worst part of the situation. Neither was her mom finding out about them. Though McKenzie had to admit that landed near the top.

No, being robbed of her peace of mind was far more catastrophic. As much as she hated it, her status as an elite athlete had forced her to get used to people recognizing her in public. But her home was supposed to be the one place she didn't have to worry about the media getting up in her face. Now that it had been stripped away from her, was any place safe?

Her arm gave out as though she were holding a pile of bricks instead of a small electronic device. The phone slipped from her fingers, clattering to the carpet. "I d-don't know where this c-came from. I had nothing to do with it."

Her mother's brows drew down in disappointment. "Well, if this bothers you, then it should be a clear signal about what kind of man you insist on dating."

Mitch promised he wouldn't say anything. She had to trust that. But if he wasn't responsible for this, who was? "Mom, that picture was taken—"

"Pack your things," Mom said, picking up her phone and slipping it back into her purse. "I think it would be best if you come stay with me for a while."

McKenzie threw up in her mouth. The bile burned all the way back down. "For how long?"

Mom fixed her with a hard look. "For as long as it takes for you to reclaim your focus."

That declaration sent McKenzie's heart plunging all the way to her toes. She trudged up the stairs to pack, though someone might as well have slapped handcuffs to her wrists and led her straight to her jail cell.

Chapter Forty-One

Something was wrong. Mitch couldn't say exactly what, only that somehow he sensed it. He hadn't talked to McKenzie since before he'd arrived in Salinas for his third tournament. Not for lack of trying on his part. He'd held religiously to his promise to call every day, but for the last week, all his calls went straight to her voicemail. And she hadn't responded to any of his texts either.

He understood their schedules didn't always match up. Deep down though, he didn't think that was the case here. They'd played phone tag before, and she'd never ghosted him like this.

Focus, he thought as he sat in the timeout box, attempting to reign in his worries. He was minutes away from playing in the bronze medal match of only his third World Tour tournament. Charlie was counting on him to have his head on straight. Good thing Mitch had years of experience in suppressing his emotions.

His right leg bounced rapidly while he soaked in the pulsing electricity of the fans on the other side of the sand. There was nothing more exhilarating than a packed grandstand full of people anticipating a big match. Mitch appreciated that enthusiasm now.

Umbrellas dotted the seats, protecting people from the mist. Those who didn't have one were dressed in ponchos. Apparently, a little rain wasn't enough to keep the good people of Salinas away from their volleyball.

Mitch raised the hem of his red sleeveless jersey to wipe the lingering moisture from his warm-up off his face. Playing in the rain wasn't the most pleasant experience, but as Doug always used to say, "Any day you get to play volleyball is a good day."

This one's for you, buddy. Ever since Mama B had encouraged him to dedicate his comeback to Doug, Mitch had found himself having these silent one-sided conversations with his friend. It gave him a weird sort of strength, a peace that he hadn't felt before in the years since his passing. Like maybe Doug wasn't too far away, after all.

Just then, the background music stopped, and the emcee's voice came over the loudspeaker. He introduced both Portuguese players first, to wild applause from the crowd. Before the cheers died down completely, he turned his attention to the men in red. As the captain of the team, Charlie was announced first. He stood, turning back to slap Mitch's hands before trotting onto their side of the court, waving to the fans.

As Mitch listened to his introduction being made in Spanish, he took a deep breath in, puffing his cheeks. He blew it out slowly, aware of the camera pointed at him.

"And now," the emcee shouted, switching to English, "he's a junior world champion, two-time junior US champion, and current record holder for the most successful digs in a single season on the junior circuit. Please welcome to the court, wearing number two, Mr. Dig Man, Mitch Skaggs!"

Mitch launched from his seat. He kissed the pads of his fingers, then turned them toward the camera on his way out to the sand, acknowledging the cheering fans with both hands. When he reached Charlie, they both jumped, meeting in a chest bump.

At the head ref's whistle, all four players trotted to the net to shake hands. As Mitch turned to make his way to the back of the court to prepare for the opposing team's serve, Charlie patted him on the back.

"You good, man?" he asked, raising an eyebrow. "I need your head on straight if we're going to win this."

Mitch hadn't voiced his fears about McKenzie out loud to his teammate, but even he could admit he hadn't done the best job at hiding the fact that something was bothering him. Now wasn't the time to get into it though. Charlie was absolutely right. Now was the time to focus. "Yep. Let's play some volleyball," he said, holding out a fist.

Charlie bumped it with his own. "You got it."

Mitch took his position near the baseline, bending his knees with his hands on his thighs. As he squinted into the rain, he attempted to push all lingering thoughts of McKenzie from his mind. There was nothing he could do about her now. In twenty-four hours, he'd be on his way home to her. Maybe then he'd be able to figure out what was going on.

For now, he had a game to play. The piercing shrill of the head ref's whistle signaled the start of the game.

Chapter Forty-Two

"You need to eat," Mom scolded Monday evening after they'd returned to the timeshare following her second training of the day.

McKenzie stopped pushing food around her plate at the small kitchen table to aim a hard stare at her mother by the sink. "I'm not hungry."

A week had passed since she'd hastily packed a suitcase with the basics and left her house with only a quick note to her roommates. Since then, her anger had only grown with every word that spewed from her mom's mouth.

The towel in Mom's hand stilled over the stock pot she dried. "Really, McKenzie. Stop moping. When you make the Global Elite team and go on to win the all-around, you'll thank me for encouraging you to stay focused."

"That's doubtful," McKenzie grumbled to the uneaten vegetable stir-fry on her plate.

Mom pursed her lips, tilting her head to the side and scrutinizing her daughter. "Is this still about that boy? How many times do we have to go through this? If you want any hope of becoming a Global Elite champion, you have no time for ... *boyfriends.*" Her tone dripped with derision.

McKenzie ground her teeth but remained silent. Yes, she wanted to be with Mitch, yet this went so far beyond him. This was about claiming her life.

The lecture continued. "If you're that desperate to be in a relationship, you'll have plenty of time to date after the Global Elites are over."

I'm not desperate for a relationship. I'm desperate to be away from you. "I'll bet you have a candidate all picked out too."

Mom paused in a crouching position, about to put the pot away in a low cabinet. "I don't appreciate your tone, young lady." She slid the dish away and stood. "As a matter of fact, Melanie's oldest son is a year or two older than you. Good kid, graduated from Stanford. I think he'd make a great match for you."

"I'm not interested."

"Honestly, McKenzie, you're acting childish. It's time for you to grow up."

McKenzie's head shot up, nostrils flaring. She was bound to crack eventually, and that moment was apparently now. "And how exactly do you expect me to do that when you've never given me the chance to? You're always breathing down my neck, making every little decision and pointing out *every little imperfection*." She accentuated the last three words as if they were each their own sentence.

"*McKenzie*," Mom gasped. "How dare you—"

McKenzie held up a hand. "No. It's my turn to speak. I've spent years trying to live up to your expectations. My entire life I've tried everything to make you proud. But I've realized something."

She clenched her jaw to keep it from trembling as she came face to face with the years of hurt caused by the woman in front of her.

"Nothing I do will ever be good enough for you." She swiped at the stubborn tear trickling down her cheek. "This was supposed to be *my* dream. But you've stolen it and turned it into something ugly. So, I'm done. I can't do this anymore."

Pushing her plate away from her, she stood so fast the movement knocked her chair backward onto the floor.

"McKenzie," Mom called after her retreating back.

At her bedroom door, McKenzie turned. "Go home, Mother. Take your money, and your toxic need to control me, and leave me to figure my life out on my own." She slammed the door so hard the walls shook.

Her breaths emerged shaky as she leaned her back against the door, attempting to ease the inferno burning through her body. Then she picked up her duffel bag and tossed it on top of her suitcase—she hadn't bothered to unpack when she'd first arrived at the timeshare —and left the room again.

"Where are you going?" Mom asked as McKenzie strode purposefully to the front door. "How do you expect to pay for yourself?"

McKenzie barely spared her mom a glance. "I don't know, but I'm looking forward to figuring it out." With that, she dragged her things out of her mother's life and into the dark night outside.

Where am I even going? she thought as she started walking. Her car was still parked at the house in Buena Hills, but the fresh air felt good on her skin, which was flushed hot with anger. Walking for a bit also gave her some much-needed time to think.

But with each step she took, the adrenaline began to wear off, and reality soon set in. Her career was over, the dream she'd worked so hard to achieve shattered. And beyond that, how *was* she going to pay her bills? She'd have to get a job, but would it be able to cover all her expenses? And if she couldn't afford to live in California, where would she go? She'd made her grand exit; she refused to go crawling back to her parents.

She walked until her legs grew too tired to keep going and her hand cramped from the death grip she currently had on her suitcase handle. Stopping suddenly, she looked around, trying to decipher her location. But the all-encompassing darkness made it impossible to see any street signs.

Where am I? she thought, the first prickles of fear settling over her. Perhaps she should've figured out her ride home before leaving the hotel premises. She unzipped her bag and dug through it until she found her phone. She hadn't bothered checking it since Mom had dragged her away from Buena Hills. What was the point with the woman constantly looking over her shoulder? At least it still had some battery left. Barely.

McKenzie toggled through her contacts until she found the number she wanted. "Please be home," she pleaded to the night, lifting the phone to her ear.

A phone call interrupted Mitch's small talk with his Uber driver on the way home from the airport. He glanced at the device held in both hands between his knees, his heart jumping to his throat. *Finally!*

He'd tried calling McKenzie after the awards ceremony of the Salinas tournament the day before, but like all his other calls and texts over the last week, it had gone unanswered. He'd tossed and turned all night worrying about her.

"Do you mind if I take this?" he asked his driver, jiggling his phone in front of himself. At the man's nod, Mitch accepted the call, bringing the phone to his ear. "Hey, there you are. I've been trying to call you. I was beginning to think ..." He trailed off at the sound of sobbing on the other end. "Zee? What's wrong?"

"I had a huge fight with my mom." She barely managed to get the words out. "She found out about us. I told her I didn't want her in my life anymore, and then I left the timeshare and started walking. Now I have no idea where I am or what to do." She gasped for breath. "It's gone, Mitch. My dream is over."

Poor McKenzie. No wonder she hadn't been answering his calls. "First of all, I need you to stop and take a deep breath." He waited while she complied. The Uber pulled into the parking lot of his apartment. "That's my girl. Hang on a sec, Zee." He tapped his driver on the shoulder as they drove past his car. "Hey, can you drop me off right here?"

"Right here?" the man asked in a thick Italian accent.

"Yeah, I have somewhere I need to be." Mitch reached forward and shook the driver's hand before hopping out and retrieving his own bags from the trunk. He didn't spare the car another look before wheeling them to his SUV and shoving them in the back. Once behind the wheel, he addressed McKenzie again. "Where are you? Are you safe?"

She sniffled. "I think so. I'm sitting out front of a school in some neighborhood I found after walking for a while."

"Text me the address," Mitch said, starting his car. "I'm coming to get you. I'll be there as soon as I can."

He ended the call, tapping his fingers on the steering wheel impatiently while he waited. A whirlwind of thoughts swarmed him, one question gaining advantage over all the rest. How had Mrs. Bowman found out?

Don't worry about that right now, he thought as his phone finally pinged. Zee was priority number one. He located the address she sent in his GPS and peeled out of the parking lot with squealing tires.

It seemed to take forever to get to the elementary school the next town over from Buena Hills. *Why does SoCal always have so much traffic? Rush hour should've ended hours ago.* He really needed to make finding an apartment closer to Zee a bigger priority.

"In two hundred feet, turn right and arrive at your destination," the voice from his GPS instructed him.

"Finally," he muttered, flicking on the blinker and turning into the bus lane. He didn't bother shutting off the engine as he threw his door open and flew out. "Zee!" he called, searching desperately for any sign of her.

"Over here," a quiet voice responded.

He spotted her on a bench a short distance away, the dim emergency light illuminating her hunched over with her head in her lap. She sat up and looked at him as he rushed over.

"I'm here." He helped her stand and folded her in his arms while she broke down in more sobs. For several minutes he held her, rubbing soft circles along her back. His heart broke for her. Everything she'd worked for, gone in an instant. "What can I do?" he asked, desperate for some way to make things right.

McKenzie pulled back, her focus remaining on the dark pavement. "I just want to go home," she muttered.

Her bleak expression tugged at him. "Okay." Reluctantly, he

dropped his arms and led her to the car, seeing her safely inside before retrieving her bags and tossing them in the back next to his.

She said very little on the drive back to Buena Hills. Her head rested against the window, and she kept her gaze directed at the blackness outside.

As they passed SoCal Elite on the outskirts of Buena Hills, he couldn't take the silence any longer. "How'd she find out?"

McKenzie didn't bother looking away from the window. "There was an article about us in that magazine you told me about. She saw it."

"What?" That made no sense. Wait a minute, the magazine *he* told her about? "Is that why you asked me if I'd had my interview? Zee, I swear I didn't say anything. I'd never betray your trust like that."

"I know," she whispered before morphing into silence again.

Mitch reached over the center console and covered her hand resting on her thigh. "We'll figure this out."

Nothing but silence followed his statement. In fact, she didn't say anything for the rest of the drive back to her house. When they pulled into her driveway, she let herself out of the car, not waiting for him on the sidewalk like she usually did. Instead, she trudged up the walk, head down, shoulders slumped. Mitch retrieved her bags and followed.

"Oh my gosh, Zee," Beej shrieked when they'd entered the house. "We've been so worried!" She, Hallie, Kendall, and Elise surrounded McKenzie, engulfing her in hugs.

McKenzie just stood there in a daze, not reciprocating the affection but not pulling away either.

Hallie took over the fretting next. "All you said in your note was that you were going to stay with your mom for a while. Are you okay?"

"I'm okay." The emptiness in McKenzie's eyes contradicted her statement. She wasn't okay at all. She appeared as though she'd given up on life.

Mitch approached her, wrapping her up in his arms. She'd once called his hugs magic. She could use some of that right now.

Although she slid her arms around his waist, he could tell her heart wasn't in it, and after a moment, she placed a hand on his chest and gently pushed him back. "I think I want to be alone for a while," she said, taking a step toward the stairs.

As she made her exit, he took in the questioning looks of the other women. Unfortunately, he didn't have much more information than they did. "Zee," he called before McKenzie could disappear completely.

She stopped halfway up, only turning her head enough to glance at him over her shoulder.

Mitch resisted the urge to ask her to come back down. "Better days will come. Remember that. I won't stop fighting for you."

She paused for a few seconds before nodding and disappearing up the stairs.

Elise's hand on his arm captured his attention a minute later. "What happened? She left a note, but it didn't say much. And she wouldn't answer our texts. Rory said Seth is especially frantic."

Mitch lifted his shoulders, then dropped them helplessly. "She didn't tell me much. Only that her mom found out about us from some article and came here to keep an eye on her. They had a big fight tonight, and that's when she called me."

"That's terrible," Beej said. Hallie and Kendall nodded in agreement.

Mention of the article had Mitch pulling out his phone and finding the *Stars of the Sand* website. There, front and center, an action shot of him during one of the tournaments stared back at him. He scrolled down to the headline. And stopped. A few expletives escaped his mouth as he began to skim the contents of the article. It read more like a gossip column than a serious news story, sharing details of her personal life and their relationship.

When he reached the picture of them sitting on her doorstep, he swore again. Did these reporters have any decency? *No wonder she's so upset.*

He held his screen out in front of him so the others could see it. They crowded around his phone to read. After a moment of silence, Hallie said, "McKenzie hates the media. Who would do this to her?"

"I don't know," Mitch said.

Elise touched his arm again. "What're you going to do?"

Mitch buzzed his lips and then shrugged. "I'm going to find out who's responsible, I guess. And wait until McKenzie's ready to talk."

"When do you leave for your next tournament?" she asked.

His heart sank. "Friday." That didn't leave him a lot of time. But how was he supposed leave again knowing McKenzie was in so much pain?

"We'll try to talk to her too," Beej said, handing him back his phone. "She'll get through this."

"How do you know?"

Elise gave him a small smile. "Because of what you said back there. You're not going to give up on her. And neither are we."

Chapter Forty-Three

McKenzie woke to a scratching at her bedroom door. Sunlight streamed through her closed eyelids. *What time is it?* She turned over, groaning at the pain splitting her forehead. *Better question, what day is it?*

She'd hardly left her room since going all psycho on Mom and sending her dreams up in smoke. Eventually, she'd have to dust herself off and figure out how to earn a living, but she needed time to mourn wasting her entire life training for something that was now out of reach.

Whispers drifted through the door. Some stifled giggles. And more scratching. What could possibly be going on out there?

McKenzie forced her eyes open as her roommates successfully broke into her room. Kendall entered first, shoving a bobby pin into her front pocket. Hallie followed, carrying a tray. Elise and Beej came in last.

"Wakey wakey, eggs and bakey," Kendall sing-songed, dropping onto the edge of the bed.

McKenzie rubbed her hands down the sides of her face and sat up.

"Actually, it's oatmeal and berries," Hallie said placing the tray on McKenzie's lap. "But that didn't have as nice a ring to it, don't you think?"

Elise set a mug next to the bowl. "And coffee with coconut milk, exactly the way you like it."

"Thanks." McKenzie bent forward, letting the steam wafting from the oatmeal warm her face. "What's all this?" She blew on a spoonful of oats and berries before sliding it into her mouth.

"It's been four days, Zee," Elise said, claiming part of the bed next to Kendall. "We've let you have your alone time like you asked. Now we're joining this pity party."

Beej bobbed her head in agreement. "Seth's worried sick about you. Will you please answer his texts so he can stop calling me?"

He *must* be desperate for information if he'd resorted to pestering his ex-girlfriend. He and Beej hadn't spoken since November.

"Mitch has tried calling too," Elise said.

That only added to the guilt McKenzie felt for pulling away. "I turned my phone off after the fifth call from Gary." The constant ringing had been enough to send her into a full-blown panic attack.

Elise placed her hand on the lump of blankets that was McKenzie's knee. "Do you know who's responsible for the article?"

McKenzie took a sip of coffee, then lowered her mug, keeping her eyes on the steaming liquid inside. "No. And I feel icky that someone was taking pictures of us without our knowledge. Especially here. Is nothing sacred?"

"It's a total breach of privacy," Hallie agreed. "That's why Mitch called the magazine as soon as he found out. *Stars of the Sand* isn't a gossip column. At least that's what his contact told him. They sacked the reporter."

McKenzie sighed, the guilt at home in her stomach making itself even comfier. While she'd shut herself into her safe cocoon away from life, Mitch had been on the outside, protecting her all along. He was too good for her.

"If that's not how they operate, how was the article even published in the first place?" Kendall rolled her eyes.

"Who knows." Beej pulled her legs into her chest, wrapping her arms around her knees. "Zee, I hope you know we wouldn't do this to you. We know how much you hate the media."

McKenzie swallowed her last bite of oatmeal. "I never thought you did. And I know it wasn't Mitch. Seth is too protective of me so I know he didn't do it. But who else is there?" She slid the tray with the empty bowl and mug down her legs so she could adjust her sitting position.

Kendall popped up to take it from her, setting it on the desk nearby. "We're your friends though. I mean, it's hard to picture anyone not liking you, but is there anyone you can think of who might be holding a grudge or something?"

McKenzie's eyes flew to her as realization dawned. "Aria." How did she not think of her earlier. For months she'd put up with her teammate's passive-aggressive jealousy, worrying about how far it would lead. She should've expected this. But what was Aria's motive? Was she only hoping to rattle McKenzie? Or had the intent been to make her quit altogether? Either way, Aria had gotten her wish.

Elise wagged a finger. "I've heard that name. Was she the girl who used to try to flirt with Mitch back when he first started working at your gym?"

"Mm-hmm," McKenzie said. "She's been jealous ever since I made the World team and she didn't."

"Petty much?" Hallie scoffed. "I'm sorry, Zee."

"She has nothing to be jealous of anymore now that I'm officially out of the picture." McKenzie rubbed at her temples, trying to ease the pounding headache. Crying was the worst. "I should start looking for a job."

The prospect left a bad taste in her mouth. She had nothing against working. She just couldn't handle the painful reminder of all the years she'd devoted to gymnastics. *What a waste.*

Kendall slid onto the bed next to McKenzie, and Beej scooted over to take up the spot on her other side.

"You're really not going back?" Kendall asked.

McKenzie leaned against her. "There's no way I can pay for it anymore. I shouldn't have overreacted, but I was so mad at my mom, and I didn't think first."

"You had every right to react the way you did," Hallie said. "You've been dealing with so much your whole life. It's perfectly reasonable for you to want your mom to give you some space."

"I feel like I've blown up my family." McKenzie ran a hand

through her hair, scrunching her nose. She probably should wash her hair at some point. "I'm not usually the one to rock the boat. That's Seth's expertise."

Soft chuckles rippled through the group.

"Look, Zee," Kendall said, her mouth still turned up in amusement. "My childhood was also rough, so I know a little of how you feel. It wasn't until I moved in with the Abernathys that I learned that family isn't always flesh and blood. They're the people in your life who know your flaws and love you anyway."

Hallie shifted at the foot of the bed, pulling her legs into a criss-cross position. "And that's what we're here for. No matter what happens, you have a place with us."

"They're right," Elise said. "Whether you decide to get a job, go to college, or figure out a way to keep training is your decision. And we'll love and support you in whatever you choose. You're part of our family now. We're sisters—always."

"And sisters never let sisters cry alone." Beej wrapped her arms around McKenzie's shoulders and pulled her down to lay across her lap. The other women crowded around them in a group hug.

McKenzie smiled for the first time in days as she gave in to the comfort of their words. "I love you guys too." She soaked in all the warmth of their little cuddle fest before reality sunk in once again. "I don't know what to do."

Hallie sat up again. "If you really wanted to give up, you could walk away with no regrets. It sounds like you still have some unfinished business to take care of."

With her head still resting against Beej's legs, she turned her face to the ceiling. "I can't go back now. Not without a way to pay for my training."

Kendall furrowed her brows. "Sure you can. The Global Elite Games are in June. Trials are in, what, a month? We can help you figure out how to make it work."

"I don't know ..." McKenzie bit her lip.

"Don't think about the obstacles right now. What do *you* want?" Hallie asked.

The answer came automatically. "I want to go to the Global Elite Games." The words emerged barely above a whisper.

"What was that?" Kendall cupped a hand to her ear.

McKenzie spoke a tiny bit louder but still hesitant. "I want to go to the Global Elite Games."

"I can't hear you!"

As loud as she could, McKenzie screamed, *"I want to go to the Global Elite Games!"* Cheers bounced around the room from the other women.

When the noise died down again, Kendall leaned over and looked McKenzie in the eye. "Then go claim your spot. But this time, do it for yourself. Not your mother, or Gary, or anyone else. Do it because you're worth it."

Beej shifted so she could pull her phone from her jeans pocket. She let out a long groan as she jabbed at the screen for a few seconds. "Seth's here. He's waiting downstairs. Seriously guys, why don't we ever lock our door?"

McKenzie entered the living room a few minutes later to find her brother nervously pacing with his back to the doorway. When he spotted her, he hurried over and wrapped her up in a hug that almost sucked the air out of her. "I'm so sorry, Zee. I've been so caught up in my own stuff I haven't been here for you. I shouldn't have left you to deal with Mom alone."

McKenzie squirmed a little until he loosened his hold enough for her to breathe, but still hugged him back. "It's not your job to solve my problems. But I love that you care enough to want to."

"I'll always care." He smiled, though the guilt didn't completely leave his face. "What are you going to do now?"

She shrugged, stepping back. "It's time I put on my big girl panties and confront my coach."

"Need some backup? I can come with you."

She shook her head. "I've been hiding behind my insecurities for too long. I need to take responsibility for this on my own." She lifted the neck of her shirt to her nose and took a whiff. "But first, maybe a shower."

Seth sniffed, his nostrils flaring dramatically. "Yeah. How long has it been since you've had one?" McKenzie punched his arm, and he laughed. "Hey, Zee?" he asked, growing serious once again.

"Yeah?"

"Rory's moving to Connecticut in August," he started. "I'll have an empty room at my apartment. Not saying you have to take it, but if you need to, it's yours. You can stay with me rent-free until you get on your feet."

She smiled up at him. "Thanks, Seth."

After all the hardships she'd faced over the years, their relationship stood out as the one bright spot through it all. He had his flaws, especially when it came to relationships, but he was the best big brother McKenzie could ask for.

It was odd walking through the halls of SoCal Elite that afternoon. Familiar, yet different. Even after only a few days away, she felt like an outsider. Thankfully, she'd purposely chosen a time when most athletes were gone for lunch, so she didn't run into anyone she knew on her way to Gary's office.

She paused outside her coach's door and took a calming breath. What if he refused to give her another chance?

You won't find out until you try. Before she lost her nerve, she knocked, then poked her head into the office. "Gary, can I have a word with you?"

He looked up from his desk, his brows raising. "McKenzie. It's not like you to skip practice for days without telling me first."

She twisted her fingers together. "I k-know. I'm sorry."

He gave her a nod. "Perhaps you'd like to tell me what's going on." He gestured to the seat in front of his desk.

McKenzie dropped her bag to the floor with a thud and sat down. "It's hard to explain."

Gary's face remained stoic and unyielding, though not unkind. "Try me."

"Well ... I ... uh." *Why is this so hard?* She trusted Gary. She should be able to talk to him. "My mom ... uh."

Gary stopped her, his face turning soft. "You know, I remember the day you first walked into my gym in Seattle. When the rest of your classmates had trouble focusing on the activity we were doing, you always followed my instructions to a *T*. Even as a three-year old, you had a fierce determination to do your best. I knew very early on you were special. And you've never proven me wrong."

You were special. Mitch had said the same thing.

"We've been through a lot together, you and I," Gary continued. "If something is going on, I want to know, and not because I'm your coach, but because I see you as another one of my daughters."

Warmth filled her straight to her core. She'd always looked up to Gary as the father she never had, and to have her feelings validated by him eased some of the ache in her heart. She took a deep breath and looked up at him. "This is really hard to talk about, but I'll try."

Then she told him everything, though not without difficulty. She spoke of a lifetime of internalizing her mother's toxic control. Her relationship with Mitch. The ultimatum. And being cut off. Through it all, Gary let her talk without interrupting, only handing a tissue when she couldn't hold in the emotion any longer.

"I don't know how I can continue training now that my parents won't pay for it," she said, dabbing at her eyes. "But I'm *so* close. I'll do anything to be able to keep going. If I have to work as a janitor, or something, before and after practice, I will."

Gary remained silent for a moment after she'd finished, his face pensive. She held her breath, waiting for his response. *My fate is in his hands now.*

"I knew your relationship with your mom has always been tense, but I didn't realize it was that toxic. And I'm sorry you've had to go through all that. I wish I'd known so I could've done a better job at supporting you."

"I was afraid she'd find out I was talking bad about her," she squeaked out. "You know how much she values her appearance."

"She's a complicated woman." Gary's mouth turned up. "And as far as Mitch is concerned, I knew you were seeing him all along."

"You did?"

He chuckled. "Neither of you were very good at hiding it with all the goofy looks you shared whenever he came into the gym. And those conditioning sessions he led? You may have thought I wasn't looking, but I saw it all."

A blush sped up her neck, and she squirmed in her seat. "Why didn't you say anything?"

"I figured as long as you stayed focused during practice, I didn't have a problem with it. And I've always been impressed with Mitch. He's got a good head on his shoulders. You couldn't do much better."

No, I couldn't. But Gary's approval didn't solve the fact that she had no money. "It doesn't matter though. If I can't find a job, I'll have to leave California."

"About that," Gary started. "I think I have a solution that will allow you to stay in Buena Hills and continue training."

A flicker of hope entered her heart. "What is it?"

"When Tamryn first started this program, she had a vision that gymnastics should be available to everyone, regardless of their financial situation. She wanted a way to help athletes showing a lot of potential in the sport but who may not have a way to pay for it."

"Like a scholarship program?" That sounded promising. "I've never heard anything about it." If she had, McKenzie would've applied in a heartbeat. Anything to get out from under her mother's hold.

Gary leaned back in his chair, folding his arms over his chest. "It's not well-known among the athletes. Tamryn didn't want anyone abusing the system. So, she left it up to the discretion of the coaches. I think you're a perfect candidate for it. I would've recommended you long before now, but I thought you were okay with the arrangement with your parents."

"Are you saying ..." McKenzie trailed off, not willing to believe it just yet.

Her coach nodded. "I'll fill out the paperwork this afternoon to get the ball rolling."

"Thank you. I'm sorry for quitting." Moisture stung her eyes, though this time, they were tears of relief, not sadness. "Um ... Gary?"

Her coach tilted his head to the side. "Yeah?"

She twisted her fingers together. Maybe she should take the scholarship and leave it at that. But there was one more thing she needed to take full control of her life. "You know that job opening for the part-time beginners class instructor?"

Gary nodded.

"I'd like to apply for it."

"I'll get you an application." A slow smile crept onto Gary's face as he came around his desk. McKenzie rose from her chair on shaking knees, forcing herself to stand tall. Placing an arm around her shoulders, he gave her a squeeze. "It's good to have you back. Let's get to the gym. We've got work to do."

When McKenzie walked into the gym for practice a few minutes later, Aria's immediate scowl made it obvious that she *was* the culprit responsible for leaking McKenzie's relationship with Mitch to the media.

A new resolve fueled McKenzie through that training session. She'd been tiptoeing around Aria for months, intentionally avoiding any kind of confrontation. But no longer. Words needed to be said if she were truly going to take control of her life. She couldn't let her teammate off the hook this time.

When Aria left practice without a word to anyone, McKenzie slipped on her flip-flops and hurried from the gym, not bothering to throw her shirt over her practice leo.

"Why'd you do it?" she called from behind when she'd caught up to Aria in the parking lot.

Aria turned to face her with narrowed eyes. "Do what?"

The fact that she still refused to fess up to her actions only stoked the flames burning inside McKenzie. "You know how much I hate the media. Why would you sell me out like that?" She had a good idea of why, but she wanted to hear Aria say it.

They stared at one another for a drawn-out moment before Aria sneered, "Because your life is so perfect. You're Gary's favorite. You win bars at nationals one time, and now everyone thinks you're the next big thing. And somehow, despite the way you are"—she circled her hands around in front of McKenzie, disgust curling her upper lip —"the most amazing guy is head over heels for you. I'm tired of you getting everything. What about me?"

McKenzie bit her lip, shaking her head against the hurt that once again gripped her heart. She was tired of hurting. And the insulting way Aria had just gestured at her, as if McKenzie was somehow undeserving of Mitch's affection was an indication of her team-mate's character, not hers. "If you knew me outside the gym, you'd know my life is far from perfect. I've had to work really hard to come back from my injury. And there's a reason Gary and I are so close, since my own dad doesn't care enough about me to be a part of my life."

She started to walk away but stopped. "You know, I can forgive you for resenting me over making the World team. I can get over the months of hurtful comments when you were supposed to be my friend. But attempting to mess with the best relationship I have ..." She squeezed her eyes shut and shook her head, willing the angry tears away. "I can't forgive you for that. I don't know if I ever will."

This time, she did walk away. And she didn't look back. She'd stood up for herself, and now there was nothing else to say.

"Gary's not letting me compete in the trials," Aria called after her. "I have no shot at the Global Elites."

McKenzie paused. That had to be a major blow for her teammate. Five years was a long time in the life of a Global Elite hopeful. She knew what it felt like to have a dream ripped away from her. For a moment, she considered marching back into Gary's office and asking him to give Aria another chance. She forced down the temptation. *Aria dug her grave. Now it's her turn to lie in it.*

Slowly, she turned around, catching Aria's defiant stare. "Good luck in five years," McKenzie said, holding her head high.

When she'd locked herself in her car, she slumped forward and rested her forehead against the steering wheel. The last few days had drained what little emotional energy she had left. Even the prospect of driving home seemed an insurmountable task. And after so many difficult conversations, there was only one voice she longed to hear.

She pulled out her phone and finally turned it on, ignoring the text messages and voicemails in her notifications—most of them were from Mitch anyway. She swiped one of his missed calls to dial him back.

"Hey, it's Mitch. Leave a message and I'll get back to you."

Her heart dropped at the sound of the beep. "H-hi, Mitch," she said, resisting the urge to sigh. It hit her that she had no idea if he was even in California or not. "It's me. Call me back when you can? I miss you."

She hung up and turned the key in the ignition, the engine roaring to life. As she left the parking lot, she said a silent prayer that things were still okay between them. It was in his hands now.

Chapter Forty-Four

"Man, that flight was rough," Charlie said once the plane landed in Rome late Saturday morning. "For a little while, I almost started praying."

"You wouldn't be the only one," Tom said, retrieving his bag from the overhead compartment. "I'm pretty sure I heard some muttering from the lady next to me."

The nine-hour flight from Atlanta had been one of the worst in Mitch's life. And that was on top of the four-hour leg from Los Angeles and a layover to boot. He couldn't wait to get to the hotel and take a nap.

As they stepped into the terminal at the Leonardo da Vinci Fiumicino Airport, he pulled his phone from his pocket and took it off airplane mode. After giving it a minute for the notifications to catch up, he glanced down at the screen, his heart stuttering at the missed call from McKenzie at the top.

It had been even harder to leave for this tournament than the last. Knowing she was suffering and not being the one to comfort her didn't sit well with him in the slightest. He'd spent so much of the last four days wondering if they were even still together. Maybe that was unfair, but he couldn't deny he was a little hurt she didn't turn to him in her time of need.

Mostly he just wanted to see her face. To know for himself she was okay.

Mitch nudged Charlie, who was half a step in front of him. "Hey, I need to make a call. I'll meet you guys at baggage claim."

Charlie took one look at his face and nodded. "McKenzie?"

"Yeah," Mitch said.

They'd spent so much time together over the last several months, it was natural to open up about their personal lives. Out of respect to McKenzie, he didn't go into too much detail about their struggles, though he did share enough for his teammate to understand the complications. And Mitch had been there for Charlie back in February when his relationship with Addison finally ended.

"Good luck." Charlie clapped him on the shoulder before continuing after Tom.

Stepping out of the way of the stream of passengers, Mitch waited for the announcement over the loudspeaker to finish before dialing McKenzie. It wasn't until the call went to voicemail that he realized his mistake. It was the middle of the night back home.

"Hey," he said after he heard the beep. He cleared his throat. "I just landed in Rome. You're probably asleep right now, but ... I miss you." The literal ache in his chest proved the truth of that statement. "Anyway, I hope you're doing okay. Call me."

He slipped his phone back into his pocket. "Time differences suck," he muttered as he made his way toward baggage claim.

Early Saturday morning, McKenzie startled awake to Mitch's voice in her room. Her eyes popped open, and she looked around in alarm, though the early morning darkness made it impossible to see anything. Her awareness returned in time to catch the end of the birthday message coming from Cuddles the Bear next to her. She must have unintentionally squeezed the stuffed animal in her sleep to make the sound go off. Maybe her bed wasn't the best place to keep the bear if she wanted a restful night's sleep.

Reaching for her phone to check the time, she let out a groan when a missed call from Mitch popped up underneath the clock that showed a few minutes after four. Why hadn't she turned the ringer up before going to bed last night? She'd willingly lose sleep in order to talk to him.

She plucked the device from her nightstand and rolled onto her back, careful not to jostle Cuddles too much, lest she set off the recording again. Leaning her head against the soft fur of its leg, she opened the video chat.

Please answer, she silently begged as the phone rang once, twice, three times. Her heart rose into her throat. She had no idea what time it was in Rome or what his schedule was for the day. But she pleaded with whatever higher power would listen for him to answer. She desperately needed to hear his voice.

On the fourth ring, her wish was granted. "Hey," he said after he'd picked up, relief immediately appearing on his face. "Isn't it early there?"

McKenzie reached over and clicked on her lamp. "Yeah. Something woke me up and I can't go back to sleep." She took a shaky breath. *This is Mitch. There's nothing to be nervous about.* But the way she'd pulled away from him—from everyone, really—he had every right to be upset. "I'm sorry I missed your call."

"That's alright. I have a few hours before I have to report to afternoon training." Mitch turned his head away from the screen and said a few words to someone in the background before leaving what looked like his hotel room and stepping outside. Blue sky filled the screen behind him, and sunlight bathed his gorgeous features. "How ... how are you?"

"Tired. It's been a rough few days." She still hadn't entirely recovered from the emotional toll of the last week. "I feel a little better now that I'm talking to you though."

"Really?"

Regret rippled in her stomach at the uncertainty in his tone. "I'm sorry for pulling away. I was so overwhelmed with everything, I didn't know how to handle it all." She blinked away the moisture pooling in her eyes.

Mitch's mouth lifted into a small smile, easing some of her nerves. "I understand that. And I wasn't mad."

"You weren't?"

He rubbed a hand down his unshaved face, a humorless chuckle escaping. "Of course not. I know you need space to process hard things. And you've been through a lot. It's okay for you to need time. I hope you know that no matter what though, I'll always be here to bring you back. There's no battle I won't fight for you."

McKenzie felt the truth of his words. He'd never given her a reason to doubt him. "I know. And I love you for that. Only Seth has ever cared as much about me as you have. Eventually, he'll probably have a family of his own and forget all about his little sister."

"Seth will never forget about you. And I definitely won't."

McKenzie didn't know how someone's eyes could hold fierce determination and soft adoration at the same time, but she saw both in his gaze.

"I promise to always be your safe space," he continued. "To celebrate your successes and be your soft landing when you fall. I mean it, Zee. No matter what happens in your life, I want to be here for all of it."

"You already are," she said with absolute conviction. "Even during all the darkness of the last few days, I never doubted you were there for me. And I really appreciate that you didn't pressure me to talk until I was ready." Her voice wobbled. What she'd give for a chance to be held by him right now. "I've really missed you, Mitch."

"I've missed you. Every single minute of every single day. And believe me, as soon as I'm able, I'll hop on the first plane to get back home to you."

He didn't actually say the words, and yet, McKenzie felt his love in the ones he did. "I can't wait. When do you play next?"

"Qualifiers start Monday morning. I expect you to wake up early to watch." There was enough laughter in his tone to know he was kidding.

McKenzie giggled. "I hope you know I love you, but you've already cost me enough sleep. I'll catch the replay."

"Can't get me out of your dreams, can you?" He made a kissy face.

Her laughter echoed through the quiet of the room, and she turned her face into her pillow to muffle the sound. "Something like that," she said when she'd glanced at the screen again. Thank goodness for her unusual wake-up call. If it hadn't been for Cuddles, she wouldn't have had time to talk to Mitch before having to get ready for the day.

"What do you have going on today?" he asked, bringing her back to the conversation.

"I have two training sessions, and then I need to fill out an application for the beginner's coaching job. If I get it, I should start right after the Global Elites are over."

"You're training again?"

She quickly sat up, pushing a hand through her sleep-messed hair, working through the tangles. "Oh my gosh, I assumed you'd already heard. Did you know about the scholarship program at SoCal Elite?"

"I didn't."

McKenzie told him all about her conversation with Gary the day she'd finally gone back to the gym. Although they were still waiting for the paperwork to be approved, her coach had assured her that the funding should kick in sometime in the next couple of days.

"I'm so glad, Zee. That's the best news ever."

"You know what it means, don't you?" She couldn't help the smile that took over her face. "We can be together. No more secrets."

"No more secrets," he repeated. By the way he looked at her, even through the phone, there was no possible way for her to feel except loved.

Mitch had to go soon after that, but they parted with the promise to talk again the first chance they got.

McKenzie lingered in bed a few minutes longer, soaking in the excitement of her new reality. For years she'd longed for someone to accept her exactly as she was. She'd loved Mitch almost since the day he'd first walked into her life but had dismissed the likelihood that he'd ever give her more than a passing glance. But now, not even the thousands of miles between them, or the obstacles that had almost torn them apart, could sever their bond.

At last, she'd found the love she'd hoped for all along. And for the first time in her life, she knew without a doubt exactly where she belonged.

Chapter Forty-Five

Six Weeks Later

McKenzie shouldn't have watched. If she'd stayed in her own world a little longer, she wouldn't have witnessed the gymnast before her stumble on vault. And if she'd left her earbuds in, "Eye of the Tiger" would've drowned out the sharp crack of breaking bone and shrieks of pain echoing through the arena.

She stood with her eyes glued to the huddle of trainers working to stabilize the gymnast's leg. Images of her own accident jostled for position at the forefront of her mind, even as she willed herself to turn away. The sight in front of her was hauntingly similar to the video footage of herself that she'd watched hundreds of times.

Gary stepped in front of her, blocking the scene from view. Too bad he couldn't also hide her from the eerie hush of the crowd or the girl's heartbreaking sobs. He placed both hands on her shoulders.

Body shaking, McKenzie slid her gaze up to him. "I can't do this. Please don't make me."

"It's in times of adversity that you find out what you're made of," he said, giving her shoulders a gentle squeeze. "What happened just now isn't your narrative. You're capable of this. Trust yourself, McKenzie."

She gulped in a lungful of air. And another. With his help, she turned away from the scene and closed her eyes. Pushing the images from her mind took all the strength she had. Would she even have any left by the time her turn came? She was already running on fumes.

After several more minutes, the trainers finally carried the injured athlete from the podium to the respectful applause of the spectators. Shortly after, McKenzie was given the go-ahead to take her place at the end of the vault runway.

Nerves pulsed through her, and her stomach flipped at the same rapid speed her body had on floor exercise earlier in the competition. She paced back and forth on the mat waiting for the green flag.

Trust your training. She'd landed the vault dozens of times in practice over the last few weeks. In the comfort of her own gym, away from the crowds and the pressure, it didn't seem nearly as scary anymore. But add thousands of people watching her, the electricity of the Global Elite trials atmosphere, and the raised competition floor—which always made the apparatus a little wobbly—and it was a whole new ball game.

Finally, the green flag went up, and she raised both arms to signal her readiness. She took a few deep breaths, pushing down the rising nausea, and started running. With each step she picked up speed, her body going into autopilot as the vault grew closer. She reached the end of the runway and dropped into a roundoff. Punching the springboard with her feet, she arched her back with outstretched arms and pushed off the vault, exploding into the air. Bent arms tucked into her body, she twisted with all her might until her feet hit the mat.

For a beat, nothing happened. Not even the slightest shuffle of her feet. Then, the whole arena erupted into chaos. Standing tall, McKenzie straightened her arms above her head, letting her full smile show. She did it. Almost nine years after the worst night of her life, she'd finally come full circle.

After saluting the judges, she jogged over to Gary. Bypassing the stairs, she leapt straight into his arms, unable to hold in the emotion any longer.

He held her tightly, pulling her off the podium as the roar from the spectators continued. "I'm so proud of you," he whispered over and over, choking back tears. "I knew you had it in you."

He was right. Even amidst the doubt she'd placed on herself over the years, her coach had always stood tall in his faith in her.

Setting her back on the floor, Gary turned her to face the crowd. "Look at them. They're cheering for you."

McKenzie scanned the packed arena. Every single person in attendance was on their feet. Coaches, gymnasts, and officials standing on the sidelines had also joined in the applause. The attention was almost too much for her to handle, and she covered her mouth with her hand, weeping openly.

She'd sacrificed so much for this dream that, at times, seemed impossible. Loneliness had been her constant companion on this journey. She'd let the voices of the doubters drown out the support that really mattered.

But she hadn't been alone after all. People were pulling for her all along.

Gary patted her shoulders. "Soak it in. You deserve this." Then he backed away.

McKenzie wiped the tears from her eyes. New ones swooped in to replace them. The elation filled her heart so completely the emotion just continued to spill out. She pulled herself onto the raised competition floor and turned in a slow circle, waving to the crowd.

As her small fan section came into view, she paused. Her parents weren't among them, but McKenzie hadn't expected them to be. She'd given up on ever hoping her father would give a care about her competitions. And she wasn't ready to face her mother yet.

But everyone else McKenzie cared about was clustered in a small section next to the vault. Elise and Hallie both wiped tears from their eyes. Rory clapped enthusiastically beside his fiancée. Kendall cupped her hands around her mouth, cheering. Beej and Seth stood on opposite sides of the group doing the same.

And next to Seth, wearing that same smile that always made McKenzie want to float away on a puffy cloud of bliss was Mitch.

He winked at her when he met her stare. Then he placed his fingers to his mouth and let out a shrill whistle.

He came, McKenzie thought, wishing the stands were more easily accessible from the competition floor. After being apart for the last few weeks, she didn't want to have to wait until the announcement of the Global Elite team to get a hug. But he was too out of reach.

Still, there had been doubts on whether he'd even make it back from his tournament by tonight. Somehow, he'd pulled off a miracle. Out of all the highlights from this truly magical night, him being here to the biggest competition of her career topped them all.

Mitch finally spotted McKenzie exiting the locker room an hour after she'd been named to the Global Elite team. Dressed in her navy USA warm-ups, with a bouquet of red, white, and blue flowers in her hand, she was the picture of radiance, her face glowing in euphoria of her incredible performance. Resisting the urge to scoop her in his arms, he hung back. This was her night to shine. He could wait his turn.

Seth congratulated her first, throwing his arms around her waist and spinning her in a circle, her angelic laugh ringing out over the low rumble of conversations happening among the other athletes and spectators. Once she was on her feet again, her roommates surrounded her in a group hug, fast chatter coming from all of them. Rory and Seth joined in on the outside.

When the group broke apart, McKenzie looked past them, finally spotting Mitch. The gorgeous smile she gave him kick-started his heart, like it was finally beating after weeks of atrophy. No, like it was finally whole.

She handed her flowers to Kendall and hurried over to him, launching into his arms. "I didn't think you'd make it in time," she said into his neck.

"Did you really think I'd miss the biggest night of your life?" He held onto her, savoring the comfort of her in his embrace. "When my flight was delayed, I told the pilot, 'You better figure out how to get this plane off the ground. My girlfriend has an important competition tonight that I just can't miss." He lowered her back to the floor.

Her laugh was pure gold. "I'm so glad you're here." She raised onto her toes and brushed a kiss to his jaw. Then she stepped back, sliding her hands down his arms to link their fingers together.

Something in his peripheral caught his notice. Reluctantly, he pulled his focus from his love as Mrs. Bowman passed in the distance, staring at them.

He frowned, slipping both arms around McKenzie's waist and pulling her to him again, ready to protect her from any vitriol her mother might send her way. "Do you want to talk to her?" he asked, gesturing with his head to Mrs. Bowman's disappearing back.

McKenzie glanced in the direction he'd indicated, and the radiance in her countenance dimmed. He could see the debate raging in her head. Even after the years of emotional abuse she'd been subjected to, he knew she felt guilty for the things she'd said to her mother. And her desire for peace would make it difficult for her to leave the situation unsettled for too long.

She shook her head, resolve crossing her face. "I know I'll need to talk to her eventually, but not tonight. I need to heal myself before I let her in my life again."

Mitch stooped to plant a kiss on the top of her head. The red, white, and blue ribbons holding up her ponytail brushed against his cheek. "I'm proud of you." He dropped a hand from her back, lacing their fingers together. Brushing her cheek with his other hand, he said, "And when you do have that discussion, I'll be right there beside you. You'll never have to face another trial alone."

"My champion," she whispered in reverence, a fond smile gracing her gorgeous face. He loved that smile.

"Always," he murmured, raising their linked hands to his lips.

"I've been thinking about that promise you gave me a few weeks ago." Her eyes found his, her gaze unwavering. "You know, about being my safe place?"

"Yeah."

"I want to make one of my own. I promise to trust you with everything I have, even when my anxiety is telling me to run and hide. I promise to be your biggest fan, to walk beside you no matter what life throws your way." She reached her free hand up to his cheek. "And on those days when your grief becomes too heavy to carry alone, I'll be your rock, like you are mine."

Mitch wrapped her in his arms, bending to bury his face in her shoulder. Holding her like this again almost made the last few weeks of missing her worth it. All was right in his world because she *was* his world. He vowed right then to let nothing pull them apart again.

After a moment, McKenzie stepped back. He kept his arms around her waist, not willing to put any distance between them quite yet. "I love you, Mitch," she said, unmistakable trust shining in her eyes as she looked at him.

She'd said those words before but hearing them now, after everything that had happened between them, they held more weight. Leaning toward her, he whispered, "And I'll love you forever."

He pressed his mouth against her forehead. Unsatisfied, he directed his attention to her lips. And like they'd done before and would do many times in the years to come, they sealed their promises with a heartfelt kiss.

Epilogue

June—Global Elite Games

The grandstands were packed at the gold medal beach volleyball match, filled with spectators anxiously waiting to see if the USA could pull off a win against the top-seeded Dutch team. Anticipation buzzed through the crowd, fueling Mitch's competitive drive.

He knew from experience the Dutch would be tough to beat. Still, with how much Mitch and Charlie had improved over the last few months, they weren't quite the underdogs they'd been at that quarterfinal back in March.

But after narrowly losing the first set, they were down by one in the second at match point. If they lost the next rally, the game would be over.

Mitch, volleyball in hand, stood at the baseline preparing to serve. Sweat covered his face and arms, and his heart beat rapidly as he bent at the waist, attempting to catch his breath from the last rally.

Fine sand shifted beneath his feet as he straightened to his full height, looking to the head ref. A whistle perched in the woman's mouth, and she watched one of the Dutch players wiping his sunglasses on the towel hanging from the net directly below her spot on the referee stand.

Mitch's eyes then strayed to the crowd, immediately finding McKenzie in the front row, her palms pressed together, the tips of her fingers underneath her chin. She'd missed his first few matches of the tournament due to her own events, but once the gymnastics competition ended, she hadn't missed a game. Her unwavering support, despite the chaos of her own schedule, meant the world to him.

The shrill chirp of the ref's whistle pulled Mitch's attention back to the court for the start of the next rally. He bounced the ball between his hands three times before bringing it up to his face.

This one's for you, Zee.

He tossed the ball in the air and jumped, sending a hard serve aimed directly between the two members of the other team. It sailed past them both, landing on the sand on the baseline.

Ace.

Breathing heavy, Mitch wiped the sweat from his face with his jersey. After the second set went on for what seemed like forever, he and Charlie finally claimed the two-point advantage, forcing the game into a tie-breaker set. Now, deep in the third, all four players were gassed, pure adrenaline and heart the only things keeping them going.

One more, Mitch thought, stretching his hands behind his back, signaling to Charlie at the service line to send the ball crosscourt. *Match point.*

At the ref's whistle, Charlie sent the ball over the net. Mitch tracked it as the Dutch team bumped it once, then twice. On the third hit, the defender spiked the ball past Charlie at the net. Diving, Mitch slid his hand between leather and sand just in the nick of time. He popped to his feet, as Charlie set the ball close to the net.

Taking a running leap, Mitch jumped and the heel of his hand connected with the ball, smashing it straight down onto the sand on their opponent's side.

As his feet landed, he clenched both his hands in front of him, and a carnal roar sounded from deep in his chest. Charlie's ecstatic yelling echoed the rumbling of the crowd. Mitch sprinted over to him, and leapt, a single fist pumped in the air. His teammate caught him around the waist, and they both crashed hard onto the sand.

Rolling onto his back, Mitch covered the sides of his head with both hands. His mouth formed an all-encompassing grin as he soaked it all in—the roar of the crowd, the cameras swarming around him capturing everything, the heart pounding elation of accomplishing what they'd set out to do.

He'd spent years working for this moment, wondering whether he was good enough, then grieving the loss of both his friend and his dream. He wished Doug was here to share in the celebration. He would've cheered louder than everyone.

Charlie reached his hand out, pulling Mitch up from the sand. "We did it, man! We did it!" he exclaimed, slinging both arms around his teammate and slapping him on the back.

We did it, Mitch repeated, another wave of euphoria pulsing through him as he returned the bear hug. Then he faced the crowd, acknowledging them with a raised fist. More thundering applause followed.

His gaze landed on his family, McKenzie in the center of them all, her hands over her mouth, happy tears trailing down her cheeks. He would've never gotten to this moment if she hadn't encouraged him to take the chance. After all they'd been through, he couldn't think of anyone he'd rather celebrate with than her.

Vaulting over the banner separating the sand from the media section, he jogged past the cameras to the edge of the raised bleachers. He jumped, grabbing onto the top of the railing and pulling himself into the stands in front of her.

"You did it!" she sobbed, wrapping her arms tightly around his neck.

Mitch embraced her. "We did it," he corrected. Then right in the middle of the packed grandstand, he bent toward her, stealing her lips in his. Everything in the background—the noise, the lights, the cameras—faded to nothing while he poured all his love into this moment between them. As she returned his affection, he reveled in the feel of her in his arms, and the sweet taste of her lips. This moment was the start of many memories to come in their life together.

"Where are you taking me?" Mitch asked as McKenzie led him up a hill at the edge of the athlete's housing.

She squeezed his hand, urging him onward. "Be patient, we're almost there. I want to show you this spot I found." She'd discovered it right after the balance beam finals when she'd needed a place to unwind from all the attention.

Her individual gold medals on bars and beam, as well as the success of the US in the team event, had launched a frenzied whirl of media appearances. Late night talk shows and news agencies covering the event all wanted a chance to talk to the "Comeback Kid," as one sports magazine had dubbed her. The attention had been overwhelming, to say the least. But she'd spent a lot of time in the week's leading up to the Global Elites embracing her journey, and how far she'd come, that talking to the media hadn't bothered her as much as she'd expected.

They reached the crest of the hill, and she turned around. The buildings housing their respective apartments for the last three weeks stretched out behind them, made to look like a cute Swiss village. The setting sun cast a golden hue across the half-timbered buildings and gabled roofs and sparkled off the fountain in the center square. McKenzie lowered herself to the grass, pulling Mitch down next to her.

"Wow, this is beautiful," he said, draping his left arm over her shoulder.

McKenzie leaned her head against him. "Isn't it?" They sat in silence for a minute, breathing in the peaceful scene.

Earlier that day, her heart had swelled with pride watching Charlie and Mitch accept their gold medals. No one deserved it more than he did after the hard work he'd put in to achieve his dream. But now, she was grateful for this time to spend with him, to decompress together after so much time apart.

"Can you believe it's almost over?" she asked, turning her face to him.

Mitch placed a light kiss on her forehead. "These last few weeks have flown by, huh?"

"I know this year hasn't been the easiest between us." McKenzie hooked her hand over his kneecap. "So many things seemed to get in the way of us being together."

"And yet, here we are."

"Here we are," she whispered, replacing her head to its spot on his shoulder.

"It's pretty incredible, actually."

"What is?"

He pressed his cheek against her hair. "A year ago, you barely spoke to me. And even though a lot of difficult things have happened to us, I'd say everything has only brought us closer together. I mean, there's no one I'd rather be sitting here with than you."

"Me too." She lifted her face to place a soft kiss on his jawline, her lips lingering close to his skin, waiting for him to reciprocate. The sweet pecks that followed weren't nearly enough to satisfy the desire working its way through McKenzie's body. She moved to deepen the kiss, but Mitch quickly pulled back, angling his body toward her. At first his sudden movement startled her, but her alarm quickly turned to amusement when she caught sight of his goofy grin.

He raised a fist to his mouth like a microphone, and in his deepest announcer voice, said, "McKenzie Bowman, you've just been crowned Global Elite champion, and named the darling of American gymnastics. Tell the lovely audience what's next for you."

McKenzie laughed and shoved him, drawing a chuckle from him. "I want to go to school. And I think I'd like to coach. Maybe even own my own gym someday. Something to make a difference in the next generation of gymnasts. To give them a safe place to learn the sport, but also to have the confidence to grow into the women and men *they* want to be."

"I love that idea." Mitch tucked her back to his side. "You'd be great at it. And I'll do anything I can to help you."

She had no doubt he would. "And what about you, Mr. Break-Out Star of the Global Elite Games?"

He shook his head in disbelief. "I still can't believe we won."

"I can. Have you even stopped to consider what you've accomplished in the last year? You went from not having competed for almost a decade to becoming a Global Elite champion. Athletes train their whole lives to do what you did in less than a year. How amazing is that?"

"I did that, didn't I?" He puffed out his chest a little.

McKenzie placed a hand on his shoulder, running it up and down his arm. "I'm so proud of you."

"This is only the beginning." He pressed his lips to her cheek.

She closed her eyes, enjoying the sensation of his nose nuzzling her neck. "I can't wait to see you in action."

"Oh yeah? How about I show you some action right now?"

She squealed as his mouth curved into a devilish smile before taking her lips hostage, cutting off any additional conversation. His hand slid into her hair, running his tantalizing fingers across her scalp.

"Are you sure you're okay with me continuing on the pro circuit?" he murmured in between kisses. "The seasons are long," —his lips lingered on hers for a moment—"and I'll be gone a lot." —they skimmed over her nose—"I'll quit in a heartbeat if you ask."

McKenzie sat back, keeping her arms around his middle. "This is your decision. I'll stand by you no matter what you choose."

"I want us to make it together. I'm hoping it will affect us both long-term."

Her heartbeat quickened. "Are you asking what I think you're asking?" They'd only been officially dating a few months. And most of those were spent apart. And yet, she couldn't imagine spending forever with anyone else.

As Mitch knelt in front of her, the term racing pulse seemed to take on a whole new meaning. He pulled a small box from his pocket, taking her left hand in his. "You once told me that better days will come." He brought her fingers to his lips. "You are my better days. My life, my future is already brighter with you in it." He flicked the box open. "I love you, McKenzie Eliza Bowman. Nothing would make me happier than having you by my side forever. Will you marry me?"

McKenzie raised onto her knees, cupping both his cheeks in her hands. "Yes! Of course I'll marry you." She didn't wait until the ring was on her finger before kissing him, deeply and passionately, hoping to communicate every ounce of her love and devotion in that one act.

Without breaking the connection, Mitch lifted her to her feet and wrapped his arms around her waist, tugging her against him. She slid her hands up his chest, savoring the caress of his lips on hers.

It wasn't until they'd broken apart that she even thought to look at the ring. Her breath caught as she studied the familiar aqua sea glass set in sterling silver prongs. "Mitch, how did you ..." She looked up at him.

An uncharacteristic flash of uncertainty entered his eyes. "Doug's mom has a friend in the jewelry business. She did it as a favor to her. I promise I'll get you a diamond when I can afford it—"

McKenzie placed a finger to his lips, shaking her head. "I don't want a diamond. This means so much more to me." She reached on her tiptoes and kissed him once more.

The Global Elites were practically over. In a few weeks, she'd officially announce her retirement from gymnastics. But she wasn't saying goodbye to the sport. Her role was simply shifting, and she was excited to find her new place in the gymnastics community.

And as the sun set on this chapter of her life, she turned her focus to a new dream. This one didn't involve competitions or winning or medals. This dream was all about a family. And a cute little house with a few kids playing in the yard—kids who looked a lot like their father.

Her husband.

Oh boy, she liked the sound of that. Not every day would be perfect. But with love, laughter, and trust in each other, she had no doubt they'd work through every obstacle together.

Seth was right. Better days *do* come. McKenzie was living proof of that. And she couldn't wait to live out her happily ever after with Mitch.

Mitch and McKenzie's story doesn't end here! If you'd like a glimpse into their happily ever after, make sure to check out the bonus epilogue by signing up for my newsletter!

https://BookHip.com/NGJFDNM

Buena Hills Series

Discovering Her Heart

Book 1

Chasing Her Heart

Book 2

Champion of Her Heart

Book 3

Stay up-to-date on all my new releases by following me on Amazon.

Acknowledgments

This book was such a labor of love for me. It had a way of both ripping my heart in pieces and putting it back together again. At the same time. It has been a joy being able to create this beautiful story.

I first want to thank you, dear reader. Thank you for taking a chance on this book. I hope you loved Mitch and McKenzie as much as I do. You are a large reason why I write, and I hope you'll stick around for more stories in the Buena Hills universe.

Thank you to my critique group—Danyelle, Judy, and Sarah—for being the ultimate hype girls. Your feedback and encouragement was exactly what I needed to get this story down on paper. I think another writing retreat is in order. But hopefully the next one will go a little smoother than the last.

To my incredible editor and cover designer, Raneé Clark from Sweetly Us, thank you for believing in this story. Your insights helped me make it even better than I could have on my own.

Thank you to my proofreader, Kimberly Steinke of Parker Mayne Editorial, for helping me polish this book and make it shine.

I couldn't write an acknowledgments section without including my family. You guys are the best. Thank you for putting up with all those dinners where I dominated the conversation talking about these characters like they were real people. And thank you to David for being my sounding board and offering suggestions even when you'd rather talk about anything else. I love you!

About the Author

Allison Gygi wrote her first official story in third grade from an old word processor in the computer lab of her elementary school. Since then she has crafted countless tales both on paper and in her head. As a mom, her days are spent trying to find a few minutes to write in between constant diaper changes, never ending dishes, and helping kids with homework. She loves fairy tales and gravitates towards books with happy endings and swoony kisses. Allison enjoys reading, hiking, and traveling the world. She lives with her husband and three children in a cute suburb of Chicago.

instagram.com/authorallisongygi

amazon.com/stores/Allison-Gygi/author/B0B27C16JN

bookbub.com/authors/allison-gygi

www.ingramcontent.com/pod-product-compliance
Lightning Source LLC
Chambersburg PA
CBHW021536250626
47154CB00006BA/2144